EACH THIEF PASSING BY

EACH THIEF PASSING BY

E.M. SWIFT

LITTLE, BROWN AND COMPANY   BOSTON / TORONTO

FIRST EDITION

LIBRARY OF CONGRESS CATALOGING IN PUBLICATION DATA

Swift, E. M. (Edward McKelvy)
Each thief passing by.

I. Title.
PS3569.W482E18   813'.54   81-5997
ISBN 0-316-82540-9   AACR2

BP

Designed by Susan Windhein
*Published simultaneously in Canada
by Little, Brown & Company (Canada) Limited*

PRINTED IN THE UNITED STATES OF AMERICA

For Sally

Some kind of love is like gold;
That is the hardest to hold,
for it catches the eye
of each thief passing by;
Some kind of love is like gold.

—from the song
   "Some Kind of Love"
   by John Stewart

AUTHOR'S NOTE

The characters in this book are imaginary, as is Kearney, Wyoming. The problems accompanying strip-mining in the American West are real, however, and they are with us as much today as they were in 1974, when this novel was started. I have gathered my information from a variety of sources, including personal observation, but in particular I would like to acknowledge K. Ross Toole's excellent book on the subject, *The Rape of the Great Plains*.

This is a first novel, and has required a seemingly bottomless well of support from my family and friends, East and West. I have drawn from that well shamelessly. In particular, thanks to G. Clayton Kyle and Alexander Stuart for their faith in the book and in me.

It has also required the imagination, insight, and guidance of my overworked editor, William D. Phillips. To him, and to Laura Evans, go special thanks. They are masters.

EACH THIEF PASSING BY

CHAPTER 1

"**H**ow *exactly?*" Papa Vic repeated. "I kept my blamed head above water is how. I swum till I could crawl into a wicker basket just like the baby Moses, then I rode on that flood till we hit a tree. Most trees were down, but this'n wasn't. Shinnied up and sat two days waitin' for the water to go down. Tied myself to the branch with my belt and chewed leaves for strength." He winked, pausing just a beat. "Well, I'll tell you, Mr. Aldridge, since you asked, when that dam broke it sounded like thunder. That water funneled down the valley like thunder. When it got closer, it sounded like an earthquake. I was upstairs in my pa's store, listenin' to the rumblin' up the valley, louder and louder, me lookin' out the window at the rain-drenched streets, the elderbushes in bloom — you remember these things. You don't forget 'em. I never forgot nothin' about that Johnstown Flood, and I'm old enough where I've forgot most things. Got to where you couldn't think, it rumbled so. And 'fore you ever saw the water, there was that big dark cloud bein' chased ahead of it, real eerie. Like a big giant train was bearin' down on the town, kickin' up dust. Then the churchbells started, all over town. That was the warnin'. I seen the first wave hit the opera house, a big brick house, and crush it like an eggshell. I'm yellin', 'Flood! Flood!' — but you can't hear yourself think. My folks and my sister Missy comes up then, and the flood hits the store. Knocks it right off the foundation. Broke it apart, bit by

3

bit, and us with it. I's swimmin' in the wicker basket like the baby Moses — I'd be nine years old — and my pa and Missy is on the roof. I never did see where my ma got to. Well, they all died, and I made it to that tree and lived, me the littlest and the weakest. Who knows why?"

Aldridge was silent. Papa Vic looked up at the newsman and then went on; "Washed the store clean away. Been twenty-five years since Sam and Kate McKenzie drove into Johnstown with a horse and a wagon and all they owned tucked in the back. Twenty-five years, with nothin' better nor worse to show for it than me. That's not much of a golden age, a lot of folks would say, but that's what my pa always said we were livin' in. A golden age. Maybe so and maybe not.

"Well. I moved in with my Aunt Cornelia on my ma's side, who was married to the Reverend. Them were lean years for a growin' boy. Kept talkin' on how that flood was the work of the Lord, cleanin' up the sin. Well, Johnstown had its share, but I say bullfeathers to that, sir. That flood was the work of some jackass engineer . . ."

Aldridge winced.

". . . who had a notion thirty years back to build the Pennsylvania Canal. That was before the railroad run in there and they abandoned the whole affair. But they left that lake and they left that dam. . . .

"Them was lean years, all right. I remember old Fiddlesticks Henshkey, the schoolmarm in Johnstown. Always said, 'Victor, you'll never amount to a hill of beans is what. Not a hill of beans.' I didn't have much notion on what she meant by that. I was at the stage where I was the fella just knee-high to a grasshopper, so a hill of beans sounded 'bout like the moon. Kind of a place ever'body'd like to amount to if they could. I don't know if goin' on the television as a folk scholar amounts to a hill of beans or no —I suspect no — but I reckon Miss Henshkey'd allow it's further along than she'd figured for ole Vic."

Aldridge sat forward, tapping the eraser of his pencil on the desk. He seemed to sense that he was losing control of the interview. "So when did you come out to this area?"

"Day I turned fifteen I hitched a wagon behind our nag Betsy and headed out of town. Stared at her east end for a month, Mr. Aldridge. That's a view I got my fill of."

The newsman laughed nervously.

"Didn't own nothin'. Didn't have nothin' in the wagon. Stopped me in a farm in Illinois and worked two years for a Welshman. His daughter, Katie, who's about seventeen, sneaks in the shed one day, unbuttons her dress, and says, 'Take me away, Victor.' Katie weren't no looker, Mr. Aldridge, but I'll tell you the truth, a buxom young girl can look pretty fair with a pouch of her pa's seed money stuffed between her breasts. And I'll tell you somethin' else, long as we're havin' this little chat, she was a sight prettier than them Johnstown women, Gawd rest her. Johnstown had some powerful ugly women back then. Might still. Somethin' in the water, is how I figured it. I saw this one lady, Mrs. Penniman . . ."

"Mrs. Penniman?"

"The same. Mrs. Penniman — and her gettin' a husband attests to the humble fate man can expect on this earth — I saw her kill one of Johnstown's elderbushes just by lookin' at it. Every leaf on that tree was on the ground in fifteen seconds. . . ."

The slope-shouldered cowboy behind the cameraman blew a long, disgusted gush of air toward the ceiling and staggered backward. Laughing, the pretty woman beside him grabbed at his hands and pulled him back. The cameraman motioned for them to hush.

". . . That lady made it through the flood, and prob'ly lived a hundred years, the Good Lord having enough sense not to want her back for a while. I mean *powerful* ugly. So I told Katie, sure, let's hightail it, which made her button up quicker than a chilly wind. We ran off to Iowa, got wed, and kept heading west till we come to the Powder River. That's where I hooked up with Jake Jenkins's outfit. And this whole damn country seemed to open up before us and say, 'Come on, McKenzie, you big lout. Come on, let's try 'er again.' And I was thinkin', yessir, here comes the *real* golden age.

"Katie, she died of pneumonia the winter of nineteen hundred five."

Papa Vic wiped his mouth on the back of his knotty hand, looked around quickly, then turned to one of the technicians off-camera. There were a half-dozen of them standing around, absorbed in the interview. "S'pose you could bring a man some coffee?"

The man he spoke to was so startled — it was a live broadcast — that, again, the young, dark-haired woman stifled a laugh. Aldridge nodded to the man helplessly, and Papa Vic smiled. "The point is, Mr. Aldridge, there never would have been a Bar V Ranch if it weren't for that flood, and there never would have been a flood if it weren't for that jackass engineer and his Pennsylvania Canal. So we McKenzies, and maybe Wyomin' too, owe a lot to that flood and the jackass both. Ain't that somethin', the way Gawd works? But we paid out a lot, too. I reckon just about everything there is owes a lot to some jackass somewheres, but's been paid for, too, one way or th'other. Then, even after it's been paid for, each blessed thief passin' by is going to try to grab it away from you. That's the way of this country."

It suddenly occurred to the young woman, Avelyn McKenzie, that the wagon he had driven west, his first possession, was the one by the gate, near the cookshed where they barbecued the calf every fall. Its wood was gray and cracked, and grass grew from its crevices, and the iron-rimmed wheels were rusted and bent. She had always thought of it as decoration. Once, Mike had mentioned breaking his collarbone against it as a boy. But she had never given it much thought. She had given so little thought to Mike's roots.

Papa Vic was talking again, his voice dry and raspy, soft, with a quality in it that stilled the entire studio. She was leaning forward, her head cocked toward him — he sat bolt upright, his face wrinkled, so distinguished-looking in his suede jacket and black string tie and gray Stetson. He was ninety-two.

"Jake Jenkins was a powerful man and a good man to work for," Papa Vic was saying. "You had to be them things. Took powerful men to take this land from the Injuns, and took good men to work for to hold it from the next fella who came along. You got to understand this one thing if'n you're gonna understand any of it. They're always gonna try to take it from him that's got it. They'll try. Sheepherders tried. Homesteaders tried. Next fella through'll try, too. But this here land, Gawd meant for cattle, seems like.

"What about the range wars?" Aldridge asked.

"Trouble with the sheepherders started down on Powder River country, 'bout nineteen hundred two. Katie and I was over in the Canyon Creek area by then. First white folks to settle in that valley. That means somethin'. Jenkins sold me my cattle. He spoke for me when he formed the Cattleman's Association, and he formed it 'cause of them sheepherders. I rode with him 'cause I owed him.

"Powder River land was the best land in the state back then. A man could've growed wheat or beets on that land, or watched the grass grow up to his chest with no more fuss than fallin' off a log. That was Gawd's backyard, and Gawd bein' a cattleman first and a Gawd second, weren't nothin' but cattle raised there.

"Then the bottom drops out of the market two years runnin', and the smaller outfits start to go under. Me, I'd've gone under with 'em, but I was just startin' off and doin' a whole lot of buyin' to build me a herd. Prices seemed swell to me. But some of Jenkins's neighbors feel the squeeze and start to sell off their cattle and replace them with sheep. Sheep business flat had more money in it then. Couldn't deny it. Still, it weren't right. That's what started off this range war thing."

"Why weren' — wasn't it right?"

"It was open range then. Sheep started grazin' the open range. No fences. You seen sheep?"

"Well, sure, I've seen sheep," Aldridge said.

"All right then. Any fool knows sheep's got sharp, clove hoofs raise hell on a pasture. They graze the grass right down to the roots, further down'n a cow, then they move forward and cut the roots with their hoofs. Grass don't reseed itself. Sheep were grazin' that Powder River country to death. This here's fragile land, about one step from a desert. Somethin' like that takes a hundred years to come back to where it was. You been down in Powder River country?"

Aldridge nodded and seemed pleased. "Sure have. Beautiful land."

"Paaa! Grass along the Powder River still ain't worth a — " He caught himself.

"I see what you mean," Aldridge said.

"Well. So Jenkins starts the Cattleman's Association to get rid of the sheep, and like I said, I owed Jake. We drove one of them flocks right over the bluffs and into the Powder River. Had us a rimrocking party, folks called it. Three thousand sheep, they said. River boiled white with 'em. Over the cliffs like lemmings. That was a sight, all right. One of them sheepherders got shot, and another stampeded. I know who shot the one, but I won't say who. I still won't. There's kin on both sides still in the area, and there'd be bad blood between 'em even now. Always been bad blood between the ranchers and sheepmen. Always will be. You want to make a rancher mad, you call him something with the word 'sheep' in it. Hee-hee-haw." Papa Vic laughed and slapped his knee. "Unless the fella's a Basque. Them Basques, they can't hear enough about sheep. Call them anything you want."

"Let's talk about the open range. It was on its way out then anyway, wasn't it?"

"Pretty near. Used to be you could ride for seven days any direction and never find a fence. That changed." Papa Vic slowly pulled a large blue handkerchief from his back pocket and blew his nose. Avelyn glanced at Mike and was surprised to see him smiling. His arms were folded, his upper body leaning back slightly, and his feet were spread wide.

"Where's that coffee?" Papa Vic asked.

The technician lurking in the wings darted on-camera and handed him the cup. Papa Vic thanked him and sipped it. Aldridge watched.

"This stuff ain't good for me," Papa Vic said.

"So what did bring an end to the open range?" Aldridge asked lamely.

"Barbed wire." He frowned at the coffee. "This stuff eats at my guts."

"What about the 'Don't Fence Me In' mentality? 'Oh, give me land, lots of land 'neath the starry skies above, don't fence me in.' "

Papa Vic looked at him and laughed. The cameraman and the technicians laughed, too. Blushing, Aldridge grinned.

"Look, this here land, Gawd meant for cattle. That pretty much sums it up. This here country, Gawd meant for cattle. Bovine creatures. Buffalo was plumb happy here, and they're top-of-the-line bovines. Once a person comes to grips with that, Mr. Aldridge, you croonin' fool . . ."

Aldridge blushed again.

". . . once he gets that into his head, well, that explains 'bout everything. Us and the Injuns. Us and the sheepmen. Us and the homesteaders. Open range ended when a man named Hardy Webster Campbell convinced folks back East that this here land was meant for dry-land farming, for wheat. Between nineteen hundred ten and nineteen hundred twenty, eighty thousand of 'em come out to try. Bought up all the private lands for sale, then the state gets thinkin', 'Sure, this here land's meant for wheat, too.' So they pass the Homestead Act in nineteen sixteen and put all our public grazin' land for sale in three-hundred-twenty-acre parcels. And folks came out and bought 'em, and up went the fences. The whole Canyon Creek area that me and an Injun up the road ranched ourselves, whole valley was scooped up by the homesteaders and farmed east to west. The Great War come, price of wheat shot up, and all them wheat farmers make more money than Carter's got pills. So they mortgage themselves out their geezers — can I say that? Geezers?"

Aldridge looked around and shrugged.

"— well, they do and then they get more land, plant more wheat, and the weather's just right. Rain falls, and by Gawd, they grow forty bushels of wheat to an acre. I'm thinkin', Victor, you young buck, time to be a wheat farmer. Ole Hardy Webster Campbell, he could've run for President and not wore socks.

"Things turned in spring of nineteen eighteen, of course,

'cause that there land was meant for cattle and bovine creatures. First sign was when Frederic Meyer run over hisself furrowing, and bled to death in his wheatfield. Poor ole Frederic — him and his wife Abbey come from Pennsylvania and settled two sections acrost from the Bar V — he run over a hornet's nest. You been stung by a hornet, Mr. Aldridge?"

"Me? Well, yes. Not recently."

"You're a lucky fella. Man stung by a hornet'll do near anything to get away, and Frederic jumped right under his tractor, which he wouldn't've done if he'd thought it out. That was the first sign. Then the war ended, a drought come, and what little wheat could be harvested brought a damn poor price. So them homesteaders packed up and cleared out, some now, some later. They left behind dustfields where good pastureland had been. Cattlemen stayed, 'cause cattlemen always stayed. Abbey Meyer, just nineteen, packed up her belongings after ole Frederic run hisself over and the crop failed, and was gonna try to get to California 'fore winter. Never would've made it, is how I had 'er figured, so I moseyed over in a neighborly way and asked for her hand. She give it to me, too. We combined our property, bought out two more homesteaders, and the Injun up the road, and by Gawd, we had a spread. Took till nineteen hundred thirty 'fore that grass come back with much respectability, but we were there when it did. And so were cattlemen along the Tongue River and the Powder River and lower Canyon Creek, 'cause that there land Gawd meant for cattle, like I mentioned.

"Abbey never did forgive ole Hardy Webster Campbell. Never blamed poor Frederic's death on them hornets for a minute. It was Hardy Webster's fault for tryin' to make this land somethin' it weren't.

"Abbey give me a son, Earl, and a girl, Willa, and I give her beef six days a week and liver on Sunday. Cattle business was as good a business as any durin' the Great Depression, if you owned your land, which I did, and liked beef, which I did. She was killed in a fall in nineteen thirty-two." Papa Vic paused, tucking his chin against his neck. "Abbey and Earl was tar-paperin' the barn roof, tryin' to get 'er done before a storm come.

Lightnin' struck the weathervane and jolted 'em off. Abbey broke her neck, and Earl landed on the rail fence and broke his arm. Went through all three rails, and him just a little guy, not eighty pounds. We got a family plot down under three cotton-woods in a nook, and I buried Abbey there beside Katie and Abbey's stillborn. Them cottonwoods're about ready to fall anymore. Any storm now, and they're goners."

Avelyn was kneeling now, listening. The small graveyard had moved her more than she could explain the first time Mike took her there. His parents, killed in an automobile accident, were buried there. She had not thought to ask about Papa Vic's wives. They had seemed so old, so far removed — though no longer. Neither had been much older than she was. Avelyn had planted bulbs there last fall, and in the spring, with the daffodils, it was a lovely spot. She thought of her name next to Mike's there, and felt oddly safe.

"You endure it," Papa Vic was saying. "You don't love it nor hate it, you endure it. Man tells you he loves this land, Mr. Aldridge, is lyin' to your face. He might believe it, but it's a lie anyhow. What you love is the water. You payin' attention to this?"

Aldridge was looking toward the cameraman, who was hold-ing a thirty-second timer that signaled a commercial break. It had just started to run. The newsman glanced quickly back to Papa Vic, with the sheepishness of a pupil caught daydreaming. "The water," he repeated.

Two technicians walked away from the set, laughing.

"Yessir. Water's more important than the land, the cattle, a woman, or a good horse. Tastes good when you're thirsty, and tastes good in cubes. And this land ain't worth horsecakes with-out it. I'm a big fan of water, Mr. Aldridge, and I got company."

Then Papa Vic stopped and leaned closer to Aldridge. "All this talk about water," he said gruffly. "I got to piss."

Aldridge's expression went utterly blank. Five seconds later, he turned and smiled feebly at the camera. "We'll break now for a word from our sponsor."

CHAPTER 2

MIKE MCKENZIE STOLE a look at his grandfather and grinned. It was a small grin that just curled one side of his mouth, that softened the steel-gray eyes for an instant and creased his brown cheek, making a face that might simply have been called rugged, or interesting, at once boyish and strikingly handsome. At such moments Avelyn was overcome with the feeling that he might say, or do, about anything — though now he was clearly trying to work up some indignation and battled to suppress that grin.

"You tell me one thing," Mike demanded. "You float through that flood in a basket or a washtub?"

Avelyn said, "Oh, Michael, don't be so literal-minded."

"Ask him. . . . Basket or washtub?"

"Might've been a washtub at that," Papa Vic said.

"Well, Moses never went down any river in a washtub."

Papa Vic brooded over that as they drove out of Billings. It was a flat, middle-class town with wide streets and uninteresting houses. They passed the trainyard and crossed the Yellowstone River, where they got on the eastbound highway. "Well, how in the hell would *you* know what Moses did or didn't do?"

"He never went down any river in a washtub," Mike said.

"Listen to him, who wouldn't know a Bible if it fell on him."

"Don't pull your holier-than-thou airs on me. I was raised in that graven image of yours." Mike pointed a thick forefinger at his grandfather.

"The hell."

"By *you*, old-timer."

Papa Vic snorted. "I may have raised you a heathen, but I didn't raise you an *ornery* heathen."

"The *hell!*" They glowered at each other, then glanced automatically back to Avelyn for support.

"Where'd you get the notion to say you got to piss on television?" Mike asked.

"I had to."

"If you'd had to crap, would you have announced that too?"

"If I'd had to *crap* — pardon me, Missy — I'd have darn well raised a flag and hollered. That particular ship comes in 'bout once a month."

Mike shook his head, breaking into that little grin of his. Papa Vic folded his arms in annoyance. They were in grazing country now and the hills began to roll. When they reached the top of one they could see for fifty miles over the spring-green grassland and the wheatfields and the rich, dark sections lying fallow. The northern Great Plains. Nowhere else had Avelyn ever felt such a sense of freedom and limitless possibility, as if a person might become about anything she wanted. It was beautiful land, and vast.

"How about if I call Lloyd and Carol and we celebrate Papa Vic's television debut?" she said. "What say?"

"Not tonight. Gonna shoot us a bear tonight." Mike saw Avelyn's face fall and curled one side of his mouth in an apologetic smile. "Last day of the season, hon."

She sat back, trailing her slender fingers against her cheekbone. "You and I will celebrate," she said to Papa Vic.

Mike shrugged. "Come along on the hunt if you like."

"There! That's it." She brightened.

"You and Denny and that fool Deacon ain't manpower enough for that little blackie, that's clear," Papa Vic said.

"That's a big bear up there," Mike said. "Seen its tracks."

"You set bait?"

"Hung the hindquarters of that steer that froze in the creekbed."

"Pretty rank?"

"Oh, it's rank."

Papa Vic laughed and clapped his hands. "Like to eat me a nice spring bear. They're tasty early, 'fore they get into all that winter-killed game and garbage. Sweet and lean. Ever cooked a nice spring bear, Missy?"

Avelyn shook her head.

"I'll learn ya if these carrion-eaters can shoot one."

"Eat, crap, piss. All you're good for anymore," Mike said.

Papa Vic leaned forward and scowled. "What'd he say?"

"He said he doesn't shoot too good anymore. Don't pay any attention to him, Papa Vic." Avelyn elbowed her husband in the ribs.

Mike cupped his hand to his ear. "Eh? Eh? Say what? You're getting plumb balmy."

"Don't call me balmy."

"Balmy sonofabitch."

They crossed into Wyoming. The Goose Creek Highway took them over the Tongue River and into Kearney. It was a small town, pretty in its way. There was a wooden boardwalk in front of all the stores, shaded by an overhanging roof. The pine pillars supporting the overhang were notched and rails had been nailed between them, perfect for sitting. It made the main street seem simple and old-fashioned. Most of the stores were log-sided and had weathered gray, and four towering spruce trees gave the street some color.

When Mike stopped in at the post office, Avelyn ran across the street to Trudy Miller's art gallery to see if any of her photographs had sold. The door was locked and there was a note taped to the window saying, "Back in five minutes." She tried to see in, but the pictures were along the dark, back wall of the store. It was silly to get her hopes up until the tourists came, she thought. Another month — and summer, backpackers, fishermen, and sightseers in their accursed Winnebagos. The tourists. She'd been one. A bored eighteen-year-old fashion model out to the dude ranch with her parents — horseback-riding, fishing, escaping from the Long Island summer humidity. Something new — a new part of the country, a new man, a new . . . something. Falling in love with Michael that very first morning, letting him help her on the horse as if she'd never seen a horse before, being so ready for love and that new something that it was like holding up your arms and falling, drifting off, wonderfully helpless. She didn't even have to try. And spending that whole next year back East waiting for the magic to fade, finishing school, and expecting to be swept away again as everyone had promised would happen. A career. A boy. It was Wyoming that had entrapped her, not the cowboy. She'd forget the cowboy. But she didn't.

He had backed the truck around and was waiting. She started back across, and as she did Ziggy Ziegler, who owned the hardware store in town, came out and made a beeline toward the pickup. He was an odd little man whom she had never seen out of his black apron with the folding rule in the pouch, a device he was in the habit of fiddling with to pass the time. They arrived at the pickup at the same time, and Ziggy nodded to her in greeting. Then he leaned his elbows on Mike's door. "You hidin' ole Vic in here, Michael? I saw you on the television this morning, Victor."

"How'd I look?"

"Looked fine. Cut quite a figure." He wore a big, leering grin that bared his upper teeth, which were black with tobacco flecks. "You won't forget your friends now that you're a celebrity?"

"Man needs balin' wire, I figure I'll remember ole Zig."

The merchant spat into the dust, making sucking, laughing noises. "That's all folks is talkin' about. Ever' man comes in the store is askin' if I seen Vic McKenzie on the television."

"Conversation always been a mite tedious in this town," Papa Vic said.

"You sure give it to him. I wished I'd had my color set in the store here. That fella looked about seven shades of green when you said —" Ziegler suddenly stopped, grinning foolishly at Avelyn. Mike said something about there being work to do and resettled himself to shift the truck into gear. "Hear about the goings-on at the reservation?" Ziegler quickly asked.

"What're them Cheyenne up to now?"

"Titanic Coal found a vein up there. Not six miles from here. Quite a find, I understand."

"Yeah?"

"Sam Benson was in here and he was plumb agitated," Ziegler said, spitting again. He was shaking his head and smiling. "Guess that lease them Injuns signed with them coal boys might not have been the best dang deal. You know Sam . . . "

"Oh, God . . ."

"I told him, 'Sam, they's Injuns, ain't they? Since when you ever heard of an Injun making a good deal by signin' a paper with a white man? Damn near a law against it.' He says when he was state senator, ever' time he saw an Injun sign a contract, he got the same feeling in his gut as watching a coyote eat a chicken. Just somethin' in him told him the chicken was getting the short end of the stick. But these eastern coal companies are a special burr for ole Sam, all their wheeling and dealing and stepping on toes. Says they've all got together and divvied up areas so's not to get into bidding wars. That Titanic was the only company interested in that Cheyenne lease."

"They sure got in there quick," Mike said.

"You bet they did. Sam can get kinda comical going on about it. 'They's just Injuns,' I'm telling him."

Mike worked his tongue across the inside of his lower lip and dropped a thumbful of Ziggy's Copenhagen tobacco in. "That'th the truth." He worked some saliva up and spit. "Work to do, Zig."

Mike was already pulling away. Ziegler called something out to Papa Vic that was lost. "Never did much like that fella," Papa Vic said. Through town, they turned onto the Canyon Creek road and headed up the valley. It was greener there. The road was unpaved and gravel slapped at the belly of the truck.

Avelyn picked up the bunch of mail Mike had laid on the front seat. "You've got a telegram," she said to Papa Vic. He grunted and looked at it. "Well. Open 'er up and tell me who died. Maybe I did."

Avelyn tucked the rest of the mail under her leg and slit open the telegram. "It's from Jimbo. 'Sorry not there. Volunteering for McGovern! Bank wants soul. Help. Luck. Love. Jimbo.' "

"Jiminy-Criminy-send-him-back-to-Bimini," Papa Vic said. "I miss that whelp. Who the hell's McGovern?"

"A nut," Mike said.

"What kind of nut would Jimmy be workin' for?"

"He's running for the Democratic nomination for President."

"Against Ike?"

"Ike's dead. He's Republican anyhow, you balmy old sonofabitch. You pullin' my leg?"

"Who is? I like Ike. Never touched nothin'. Never interfered. Sat back and played golf with the rich folks. Polished his medals and his head."

Avelyn laughed, shaking back her hair. Mike looked at his grandfather in disapproval, unsure whether Papa Vic knew what he was talking about or was just leading him along a playful path.

"McGovern's a nut, eh?" Papa Vic said, winking at Avelyn.

"Been saying nutty things for months," Mike said.

"Jimmy's always showed good sense. I might just vote for him. I ain't voted in about thirty years."

"Well, don't start now."

"Kinda like to see a regular nut in that office."

"If you listened to McGovern for an hour, then listened to a fencepost, you'd vote for the fencepost," Mike said.

"Might. Damn few Presidents could've won my vote from a good fencepost." Papa Vic removed his hat long enough to run his hand over his hair, which was mottled with streaks of gray, brown, and white and was still full. "I recollect votin' for Teddy Roosevelt on account of he got his ears wet in Dakota. Oh, I liked him, Michael. Things got ornery, little Ted was just guaranteed to give you a laugh. Smart fella gets in the White House, first thing he does when things get tight is start a war. Ole Teddy, little comical guy in a top hat, he'd say 'bully' and drop his monocle. Then things'd seem pretty swell again. Don't take a war. Just takes a monocle and a person in a top hat saying 'bully' at the proper times. Course, a lot depends on *how* you say 'bully.'

Ole Teddy could flat give you a 'bully!' This McGovern fella, he wouldn't wear a monocle?"

Mike ignored him. "I can't believe old buddy boy is doing volunteer work for that nut," he said.

"Hee-hee!" Papa Vic laughed, slapping his knee. "You're *against* him, ain't you? Since when you and your baby brother agreed on anythin'? Since when, Michael? You tell him the sky is blue and he'd say, 'That depends.' Gawd, I miss that whelp. What you got there, Missy?"

She looked up from the letter she was reading. "It's from Mummy."

"What's 'Mummy' have to say?" Mike asked.

Avelyn ignored his tone and continued reading the letter. When she finished she folded it carefully back into the envelope. "She says that any time I choose to admit my mistake I'll be welcomed home with open arms."

"That it?"

"She's the only woman in Oyster Bay with a bumper sticker that says 'Eat More Beef.' "

Mike nodded. "She's all right, your ma. They coming out?"

"Daddy's taking her to England on business. They've a chance to see Wimbledon, and my mother prefers strawberries to cow-dung every time."

"They eat little strawberries there, that's right."

"I went once," Avelyn said. "They can have it. The weather was not to be believed — rain and damp and wind. My sister and I were with a friend from boarding school, and the three of us snuck in on two tickets. We squeezed together into two seats, or tried to. It was hysterical. Finally this pleasant little man with a pipe who was beside me said in the most apologetic way, 'Madam, your hips are too large.' "

Mike smiled. "Your sister gonna visit?"

"She hates horses; I told you that. It doesn't matter. It's their loss, right?"

On the left-hand side of the road a broad mesa rose steeply. It was smooth and flat and treeless on top. The McKenzies grazed their cattle there in the summer, leasing the land from the state. It was a good place to ride, and from the top you could just make out the chimney of the ranchhouse up on the opposite ridge, surrounded by cottonwoods. Beyond, farther south, the snow-capped tips of the Bighorn Mountains showed against the sky. The sky was what you noticed. Not the flatlands toward Sheridan or the foothills or those jagged white peaks. The sky. A depth of blue such as you've never seen.

Mike turned through the Bar V gate, two thick pine pillars with a third notched across the top. The dirt drive was rutted from the spring runoff. They climbed through the south pasture, then dipped as they reached the hollow below the house. A spring trickled there and beside it the three old cottonwoods grew, hiding the graveyard. Stormy, Mike's German shepherd, lay in the shade, wagging its tail as the truck passed. It bounced across the cattle guard and into the yard. "You boy," Mike called, and the dog got up to follow.

Deacon Bueller, their foreman, was tinkering under the hood of the tractor. Deacon had been a world champion bareback rider in 1958, but a bad fall four years later had ended his rodeo career and Papa Vic had hired him on after finding him drunk one night in a bar. He stuck directions to the ranch inside his shirt pocket and four days later Deacon showed up sober and ready to work. That was ten years ago. Deacon's beer belly pushed his pants low in the front so that his championship belt buckle, a huge silver and gold oval, pointed straight toward the ground. He was wearing his stained baseball cap and a dirty white T-shirt, and his broad grin upon seeing Papa Vic revealed a gold-capped front tooth.

"What the hell possessed you to say 'geezer' on the television, Papa Vic?" Deacon asked, pulling his head away from the tractor.

"Did I say geezer?"

"You sure did. Just like that. 'Geezer.' " Deacon spoke in rapid spurts and winked when he smiled.

"You making any headway there?" Mike asked. He nodded toward the tractor.

"Think I got 'er licked. Grounding wire 'tween the alternator and regulator got jostled out of whack."

"Hell of a deal, Deac. You do good work. Denny rigging up a siphon for them new steers?"

"He's down there. Goddamn that Denny, he seen you come on the television and I thought, by God, he's gonna talk. He's gonna get himself so plumb excited he's gonna utter words. I'd've keeled right over and died. I never seen nothin' like it. Big old lout shakin' and twitchin' and movin' his big mouth, pointin' at that television like he sees the face of God. He keeps looking over at me with that goofy expression he gets, and I finally say, 'Hell, Den, *I* know that's him. I'm the fella set you down here if you recall.' That boy was a sight all right. Give me the willies, seein' him movin' his mouth like a fish."

"Better see how he's making out," Mike said. "Papa Vic, you up to walking down to the arena and seeing the Mexican steers?"

Papa Vic walked stiffly past him. "I ain't waitin' on you."

"By God, it moves."

"Damn your insolence anyway."

Avelyn started inside, then Deacon remembered something. "Marjorie Fox called. Said she'd like to see you."

Avelyn picked up his change of tone. "That all?"

"Well." Deacon lowered his eyes. "Just better see her, I guess."

"Is it Hepp?" Deacon didn't answer her. "Is it that awful Hepp again? Deacon? Oh, dammit all."

"She didn't say anythin' about it," Deacon said. "She didn't sound too good though. I guess you'd better see her."

"When did she call?"

"This mornin' early. I'd guess it happened last night."

"All right. Tell Mike where I am." She went inside to get the keys, then drove back down the road.

CHAPTER 3

MARJORIE FOX'S LEFT eye was swollen to a slit. The tender reddish crescent was beginning to deepen to purple, and her lower lip was puffy and split. It took a long time before she would lower the ice pack to allow Avelyn to look. Then they had a cry together.

After a while Marjorie pulled back and faced her and shrugged with resignation. "I told him I weren't married to this ranch. I told him that. I told him I'd leave this goldarned ranch in a minute and he'd better not doubt it. I didn't say 'I do' to any fool ranch."

She cried again, and Avelyn held her. She could imagine the argument. Marjorie and Hepp could go along evenly for months, quietly storing things up against one another, so that once they got into it they began ripping at the old scars, both going back as far as their memories would let them. Old ghosts far better forgotten. It always ended with the same not-entirely-empty threat: that Marjorie had never said "I do" to the ranch, and that she'd leave it, with or without him, and take the kids with her as far west and south as she could go. He'd better not doubt it. Which is when Hepp would hit her and run off to wherever he would disappear to for a week or so. Hepp's mother had left his father, old Jake Fox, for a traveling soap salesman, of all people. That was behind it. Old Jake had turned to drink and to whipping Hepp and Hepp's sister, Patty, until one night he choked on his steak right there in front of the kids. But he'd already whipped in the meanness. After a week or ten days, Hepp would come back, repentent, and Marjorie would take him back in, and things would go all right until the next time. But every time they went into town, she made him pay for it. Pretty and blonde, Marjorie would put on makeup and a tight set of clothes and would carry herself in a teasing, sexy way, playing up to Hepp's friends as if in open invitation. She'd smile and leave her mouth parted in a willing and vulnerable manner, so that Hepp was afraid to leave her alone. So that he was afraid to trust her with anyone. So that every Saturday night in town became an ordeal, something he dreaded. To Avelyn's knowledge, her flirting was just show, her way of getting back at him. But it kept the vicious circle spinning, and things would build and stew until the next time, when all would boil out in a rage.

"You okay?" Avelyn asked when she'd stopped.

Marjorie nodded, wiping her face with a Kleenex. Kneeling on her bed and biting her lip, she looked little more than a young girl.

"Are the kids all right?" Avelyn asked.

"Timmy's off at school. I told him I fell against the doorknob. He'd go right after his daddy if he knew the truth." Marjorie sat back and reached for a pack of cigarettes. They sat thinking for a while.

"You take my advice and wait on having kids till you're good and ready," Marjorie said. She inhaled and blew out a long stream of smoke. "Here I am giving *you* advice. I'm the one who needs the advice, honey. *Needed* it. How come you and Mike's so smart, anyhow?"

"I'm not ready for children," Avelyn said.

"Well, I guess I weren't ready for children either but they was sure enough ready for me." She blew cigarette smoke from her nostrils. "I'll bet that Mike's ready enough. I'll bet that. You don't mind me askin', do you, hon?"

"I don't mind. Sure, he's ready. I'm not."

Marjorie laughed. "That's my girl. You take my advice and wait till *you're* good and ready. Well, listen to me, telling you advice again. Look at me with two kids; and look at you, free as a bird. Look at *me* telling you. That's a stitch." Marjorie tapped her fingers on the bedspread and looked vacantly out the window. "I used to be sweet on Mike, you know that? Sure I did. He was captain of the football team. I had the pick of anybody in the high school, and I was sweet on Mike. Well, he was the star of everything, really."

"Wouldn't he just love to hear it."

"Well, he knew it, hon. Not in a bad way, but when you're all-state this and all-state that —"

"And the best-looking cheerleader in school is after you —"

"There you go. And senior year . . ." Marjorie whistled to show how torrid the romance had been. Then she waved her hand as if she were teasing. "Mike's a good guy. You married a nice fella. Everyone says so."

"I know I did."

"Did you know? Did you —?" Marjorie stopped and pulled another Kleenex from the box and dabbed at her eyes. "Eastern girl like you, fancy girl like you . . . Did you know what you was getting into, hon?"

"Oh . . . What do you know when you're twenty, anyway?"

"Ain't that the truth," Marjorie said. "None of us knows what she's getting in for, really. I don't care how old you are." She was quiet for a long time, staring down at the folds in the bed. "You take Lucy Preston. When she married that Billy, well, he was the nicest, politest boy you'd ever want to see. Everyone was falling all over themselves for happiness. Now just look at him. He's making all that money at that construction company of his, and instead of things going good for Lucy, well, he starts carryin' on with other women just as soon, just exactly as soon as he starts makin' money. He's carryin' on with Hepp's sister Patty now, you know that? Well, he is. That Patty, she's a one. She's gonna get her neck wrung good some day." Marjorie had smoked her cigarette nearly down to the filter, and she snuffed it out. "Well, Patty's a nice enough kid, but she oughta have enough sense to keep clear of the married ones, you know? Ain't my affair to get mixed up in. But you see what I mean, don't you, hon? Ain't none of us really knows what she's getting in for."

"Are you all right, Marge?"

"Sure I am." She laughed. "Hell, I'm fine, hon." She lit another cigarette and gave it a quick puff. "Us Wyoming women is born tough, you know? We may not be born smart, but we're born tough. Born to survive, you know? Real survivors." She laughed sarcastically. "I'm swell. Only —"

"What is it?"

"Well, my marketing. You don't s'pose . . ." Her voice began to choke up. "Hon, you don't think you'd be able to go into Mailer's and . . . do my shopping for me, huh?" She was crying again. "I don't much feel like going into town for the next few days. . . ." She covered her eyes with her hands. "Could you do that, hon? The list's stuck right there on the fridge. You're a real good friend, Avelyn. You married a real nice fella, you know that?"

CHAPTER 4

THAT NIGHT WAS the bear hunt. Avelyn's hands were crammed into the pockets of her parka, and she snuggled her shoulder against Mike's. The slope below them was scabbed with rocks, and at the bottom was a huge boulder at the edge of a forest of aspen. The hindquarters of a steer hung from one of the first small trees.

"It's freezing," she whispered. She liked being there in the chill, with night falling, with the others.

"Shh."

"What time is it?"

Mike glanced at his watch. "Eight-thirty. Best time's from here till dark. The wind's right."

It was blowing in their faces. "The wind's been right all night. It's *freezing*." Avelyn tried to find his hand to hold. She reached into his lap and hit the rifle. "Mmm. Hard."

Mike glanced sidelong at her. She returned his look brightly. He watched the hollow. "You wouldn't be bored if you'd brought a gun."

"I'm not bored. I'm freezing."

"Go sit in the car, then."

"There's bears out here, my love. Escort me?"

"Ask Denny." He took his eyes off the hollow long enough to nod toward his deaf-mute cousin.

25

"No. *You.*" Avelyn bared her teeth and brushed her tongue against his neck.

Mike pulled back. "Now *quit.* We're hunting. Hush and look."

"It doesn't seem like we're hunting."

Deacon leaned forward and offered Avelyn the bottle of Jack Daniel's he was sipping from. "Belt this down, sugarbabe." The whiskey had put a bright glaze to his eyes.

"I've half a mind to," she said.

Mike nodded at Deacon. "That's all it takes, half a mind."

"All right then." Avelyn wiped the mouth of the bottle with her palm and took a respectable belt. It was cold in her mouth and burned going down and then started to warm her from the inside out.

It would be pitch-dark in thirty minutes. Mike thought he saw a movement down by the aspen and touched Deacon on the knee to quiet him. The gray-green lines of the tree trunks swam into one another, and Mike closed his eyes, then looked up at the sky for a moment to clear his vision. When he looked back down, he could see three coyotes sniffing beneath the rotting carcass of the steer. "Coyotes."

Deacon squinted. "Well. Hell, let's shoot some coyote."

"I want my bear."

"Your bear ain't comin'. Let's shoot some coyote, boss."

"He sure ain't coming if we do that."

Deacon pondered. "Be a fine feelin' to shoot them coyotes." He took another drink of the whiskey, wrinkling up his bristly face as he swallowed, then smiling through tightened lips as it hit bottom. "Be a fine, fine, feelin'. Still got their nice winter coats, an' ole Deac would spread 'em out in front of the wood-stove in the bunkhouse, and sugarbabe would sneak on over when the bossman was sawin' logs, some cold February night, and we'd rub our knees together on them skins. Be a fine, fine feelin' to shoot them coyotes, boss."

"That sounds wonderful." Avelyn laughed. "Shoot away."

Deacon put his eye to the sight of the gun. "Give ole Deac the nod, boss. Bam! Bam! Bam! I'll mow them chicken thieves down and dirty. We'll skin them dogs and roll in their fur like pups. Be a fine, fine feelin', wouldn't it, sugarbabe? Come on, boss, what say?"

"Pipe down."

"I want to shoot a coyote. I want to shoot three coyotes."

"You couldn't hit old Ironsides with a magnet if you were locked in the hold. We're here for bear."

"Bullshit," Deacon said. He took another swig of whiskey.

"Will you hush!" Papa Vic said at last. "Go smell your feet."

Deacon curled his lips and thick jowls. He scratched the back of his head. After a minute he muttered, "That'd quiet me, all right. Knock me flat out."

Suddenly the heads of the coyotes jerked up and turned toward the woods. They posed stock-still. As if on signal, the trio trotted around the boulder and out of sight. Mike leaned against the rock in front of him. It was nearly dark, moonless.

A black bear appeared among the gray of the tree trunks. It moved cautiously, holding its nose high. They waited as the bear moved out past the carcass. The others watched Mike. He sucked in his breath and raised the rifle to his shoulder as the bear stood slowly upright. It lifted its nose into the breeze, swiveling its head from side to side.

Mike saw black in the sight. He swung the rifle to the side, and the gray outlines of the trees became clear. He realized he had been directly on the body of the bear. He swung the rifle back, across the blackness, until the gray showed on the other side. Then he eased the barrel back. He raised it a fraction, steadied, and squeezed. The rifle kicked back and up with the explosion. *Keeerrrackkk!*

The flash of light blinded them for an instant. Deacon fired four quick rounds in the general direction of the bear. Suddenly he broke out of his crouch and ran gimpily down the hill. "Whoooee! Whoooee! We got 'im, boss!" Deacon fired another shot from the hip.

Laughing, Avelyn followed, just eluding Mike's grasp as she ran by. "Goddammit!" Mike yelled.

"Whoooee! Whoooee! Stop or I'll shoot, bear!" *Keeerrackkk!*
Keeerrackkk! Keeerrackkk! "We got us a blackie. Big ole blackie!"
Deacon's voice was getting more distant.

"Avelyn, come back here, dammit!" Mike yelled. He and Papa
Vic were ducked behind the outcrop. Denny had also started
down the hollow. Mike heard their boots scuffing the dry, pebbly
ground of the hillside. He poked his head up, then ducked it
down again as Deacon fired another shot.

Keeerrackkk! It echoed all around them.

Mike put his arm over his head. "Avelyn, you take cover!" he
yelled, his forehead pressed against the ground.

Papa Vic had never budged. "Someone shootin' back at him?"

"I hope so."

"You dock him a week's pay, Michael." Mike nodded at his
grandfather.

"We got him, boss! We got us a blackie! Whoooee!" Deacon
sounded out of breath. Mike listened, his head behind the rock.
"Shit," he heard.

"What's going on down there? Honey? You okay?" He eased
his head up.

"I'm okay," Avelyn said. She, too, cowered behind a rock halfway down the hill. Denny was beside her.

It was too dark to see Deacon. "You through down there?"
Mike called. "Bueller? What's going on?"

"Out of ammo." Deacon was at the boulder.

"There any hide left on that bear?" Mike could just make out
Deacon's hunching figure squinting into the woods.

"Blamed if I know. Think he skirted behind this rock and
died. I got 'im good, boss."

"I'll bet. Hold on now. Don't you reload, you dummy." Mike
started down the hill.

Deacon began to creep behind the boulder, holding his empty
rifle ahead of him like a spear. After a few seconds, Mike saw
him come around the other side, glancing this way and that
nervously. No bear was in sight.

"Behind you, Deac!" Mike shouted.

Deacon jumped forward and fell. His feet churned in the

grass. He tried to crawl. "Help me," he whined, scrabbling ahead. He reached Mike and crawled behind him.

"He's gone now," Mike said.

Deacon slumped. He rolled onto his back and they laughed.

Fifteen minutes later they found the bear a hundred yards into the woods, a single bullet wound in its neck where Mike had hit him.

Mike took his knife from the sheath on his belt and instinctively felt the edge with his thumb. He had honed it two nights earlier while waiting with Denny and Deacon for the bear, and the fine steel blade scraped against the grooves of his thumb. That knife had a good feel. His father, Earl, had skinned with it thirty years ago. When you held a good knife like that, it felt like part of your hand.

Avelyn was returning with the Coleman lantern, her flashlight bobbing in the woods. He whistled to direct her. As she neared, he pulled a match from his shirt pocket.

"You sure he's dead?" she asked.

"Dead as mutton." Mike hooked the lantern onto his knife and flicked the match with his thumbnail. It caught and he lit the lantern, setting it on the sandy ground beside the bear's head.

"God, Michael. He's *big*."

He put his boot on the bear's shoulder and felt the folds of muscle and skin give way. The bear had a ripe smell, almost sweet, like rotting apples. Mike made a long cut up the belly. The skin, a half-inch thick, was tough and elastic. The entrails spilled out, steaming in the cool night air. Papa Vic rolled up his sleeves and reached into the body cavity for them. He cut out the mountainous string of intestines and dragged them farther into the woods. The blood smell became thick.

Mike cut the skin down the four legs, then gouged out the claws. They were smooth and hard, each one nearly as big as a finger. Beginning at the paws, he rolled the hide away from the muscle, scraping it free with his knife. Beneath the coat, still thick from hibernation, the flesh was pink. The work went slowly, and despite the chilly air, he began to sweat. The carcass had stiffened, which made the skinning easier, and soon the four legs were sleeveless.

He dropped the knife and rolled the bear onto its belly. Papa Vic had already salvaged the heart and liver and was cutting open the stomach. The smell was terrible.

"Jesus," Mike cursed. Avelyn turned away.

"Been eatin' garbage." Papa Vic poked around with his fingers. "Winter-killed game, I reckon. Some ole deer."

"Jesus!" Mike walked away from the bear. His forearms were red from the blood. It was splattered on his shirt and the front of his pants.

"Pretty grim, all right."

Papa Vic carried the stomach into the woods. Mike came back, muttering, and began scraping the skin off the back. When he reached the neck, he unfolded his skinning saw and sawed through the neckbone. He removed the head intact, the skin dragging behind. Then he quartered the carcass.

"That bear died quick," Papa Vic said. They were waiting for Denny and Deacon to return with the packhorses. "You can hit a bear through the heart and it'll run further'n this'n. That shot hit 'im right through the windpipe. I don't reckon I've seen a bear shot through the windpipe before. Hit one in the skull, and you might just as well hit a rock."

Mike was catching his breath. Papa Vic opened his pocket knife and cut a piece from the bear's heart. He stuck it on the blade and offered it to Avelyn.

"Don't be revolting."

"Paaa!" Papa Vic spat. He ate the piece himself. Then he offered one to Mike, who took the meat and ate it.

"Indians used to try to get it while it was still beatin'," Papa Vic said. "Give warrior plenty courage. Person'd live forever if he could chow down on bear hearts ever'day. Them vitals is chock-full of good things. Try a bite, Missy?"

Avelyn paused. "Is it really necessary?"

"Plenty courage."

She took the strip of meat off his knife and held it reluctantly.

She closed her eyes and bit it in half. It was the texture of raw liver and rich with blood. She swallowed it and instantly felt queasy. "That's awful." She handed the other half to Michael.

"Plenty courage, that girl," Papa Vic said. "Damnedest bear-hunting story I ever heard happened 'round nineteen twenty. It's a true story, too. You know that bearskin down at the Bison hanging on the wall? That big flea-bitten nine-foot grizzly? That was the bear. Tommy Phelps, Senior, used to have the clipping tacked right there next to it. Don't know what happened to the clipping, but used to be there. Told the whole story."

"Deacon run off with that whiskey?"

Avelyn had the bottle. She gave it to Papa Vic, and he took a drink. Then he sliced off another piece of the bear's heart. "Tommy Phelps, Senior, had a brother name of Charlie who was up hunting out of that cabin at the base of Black Tooth. Up there by hisself. When he didn't come out, Tommy went up there to get him, and found ole Charlie mauled right inside the cabin. Place had been ripped apart, and the biggest damn prints Tommy'd ever seen was all around the camp. So Tommy packed his brother out of there by wrappin' what was left of the body in a blanket and layin' it acrost his saddle. Then he walked out. Took him a day and a night, but when he come back into Kearney he rounded up a half-dozen men with guns, includin' me, got some good dogs, and we come back up to get that bear.

"Hunted it for two days before we lost the trail. Ever'body wanted to catch that ole griz pretty bad. There'd been stories over the years of a renegade bear that broke down corrals and killed colts and ever' damn thing. Figured this to be the same one, don't know why. But once we lost the trail, there wasn't any point in stayin', so ever'one but Tommy went home. Tommy said he was goin' to make that griz come to him, and if he wasn't back in a week, to come back to bury what was left. Save a man some whiskey, Missy."

Avelyn sheepishly took the bottle from her mouth. "It's cold."

"Reckon it is." Papa Vic drank again, then passed it on to Mike. "So. Ole Tommy left a lot of food around and cooked bacon all day long to draw the big fella in. On the fourth night, after waitin' past midnight, Tommy started to tip a bottle like Avelyn there, for company or courage or both. Maybe it was cold. Anyhow, he flat passed out, and maybe three, four in the mornin' somethin' wakes him up. First thing he feels is a cold breeze, so he realizes the cabin door is wide open, then he smells somethin' like two-day-old garbage. He doesn't move, not even to open his eyes, and in a second Tommy feels hot, stinking breath on his face. He was holdin' the rifle in his hand, but the bear was right over him so's he couldn't even lift the muzzle.

"Ole Tommy figures the next thing he'll feel is his face bein' eaten . . ."

"Papa Vic, spare us," Avelyn said uncomfortably.

"That's what he figures. But he lays there and inches his hand down his side, little by little, to where his forty-four is hangin'. It takes him ten full minutes to draw it from his holster, that bear kind of standin' there, sniffin' around, lickin' the bottle of whiskey. Then he points the gun upward and fires. Didn't aim or nothin'. Just hopin' to scare the tapeworms out of that bear. And before he can move, that big ole griz crashes down on him, a ton and a half of dead weight. Tommy'd hit it right beneath the throat, and somehow the bullet went up through its head and into its brain. I've seen a lot of bears shot, but I never heard of one dropping like a cow. 'Specially a griz. You can't shoot them buggers in the brain 'cause their skull's too thick. Kinda like Michael here. But from right beneath one, I reckon you can, 'cause that bear crashed down on Tommy like a ton of brick, and he couldn't move. Couldn't move a muscle. We found him like that two days later, trapped beneath the carcass of the biggest bear ever shot in the Bighorns. Dead or no, when I saw that griz lyin' there, I wanted to come in shootin'. Then ole Tommy kind of waves a foot at us. Near scared me to death. Can you beat that?"

"Is that true?" Avelyn asked Mike.

"What the hell you askin' him for, woman? He weren't there."

"All right then. Is it true?"

"Course it's true."

Avelyn looked at Mike. He shrugged.

"Gawddamn, don't you shrug at me. That's a true gawddamn tale. That *happened.*"

"I'd like to see the clipping," Mike said.

"I'll clip you, you insolent gawddamn —"

"All right, all right." Mike winked at Avelyn, who was finishing the Jack Daniel's. "Balmy sonofabitch."

"Don't you call me balmy."

"There's Deacon." Mike whistled, and Denny and Deacon, each leading a packhorse, came to them through the woods. The horses were nervous from the smell of the bear.

"Better cover their eyes," Mike said. He took off his down vest and Avelyn put it over the head of the first horse while they tied a quarter onto the pack saddle. Then she and Denny led it up to the truck.

When the four quarters were loaded, she took the pack saddle off Jacks, Mike's gentle bay horse, and bridled him. Mike gave her a boost up, and she rode Jacks bareback, leading the other by the halter. In a moment the truck drove past. She watched its red taillights until they were out of sight. Then she listened to the clopping hooves of the two horses on the dirt road. She spoke to Jacks as she had heard Mike do.

"Hmmm, you Jacks. You good Jacks."

Her head was light from the whiskey, and clear from the night air and excitement. She was no longer cold. The truck reappeared as it crossed the south pasture, its headlights diving down then up as it crossed the ruts. It went up the drive, then vanished over the rise. Before long the lights from the ranchhouse came on, yellow beneath the white sea of stars. The night sky pulsed with them.

She began to sing: " 'Hmm-hmm-hmm-hmmm git along little dogies; It's your misfortune and none of my own; Hmm-hmm-hmm-hmmm, git along little dogies; You know that Wyoming'll be your new home . . .' "

CHAPTER 5

I T WAS FIVE in the morning when she awoke. She pushed in the alarm before it could go off and rolled over to look out the window. The upper end of the valley was beginning to glow with orange, seeping just high enough into the predawn gray to silhouette the pines on the ridge. It was cold. She pulled the blankets around her neck. The screen door slammed downstairs, and Denny's heavy footsteps crossed the yard as he went to get the horses. They would be moving the cattle to their summer pastures today. She heard the horse in the corral stomp its hooves as he approached.

Avelyn slid from bed and moved quickly to the bathroom. When she came out, she slipped into her cold jeans without removing her nightgown, squirming to get them over her hips. Mike was awake, watching her.

"Madam, your hips are too large," he said.

"Cold." She put her shirt on the chair and slipped the nightgown over her head. She had not quite untangled her arms when Mike reached out and pulled her, struggling, back into bed. He rolled on top of her, twisting the nightgown so she could not get her hands loose. Her skin was goose-bumped. He smiled at her.

"Let me go, you." Avelyn kicked helplessly with her feet.

Mike kissed her cheek, then her neck. She arched her body

beneath him. Her breasts were firm and hard beneath the weight of his chest. "Let me go," she said, more softly.

"You're less dangerous tied up."

"Michael." She pursed her lips and relaxed.

"Quiet." He kissed her. He ran his free hand down her side and pressed his fingertips into her back. She squeezed against him, opening her mouth to rub her teeth into his neck.

"Your hands are cold," she whispered. He released the nightgown and she slid her hands free and wrapped them around his back, moving them across his cool skin. She dug her fingernails in, first gently, then harder. She kissed him, then lay back as he pulled off her jeans. Naked now, Avelyn rolled on top of him, trying to pin him down. She locked her knees around his hips and nuzzled her face into his neck, biting softly. He touched her with his hands, then lifted her off him, onto her back. The quilt was silky and cool.

Afterward, Avelyn lay with her cheek on his chest. "Mmm. Michael. Sweet." Her skin was warm now, and her head felt clear. She kissed him on his chest, rubbing her lips against the soft hairs. Then she began to dress again, more slowly. She watched him watching her. She pulled on her boots and brushed her hair quickly in front of the bedroom mirror, tying it back with an elastic. Then she went downstairs to start breakfast.

They ate slowly and well — ham, biscuits, gravy, fried eggs, and coffee. By quarter past six they were saddled and on their way. The sun had cleared the ridge and was beginning to blunt the chill, but they wore down jackets. Avelyn, Deacon, and Denny would drive two-thirds of the herd — two hundred cows and their calves — up to the mesa. Mike and Papa Vic had the rest, which they'd push to the lease above Custer Lake, seven miles away. It was a long ride for Papa Vic, but he liked to prove he could do it, liked being out, liked staying active. He still sat a horse well, his back straight and his boots plugged into the stirrups, heels down. He kept his toes turned outward so the barest twitch would rub the rowels of his spurs against the horse's flanks. He carried his reins in his left hand, his right arm hanging freely at his side.

Mike helped him get the herd moving, then he rode ahead to open the gate to the Canyon Creek road. Papa Vic's voice was too old and weak for hollering, so he had brought a whistle which he blew on forcefully, startling both the cattle and his horse. He waved his hat in an easy manner, as if to fan off flies. Stormy ran at the trailing cows, snapping at hind legs, then running off as they circled together to protect their calves from him. The lowing began as cows and calves were separated, and dust in the pasture kicked up to the height of their backs.

Slowly, the herd funneled through the gate. Mike waited just below, shooing them up the valley. "Up now, boys. Hey! There you go, there you go!" The lead cows moved lazily off and grazed to the side of the road, their calves pressing against their flanks. They milled there until the last of the cattle were through.

"Know what I think?" Papa Vic let his whistle fall from his lips and waited while Mike closed the gate. "That dog of yours is gonna get kicked."

"No, he won't." Mike remounted and started to shout. "Hey, get up there, boys! There you go, there you go!"

Papa Vic blew his whistle, and Mike's horse jumped sideways. "Goddamn that!"

Papa Vic chuckled. "Sit tight, Michael."

"Leave off that goddamn whistle for two seconds."

Just then Stormy nipped at a cow's hock and was kicked flush on the side. The dog yelped and pulled back. Papa Vic slapped his knee and laughed. "Saw 'er comin'!"

Mike shouted at the cows again, slapping the hindmost ones on the back with his rope, eyeing his dog to see that it was all right. He scowled at his grandfather.

"Never did much care for them shepherds," Papa Vic said matter-of-factly. "Ever since, oh, been about nineteen hundred ten. Jeremiah Cott of the NX Ranch had two shepherds, just like yours, used 'em as cattle dogs same as you. Smart as a couple of whips. Good cattle dog was damn near as valuable as a good horse back then, and a good horse was more valuable than a good man. Real workin' horse fit this country, and you fit the horse. It was a fine thing. Well, I'm down there one day when

Jeremiah's best mare foals out in the pasture, and them shepherd dogs get the devil in 'em and chased that foal ever' way
but loose, barkin' and raisin' cain. Foal was still wet. Time we
got there, that foal's legs is too bent to turn a pig in an alley.
Tore him up to see a good foal ruint. Them dogs is waggin'
away, about happy enough to shit to see Jeremiah. First he shoots
the dogs, and then he shoots the foal. He was plumb fond of
them dogs, too."

Mike uncoiled his rope again and flicked it toward a trailing
cow. "Storm's a pretty good cow dog."

"I seen that," Papa Vic said.

"Sssss-ssss-ssss, get up now! Hyaaa! Hyaaaah!" The lowing
began again as the herd moved up the road through the thick
dust. The sun was beginning to heat up, and Mike removed his
jacket and tied it to the back of his saddle. "Hey! Get up now!
There you go!"

It took them an hour to move past Lloyd Paxton's ranch, the
Quarter Circle T. The cows were strung out in threes and fours
across the road, moving steadily now. The most important thing
to a cow was continuity. If it was lying down, it wanted to stay
lying down. If it was feeding, it preferred to keep feeding. Now
that they were moving, they would keep moving until they were
forcibly stopped.

Just beyond the Paxton ranch was a four-hundred-acre parcel
that Papa Vic owned called the Parker place. He had bought it
from a Sioux Indian called Not Afraid Parker back in the 1920s,
and the old homestead cabin still stood next to a weathered gray
barn surrounded by bent reaper reels and rusted mowing ma-
chines and hayrakes. They leased the hay pasture to Lloyd Paxton, and hunted sage grouse and deer there in the fall.

"Lloyd asked me about selling this place again last week," Mike
said as they rode past.

"There's a man won't take no for an answer. Spare some
snoose, Michael?"

Mike handed Papa Vic his tin of snuff. "Says it fouls up his
fencelines."

"Hee-hee. Good ole Lloyd. Them fencelines was here 'fore he

was, the rummy. Ain't good policy to sell land. Specially land you're right fond of. I'm right fond of the Parker place, Michael. Not Afraid Parker's buried right here. I ever tell you about Not Afraid? Rode with Major Reno at the Battle of Little Bighorn, he did. Scout for the U.S. Army. Kept tellin' Reno after he and Custer split up, 'Heap big mistake, you and Yellow Hair make . . . plenty Injuns down there . . . plenty guns . . . plenty trouble.' Hee-hee. Truth to tell, Michael, ole Not Afraid was shittin' ten-pound bricks, is what. Plenty Afraid. Course, he was right, too, and Reno knew it."

"Never understood how you come across this land," Mike said.

"The Parker place? Hell, Injuns weren't allowed to *own* land then. Not Afraid never had a deed or nothin'. Just squatted up here and lived. Had him a squaw and a little ankle-biter of a son, lived there, died there, and buried there. Me, I owned it and I'm right fond of it. You go ahead and sell it to Lloyd when I die if you like, but it ain't good policy to sell land, Michael. That land's got a spring, too. Good land."

"You're too old to die."

"I'm too old to shit, I b'lieve."

A mile farther up, the road stopped abruptly at the ranger station. The lowing of the cattle brought the ranger out, a short man with a pug nose and dark eyebrows on an oval face. Mike knew him and nodded a greeting.

"Moving 'em out, eh? By golly, the first of June," the ranger said. "Mornin', Mr. McKenzie," he said to Papa Vic. "Saw you on the television yesterday."

"How'd I look?"

"You were fine. Just fine." They had to speak loudly because of the water spilling out of the Custer Dam into Canyon Creek, just behind the ranger station. "You be careful on that Piney Creek Trail, Mr. McKenzie. There's some trees down the boys ain't had time to get to."

Mike grinned at his grandfather. "Maybe you'd best stay behind, Papa Vic. Visit with Barney here."

"Gawddamn your young butt." Papa Vic turned his horse back toward the trail.

"Yaaah!" Mike yelled, laughing. "Get up, you! Sssss!" They herded the cattle onto the narrow, rocky trail that ran along the lake above the dam, and Mike rode up to the front to keep the leaders from slowing down. The cows were spread in ones and twos now, and more were separated from their calves. Stormy ran back and forth through the woods to keep the cows from doubling back off the trail. "Get 'er, Storm. Get her back there, boy. Up now! Sssss!"

At the head of the lake a tent was pitched, the first of the summer backpackers. The trail became steep there, but it was dry and the footing was good. The rocks on the trail were flat and not hard on a horse's feet. The cattle slowed, and Mike stayed up front, flicking the cows with his rope when they balked at a fallen log, shouting and hissing them on, listening to Papa Vic's whistle from the rear. Piney Creek fell off below, cascading, then leveling into log-strewn pools. At some points the bank was eroded away completely, and only a steep, root-scarred slope separated the trail from the creek. It was cooler in the woods.

"Up now! 'M'on you, get up there!" Mike waited at a fallen log. Each cow came to it, sniffed, tried to turn back, and was pushed into jumping over by the cow behind. The calves scrambled after their mothers one leg at a time, some of them toppling chin first over the log. "Ssss-ssss-ssss! Get going, you!" Mike flicked out his rope and over she went. The herd was trailing better now, and he waited for Papa Vic.

After a while he came into sight, looking tired, waving his hat in an easy manner as his horse picked its way up the steep trail. It scuffed its hooves crossing the log, and Papa Vic had to catch himself on the horse's neck.

"You okay, old man?" Mike asked.

Papa Vic spat. "Hell."

"Should we rest a spell?"

"You rest. I'll shoot on ahead and open that gate."

"I'll do that. You sure?"

Papa Vic spat again, eyeing him scornfully. He blew his whistle. Mike reined his horse toward the woods and kicked it up the soft clay bank.

What happened next came very fast. Mike's horse slipped on the clay. He felt it claw for a foothold, then strike a rock at the top of the bank with its hoof, dislodging it. The horse surged beneath him and up to the woods, but behind him there was a sharp crack as the dislodged rock bounded into the trail. He turned, seeing Papa Vic's horse bolting sideways against the bit, whinnying, its hind legs stumbling over the edge of the embankment. Papa Vic kicked at the horse, tugging its head back toward the center of the trail as it lost its footing and began slipping backward.

"Papa! No!"

The horse slid very suddenly down the slope with a terrified squeal, falling out of sight.

"Papa! Papa!" Mike leapt from his horse, running to the edge of the embankment. The horse had stopped at the bottom of the gully, against the rocks. It thrashed with its legs, trying to rise. Papa Vic was still.

"Papa!" Mike slid down, braking with the heels of his boots, scraping his palms raw. The horse was lying on his grandfather's leg. He cursed it, grabbing its ears and pulling. The horse squealed and lurched off Papa Vic, pawing to get its hind legs under its body. One of its front legs was broken.

"Papa! You answer me!"

He knelt and propped the old man's head into his lap. Mike was trembling. "Papa? You answer me. It's me, Papa." He spoke more softly, his voice tight. "It's me, Papa. It's all right. It's me. You hurt? Tell me where you're hurt. It's Michael. Tell me where, Papa."

Papa Vic opened his eyes. They were glazed over. Then they closed again. His mouth hung open. Mike held him, stroking his head. The horse thrashed a few feet away, still trying to rise. "Papa? Where're you hurt? Come on now." He looked down at the leg that had been trapped beneath the horse and saw that it had an odd bend below the knee. "Can you move? Can you move your leg?"

Papa Vic opened his eyes again and moved his lips.

"It's me. It's me, Papa."

The old man closed his eyes then opened them.
"Can you move?"
He moved his lips and whispered. "Michael?"
"It's me, Papa. It's all right."
He closed his eyes. "Michael."
"I'm sorry. God, I'm sorry. You set now."
Mike lowered his head onto a flat stone. He ripped his shirt into strips and fashioned a splint out of sticks around Papa Vic's leg. Papa Vic was muttering, and he tried to quiet him.
"It's all right, now. I'll take you back. You set still."
Mike's arms were still shaking. He slipped them carefully beneath his grandfather and picked him up. He was surprised at how light he was. "You hush now."
Papa Vic opened his eyes again. He groaned. Mike started up the slope, but it was difficult to get a foothold because of the steepness. He dug in with the side of his boots and inched along. The horse with the broken leg whinnied from the bottom of the gully. It craned its neck, watching them leave, and somehow wrenched itself to its three good legs. It tried to follow, but its hind legs slipped on the sandy bank and it fell to its knees. Then it whinnied terribly, trying to rise.
Papa Vic turned his head so that he could see back down the slope. "Michael."
"Just stay quiet."
"Kill my horse for me."
Mike could barely hear him. "I'll come back."
"It's tryin' to follow."
"Just stay quiet. I'll be back."
"No." The talk was exhausting him. His face was gray. There was a thin line of sweat above his upper lip and under his eyes. "I won't leave it. Just put me down and do it." He saw Mike's reluctance. "I ain't gonna die on you."
Mike stopped. He was cradling Papa Vic in front of him. "I'll be back for it. I swear."
"Now." Papa Vic let his eyes close. "It don't want to die alone, Michael. Go on."
Mike laid Papa Vic on the bank and walked down to the horse.

It was still on its knees, breathing heavily, dripping with sweat. The horse's eyes were bloodshot and frightened. Mike picked up a smooth, heavy stone.

"Talk to it, Michael. Talk to it nice."

"You just lay quiet," Mike told him. Then he talked to the horse in a low voice. He lowered its head with the reins and raised the stone. He brought it down powerfully on the top of its skull. The horse lunged back, twitching, then fell heavily on its side. Its eyes were still open, and it was watching Mike. He knelt beside the horse, talking to it softly, and took out his knife. He slit its throat, then put his hand on its neck. He stayed with the horse until it was dead.

Papa Vic was barely conscious. Mike leaned down to pick him up, and the old man opened his eyes halfway. "Don't carry me, Michael. You can't make it with me."

"Hush up now. It'll be fine."

"Go on and get help. It's too steep, son. Go on."

"You hush, Papa Vic. You rest up. I got you now. I got you."

He started up the slope backward, digging in with his heels. It got steeper, and he slipped and fell, buffering his grandfather in front of him.

"You okay, Papa? You okay? Answer me."

"I'm poorly. 'Fraid I'm poorly."

It was too steep to climb, so Mike lay down and slid along on his bare back, pushing with his heels. The rocky slope tore at his skin. He inched his way upward. Papa Vic did not complain of the pain anymore. It took them a long time. When they reached the trail, Mike stood up and started down the rocky path to the ranger station. His back was bleeding. Papa Vic mouthed a faint curse, and Mike knew he was alive.

CHAPTER 6

JIMBO MCKENZIE STARED out the window. The landscape was black except for the dot of light from a distant farmhouse, slowly falling behind. The darkness was soothing. The night light at the foot of the door bathed the compartment dimly, like moonlight through a curtain.

They passed a crossroad. Jimbo listened to the dingdingdingDINGDINGDINGdingdingding followed by the clacking of the wheels over the joints in the rails. The train had a gait like the lope of a horse. He leaned his head against the window. The town receded. The lights receded. Then the dark.

He was facing the rear of the train. "You won' know where's you goin', but you sure knows where you been," the smooth-skinned, walnut-brown porter had told him. That's fair, Jimbo thought. That's more than fair. That's more than I know. The window was cool against his cheek and the rails clacked.

It was late, and traffic in the corridor had stopped. Jimbo absently rubbed his fingertips down his sideburn and jaw. *You sure knows where you been.* He thought about the girl. She had wiped her eyes and kissed him wetly and made a joke about his haircut. Do a great thing someday, she had said.

— With a haircut like this?

— Do a great thing someday. You're so bright you don't even know it. Then she backed away and gave him the peace sign to make him laugh and mouthed "thank you" with her lips.

He wished it had not been so rushed. He wished he had had the time to say goodbye to more of his friends. He did not think he was coming back and he wished the leaving had not been so rushed.

— We knew, she had said. I always knew. There is too much cowboy in you to have ever been a banker in this town. Do a great thing someday, huh? You're a good guy, Jimbo. You've brought me to life.

— No, I haven't. I'm a hacker. You're an oiled gate.

The countryside was dark. The train jolted and his cheek bumped against the window. There was fresh air from somewhere. He thought about Papa Vic. It had frightened him to learn of the accident. It had frightened him to think he might never see his grandfather again. He had always figured that nothing in Wyoming would change until he was ready to go back; that life would go on and on and on the same every year, the way an ocean does. Not dead or still, but moving. That was the way he thought of it: that the people and horses and cattle and game lived and died there, but were always replaced by more people and cattle and horses and game. So that if a person could have sat in a bubble for a century, everything alive would have seemed just as permanent as the mountains and springs and boulders. Even the families never changed. There was a sense of permanence.

He remembered Papa Vic talking about change: *Jimmy, you was born in nineteen hundred and forty-eight, the year of the dreaded blight. I ain't sayin' you brought the blight, and I ain't sayin' you didn't, but you came, then it came; so there ya go. Person learns to expect such things. Last drought we'd had was in nineteen-eighteen — year I married your grandma. Lasted two years, and that were a bad'n. Made forty-eight look like a day at the beach, 'cause the grasshoppers come in nineteen hundred and eighteen. Then, you come in forty-eight, and lots of folks, includin' your ma, would say tit for tat. Them hoppers teach Gawd to a man quick.*

Drought 'fore that one was in eighteen ninety-nine. I was workin' for Jake Jenkins then. Ever' twenty-five years or so, you can count on one. Just the way Gawd Almighty works things. Be another around nineteen seventy-four. Lord, Lord, I'll be dead by then, Gawd willing. But you remember I said so, Jimmy, and if you sire a son, you scurry out and drown him quick or he'll turn out the spittin' image of you. Them blight childs are plumb bad news. But don't worry on your cattle or your land. Little secret I learned is things ain't nearly so bad in the bad years nor so good in the good years as folks 'round here like to pretend. Folks themselves ain't so bad nor good, neither. They got a kind of equilibrium. Get it from the land. They see lots of change 'round 'em, usually for the worse, but if they're good folks, they'll wait it out, 'cause things'll sure change back. Remember that, Jimmy. Good folks don't change when the weather turns better or worse. They hunker down and wait it out. Ever' twenty-fifth year, Gawd Almighty squats down on these folk just to show who's boss. Squats long and squats hard, like a pig in mud. When he gets back up, the good folks're still here, the land's still here, and the cattle are still here and plumb hungry. . . .

The train clattered through another crossing, another town. He was glad of the airline strike, glad to be going back by train. It gave him time. Things had been so rushed. It gave him time to think about where he'd been. He would not miss that bank, but he would miss that city now that he had left it.

He had never thanked Papa Vic for his education. Papa Vic had said, "If any institution of higher learnin' is fool enough to take a fallow-brained McKenzie like you, I guess I'll go along with the program and foot the bill. Just don't be talkin' to your perfessors in the outside breeze, Jimmy. You rattle in a fair wind." He had worn a satisfied, approving look on his weathered face for days, talking to Jimbo in a slightly different tone of voice, shifting gears up a notch without a trace of effort. Papa Vic had more gears than any man Jimbo knew. He had one tone of voice for a congressman and another for a senator. He wanted to see him again.

They passed another silent town. The lights receded and the blackness returned. The window was cold to his forehead. The train loped on: clackety-clack, clackety-clack.

He had changed, he thought. Yale had been his chrysalis, and he had emerged a moth, flying madly at lightbulbs in the night. *You won' know where's you goin', but you sure knows where you been.*

He had been to Europe. He had worked on a Portuguese freighter. He had worked in a bank. He had not been home but he was going home now, as he had always known he would, creeping back caterpillar-like on a long, slow train; and nothing would have changed except that Papa Vic was dying. Though *he* had changed. But nothing else.

The bed was folded above the seat, snapping into the wall. He wished he could lie in bed and look out the window, but the bunk was too high. He was tired. No, his body was tired, but his mind was anxious to get home. He had not seen any of them since the wedding. It had been a good wedding, with lots of pretty women and elegant clothes and early mornings. Most of what Jimbo recalled from that Long Island weekend was hazy-drunk memories like smog over the Sound. But the service he remembered.

The ceremony had started with the congregation seated and the ushers and bridesmaids standing stiffly around Mike and Avelyn in tails and yellow gowns. Avelyn composed and lovely, truly radiant; happy; so fresh and uncomplicated amidst all that opulence; Mike more nervous than Jimbo had ever seen him, shuffling his shined cowboy boots below his cutaway, his huge, hard hands opening and closing, the fingernails thick as buttons. The minister started the service, wearing robes and a bucolic expression that never flickered, except the moment he asked the part about "Let him now speak or forever hold his peace," at which point he sternly peered over his glasses and listened. (At which point, too, Jimbo looked over to Deacon, who had vowed the night before to unearth some bit of information from Mike's past that would prevent any man of God from wedding Avelyn to him in clean conscience; though Deacon just winked and remained silent.) Then the minister continued, "Will you, Michael, take this woman to be your wedded wife . . ."

"I will," Mike announced, prematurely.

Jimbo remembered the panic creeping swiftly into Mike's eyes as he realized that he had spoken out of turn. Mike looked so flustered that Deacon laughed aloud, making everyone grin. The minister curtly admonished Deacon with a shake of the head. He continued: ". . . to live together in Holy Matrimony? Will you love her, comfort her, honor and keep her, in sickness and in health . . ."

He recalled Deacon's face: scarlet, veins bulging purple as he watched Mike burning with embarrassment and tried to keep from laughing. Deacon, their stumpy, overweight foreman, whose shaking, silent convulsion was having its effect on the entire congregation. And Papa Vic, erect, dignified, scowling at the performance from the front pew. Avelyn had raised her hand to the corners of her grin, as if to stop its growth by force; and Jimbo himself had lowered his eyes to the floor, biting his lip, praying that Deacon would not utter a sound.

Then the minister said, ". . . so long as you both shall live," and stopped. The church was left, not in silence, but shimmering, as every member of the wedding party and most of the guests fought their private battles against the incipient laughter. And it suddenly became obvious to everyone, including the minister, what Deacon had known all along — that Mike, in his embarrassment, had stopped listening.

As best man, Jimbo waited until he could wait no longer. "Mike —" he whispered. Mike made no sign of acknowledgment. So there it was: the groom dumbstruck at the pivotal moment of the service, the minister determined to wait him out, and the entire congregation held on the precipice of hilarity by the sleeve of a tuxedo, which was now stuffed into Deacon's mouth.

There was a thud. Mike's jaw went slack and he grunted.

Avelyn had elbowed him in the ribs. After the shock had disappeared from Mike's face, it was followed in rapid succession by expressions of pain, anger, and finally confusion. The confusion lingered, not because he didn't know what he had been asked, but because he was now trying to decide what to answer. And while doing so, he looked from the minister, to Jimbo, to Deacon — still making muffled ululations into his arm — and finally back to Avelyn. "I still will," he said. And they were married.

Two and a half years ago. Jimbo had not seen any of them since the wedding. *You sure knows where you been,* the porter had told him. The moon began to rise. Two giant silos loomed briefly over a field, then fell behind. He remembered Papa Vic talking to Mike when they were much younger, telling him why the upper end of the Canyon Creek area was so much more fertile than the lower end — which was why he had built the Bar V where it was. "Better land on this end of the valley," he'd explained to Mike with a knowing nod.

Mike, who never believed something until he had grasped it in his own two hands; and Papa Vic, who abandoned truth remorselessly the moment it became dull — the pair they made.

"How's that?" Mike had said in a doubtful tone.

"Closer to Gawd."

Mike had snorted in disgust. "Don't bull me."

"It is."

"Lady down at church says God's everywhere, Papa Vic, and you know it; so just quit."

"Paaa!" Papa Vic had raised an eyebrow and narrowed an eye, knowing how Mike loved to doubt things and so catering to that: "You believe that foolishness? How can Gawd be ever'where, tell me that? He may have *been* ever'where, I ain't gonna argue that, but that don't mean He *is* ever'where. I imagine President Eisenhower may have been just about ever'where, but he still can't be two places at once. Gawd's no different than President Eisenhower."

"I'm just telling you what the Sunday school lady said. I didn't say I believed it. I didn't say I believed you, either."

"Well, land's better up at this end of the valley, you believe that?"

"Maybe."

"And you got an explanation why?"

"No. But it ain't 'cause it's closer to God."

"Sure it is." Mike had tightened his mouth at Papa Vic's stubbornness, and Papa Vic winked. "You know where that eagles' nest is on Custer Lake?"

"In that old pine sawed off by lightning?"

"Yessir. That's where Gawd lives."

"Papa Vic —"

"Just in the winters when the eagles ain't there. Rest of the time He camps on the mesa. Gawd's got real tender feet, so He grows the grass at this end of the valley good and long."

Papa Vic had stood there grinning as Mike tried to think of something to say. That was the way of their childhood. No matter how outrageous the story, the moral remained: You are blessed; we are blessed; this land is blessed by God Almighty, Cattleman, Gentleman, Imbiber of Whiskey.

The moon was clear of the horizon now, and the train rumbled west. Jimbo nodded off to sleep in his seat. When he awoke, the train was pulling into Pittsburgh. It was six o'clock. His head felt thick from jostling against the window during the night as the train wound through the time-gnarled hills, tunneling through the plush hardwood forests of Appalachia. There were some names, all right: Monongahela, Susquehanna, Kiskiminetas; the oldest rivers on the continent. They must have passed Johnstown already. He would have liked to have been awake going through Johnstown. He had a very clear idea of what it would look like from Papa Vic's stories — a sleepy mining town set above the junction of two strong rivers, with lovely green hills stretching up the valley and dozens of steeples and blooming elderbushes along Main Street. They would have crossed over the great stone bridge where his great-grandparents had drowned in the flood. The Flood. He would have liked to have seen Johnstown, all right.

There had been an old trapper named Red Coughlin who lived around Johnstown and took Papa Vic under his wing. He taught him to shoot and hunt and skin. One time Mike and Jimbo and Papa Vic rode past a dead skunk — Jimbo would have been about eight; Mike twelve — and Papa Vic spat tobacco juice into the road. "Gawddamn shame," he had said.

Mike had looked at him suspiciously before asking, "What is?"

"Skunk gettin' run over like that. Gawddamn shameful waste."

"Ain't a waste."

"Ain't a waste? Michael, you're turnin' into a pretty fair hand, but you're ignorant as a post. We trapped skunk back in Johnstown ever' fall. Me an' ole Red Coughlin."

Mike had ridden on a few yards, mulling that over, before saying, "A trapped skunk'd spray you silly."

"Had me a method."

"Bull." But in a minute he had asked, "What method?"

"Red learned it from an Injun gal named Running Foot. She made him a happy man for four bits and a pint of whiskey . . ." Papa Vic, for whom memory was a playground and a classroom; for whom time was not a boundary, but a gate to be passed through again and again. He launched into a story about Red Coughlin's still, Mike twisting his mouth impatiently, waiting to hear about the skunk, finally breaking in with an impassioned plea, "So what was the method, already?"

Papa Vic had smiled, knowing that the hook was set just so, and said, "Put a barrel in the woods half full of water and floated it full of rotten apples. Then you kinda stacked a stairway of rocks up the side. Ever seen slugs climb into a glass of beer? Same idea. Skunks climb to the brim of the barrel, dive in, and drown. Time we come around to check the trap, if they weren't already drowned, we'd just force the skunk under with a forked stick." Papa Vic had leaned over the neck of his horse and spat more tobacco juice into the road. "Gawddamn marvel of a trap, Michael. Skunk's the only creature in the world who'll kill hisself for apples. Bear'd do it for honey, rabbit for spindly carrot greens, mouse for cheese, man for lots of different things — usually money, sometimes land, always women. Ain't a critter in this world ain't got his weakness. That was the skunk's: apples."

"I don't believe you."

"True."

They had ridden on for a while, Mike brooding, when he turned and asked, "When you're drowning them . . . don't they make that smell?"

"Nope. Don't know why. Too busy drownin's my guess. That or they won't ruin good apples."

"Why'd you trap them?"

"Eat 'em. Sell the pelts. Same as anythin'."

"Eat them!"

"Sure."

"You didn't eat them."

"Course I did. Me and the whole family."

"You ate skunk?"

"Course we did. Same as eatin' a possum. Same as eatin' a squirrel. Same as eatin' a rabbit."

"Get out."

"Very same."

"You ate all that crap?"

"Well, sure I did, and it weren't no different than eatin' a skunk."

"Man who'd eat skunk is a sick man before and a sicker man after," Mike had said, making Papa Vic rock with laughter.

"For Gawd's sake, boy, you ever eat pig?"

"Eaten my share."

"There. You ain't sick. It's the same thing."

"As eatin' skunk? That ain't the same thing at all."

" 'Cause of a skunk's smell?" Mike had nodded, and when Papa Vic glanced at Jimbo, he had nodded too, trying to look just as cocky and assured as his brother. "You ever smelled pigshit?" Mike said nothing, so Jimbo'd said nothing. "Does bacon smell like pigshit?"

"Just the idea of eating a skunk . . ."

"How's the idea of eatin' a month-dead mule strike you? Hog'll do that. Skunk won't touch him. Hog don't care. Hog'll eat slop; hog'll eat snakes; hog'll eat babies. Hog just flat don't care. But you'll eat pig. Ever'body in the whole country'll eat pig. A hog'll eat eggs. So will a skunk. Only difference is the hogs eat theirs rotten, while a skunk sneaks in and steals his fresh. You won't eat rotten eggs, but you'll eat pork till your eyes cross."

Papa Vic had waited, but Mike had had enough. Then he'd leaned closer. "Ever eat chicken?"

"You know darned well I've eaten chicken," Mike had said with an irritated squint in his eyes.

"Okay, okay, I'll drop it. But a chicken's worse than a hog."

Mike asked, "How's that? And I already don't believe you."

"You know how corn'll go through a goose? You know how

they say that? A chicken'll follow a goose around and wait for that corn. Peck, peck, peck, gobble 'er down. And if what comes out ain't corn, well, chicken don't mind; goose don't mind; and you don't mind when you eat it.

"Ever hear of a stinkbug?"

"Nope."

"Stinkbug's just like a skunk, only it's a bug, about yea big . . ." He had held his fingers far enough apart to hold a ladybug. "Skunk'll eat insects, all right, but it won't eat a stinkbug. Only thing in the world'll eat a stinkbug is a chicken. Chicken don't care. Chicken's the stinkbug's only natural-borned enemy. And you'll eat chicken till the cows come home, and you'll eat it on the Lord's day. But la-dee-da, 'the idea of eatin' a skunk . . .' Paaa!"

Mike had finally cracked that little grin which he was already famous for, looking up and asking with a sort of gallows humor, "All right. What's it taste like?"

"Skunk?" Papa Vic had said with a broad wink at Jimbo. "Oh, kinda stringy like pork and oily like the leg of a chicken. 'Bout like possum, I s'pose. Ain't worth a shit."

Which, as always, brought peals of laughter. Jimbo had laughed at the cussword, and because he saw Mike laughing, and because all Papa Vic's tales ended with laughter. But Mike was laughing at something else, at something Jimbo was still too young to understand. He was laughing at the indiscriminate way that Papa Vic poked his finger into the ribs of the World. Skunk? *Ain't worth a shit.* Gawd? *No different than President Eisenhower . . . got real tender feet . . . squats long and squats hard, like a pig in mud . . . just to show who's boss.* And yet there he was — as he was the first to tell you — living in *God's Country,* trapping skunk, eating it, hunkering down, and waiting out those long, hard squats. *Little secret I learned is things ain't nearly so bad in the bad years nor so good in the good years as folks 'round here like to pretend.* He lived that. He didn't just believe it, he lived it and tried to pass it on. How *could* a youngster who had grown up with such a man ever take himself too seriously? Further, how could he grow up in awe of a world when Papa Vic was there at every turn poking fun at it? *You ain't such hot potatoes, neither!* The whole business probably stemmed from that Flood, when Papa Vic, the youngest and weakest, was carried off safely on the churning waters while the rest of his family were swept to their deaths — *and who knows why?* So that he lived the rest of his life as if he was being borne helplessly along on a floodwater, and if what befell him was good, so be it. If it was bad, so be it. But — *by Gawd!* — don't put any of the blame on him, or the credit either, for there were greater forces at work here. Papa Vic was still the youngest and weakest in his own eyes, and if someone wanted to take him for a ride on a floodwater, he was at least going to enjoy it. And all that he passed along to Mike. So — you see? — the cavalier manner in which Mike treated his various honors — all-state awards and rodeo championships and the Bronze Star he earned in the service — interpreted by many as arrogance, was in fact the result of Papa Vic's belief, painlessly drilled in from birth, that anything under God's sun was subject to and probably worthy of ridicule, excepting, perhaps, the land itself, which sustained them (. . . *the good folks're still here, the land's still here, and the cattle are still here and plumb hungry* . . .).

The problem was, you could understand all these things, you could laugh at the stories and swear not to take yourself seriously, but that did not mean that you lived it. That did not mean that when you closed your eyes at night you did not try to imagine a special and unique spot for yourself in the very world you poked fun at. And always, when Jimbo had done so, there was Mike.

Somehow, try as he might, he could not help taking his older brother seriously. He could not help being awed by his achievements, by his strength, his popularity, his knack of telling a story, his looks. It didn't seem to matter that *Mike* didn't put much stock in those things, that he, like Papa Vic, lived life as if swept along by a floodwater and wanted neither the credit nor the blame for wherever it took him. It was enough that Jimbo fell short in his own mind, and that, having put his brother up there on the pedestal, no niche was left that was special or unique enough. So he'd gone East.

It occurred to Jimbo that if he had ever told Mike that he had moved there to escape from his shadow, Mike would not have believed him. He probably would not have even grasped what he was talking about, for there were no shadows in Mike's world. None. It was black and white. There was one incident Jimbo kept going back to, a basketball game, the semifinals of the state high school tournament. High school sports were a very big deal in Kearney, and Mike had led the team to their best record in some twenty-five years. They had never won the state. Against Casper, the number one seed, Kearney led by five points at the half, and Mike had scored something like thirty points already. He had been fabulous. But he also had the reputation of being a hothead, and the other team knew it. In the first minute of the second half, one of the Casper players spat in his face. Mike knocked him out with one punch. Another player might have held back, might have thought it through: If I hit this guy, I'm out of the game, and the team loses its chance at the state title. But black was black and white was white. The entire gymnasium fell silent, and Mike stood there at mid-court, glaring, seeming to dare anyone, even the refs, to touch him. Then before anyone even had a chance to tell him he was gone, he walked off the court without a word, blatantly without regret for his action — suddenly aloof from and somehow above the scene he had created. Jimbo had been watching with Papa Vic, and Jeb Miller, the father of the team's center, started cursing about that goddamn lousy temper of Mike McKenzie, about how he'd let his teammates down, and the town, and all those people who were depending on him. Papa Vic leaned forward and said to Jeb: "Now they're going to depend on themselves for a change," and he gave a little laugh. Casper blew them out in the second half, but Kearney had never been more of a team than it was that day, and after the tournament they elected Mike captain for the following year. His was not such a bad shadow to be in, as long as you were willing to depend on yourself. Mike was truly not his brother's keeper.

So he'd gone East to learn to depend on himself.

And, Jimbo supposed, the train rattling along, by doing so, by carving out his own niche that he could laugh and poke fun at, he had escaped the shadow that haunted his adolescence. He supposed.

CHAPTER 7

HE COULD SEE THE bluffs to the west of the city, where the airport was, where he would have landed yesterday morning had the airlines not been on strike. It was no matter. It had been a good trip. He had met an amusing piano salesman in the club car, and later his daft mother, and the three of them sang and took turns playing Jimbo's ukulele until the conductor closed the bar in Bismarck. Now the odd but engaging pair waved and affected exaggerated frowns as he stepped down to the platform. They were on to Seattle.

Jimbo walked with his bags to the street in front of the station. There was no sign of Mike. The stockyards were just down the road, and he could smell the cow manure, a good fertile smell. The street was dry and wide and unhurried.

He sat in the shade of the station house, absorbing the difference of pace. In a few minutes a pale green Travelall pulled up to the curb. Mike got out, wearing sunglasses. His square, heavy shoulders and thick arms gave a fullness to his white western shirt; his neck was lean and muscled like a celery stalk, sunburned below the back brim of a crumpled straw cowboy hat, which had once been white but was now soiled and discolored from the sweat and dirt ground in, like the tile of a gas-station washroom. It was the same Mike, all right — as if he would ever change — ten minutes late but swaggering forward

with that easy smile that made you forget he had kept you waiting, that made you want to please him as much as his presence
pleased you. Jimbo was surprised at how much pleasure he got
from seeing his brother, from seeing that his memory of him
was true. He was not quite larger than life, but there was an
aura about him, a confidence, that Jimbo recognized at once and
admired. "You're late, cowboy," he said.

Mike slowed his advance. Denny, huge and dark, eighteen
years old now, stood shyly behind him. Mike folded his arms
and made a show of looking Jimbo over, then simply said, "Ole
buddy boy" — the name he had called him since they were
kids — the implication being that no, he hadn't changed, at least
not in Mike's eyes.

"You look good, Mike."

"Can't complain."

"You do. You really do."

Mike grinned. "So do you. Figured you'd look like one of
those fancy-assed New York bankers."

"Not anymore."

Mike picked up his duffle. "Well. We'd best go, eh? Everyone's
about excited enough to shit you're home. Even old Deac."

"Old Deac. Papa Vic home?"

"He's home."

"Is he . . . well, does he talk and stuff?"

"Sure he does. You'll see him. Get in. Get in, Den."

Denny got in the back. Jimbo unrolled the window in the
front. "Jesus. The Big Sky Country." He turned so Denny could
read his lips. "You've gotten so *big*. They feeding you hay or
what?"

Denny smiled and looked to Mike in the mirror. Mike raised
his lips so he could see them. "Ole buddy boy says you smell like
a pig."

Denny rocked with silent laughter. He looked older than his
age because of his size and the heavy shadow of his beard. His
eyebrows were bushy and commanding, drawing attention away
from his absolutely brilliant blue eyes.

"You savvy?" Mike repeated. "Like a pig." Denny was shaking his head no. "Yes. That's what he said. Oink-oink-oink-oink-oink."

Grinning, Denny covered his eyes with his hand and continued shaking no. Mike leaned back over the seat and punched him on the knee, then pointed to Jimbo when Denny looked up, as if he'd done it. Again, Denny shook his head no. He was beaming.

"He seems good," Jimbo said to Mike.

"Den's all right." Mike looked back to the mirror and held his nose. "Like a pig. Oink-oink-oink."

Billings had grown. A string of Pizza Huts and Taco Bells ushered them out of the city. The radio was talking about the weather in "The Magic City," a nickname the town had embraced as a link to its more glorious past, when it had magically mushroomed into existence following the discovery of gold in 1882.

"Prodigal son returns to the Land of Oz," Jimbo said.

Mike gave him a cockeyed look.

Jimbo laughed self-consciously. "All that Magic City crap. You'd think it were run by elves or hobbits or something."

Mike shrugged. Jimbo stared back out the window and tried to think of something to say. He watched a herd of black baldies standing by a barbed-wire fence, swishing at flies.

"So, how you been?"

"Pretty fair," Mike said.

"You'd think after two and a half years I could think of something to ask besides 'How you been?' "

Mike smiled. "Well. How *you* been? Let's try that."

"I thought you'd never ask. Pretty fair."

Mike nodded.

"And Avelyn?"

"Pretty fair," they said together, laughing.

"No, how is she?" Jimbo persisted. "She like it here?"

"She's doing good. It ain't the country club life, but she likes it fine. Looking forward to having another Easterner around."

"That what I am now? Another Easterner? Well, hell, maybe

I am. I liked it back there." He put his hand out the window and opened his palm so that the air forced it back. "She's not pregnant or anything?"

Mike flashed that little grin. "Anxious to be an uncle?"

"No. Well. I'm just asking. Just passing time. Anything but silence."

"No. She's not," Mike said.

"So how's Papa Vic doing? For true."

"He's pretty sick, buddy boy. He's a tough old bugger, but he ain't well. Laid up in bed. He's likely to be there for some time. We got him a wheelchair, but he won't get in it. Calls it a rolling coffin. Won't touch it. His mind's good. He asks about you. Always has."

Jimbo waited. He wondered if Mike meant for him to feel guilt. "Did he think it strange that I stayed East?"

Mike shrugged.

"Did you tell him I quit my job?"

"You really did, eh? What about McGovern?"

"McGovern can govern without me."

"That'll break Papa Vic's heart. Break that news to him gentle. He won't care you quit your job, but he was all hot-to-trot over McGovern. Kinda liked him being a Dakotan. Reminded him of Teddy Roosevelt. He was all set to vote for that nut."

Jimbo smiled. "Nut, huh?"

"Nut."

Jimbo sang in a mutter: " 'I'm proud to be an Okie from Muskogee, a place where even squares can have a ball . . .' "

"Nut."

He laughed. "It's all relative, big brother. You know, out East everyone thought of *me* as a redneck cowboy."

"That right? How was it out East? How come you never looked up Avelyn's sister?"

"Jesus, I don't know. That was dumb."

"That *was* dumb."

Jimbo thought for a while, watching the grassland. "Lots of people back there. Lots of different types. I never knew different types of people before. I kept waiting to get a grip on things, you know, like every morning when I was on my way to work, I'd think, today it's all going to fall into place. I'm going to understand just what the fuck I'm doing here with all these goofy people." He looked at Mike, looked at the strong profile. "Of course I never did. I wonder if anyone really does. I'd like to have had Papa Vic back there to see if he could have figured it out. You know what I liked? I liked those little rickshaw deals that those sorry swaybacked horses pulled down Fifth Avenue. I used to follow those things around and wait for the horse apples to fall and step in them when they were still fresh. Just to get a little flavor of home. I missed you guys."

"Us horse apples."

"Yeah. One Saturday when things were *especially* low, I sat through six straight showings of *True Grit*. Somebody should look into that as a humane sort of way to get confessions."

"How come you never came back for a visit? I guess you had your reasons," Mike said.

Jimbo wondered if Mike had any idea what they were, if he guessed for a second that it had anything to do with him, with that great long shadow he was seemingly unconscious of. "I don't know. Inertia."

"It doesn't matter." Then: "Avelyn thought maybe it was her."

"*Her?*" Jimbo resisted the impulse to laugh.

"Didn't make any sense to me."

"Oh, God. It sure didn't have anything to do with her."

"She thought maybe it was. You just never came to visit once we were married, so that's what she figured." They were quiet for a while. Mike asked, "You plan to stay around awhile?"

Jimbo wondered if it mattered to him one way or the other. He felt strange, not nearly so independent as he had on the train. Or in New York. "Depends on Papa Vic, I guess."

"Well. We could use a hand if you decide to stay on."

Jimbo looked at him. "Yeah?"

"We could keep you busy."

"I wouldn't want to put you out."

"I'm just tellin' you you're welcome to stay, if that's what you like. Play it by ear."

"Appreciate it."

They turned off the highway. The road to Kearney was paved now to accommodate the trucks running in and out of the new strip mine on the Cheyenne reservation. At the edge of town a new rectangular building stood, topped with a big sign: Preston Construction Co. There was a development going up along the Tongue River. An aluminum trailer had been turned into a diner — Millies Eat: Sno-cones, Soft Ice, Shakes, Malts, Burgers, Footlongs, Sundays (sic), THE BIG MILLIE! You've Got to See Her to Believe Her! — beside the movie theater.

"The town's changed," Jimbo said, taking it in. A vaguely unsettled feeling welled inside him, and he worked his palms together, back and forth, slowly. "I just never imagined this street changing at all."

But on the Canyon Creek road, all that disappeared. The familiar landmarks, coulees and springs and outcroppings, leaped out at him. The pinging of the gravel against the bottom of the vehicle, the tunnel of dust behind, the tall grass, and the irrigation ditches teeming with water — it was just right, all of it. Just as he had pictured it a dozen times since boarding that train, just as he had recalled it a thousand times in the past thirty months. They didn't talk. Mike drove, and Jimbo drank it in, blinking more rapidly and feeling his breath come short as they neared the Bar V, everything seeming so *right* all of a sudden, as if things had been slightly out of joint for as long as he had been away. The Herefords looking up with their trusting, confused expressions, the magpie squawking from the fence rail, the cottonwoods growing along the creek, silhouetted by the south ridge — it was as if everything had turned out for his benefit alone. He had forgotten so much, he thought. He could never have stayed away so long had he remembered all this.

"*This* hasn't changed," he said softly.

"Well, we don't work real hard out here in the country."

They turned through the gate. Jimbo rested his eyes on the south pasture, on the one odd oak tree in its center, on the crosshatch of ditches and the coil of rusted barbed wire beyond the fence. Stormy, a pup when he was last home, was lying beside the cattle guard, and he trotted along behind when the Travelall rattled over. They came up the last little pitch to the yard. The screen door swung open, and Avelyn stepped out, her dark hair pulled back and hanging below her shoulders. Since he could remember, there had never been a woman on the Bar V, and she looked absolutely stunning, absolutely right in her plaid shirt and jeans. He was out of the car before it was parked, grinning happily, full of energy, and he ran forward and hugged her.

"Hey! Sister-in-law!"

"Hey! Brother-in-law!" she said, slightly taken aback.

He kept moving, right on by, and she took a couple of steps after him, sucked along by his enthusiasm. "Can I see Papa Vic? Is he in his room? Is he asleep or anything?"

"Don't wake him if he is."

"No, no. Don't worry."

He went inside, bounding up the stairs. He knocked twice on the bedroom door, then opened it. Papa Vic was propped up in bed, a half-bottle of whiskey and a two-hundred-fifty-tablet jar of aspirin on his bedside table. His leg, in a cast, was lying on top of the bedsheet. His face was gray. He is dying, Jimbo thought, knowing it beyond doubt.

Papa Vic recognized him and squirmed up straighter in bed. Jimbo closed the door, and they watched each other. Then Papa Vic wiped twice under his nose. "Well, well, well," he said in a gruff, serious manner. "The blight child."

"Come home to roost. How are you, Papa Vic?"

"How am I? Jeeminy Christmas, boy. I feel like *shit*." Papa Vic reached over and opened the whiskey and took a drink. "Well, come on over and shake my hand. You want a drink?"

"No, thanks." They shook hands. Papa Vic's grip was weak now, and his hands were very thin.

"The child is father of the man, Jimmy. That's real poetry. First thing I thought when I seen you as an infant, was you were about plain enough to roll a wagon wheel acrost. Still are. I told your pa to name you Wheeler on that account. Wheeler McKenzie. That's kinda nice. Said so then and I still say so."

He'd heard it a dozen times. "Well. Old Wheeler's home."

Papa Vic allowed himself a smile. "By Gawd, he is." Then he asked: "You learned much?"

"I guess I learned some."

"Tell me what you learned."

Jimbo stammered, trying to think of something worthy.

"Don't tell me ever'thing you learned. Just one thing."

"I learned I didn't want to be a banker. Least not in New York."

"That's a good thing to learn. What else?"

"I learned how to play the ukulele from Manny Orta."

"That's a good thing to learn, too. What else?"

"Papa Vic . . ."

"Just one more thing."

"Any field in particular?"

"All right. Gawd."

"I didn't learn anything about God."

"Me neither. Even when I was 'neath that horse, dyin'. I always thought as I got older I'd learn somethin' more about Gawd than the fact that He lives in that eagles' nest. But I haven't. Last thing I learned about Gawd was that when coyotes howl at night, that's who they're howlin' to. I learned that a long time back. Well. Let's try women."

Jimbo grinned. "I've missed the hell out of you, Papa Vic."

"That don't count. Tell me what you learned about women. That's important."

He thought. "They're a damn sight different than men. They're a different species altogether. They think different."

Papa Vic wheezed with laughter. "That's morc'n your brother knows. You're gonna be all right, Jimmy. I see that. I ain't gonna worry on you no longer."

CHAPTER 8

IN THE MORNINGS, Jimbo would lie in bed smelling the coffee. He had never brewed coffee for himself in New York, and even if he had, it could not have smelled so delicious as that coffee, which mingled with the cold dawn air and the light piny fragrance of the house itself, which made you want to leave the warmth of the bed and dress quickly in the chill for no better reason than to go down and taste it, sipping it and rolling it on your tongue to get all the flavor. The kitchen would heat up with the smells of bacon and Avelyn's biscuits and eggs splattering in the bacon grease, and they'd drink their coffee and talk about the day. Deacon would stomp in from the bunkhouse, then Denny with his eyes puffy and hair mussed, quiet and hungry. It was the best time of the day, really. Out East breakfast had been a hurried, unpleasant affair, silent but for the rustling of newspapers, a meal to put behind you so that the day could begin. On the ranch, it *was* the beginning. It was lingered over. The day's chores were laid out, and the talk was light; though as Papa Vic worsened, the morning's giddiness disappeared.

The greenness left the hills at the end of June as the hot, dry summer sun began to cure the grass. In the valley, where it was irrigated, the hay pastures recovered from the late spring. The wildflowers wilted in the fields, and the ivory-colored yarrow and purple bull thistle came up along the roads. In the evenings Jimbo would wade up Canyon Creek, throwing a dry Joe's Hopper beside the bank, where the trout hid. Or, if Papa Vic were

64

still awake, he would sit up with him. Papa Vic was living on whiskey and aspirin, and as the day wore on his eyes would glaze and redden and sink deeper into his weathered face. But he never spoke of pain.

He tired quickly now. Sometimes Jimbo came in and stood and watched from the doorway, so still that Papa Vic wouldn't know he was there. Just standing and watching. Papa Vic had had them move his bed in front of the window, where he could look out on the south pasture, and the two of them would look out of it as if alone. Then Jimbo would come in and talk, or sometimes, if Papa Vic were tired, he would stand there awhile and then leave, never saying a word. He wanted Papa Vic to move back into the hospital, but he wouldn't go. He'd perk up and snarl that any fool bunch of doctors who'd let an old man's constipation lick them for eighteen years weren't qualified to postpone a man's natural time of death. "Like my bowels, Jimmy, I ain't movin'." Mike backed him up, too. He belonged home.

In the morning Papa Vic ate a bowl of fruit, but his lunch and dinner went untouched. Once a day he'd crutch to the john, and when he returned he'd let Avelyn shave him. Then he'd sip whiskey and read and stare out the window, and when Lloyd Paxton or Sam Benson or one of the other ranchers came by to visit, she'd bring in another glass, smiling at the way he'd slipped on his hat for his guest. When he napped in the afternoons, Avelyn had a chance to go to town for supplies. Everywhere she went, people asked how he was coming along, and asked to be remembered to him. Old people. People she barely knew, and who barely knew her.

"He's just resting up for hunting season, so he says," she'd say.

"Ole Vic . . ." with an admiring wag of the head.

Late in the afternoons she started bringing him some bread or soup or oatmeal, knowing he wouldn't eat any dinner. He'd shake his head and sip his whiskey, and in an hour or two she'd be back to take it away.

Finally she scolded. "You've got to eat something. You need to build up your strength."

"Man don't need strength to die, Missy."

"Don't say that. You're too old to die. You've said it yourself. Now eat something."

"Once ole Wes Smith up in Birney got drunk and figured how a man growed old. Said a man's got so much energy in him, no more, no less, and ever'time he gets in a fight, ever'time he sleeps with a woman, he uses some up. Fella can't get 'er back; she's gone for good. Told me that's how some of these fellas live darn near forever — never had any fun. Well, this was forty-some years ago, and I believed him. Ole Wes died 'bout two years after, and we gave a helluva party for 'im. Man dies young like that prob'ly had one damn fine life."

"Papa Vic."

"He was right on one count, though. Gawd Almighty ain't against a little sin and hellin', but He'll only let a man back to the well so many times. Then she's dry. Some men got a real big well, and some have a little one. When she's dry, she's dry. Don't mean you're dead; just means you ain't gonna get no older. Means she's dry. Plumb dry." He raised the bottle up in a toast. "Ole Wes figured that out while stiff as a boot."

She squeezed his hand.

"Well. She's dry."

"That's whiskey talk."

"Where's Michael? I got to find out what he's gonna do with the calves."

"I'll get him."

Mike came and they talked about selling the calves. Prices were low. Mike thought they should keep half through the winter and sell the rest that fall. Papa Vic doubted prices would be much better in the spring, but thought that was the way to work it. Mike had good business sense that way. They drank some more whiskey and then Papa Vic asked him to get Jimbo.

Mike left the two of them alone. Papa Vic looked at him, his eyes red and glassy. "You made plans? After I'm gone, you made plans?"

"Papa Vic, don't . . ."

"You made plans yet?"

"Don't talk like that, Papa."

"I'm just askin'. I'm just wonderin'. I had a thought you might think about a run for county commissioner, since you showed an interest in politics. I served that post twenty-four years. It's a good post. Lot of power there for the right man. McKenzie name prob'ly won't hurt you none, but you could win it on your own merit, Jimmy. Well, I's just wonderin'. Don't matter."

"I don't really have any definite plans, Papa Vic. I'd sure talk to you about them if I did. I'm still feeling out if I belong."

"You'll be fine, Jimmy."

"Papa Vic."

"McKenzies had ought to keep a hand in the working of the town. That's the thing. They ought to help shape it. Michael, he give up the head of the Cattleman's Association last year. I give him hell for that, lousy as that outfit is anymore. Course Michael ain't just the right cut for that sort of thing, bless him. Well . . ." His voice trailed off and he stared back at the fading light outside. "Your ma's brother, Sam Benson. He come by this afternoon. He was state senator, you know. Eighteen years. He'll help you if you should like. Just a thought."

"All right, Papa. Thanks."

"I'll get some sleep now."

In the morning Avelyn brought him his fruit, but Papa Vic let it sit. He was weak now. He smiled at her and said, "You like to take pictures, Missy. I seen you trompin' through the marsh there sometimes."

"The moose feed through there," she said.

"You best watch yourself around them moose. Right time of year, a bull moose is just as dangerous as a grizzly."

"I'm not afraid of moose, Papa Vic."

"I seen that. That's why I tell you. Bud Travis got hisself killed one fall after wounding a moose."

"I'm not shooting at them. Have some fruit, Papa."

"Moose don't know that. I'll tell you a story 'bout a moose. Happened right out here by the Bar V gate. Tourist fella from Michigan pulls toe to fender with a big bull moose one fall, makes him a happy man: I seen him snapping pictures right through the windshield of his little bitty Volkswagen. Moose had a considerable size advantage as you might imagine, hauls off and butts that car right in the kisser. Whammo! Well, tourist fella like to swallow his camera he was so surprised, and he honks on his horn to beat the band. Moose don't care. Whammo! Butts him again. Headlights busted all over the road. Oooh, that made that fella mad. He's cursin' the moose to clear out of the road or by Gawd! Honking that bitty horn, the big ole moose bustin' it one ever' time he so much as slips that car into gear. They're territorial as a woman. Tourist finally backs around and drives back to Kearney. Moose stood and watched him clean out of sight, and I'm in my pickup near enough to spit on him in a good wind. Moose looks over and sees me, and I'm thinkin', 'Lord love me, I'm next,' when that damn critter takes off across the creek and through the willow bushes, up toward the mesa with that goofy moose lope of theirs, and who knows why? One of them moose gets a notion, there's no ungetting it." He smiled at her. "Kind of like your fella Michael."

She squeezed his hand. "Here. Eat something."

"You know that about him."

"I know it."

"You'll be a good woman for him, Missy. Good strong woman. Man needs that." He wiped his nose. "I ain't very hungry this mornin'. S'pose you can find them two boys?"

"I'll get them. I'll leave your breakfast here on the table for you. Try to eat something, Papa Vic."

She caught Mike and Jimbo on their way out, and they came back to see him. "How do you feel?" Mike asked.

Papa Vic's face was hollow and gray, but he smiled thinly. "Proud. Proud as a donkey on a mare."

He held that weak grin, but Mike ignored it and plunged ahead. "How's that, huh?"

"Broke me a Yellowstone County record this mornin'." Papa Vic sat up a little straighter in bed. He threw back his shoulders like an old rooster. "Went fifteen days without takin' a crap. Nurse down at the hospital says that were a record. Says lots of old cantankerous sorts like me clam up at the sight of a bedpan, but all of 'em gave in by fourteen days. Well, I set my sights on fifteen, and today were the day."

Mike grinned at him. "Bullshit."

Papa Vic's face glowed for an instant. "Ain't bullshit. Ain't bullshit or any other kind of shit neither for fifteen days."

"I don't believe you."

"I don't either," Jimbo said.

"Can't be done."

"If you two ain't a pair of doubting Thomases to beat 'em all. What I'm tellin' you would hold up in a court of gawddamn law if it had to, me bein' a dyin' man and all."

"You'd be a dead one if you hadn't crapped in two weeks," Mike said.

"Fifteen days! Don't you forget it, neither. I just flat put the lid on 'er. You call up that nurse. Nurse Kobliskey. Big fat ole gal, Deacon's type. Give me that phone, damn your insolence. Hell's bells, I can't get my own flesh and blood to acknowledge a true and hard-won record. I been constipated since I was seventy-five, and I'll tell you true, fifteen days ain't nothin'. Ever' fifteen days, and I've got the durn runs. I ain't even warmed up till I hit three weeks, and I consider myself regular when I match cycles with the moon. And there's your wife, Michael, ever' mornin' tryin' to trip me up by slippin' prunes into my fruit bowl and that. Well, didn't work. Record's mine." Papa Vic nodded at Mike's smile, and sank deeper into the pillow. "Now I've given you boys somethin' to shoot for."

He held out his hands and motioned for Mike and Jimbo to take them. He was looking out the window, not at anything, just out, toward the light, his eyes glazed. "She's a good ole ranch, this is. Good ole house. I built her up here on this ridge so's it would stand up and face ever' damn thing Nature wanted to throw at her, up high where you knew what was comin' and not tucked down in some little nook where something might sneak up on you like a thief. Flood taught me that." He coughed. The cough tired him. His voice was lower. "That ain't the worst way for a person to live, neither . . ."

Papa Vic turned his head to face Mike. "She's good land, this. She works her way under your skin. Protects a man from whole lots of things. Gives a man a skin like a gawddamn rhino." He smiled briefly. "Be all yours now, fellas."

Jimbo's eyes blurred and his throat went thick. "Don't you worry," Papa Vic said. He grinned from one to the other. "I'll be watchin' to make sure you don't screw things up too bad."

He waited. "You understand?"

"Sure," Mike said.

"That hay comin' up?"

Mike nodded. "Be a fair crop, I guess."

"Jimmy? Don't let him work you too hard."

"No," he said.

"Well. Go on now. I'm gonna nap."

That afternoon he died. He was in the same bed his first wife, Katie, had died in sixty-seven years earlier.

Mike fell quiet, letting Avelyn and Jimbo take care of the funeral arrangements. He seemed to throw himself into his ranch work to numb the loss, not even stopping for lunch beyond eating a sandwich on the tractor. At the end of the day he would have a couple of beers, eat his dinner, then take the paper up to bed, never saying more than two or three words at a time. Jimbo wondered if he was talking to Avelyn at night, getting the sadness out of his system when it was black and quiet. Or maybe he was the same way when they were alone, silent and hurt, as if he had never considered the possibility that Papa Vic was mortal after all, as if things might have gone on as they always had forever, simply because he willed it so. Jimbo didn't ask her. They all felt a monumental void, and Avelyn, too, was subdued.

Papa Vic was buried in the family plot, between his wives, Kate and Abbey. It was a clear, hot day, the sun glinting off the windshields of the trucks driving up the valley for the funeral, just enough of a breeze to blow the cotton off the cottonwood trees. Ladies and cowboys Jimbo had forgotten the names of milled in the yard, then filed down behind the minister to the small fenced graveyard bedecked in flowers. The men, heads bowed, hair neatly parted, stood with their hats held before them. Their faces were sunburned, but the tops of their foreheads were white. The women wore muted dresses just below the knee, their thick legs narrowing into tight Sunday shoes.

They walked with a sort of studied care to avoid toppling forward — so altogether different from the New York women whose chic and grace had so dazzled Jimbo. And among these was Avelyn, who carried herself fluidly but without self-consciousness, like an athlete more than a dancer, a black cotton dress cut low in the front, sleeves ruffled and puffed just enough to give the dress a soft angularity. She stood beside Mike, her dark hair combed down in waves, one arm slipped through the crook of his elbow, laying her fingers on his forearm. Mike was still. There was a tension in his face as the minister spoke of life after death and life on earth, as the ex-governor read the eulogy, as they prayed, "Our Father . . ." His hands were clasped in front of him, gripped so forcefully that the veins showed. There was a tightness around his mouth. Jimbo saw Avelyn rubbing his forearm to relax him, but the tightness stayed.

The guests that came back to the house afterward were subdued and respectful. They spoke to Mike, automatically treating him as the new leader of the family, a new leader in the community. Most sought out Jimbo as well, welcoming him back. Faces tough and dry from working in that climate. Hard hands. Bad teeth. There was a sincerity about them more than a sadness. It made him feel good for his grandfather. It made him feel good to have his name, the kind of a feeling that made you want to do something with your own life that might make someone feel good to have yours someday, that might bring out sincerity more than sadness — the sadness that came from a life left unfinished or wasted. So that even in death, Papa Vic's moral remained: *You are blessed; we are blessed; this land is blessed by God Almighty, Cattleman, Gentleman, Imbiber of Whiskey* . . . which was his written epitaph.

And he made one final statement in the form of an unusual provision in his last will and testament. Papa Vic asked to be cremated and fed to his cattle. He wanted his ashes to be scattered in a half ton of grain and fed to the entire herd. He wrote: "I've spent my whole adult life eating these critters, and I figure I've got this coming."

It turned out to be illegal. Had the Department of Health

stayed out of it, though, Papa Vic would in effect have been spreading himself over every acre of land he had ever owned. They ran the bulls in the home pasture in the fall, the stockers and heifers in the north pasture, and the cows in the south pasture. And he would have done so while settling an old score with the blight of constipation.

Well, Jimbo thought, the cows still owed him one, and he still owed constipation one. Maybe next time around it would all even out.

CHAPTER 9

JIMBO STAYED ON. Fall came, and the aspens up the valley began to turn. The hollow where Mike had shot his bear became a shimmering bowl of gold, and from that very spot Denny got his first elk on the third of October. Avelyn also had some good news that week when the Sheridan bank bought her entire series of photographs from Trudy Miller's gallery, her first sale.

But it had not been a good year financially. The hundred fifty calves Mike took to auction fetched a disappointing forty-six cents per pound. They had put up nearly a thousand tons of hay — just fair — which would get the rest of the herd through the winter with little to spare. They had seen far worse years, though, and now there was winter to attend to.

Deacon and Denny loaded the Mexican steers into the stock truck to sell in Sheridan, and Jimbo, who had been cutting and stacking wood all week, was sharpening the chain saw in the workroom of the barn. Mike was in the shoeing stall, trimming the horses' feet, replacing worn and thrown shoes while it was still warm enough to work without gloves. They owned seven head, and except for Mike's old roping horse, Jacks, they were all good horses to work with.

Mike brought Jacks in last. The horse had turned kid-gentle with age, and would lean on whoever was working on him like a drunk on a lamppost. Mike had to change the left front shoe, and as he shaped the new one on the anvil, Jimbo could hear him talking to the horse. "You be good now, boy. Don't you lean on me or I'll whale on you. Jacks boy? You hear?" The clanging of the anvil was a good sound.

In a little bit it stopped, and he could hear Mike flat-filing the bottom of Jacks's hoof with a rasp. The strokes were quick at first, then more careful as the conformation of the hoof became better and better. Mike was panting now, sucking in his breaths unevenly as Jimbo imagined him straining under the horse's lazy weight. "You quit!" Mike muttered. "Jacks boy, you get back!"

There was a thud as the horse's foot fell and Mike stepped back to catch his breath. Jimbo poked his head in from the workroom. "Old Jacks taking a little nap?"

"Fucking horse."

"He's just overfond of you, Michael."

Mike cast him a warning glance, and Jimbo disappeared back into the workroom. He was almost finished with the blade of the saw. In a moment he heard the tapping of Mike's hammer as he nailed on the new shoe. He always held the extra nails in his mouth, and he was mumbling through them: "You be good, you be good . . . be good . . . be good."

There was mounting panic in the tone and Jimbo could not resist. He peeked through the doorway again, and there was Mike, crouched over, struggling against the shifting weight of the horse, the two of them working exactly against each other like beginning dancers, until he finally blew the nails out of his mouth and spun around, kicking Jacks in the belly as hard as he could.

"Fucking horse!"

Jacks skittered sideways and snorted angrily, and Mike waved the hammer in front of his face with menace.

Jimbo ducked back into the workroom, smiling to himself, and things were quiet for a while as Mike waited for Jacks to calm down. It happened every time with that horse, no matter who was doing the shoeing. He was a bitch, Jimbo remembered that.

The tapping of the hammer started again, Mike muttering, "Be good . . . be good . . ." between breaths. Things seemed to be going smoothly, Mike saying, ". . . almost through now . . . be good . . . be good . . ." when suddenly he called out, "You! Get over there!" Jimbo poked his head around the corner. Mike was leaning against the horse with his shoulder, holding up the one leg while still trying to hammer.

"You Jacks! Dammit!" Mike cursed, his breath coming in quick snorts. He dropped the hammer and repositioned his feet, grabbing the horse's leg with both hands. "I ain't letting this down, dogmeat! You wake up!" He cranked the leg upward.

The horse lost its balance. Jacks's front foot hopped right, then left, and landed on Mike's boot. Mike straightened up with a sharp hiss of pain, dropping the hoof he was holding. It fell on his other boot.

"No, no! Oh, God!" His mouth twisted in pain. Eyes clenched shut, he groped wildly with his hands. He hit upon the hammer. Before Jimbo could move, he lashed over his shoulder with it, thwacking Jacks in the face three times before the horse finally reared backward. His feet freed, Mike toppled like a toy soldier off its base.

Jimbo watched him writhing on the floor of the barn. "You okay?"

"*You goddamn Jacks!*" Mike sat bolt upright and raised the hammer high, winging it past Jacks's bleeding cheek so that it crashed through the window across the barn. The shattering glass spooked the horse so that it bolted forward, toward Mike. Jimbo jumped between them, waving his hands, and Mike rolled back, kicking his feet in the air. Jacks reared up and broke his halter rope, then dashed breakneck out of the barn, through the yard, down the drive, and out of sight.

Jimbo started to laugh. He turned to Mike, who was rocking on his back, clutching his feet.

"It ain't funny, you prick." Mike lay back and groaned. Jimbo smiled despite himself. Mike saw this and lashed out, "And where the hell were you, you . . . you . . . *banker!*"

Jimbo stiffened. "I was here."

"Goddamn eastern banker." Mike's eyes were closed and his face was lined with a faint grimace. Jimbo watched him, stung. But before he could say anything he heard a heavy footstep and turned to see a huge man in a three-piece suit standing hesitantly in the doorway. He and the stranger stared at one another, each waiting for the other to speak. The man had intelligent eyes that were neither friendly nor unfriendly, black curly hair receding at the temples, and one of the largest heads Jimbo had ever seen.

The man wrinkled his brows. "Looking for Mike McKenzie."

Jimbo nodded toward his brother, who was still supine.

"I'm afraid my timing's not very good," the man said, taking a step forward.

Mike looked at him once, then sat up and rubbed his feet.

"I drove down from Decker," the man said. He waited. "Are you all right?"

"No thanks to this one," Mike said, nodding toward Jimbo. Jimbo said nothing.

"I should have called. My name's Zach Thorndike. I'm with the Titanic Coal Company."

Mike looked at the man more carefully this time, then went back to rubbing his feet.

"I'd like to talk to you."

"You've got a plumb captive audience, pal. I can't even walk."

"Are you sure you're all right? Listen, this is awful timing. I'll come back, if I may."

"Go ahead and talk."

"Well. You may know this: my company is pretty active in pursuing coal in this region. Our field people, geologists and geophysicists and all those types, are interested in taking a few samples from this valley. They're doing it everywhere; it's unbelievable. There's a million square miles out here they'd love to take samples from. Anyway, I've got an offer to make on the company's behalf."

Mike frowned at him. "All right."

Thorndike glanced at Jimbo, then back at Mike.

"My long-lost little brother," Mike said. Thorndike and Jimbo shook hands. "Go ahead," Mike said. "What's this neat little offer?"

Thorndike pulled a folded, legal-sized document from his pocket. It was an exploration lease.

"For coal?" Mike asked.

"And oil. Gas. Certain minerals."

It was fourteen pages long. Mike flipped through and started to hand it back.

"Should I go over the key points with you?" Thorndike asked.

"Quickly."

"Um . . . all right. We'll pay you three dollars an acre up front; thirty-five hundred acres, ten thousand five hundred dollars. For that we take an extremely limited series of core samples. In and out in a week or two once we start. That's all filled in again, no problem with running the ranch. If we find anything — maybe one in ten times we do — well, that's the next step. If we do happen to end up mining something, your royalties come on a percentage basis, and let me tell you, Mr. McKenzie, that runs into some pretty heady sums. You'd be set for life if we came up with something like, say — well, say, the Cheyenne mine. Just six miles away? Man, oh man, I don't want to get your hopes up, but you never know. That thing's worth *millions*. But in any event the ten grand is yours to keep."

Mike nodded. "Anything else?"

"Well, those are the essentials. It's all in there."

Mike tossed the lease back to him. "Then thanks for your trouble." He struggled to his feet and hobbled gingerly past Jimbo and Thorndike.

Thorndike followed. "It's natural that you should have some reservations. By all means, talk it over with your brother and your wife. But if it's the running of your ranch you're worried about, I assure you taking a few core samples won't bother your operations in the least."

"It won't, eh? Look, mister, my feet are very sore."

"I'm sorry about the timing of this. Perhaps if I came back another time, after you've had a chance to look this over —"

Thorndike tried to hand the lease back to Mike, but he was

already hobbling toward the house. Thorndike followed him. "Why don't I give you a call in a few days?"

"Suit yourself."

"Fine. I'll do that. I hope your feet are feeling better."

"I hope so." Mike stopped and turned around. "Not that it matters. Not that it matters, Mr. Thorndike, but I happen to know the terms of that Cheyenne lease. Not that it matters."

Thorndike was clearly caught off his guard, and he smiled foolishly.

"Not that it matters, 'cause it doesn't. You know Sam Benson? Sam Benson, state senator from these parts for the last eighteen years and no fan of your company, Mr. Thorndike — he's a pretty close friend. Happens to be my ma's brother, old Sam. I had a drink with Sam a couple of weeks back, and he told me your company give the Cheyenne *ten* dollars an acre for the exploration rights. That's, what, about three times what you're offering me? Not that it matters, 'cause it doesn't, but you must think of me as quite a rube."

"No, I don't."

"Sure you do."

"I don't. The Cheyenne situation was entirely different."

"My brother here went to Yale, you know. Maybe you think he's a rube, too."

"I don't think anyone's a rube."

Mike looked away and rubbed the flat of his hand against his cheek, making a scraping sound against his unshaven face. He gave a little laugh. " 'Member old Jake Fox, buddy boy? Hepp's old man? Old drunk whose wife run off with that soap salesman? Fella like him is who Mr. Thorndike's looking for, ain't that right, Mr. Thorndike? Some old drunk who'd sign some piece of paper without knowing any more about it than it'll bring him enough money for booze for the next ten years. Long as the fella who showed it to him was all dressed up in a suit and seemed like a nice enough fella, and had cash money to give him just for the okay to drill a few holes.

"You're not welcome back here, Mr. Thorndike. You understand me?"

Thorndike opened his giant palm in a gesture of conciliation. "I'll see if the company is willing to come back with another proposal, if you like; but frankly, I doubt very much if they'll be interested. That Cheyenne situation was entirely —"

"You're not welcome back here."

Thorndike backed away, raising both palms this time. "All right, all right." Then: "Good morning to you both."

A week later Titanic Coal, via Thorndike, raised its offer to ten dollars an acre plus royalties of twenty-five cents a ton for coal and twenty percent of the market price for oil, up from twenty cents and seventeen and a half percent respectively. Mike turned it down. Ten days after that, Titanic offered a bid of twenty dollars per acre — seventy thousand dollars up front — plus the royalties. Mike turned that down, too.

That was the final offer. Two weeks after it had been refused, a man from the U.S. Geological Survey crew arrived with a court order allowing the government to make a mineral study of the entire valley. Most of the mineral rights in the Canyon Creek area were still owned by the state, though not those of the Bar V. Still, by right of eminent domain, the state had the right to determine what was there. With the energy crisis pending, Wyoming was making a concerted effort to establish its available fuel resources, and that took priority over the Bar V's deed.

By December drilling rigs were taking core samples all up and down the valley, rumors of a huge coal find were circulating, and out-of-town speculators were buying up available lots in Kearney at unheard-of prices. Change was in the air, and some excitement, too. Mostly, though, just winter.

CHAPTER 10

I T WAS ONE of Nature's quirks that a dry summer was nearly always followed by a bad winter. The first storm came through in late October, and that had no sooner melted off than another followed on the tenth of November that kept the ground covered the rest of the winter. By mid-December the ice had built up enough that the stock could not paw through to the grass, and Mike began feeding twice a day by pitchfork off the sled, throwing the hay behind while Denny drove the team. It wasn't light until seven-thirty, and it was dark again by four, and the feeding took up most of the precious daylight hours. Jimbo went out every morning to chop a hole in the ice so the cows could drink, and when the really cold temperatures came in January, he chopped in the late afternoon, too, so the ice wouldn't grow too thick to break. There was the drive to keep clear, the saddles and bridles to mend, the rakes to sharpen, and the calving shed to clean out and ready. In the long hours of darkness, there was much time to read.

The first calf was born February 7. Before daylight on the eighth, another was born, and then three more during the day. The first week, the calves came in fours and fives, but by the fourteenth they began to average about nine per day. Eighteen were born on the fifteenth, two of which died. The weather was cold and dry that week, but a light storm hit on February 17, and the night of the twenty-first another came through and dumped over twenty inches of snow. A young cow wandered off during the storm to give birth, and Deacon found her at four in the morning hemorrhaging in the snow. She had had a breech delivery, and one of the calf's front feet had broken through her uterine wall. They saved the calf, tending to it by hand for ten days. Then Mike put the mother of one of the calves that had died into its stall, wrapping the orphaned calf in the dead calf's skin so that she would accept it.

The last three days in February the weather turned mild, and it continued in the thirties through March 7. During those ten days, a hundred eleven calves were born, twenty-four on March 2, making the total on the ground two hundred nineteen. Two heifers were given cesareans by the vet, and Mike gave one emergency cesarean on the ranch. One calf was born blind.

They were exhausted. They slept and watched the calving pen in shifts. Mike had taught Avelyn how to tell when a cow was near her time. Sometimes it was a physical sign like the secreting of mucus or dilation of the vagina, and sometimes the cow would get restless and walk away from the herd to find a niche somewhere. That was the surest sign. Or her bag would be so full that her teats would secrete milk. Mike could tell by a change in the way the calf was sitting inside its mother and the swelling of her barrels, but Avelyn couldn't see that. The most important thing was to know which cows were near their labor and to watch for any change or trouble. If there was bad weather coming, they would move the cow to the calving barn, where Mike and Deacon had built ten stalls in the summer. Once the cow started to give birth, Avelyn would wake Mike, and he would watch the cow through it to see that she tended her calf afterward. Sometimes the mother would not lick the calf dry or would leave it altogether before it could get up; sometimes she wouldn't let the calf suck; and sometimes the teats were dry. The milk in a cow for the first couple of days after she gives birth is actually a substance called colostrum, which activates the antibodies in the newborn's bloodstream. Without it, the calf is susceptible to almost any disease or infection. When a calf was born dead, Mike milked its mother and stored bottles of its colostrum in the freezer. Then he thawed it and fed it to a newborn calf whose mother was dry or had died or wouldn't let it suckle. There were good mothers and there were bad ones. You just had to watch. But once a calf had suckled that good milk, it would live. Mike said then you couldn't kill it with a hammer.

He could tell Avelyn each cow's history and personality at a glance. He knew which were reliable and which had experienced trouble in other years. He warned her which ones to watch closest. If any of the heifers were coming near their time, Mike insisted on being awake for it. Heifers were the females that had never given birth before. They needed the closest watching, being small and untried, and Mike moved them into the calving barn when their time was near. Often a heifer's calf had to be pulled from it, and Mike had shown Avelyn how to do that, too. She watched for the cow's muscles to contract as it pushed, then she pulled on the calf's legs steadily and as hard as she could, downward. When the cow eased up, she eased up. If the calf was obviously too big for its mother to bear, they could give her a cesarean (long ago, Papa Vic had kept a long, hooked knife that was used to cut the unborn calf to pieces inside the uterus, so that it could be removed and the mother saved).

The McKenzies had always calved in February, although many outfits waited until March. In February's brutal cold the snow was fine and dry and helped shelter the newborns. On the very coldest days, there was seldom any wind, and the air was dry. The worst storms came in March, when the temperature rose into the thirties. A wet snow or sleet that started in the day would ice up at night. It was that wet cold that froze an animal, in those first two hours after it was born, when it was still too weak to get up and drink. The more calves that were on the ground by March, the better Mike liked it.

A bad storm did hit on the twentieth of March, and they took the cows with the youngest calves to the barn. It snowed fifteen inches, then the rain came in the afternoon so that the world iced up overnight. The glaze over the snow was thick and hard enough to support a horse, but its slickness made it too dangerous to ride on. Jimbo and Denny went out on snowshoes and brought in a calf that had been born early that morning. It hadn't been on its feet yet. Mike heated up a bottle of colostrum-laced milk and tried to get the calf to drink from a baby bottle. It wouldn't suck. The calf was shivering and wrapped in blankets. When it stopped shivering they thought it was going to die, but Mike held its mouth open while Avelyn spooned the warm milk down its throat. It coughed on it, but she kept spooning. It lay still for an hour, and then they spooned down another bottle. After another hour the calf struggled to its feet and drank from its own mother, and Mike left to help Deacon feed the rest of the herd. Once a calf drank on its own, it would make it.

The last calf was born the tenth of April. There were only three April calves. All told, two hundred sixty-four calves lived. Eleven had died, and the one cow. The thirty-five cows that the vet had found barren had been sold in the fall.

It snowed only once after that big March storm, and then briefly. The warm winds from Colorado melted the snow on the ground by the first of April, and the ice in the rivers broke up. The bulbs in the garden that Avelyn had planted in the fall began to appear, slender green shoots, and slowly the days became longer. None of them had slept a whole night through since the fifth of February, but with April the pace began to slow back to normal.

It was a time you loved and hated. When Avelyn thought of their ranch life, she thought of the calving. Everything seemed important. The smallest chores made sense. There were never enough hours in a day, and the nights were at once endless and hopelessly short. Yet even nights when she would sit alone in the kitchen brewing a pot of coffee and reading while Mike tended to a cow, she felt like a vital part of things. The entire ranch revolved around the birth of each single calf, and the success or failure of that birth was shared. Everything was shared then. It was easy to forget that feeling during other times of the year, when the sharing came less easily, when you had your job, and they had theirs. It was the calving that she thought of when she felt most alone.

CHAPTER 11

IT WAS DEACON who first told him about the coal. Not Mike. They were riding back to the ranch after checking to see how the fences had wintered — it was the first week in May — when Deacon gave him that jowly, amused look and said, "You know how them coal people was swarmin' around the south pasture last winter like maggots on a hog's head?"

Jimbo nodded.

"Just so happens the Bar V is settin' on top of the richest coal field in the whole damn state. The *whole damn state*."

"What's that mean, 'settin' on top of'?"

Deacon narrowed his eyes. "What's that mean? What's it mean when a babe is settin' on top of your face? Same damn thing, only that coal ain't puffin' and gruntin' for air like a pig in a slop bucket."

"What are you talking about?"

Deacon looked at him in amazement. "Ain't you never had a babe on your face, buck?"

"Not that. The coal."

"Ain't you?"

"*Jesus.* Yes! Now what about the coal?"

"I just told you. Biggest deposit in the state's under this damn land! Right here! Zingo!"

"You're full of shit, man."

"Go ask the bossman."

He found Mike in the upstairs bath, the brim of his hat pulled

84

low over his eyes so he could rest the back of his neck against the porcelain tub. His feet were propped on the hot and cold faucets so he could work them with his toes, and in one hand he held a bottle of Coors, in the other a yellow rubber duck. He squeezed the duck. "Quaaack-quaack-quack-waaa-waa-waa . . ." he called, letting it fade out softly. In the fall Mike could bring in mallards or geese or canvasback, and he practiced in the bath. "Shut the door, buddy boy, ducky don't like a draft." He gave the tub a quick shot of water with his foot. Then he sat up, pushed his hat back, and carefully floated the duck right side up. He put the beer on the counter behind his head and began lathering his arms and chest.

"Jesus Christ, Mike. Are you for real?"

"Goddamn, I itch. Been driving that tractor all day, seeding that north pasture. I hate it. I hate that tractor. Makes me itch like an old dog. Makes me itch like Deac. Lord, I itch. Put down five hundred pounds of brome, five hundred pounds of alfalfa. Two kinds of alfalfa, truth to tell. Damn good mix, really." He took a sip of beer. "What's up? You look glum."

Jimbo sat on the hamper and slid his boot through a puddle of water, back and forth, watching it. His anger was gone, but there was still a hurt. He was hoping Mike might say something about the coal, might confide in him right then, might do something besides drink his beer and play with that damned duck.

"I live here now, Mike. I've an interest in things."

Mike looked at him, surprised.

"Deac told me about the coal."

"That right?" Mike put the beer down and scraped at himself with a washcloth.

"So what's the deal?"

"Ain't no deal. Lots of folks might want to make a deal, but it ain't no deal at all."

"Don't you think I ought to know what's going on? Deacon didn't tell me a damn thing, really, except they found a lot of coal. So *what's going on?*"

"I was going to show you the letter, buddy boy. Don't you fret about that."

"I'm not fretting about anything. It's just a little bit irritating to get all this secondhand from Deacon."

"He doesn't know anything."

"He knows a helluva lot more than me."

"All right then. Relax."

"Relax? Just tell me what the hell's going on."

Mike grinned and started to wash his ears as if he were trying to kill something in there. Jimbo waited until he'd dunked himself — carefully removing his hat — and lay back in the water again with his beer.

"Your duck tipped over."

"Thanks." Mike righted it and gave a quack.

"How much coal did they find?"

"Read the letter. I left it with Avelyn."

"Okay. But how much — about?"

Mike cocked his head and winked. "There's lots, buddy boy, by the sound of it. But it don't matter."

"It may not matter to you, cowboy, but I'm sure it matters."

"Nope. Don't matter. And what's this 'cowboy' shit?"

"What's this 'buddy boy' shit?"

They looked at each other. Mike shrugged. "Shut her tight," Mike said as Jimbo turned to leave. He could hear the quacking start again as he went down the stairs.

The government survey had discovered a horseshoe-shaped seam of coal between twenty-five and eighty feet thick that curved through the Canyon Creek area. The closed end of the horseshoe started at Lloyd Paxton's property while the shanks extended in thinner and thinner degrees back down the valley toward Kearney, running for four miles along both the north and south ridges and cutting through the properties of eight ranches. The heart of the seam, however, lay up near the closed end of the horseshoe, underlying more than two thousand acres of McKenzie land. The government estimated that between one hundred fifty and two hundred million tons of coal stretched beneath the Bar V alone, and that the entire Canyon Creek deposit ran twice that. It was the largest privately owned deposit of coal in Wyoming.

Jimbo finished the letter and looked up, amazed. Avelyn was watching him with an understanding expression, an expression that was neither happy nor sad, an expression that pretty much reflected his own feelings: that a door had been opened which maybe should never have *been* opened, even though he had no idea where it would lead.

"I don't know what to say," he said. She smiled a little. He must have looked ridiculous. "What did *Mike* say?"

"He hasn't exactly spent a lot of time brooding about it. He's sort of ignored it, if you want to know the truth." Then she breathed a little laugh. "He showed me the letter and told me not to drop any matches down deep holes."

Jimbo looked at her incredulously. "That's all?"

"Well, he's not thinking about selling. You know that."

"Has he had an offer?"

"Two weeks ago, before we got the letter, that Thorndike man made an offer to buy. Nine hundred dollars an acre, or something. It came out to over three million dollars, I remember that."

"But he didn't mention coal."

"No."

"Those guys really are something. He had to have known." He looked back down at the letter for a while. "I need a drink."

"Yes. I'll join you."

Jimbo made martinis. He took a long swallow. "So what do *you* think?"

"Since when does that matter?" She laughed. "Jimbo, I didn't marry Mike for his money. I knew the life I was getting into. I don't want to change it." She shrugged. "What does two hundred million tons of coal look like? How much is that? My God, what a number."

He wondered if she truly had known what she was getting into when she moved out to little Kearney. How could she have? She was a game one, though, his brother's wife. One game lady. She was drumming her slender fingers on the side of her martini glass, her lips in a little pout, trying to picture two hundred million tons of coal. Already learning to cope with it, as she no doubt had had to learn to cope with so many strange things in the past three years. "I've seen the Decker mine," he said. "I don't know how many tons of coal that is, but it's a damn big strip mine. The seam's maybe, say, seventy-five feet thick and about as wide as our north pasture. It goes on and on and on to the horizon. Not that they mine it all at once. They don't. They work like window washers on a skyscraper: down one side, up the other. It kinda creeps. They got huge spoil banks around the edge of the pit, and down about a hundred feet, there lies the coal. A great flat plateau of black with these dinky-toy trucks zipping in and out loaded with coal. It's so big it's unreal. You can't describe it. It's like putting Hank Aaron in the middle of the ocean and telling him to hit a long fly. You can't do it. It's too big."

"Well, it's too big for this little imagination," she said. "Let me see if I can relate to how much it's worth. What's a ton of coal sell for these days, Jimbo?"

"It depends if you have it delivered."

"Clever boy. Actually, all I'm interested in is the royalties. What, twenty-five cents a ton? What's that times two hundred million?"

"Fifty million." Jimbo shook his head and finished his drink "And he ignores it."

She, too, drank up. Then she smiled prettily. "You'd have to, though, wouldn't you? You couldn't think about it."

"I suppose not, no." Then: "Say, what's this about you thinking that I stayed East all that time because of you? Is that what you thought?"

"Who said that?" Avelyn said, blushing.

"Mike. The day I came home. Said you figured it was you who was the reason since I never came home after your wedding."

"He's got a big mouth, he does."

"It wasn't you. If you want to know the truth it was him. I don't know why. I just wasn't ready to be anywhere around him; to be, you know, his younger brother in everyone's eyes. I just wanted to let you know. It wasn't you. You're perfect here. The first time I saw you come out that door I knew you were perfect for the ranch; the one thing it had always been lacking. Mike's very lucky. I think he knows it, too, for a change."

Avelyn pulled his head down and kissed him on the cheek.
"You're a sweet brother-in-law."
"You're stuck with me."
"You'll do fine."

He took a walk that night after dinner. *You'll do fine.* Papa Vic
had told him that, too. *You're gonna be all right, Jimmy.* The air
was perfectly still and cold, and he watched the sky for a while
and saw two stars fall, one after another. That was good luck.
The Milky Way was a clear speckled band of silver dots. Then
what am I doing here? he wondered. If I'm going to do so
wonderfully, what am I doing here, an overeducated hired
hand? He heard the sharp, howling cry of a coyote, and then
the many others who joined in. That signified a kill. They
stopped and started up twice more, and he thought about Papa
Vic, and his coyotes howling at God. Yes. Why not? Whom else
would they be howling to in such a ritualistic manner? Jimbo
listened until the coyotes stopped for good, then he went to bed.

In the morning he drove Denny down to Gillette, where Aunt
Willa Torgeson, Denny's mother, lived in a nursing home. Aunt
Willa was Papa Vic's only daughter, and she had been confined
to a wheelchair since a stroke had paralyzed the left side of her
body. Jimbo stayed for a while and talked, then he left the two
of them alone and went to buy the supplies for tomorrow's
branding.

He remembered the last time he had seen her. It was seven
years ago, the day they went to pick up Denny. Mike had been
home on leave. He remembered waiting in the reception room,
and Aunt Willa being wheeled in with Denny beside her, already
much bigger than she, his hands huge for a twelve-year old's.
The left side of her face drooped involuntarily, and she had to
speak out of the corner of her mouth. She was forty-six then,
but looked years older.

Her first boy had been killed in a hunting accident, and she
couldn't seem to keep her eyes off Mike. Perhaps there was a
resemblance. She reached out with her right hand to squeeze
Mike's, saying without sadness, "You look so fit. The service
always makes young men look so fit."

"Fit to be tied," Mike had said.

She asked Denny if he remembered his cousins, and introduced everyone by name. Denny just looked at her, frightened. Aunt Willa turned to Papa Vic and said, "He can't understand me anymore. My mouth doesn't move right."

Mike, tight-lipped and curious, was looking Denny over, the way he might have looked over a horse or a bull before buying it — carefully taking things in while maintaining a certain distance. Aunt Willa asked him a few questions about the army — where he was stationed, whether he had a girl, if he was going overseas — and it so happened he was en route to Vietnam, which he told her. That was the one time the whole morning Aunt Willa showed any sadness. "You be careful, Michael," she had said. "You take care of yourself."

"I'll be careful."

Then her face brightened and she said, "You'll do fine" — turning right away to Denny and telling him how fine *he'd* do at his grandfather's ranch, how much he'd love it there with his cousins. What a tough lady she was, Aunt Willa. How much her father's daughter.

Pretty soon Denny had started to cry, and Aunt Willa allowed it was probably best if they said goodbye then and there. He was holding on to her arm — her bad one — and with her right hand she unwrapped his fingers one at a time, saying, "It's all right, son. It's all right. You'll be fine. I'll write very often. Go on with Papa Vic."

But he wouldn't have gone. He never would have. Then Mike put his hand on the back of Denny's neck and turned him away just as easily as if he'd had him on reins. Denny looked back as they opened the door, and Aunt Willa waved to him; but Mike kept his hand on his neck without any pressure, as Jimbo had seen him do on the nose of a colt he was working with. He kept it there as they walked out, and until they were seated in the car, never saying a word, Denny beside him with tears running down his face. Ever since that day, Denny had treated Mike like a father.

The year before her stroke, Aunt Willa had sold her ranch

in Gillette to Titanic Coal. Her husband, Joe Torgeson, had died a few months earlier, and it was too much for her to handle alone, Denny being then only eleven. She got a good price for it, too, which she needed once she had her stroke. But it had haunted her. Jimbo remembered her saying to Papa Vic that morning they picked up Denny, "I don't know if I did right selling the ranch, Papa. Joe never would have. I wish I knew if I did right. Joe, he used to say he had enough trouble not doing wrong without worrying about doing right every waking hour. But I wonder about it, Papa. I wonder if I did right."

Titanic Coal had opened their strip mine there three years ago, and now Gillette was a boom town. A hellhole, maybe, but still a boom town. The population in those three years had grown from three thousand to fifteen thousand, and those weren't just miners. It took only two hundred men to work a strip mine. But those two hundred men meant a payroll of sixty thousand dollars a week, and behind them came new restaurants, department stores, bars, car and mobile-home dealerships, you name it. Now, Wyoming Power had announced plans to build two coal-fired generating plants outside Gillette to send the power back East via high-tension wires, instead of chugging the coal to Chicago by rail. There was plenty of coal to fire, that was for sure. There was the Decker mine up north, the Cheyenne mine, and now the word was spreading about a new find in Kearney, bigger than any of them. And the mine right there in Gillette. Yessir. Once they got those generating plants built, the town would be set. And news of that brought more men in. More construction. More businesses, housing, cars, and motorcycles. More trailer camps filled with truckers and crane operators and pipe-fitters. There were plenty of jobs for a man who liked to work; for a man who didn't mind a little winter when the time came; blizzards like you've never seen blizzards; eye-stinging, face-burning, ear-numbing blizzards that blew the polyethylene strips from the windows and the TV antennas from the trailer roofs; that came up through the floorboards and made them like ice. You couldn't ever keep those trailers warm in the winter, but in the summers they weren't bad. And come fall you could take off to the hills and find lots of antelope and deer and elk if you knew where to look. And you couldn't beat the money. No sir. Twelve dollars an hour, and that was to start. Two or three years, that's all a man could take of those kind of winters. But Gillette wasn't a town to settle in anyway. It was a place to make your money in, and then move away from.

The old residents, the people like Aunt Willa, had long since sold out and moved away. As new people poured in, real estate prices soared. The population became transient, without roots in the community, and the summer nights became alive with girls clinging to the backs of leather-jacketed, unshaven youths, hair whipping out behind like ponies' tails, laughing and racing their bikes down the quiet, flat streets, drinking their beers, and throwing the cans into the square little yards with the unhappy trees.

The growth had come so rapidly. There was no time for new schools, new hospitals, new prisons; so all were overcrowded and inept. Construction companies had their hands full trying to keep up with building new homes and new streets and new waterlines; city officials needed time to study each new proposal, needed time to rezone districts, to solicit bids, to meet government regulations. Still, the people flowed in, escaping the recession in which the rest of the country was mired. The crime rate grew, as did the inflation rate, divorce rate, and suicide rate. And yes, wages grew.

It wasn't just Gillette. Jimbo had read about the others, too. Rock Springs. Decker. Colstrip.

There was a sudden need for energy, and western coal was a solution. It was low enough in sulfur to meet federal pollution standards when burned for industrial purposes, and there was a nearly limitless supply that could be reached cheaply. Two hundred years' worth, according to the estimates he'd seen. But it wasn't going anywhere. That was the crazy thing. What the coal companies had done was convince the country there was a sense of urgency involved. Tighter reclamation standards were on the horizon, and they were trying to sweep in enough long-term leases to last them — what? A century? Titanic Coal had coal leases they wouldn't touch until 1990. Federal leases. State leases. Private leases. They'd been garnering them for years, before anyone had heard of an energy crisis. Yet no one knew for sure — *no one* — what twenty-some years of stripping would do to a fragile yet fertile area like the Great Plains. Ecologies could be studied, slopes charted, water tested by coal groups and by environmental groups — *but nobody really knew what the effect would be.* Land reclamation projects in the Midwest, in Appalachia, in Germany, in Australia, had no more bearing on what might happen in the climate of the Great Plains than Wyoming's grapes related to the vineyards of France. And when the coal was all mined and the companies had moved out — what then? he wondered. Boom to bust? More "Magic Cities" ghosting about in search of a glorious past? What then?

Still, the leases were granted as fast as the companies could apply for them. Foreseeing an oil crisis, the coal interests had gathered them up by the dozens, providing themselves with solutions before the government or citizens groups even knew there would be problems. Problems of reclamation. Problems of water tables. Problems like Gillette. It was easy for them. They'd been through it all back East, when Appalachia was stripped in the 1950s. The principle was simple, basic, one that he'd learned at the bank: if you pay a man today, he will close his ears to the problems of tomorrow. When tomorrow comes, he will have adjusted, or he will have gone.

CHAPTER 12

IT WAS STILL dark outside when Jimbo opened his eyes. There was a hand on his shoulder shaking him. It was Deacon. "Come on, buck. Shake a leg. We got us some branding to do today."

Jimbo closed his eyes again and turned his head away. Deacon stripped off his covers and a rush of cold chilled him. "Go away," he said.

"Come on, you huckle-fucklin'-stud-buck. Open them lids. I brought somethin' for you to chew on that'll plumb get you goin'."

Jimbo reopened his eyes. Deacon was shining a flashlight on his championship belt buckle. The thing to chew on was hanging beneath it.

"Make me puke."

Deacon laughed and tucked himself back in. "Let's go now. Get up and function. I got coffee on at my place. We got time for one quick cup. Then we'll get the horses."

Jimbo put on his oldest shirt and jeans and slipped into a ratty brown parka that had belonged to his father. His boots were stiff and cold. He followed Deacon into the frosted morning air, rubbing sand from the corners of his eyes. The stars were still out, and a horse stamped its feet in the corral. Deacon's work-boots were the color of campfire coffee and splattered with paint. He walked quickly, with a painless limp, past the barn to the

94

bunkhouse, a long thin hut that had been built as a stable. It jutted from the back of the barn and faced the home pasture.

Deacon's limp was from the broken hip he had suffered in 1962, when a bucking horse came over on him. That was the last rodeo horse he had ever ridden. Deacon had a picture of himself on that horse hanging in the bunkhouse. It was bucking, absolutely vertical, its black mane flying. The horse's legs madly pawed at the sky while Deacon's spurs dug at its neck. The horse was barely out of the chute. It was a green horse and had never been ridden in a rodeo before. The man who had pulled the flank strap — a leather thong tied around the horse's loins that made the horse buck — had pulled too tightly. A green horse hardly had to be flanked at all. Which was why it had bucked itself over backward. The cowboys leaning over the chutes were just beginning to realize that the horse was going to come over on Deacon, and the photograph had frozen their faces in the transition between cheering and fear. Clearly, there was no sense of danger on Deacon's face. It was drawn tightly with determination. The horse was blindly furious, and the flanker was shouting. It was a remarkable photograph.

The picture hung in its dusty frame above Deacon's trunk, which was in the far corner of the bunkhouse. The burlap curtains were drawn, and the room was lit by naked, pull-chain bulbs hanging from the ceiling. There was nothing on the plywood walls except Miss January, 1967, whom Deacon had met when she was rodeo queen for Cheyenne's Frontier Days. The next year, when she returned to pass on her crown, Deacon had her sign the foldout: "To the Big Fella, Love Always, Sherrie."

Two bunk beds were side by side along one wall of the bunkhouse, and on the opposite wall there was a beat-up bureau and a gas stove where he had the coffee heating. Deacon poured out two mugs and stepped to the door. It was four-forty-five in the morning, and streaks of gray were beginning to color the pitch-black sky to the east. Jimbo sipped the coffee and watched Deacon rub his unshaven stubble.

"How long's it been since you been back for a branding, buck?"

"Six, seven years," Jimbo said.

"Long time. How come you never come back for a branding?"

"We always had exams in May. I'd've rather been here than there."

"Bet you were a good student, eh? You always struck me as that type. Good, smart, thinkin' type. How come you're drinkin' Joe with a shithead like me 'stead of bein' back East makin' a million dollars? Maybe you ain't so smart."

"I missed you, Deac."

"Bullll-shit. Got a girl knocked up is my guess." He drank his coffee, thinking. "Last time I was out East I rode in Madison Square Garden. Rodeo had a whole eastern tour. Boston; Buffalo; Chicago. The whole bit. Oh, I broke me some hearts back East, buck. Me and Lenny Barrett got throwed into the street one time in New York for cookin' up some steaks in our hotel room bathtub. Used the pillow for kindling and chopped up a chair for firewood. Set the damn sprinkler system off. I 'member ole Lenny hollerin' to the house dicks, 'Come on in, boys. Got beer aplenty, but you'll have to dig up your own beef!' God, I laughed." Deacon sipped his coffee. "You liked it back East, eh?"

"I liked it all right."

"Boss told me you was a banker, and first thing I thought was you'd improved your pool game. Never would've occurred to old Deac you'd wind up a money-type banker."

"They were hiring."

Deacon glanced out the window. The sky showed more gray now. "I outfitted a baseball scout after elk a few years back. Told him you was one hot prospect at short. Said he'd check up on you. Fella from Pittsburgh. You recollect ever hearing from him?"

"I couldn't hit, Deac."

"You couldn't hit the curve." Deacon wiped his nose and sniffled the cold air. "Ole Mike, he could hit. Couldn't run like you, but he could hit a ton."

"Sure he could. He's our hero." Jimbo smiled.

"Well." Deacon finished his coffee with a gulp. "Let's go get us some horses. Whoooeee! We got us a day for brandin' that's gonna be hotter'n French love by noon!"

Jimbo set his mug down on the trunk. His eyes returned to

that rodeo photograph, the furious horse pawing upright, as if to strike fate a final blow. "What ever happened to that horse?"

"Dogmeat. Canned him within the week, I heard."

They saddled the two horses they had left in the corral and trotted them into the home pasture. It took forty-five minutes to herd the cattle into the arena, then they rode back for breakfast. It had felt good breathing the cold air, and Jimbo was hungry.

Avelyn had set out separate platters of eggs, bacon and sausage, and fresh-baked biscuits, with a bowl of chicken-stock gravy. Jimbo loaded his plate up with biscuits and gravy and ate quickly. The other cowboys would be arriving soon.

"Jimbo, it's a joy to watch you eat," Avelyn said. He was running his fork along the bottom of the plate, sopping up the thick gravy.

"It's a bigger joy to eat."

"I don't think so. I get more pleasure watching you eat those biscuits than I'd ever get eating them myself."

"That's mighty queer. And it's equally queer that a fine New York girl can learn to cook so good." He rubbed his belly. "Ugh. Me full."

Mike said, "You must have a tapeworm the way you eat and stay so thin, buddy boy."

"I digest rapidly."

"Unlike Ike," Deacon said. "Who don't digest at all. Is blubberface comin' today?"

Mike nodded.

"Oh, Lord. Better kill a cow."

Mike smiled over his coffee. "He can eat, can't he?"

"That's the only reason he ever comes," Deacon said.

Mike said to Avelyn, "Hon, remember last year he damn near ate that whole rhubarb pie?"

Deacon said, "Hell, before he even got around to that pie it looked like a chicken died right there on his plate. He plumb went after that chicken. I won't forget that. That man can flat eat a chicken."

"I've cooked another rhubarb pie," Avelyn said. "Should I hide it?"

"Hide it." Deacon nodded.

Mike yawned loudly, stretching his arms behind his head. "Better let him have it or he'll eat up the furniture." It was light outside, and he pushed back from the table. They would be starting soon.

The first calf was branded by six-thirty. They branded early in order to finish before the midday heat. Mike was roping off his new gray horse, dragging the calves bawling and bucking away from the rest of the herd so that someone could throw them and take off the rope. Two cowboys held each calf down while Deacon vaccinated and castrated, slicing the scrotal sack with a knife, then burning the testicles off with a hot iron. Lloyd Paxton and Ike Jessup were working the branding irons, and Sam Benson roped off old Jacks.

They averaged fifty an hour. By midmorning they were soaked and reeking with sweat and manure. Jimbo's eyes and mouth were caked with dust that his sweat had turned to mud. There was a burning-skin stench in the air, acrid and clinging, that hurt his lungs. The cattle lowed continuously, and the cowboys cursed. It was not angry cursing. They cursed Mike for missing a loop, or a calf for being covered with manure, or one of the younger boys for letting a leg kick free.

The calves had a human sound when they cried out. They bellowed as the irons burned through their skin, tongues wagging out, eyes rolling up into their heads so that just the whites showed. It always surprised Jimbo when they clambered to their feet so quickly after being released, how soon they stopped their moaning.

Avelyn was watching from the fence with Marjorie Fox and Hepp's sister, Patty. Jimbo came over and poured himself some lemonade. His knuckles were bleeding where a calf had kicked him. The inside of his head felt baked. "Take my turn this time, will you, Patty?" he asked.

Patty was eighteen and slender, with a lovely body. But she did not have a pretty face. She worked at the Dairy Queen that had opened last summer. "No way, Jimbo."

"Try it."

"I try it every summer at our place, thanks just the same."

"How about it, Avelyn?"

"No, thank you."

Deacon yelled to him to get over there. "Come on," Jimbo said to Avelyn, "I'm petered out. You ever done it before?"

"Not exactly, but . . ."

"Not exactly?" Jimbo grabbed her hand and pulled her off the fence. "Well, come on, then. Let's get on with the program. Mike! Your wife here wants a nice gentle calf whose mama gave milk."

"No, I don't."

"Yes, she does." Jimbo pulled her struggling to the center of the arena. "Here. Give me your watch."

"Damn you, Jimbo McKenzie." He held her while she slipped off her watch. "What the hell do I do?"

"Denny will throw the calf. Once it's down, you get down and grab the top hind leg with both hands. Use your foot to push its bottom leg forward. Kind of stretch it out."

"I'm going to wring your neck."

"Here it comes. Get ready."

He stood behind her so she couldn't run away. Mike was dragging a calf out of the herd, kicking his gray horse gently. It was not a big calf, but it could not have been more covered with slippery green manure if it had laid beneath a tap. "Michael, you did that on purpose!" she cried.

Mike winked. Denny and Avelyn ran forward toward opposite ends of the calf, Denny throwing it on its side, then pinning down its head and front feet. Then he slipped the rope off. Avelyn was standing just out of range of its kicking hind feet.

"Get in there and grab it! Grab it!"

She eased forward and took three good whacks on her left leg before getting hold of the calf's bottom leg and falling into the dirt.

"You got the wrong leg!" Jimbo yelled. "The top one. Grab the top one."

"Screw! You!" She released the leg she had hold of and tried to grab the top one, which was kicking her around the arms and shoulders, ripping her shirt open down the front. She swore at the calf. Seated, she kicked back at it. Finally, the calf lay still long enough for her to reach the top leg and pull back with all her strength, simultaneously pushing its bottom leg forward with her right foot. The calf jerked twice, then lay back helplessly. Avelyn had a streak of manure down her face from the calf's tail, and her shirt was torn, but she was laughing. Everyone applauded, and Deacon came over to vaccinate. He looked down for a moment and scraped the manure on its hip away with his foot. Then he said to Mike, "This one's already branded, boss."

Mike smiled. "All right. Let it go."

They finished with the last calf just before one o'clock. The men, soaked through with sweat, bruised, tired, and happy, sat around the tub of beer in the back of the pickup and talked. Avelyn, Marjorie, and Patty went up to the house to cook dinner.

"Nice big crop of calves," Sam Benson noted.

"February calves," Mike said.

"Yeah. Jerry Jay been around?"

Mike nodded. Jerry Jay was the local buyer, representing three feedlots in Nebraska and Iowa. If a man didn't want to take his chances in the fall's auctions, he could contract in the spring or summer for delivery in the fall.

Sam was squatting on his haunches, drawing Bar V's in the dirt with a stick. "Make you an offer?"

"Yep."

"Fair offer?"

"Nope."

Sam smiled at him. Sam knew Mike. "Take it?"

Mike smiled back and nodded. "You bet."

The others perked up. "That right?" Ike Jessup asked.

Mike nodded.

"Prices been pretty low, ain't they?" Ike said.

"You're the president of the association, Iker. What would you say?"

"I'd say they been low."

"That's what I'd say."

"Jay come by my place last week and offered forty cents for calves, thirty-six for steers."

Mike looked at him for a while. Then he said, "Sounds right."

"You can't break even on that," Ike said.

"Nope." They were quiet, drinking their beer and spitting in the dust. Mike said, " 'Member last year Jay was offering fifty-two cents, and I ended up with forty-six at auction?"

They remembered. They also remembered that two years ago they were getting ninety-two cents. "I don't believe it's bottomed yet," Mike said.

"Hope you're wrong on that count," Ike said.

"Might be."

"I'm headed down to Denver this week for the association," Ike said. "Big meeting down there. Our national meeting."

"Talk about prices?" Sam asked.

"I guess."

"How you figure it, Iker? Figure they'll hold?" Sam asked.

Ike shrugged. "I heard like McKenzie here — won't hold worth beans. Bottom might plumb drop out 'fore fall."

"Figure the good ole association'll plug the bottom back in, Iker?" Mike asked facetiously.

"Aims to try."

"That oughta make the rest of these boys rest easy."

Ike let the comment pass. "Gotta do somethin'. Lot of these outfits are gonna be hurt if things don't turn pretty quick."

"Well, you go get 'em, Iker." Mike saw that the gas burner had been left on, and he went to turn it off. The V-shaped branding iron was still heating up and he eased it out of the burner and dangled it behind his back as he returned.

Ike was complaining to Hepp and Sam about prices, and Mike slipped up behind him. "You light a fire under those boys in Denver, Iker."

"Well, we'll sure try to figure somethin' out."

Mike pressed the branding iron against the seat of Ike's jeans. There was a bulge there so that it burned all the way through without touching the skin. Mike pulled the iron away, then leaned forward to blow on the smoldering edges of the brand. A small flame appeared at the base of the V.

Mike walked back around in front of Ike, pretending to listen to his spiel on prices. Ike stopped. "What the devil's wrong with him?" he asked, pointing to Denny.

Denny, off to the side, was staring at Ike's pants with a lunatic grin.

"Got me," Mike said.

"Them deaf-mutes is weird," Ike said. Then his eyes went wide, and he spun to look behind him. The seat of his pants was engulfed in flames.

"Ike!"

"My God!"

He spun again, beating the seat of his pants with his hands.

"Fire!"

"God! Help!"

Fat Ike dropped to his rear, squealing. He dragged it through the dirt, smoke and dust trailing behind.

"Hang on, Iker!" Mike came running with the tub of beer.

Ike rolled onto his back. Kicking his feet in the air, he tore off his pants. He leaped to his feet and beat at his undershorts.

"Jump!"

Ike fell back into the tub. He yelped from the cold.

In a moment he climbed back out, still unsure what had happened. The others laughed helplessly. He looked from one to the other, then went and picked up his smoldering pants. A hole the size of his pocket had burned through. He looked suspiciously at Denny.

"That must have been one helluva rank fart, Ike," Deacon said.

Avelyn brushed her hair at the mirror. She shook it down in front of her and, combing, noticed a scrape on her rib where the calf had kicked her. She looked at herself in the mirror and touched the scrape with her fingers. It was tender. The strap of her bra would irritate it, so she decided not to wear one. With her figure she wondered why she ever wore one. In New York she wouldn't have. Horseback-riding, she thought, smiling and brushing again.

She slipped on a clean shirt and went downstairs. The table looked nice, but she wished they had used their good silver. Michael had thought it too showy. Even if it *was* too showy, it would have been nice to use it just once. When else would she? It had been a wedding gift from her grandmother, the entire seventy-five-piece set. She knew she should have told her to get something more appropriate to the life they would be living, but her grandmother had insisted. Of *course* she would need silver. *Every* new bride needs silver, silly goose.

Avelyn took the turkey from the oven and set it on a carving board to firm. Then she put the corn muffins in to bake. Patty was outside cooking the hamburgers on the grill, and Marjorie was mashing the potatoes. She had borrowed an apron and had her sleeves rolled up.

"I shouldn't make you do that," Avelyn said.

"You ain't *making* me do nothing, honey," Marjorie said. She laid the potato masher on the plate beside her and poured in some milk.

"And Patty, too. You girls are saviors."

Marjorie glanced out the door and saw Patty standing over the grill. "You see that mouse 'neath Patty's eyes?"

Avelyn hadn't noticed.

"It's gone down some. You can still see it though. Three days back Lucy Preston slugged her in the gal's room at the Bison."

"No."

"Saturday night," Marjorie said. She put the bowl of potatoes down, scooping a bit from the spoon with her finger. "They been heading for a run-in for a long time now. I've drove past that Dairy Queen myself with it closed up and Billy's truck parked out back. Lucy ain't blind. She's let that man of hers carry on and carry on, and Saturday night she gets her fill and hauls right off and smacks her one. That Patty ought to thank her stars she didn't get worse." She watched her through the screen. "She's just a kid, really. She don't even know what she's about."

"Maybe you should have a talk with her," Avelyn said.

"Me? Ain't my affair. Hepp, he hollers to her to stay away from Billy 'bout twice a week. What she needs is some fella to take her out of circulation. She's down there at the ice-cream stand making eyes at truck drivers and ever' fool guy in pants. She'll get herself in trouble, that girl. I'm worried on Patty." Marjorie stopped whipping the potatoes and pointed the spoon at Avelyn. "I wish that dang Jimbo'd take a liking to her. What's *his* problem?"

Avelyn shrugged. "She's kind of young."

"Kinda young? Well I ain't seen him runnin' around with anything older lately, have you? What's he doin' hangin' around, anyway? Mike don't need another hand. Just one more mouth for you to feed."

"What's he doing? He lives here. It's his home."

"Well, you're the one has to cook and clean up after him, ain't you? I wouldn't put up with runnin' a boardinghouse for a whole dang family by myself."

"I don't mind. I wish everyone in this family were as neat as Jimbo is."

"Thank God for small favors."

"He's part owner of this ranch, Marge," Avelyn said testily. "What'd he ever do to you, anyway? I happen to like having him around. He's no trouble at all."

"Sure you do, honey. What're you getting so upset about? I'm just flapping my big trap."

"I'm not upset," she lied. She waited until her irritation subsided. "Anyway, he's talking about going back to school in the fall."

"Back to school? Cripes, why don't he just get a job somewheres?"

"He wants to get his master's in education. Then he wants to teach, I think. He'd be a good teacher." The water on the stove was boiling, and she put in the beets.

Marjorie asked, "Avelyn, what do you and Mike think about all this coal?"

Avelyn had her back to her. "Don't know what to think, really," she said in an offhanded way. "Quite a surprise, though."

"You ain't just whistling Dixie."

"Why? What do you and Hepp think?"

"I think it's damn swell news. I think it's about the swellest news I've heard in years. Anything worth as much money as I hear that coal is worth can't be all bad, can it, honey?"

Avelyn laughed. "Sure it can."

"Not in my book." Marjorie walked over to the stove and lit her cigarette from the gas flame. "Jeez, it'd be nice to live in California or someplace with a lot of money, wouldn't it? Near the ocean with a swimming pool. I'd like that. I look pretty good in a swimsuit."

Avelyn smiled. "I'll bet you do."

"Awww. Don't let on like you don't, honey. Men like to look at skinny girls as much as they like to look at a bust. Don't pretend they don't. Heck, we went to Hawaii on our honeymoon, and Hepp turned green with envy when I wore my swimsuit in front of all those other men. It was just a bitty thing. He bought me another, but I wouldn't wear it. Jeez, did I come back with a tan." She took a deep drag on her cigarette and blew the smoke out slowly. "He'd never want to move to California for fear of me walking around all those men in a swimsuit." Then she smiled. "He would if I told him to, though. Jeez, but he'd be miserable."

"Poor Hepp." Avelyn wiped her hands on her apron. "I think we're all set." She walked out the back door where Patty was cooking the hamburgers. "How's it going?"

Patty looked up, and Avelyn noticed the bump beneath her eye. "They're done," she said.

"Thanks so much for helping."

"Oh . . . it's all right." Patty shrugged. "I like to cook."

Avelyn walked around to the post out front and clanged the dinner bell loudly.

Mike took the pail of Rocky Mountain oysters into the bunkhouse and covered them with hot tapwater to warm them. When the dinner bell rang, he carried the pail up to the house, setting it behind the kitchen door. The others were already there. Avelyn was in the dining room arranging the buffet on the side table, platters of roast beef, ham, hamburgers, squash, potato salad, mashed potatoes, and creamed baby onions one beside the other. Jimbo was carving the turkey, and the guests lined up.

Avelyn waited, then got in at the end of the line. Mike came up beside her. "You sit down," he said. "I'll get yours."

"Don't be silly."

"Go sit down, hon. You've worked your butt off already. Here." He took her by the arm and seated her next to Ike Jessup, whose plate was heaping. Her back was to the kitchen. "Any special requests?"

"This is sweet, Michael."

"White meat or dark?"

"White, please. Thank you, my sweet. I'll save you a place."

Mike nodded, then returned to the end of the line. He waited until she was talking to Ike, then sneaked into the kitchen with a plate. He went through the back door and plucked four of the Rocky Mountain oysters from the pail. They were pale and oblong and laced with thin blue veins. He cut them in half and smothered them in the extra cream sauce left warming in the oven. Steaming, they looked identical to the creamed onions. Mike crept out and got back in line.

Ike's appetite hadn't suffered from the excitement of his pants catching on fire, and by the time Mike was seated he was already in line for seconds. He saw the rhubarb pie. "I 'member that rhubarb pie of yours, Avelyn," he said from the side table.

"Damn good deal, Ike," said Deacon, across from Avelyn. "Nobody else does, 'cause nobody else had a crack at it."

Ike came back with his second plateful, and began eating a turkey drumstick from the top, like a Popsicle. Deacon studied him. "I never seen a man try to inhale turkey before."

Ike's mouth was plugged with the drumstick. He retracted it and chewed slowly. Then he said, "This is good, Avelyn. Mighty good vittles." He licked his pudgy fingers one at a time, starting from each knuckle.

Deacon said, "I never seen a man eat like you, Ike. I ain't hungry no more, watchin' you eat."

"Too bad for you. More for me," Ike said, chuckling.

"That's a fine imitation of talking lard."

"Oh, pipe down, Deacon," Avelyn said. She was eating her turkey.

Mike wiped his mouth. He puckered his lips around. "Them onions is good, honey, but a little bit tough."

"Tough?" Avelyn scooped two of the creamed Rocky Mountain oysters onto her fork and popped them into her mouth. She chewed for a moment, then her face began to wrinkle.

"Kinda chewy," Mike said.

"Umm." She nodded. She looked worried. "They *are* tough."

"Kinda gristly and fatty."

Avelyn slowed her nodding. She suddenly realized she did not have onions in her mouth. She stopped chewing. "Michael," she said cautiously. Her mouth was filled, and the word came out a garbled *Mwaakahhl*.

"What's that, honey?" he asked, leaning closer. "You say something?"

"Mwaakahhl, wah' ha' you done?"

"Done to what, honey?"

Avelyn still hadn't swallowed. She looked around and found Jimbo sitting across from her. She pointed to the creamed onions. "Wha' ha' he done?" She had a panicked look in her eyes.

"Has my big brother pulled a funny? Mike. You *didn't*."

"Di'n' wha'?"

"You *didn't*. You *couldn't* have." Jimbo stood up and leaned over the table. He put a fork into one of the onions on Avelyn's plate. "You did."

Avelyn hit the table with the butt of her fork. "Di' wha'?"

"Avelyn, you're eating one of the delicacies of the West. Rocky Mountain oysters."

"Wha?"

"Calf balls," Deacon said.

It took a fraction of a second for that to sink in. Mike was turning to explain just as realization flooded into her eyes.

"Eauyyyukkk!" She spat her mouthful into his face.

Mike's palms shot up and he cried out in pain.

"Yukk! Yukk! Yukk!" Avelyn gouged at her lips with a napkin. "You pig!"

"Gawddamn, I'm blind. You blinded me."

"Giving me . . . eauyukkk!"

"You blinded me." Mike squinted his eyes open and shut.

"Good!" Avelyn hit him with her napkin.

"Ow!" He curled up into a ball, his arms over his head. She whipped at his back harmlessly. "Leave me alone. I can't see."

The futility of hitting Mike with a napkin made her all the angrier. She looked around for the first solid object she could lay a hand on, which happened to be Ike's turkey drumstick. He hollered in protest as she jerked it from his hand. Then she whacked Mike on the head with it.

"Owww! That hurt!" he yelled in earnest. He sat up and tried to glare at her, but he couldn't open his eyes.

"Good!" She hit him again.

"Goddammit, woman!" Mike ducked and covered up.

"Give it to him, sugar!" Deacon yelled.

"Beat the louse!"

Mike was waving one hand above him in an effort to deflect the drumstick, and wiping at his eyes with the other. "I give!" He pushed back from the table and tried to retreat from the room, bumping into a chair as the drumstick crashed down — splat! splat! splat! — on his gravy-covered head. "Goddammit, woman, now *quit!*"

"You little bastard!" Avelyn whacked until the drumstick mercifully broke off in her hand and dropped in a pulpy mess to the floor. Undaunted, she threw the nub at Mike as he finally squirmed out the door. "You're foul! You're just foul!"

The room burst into applause.

Two minutes later Mike waved a white handkerchief through the doorway and poked his head around. His eyes were bloodshot, and his face was still covered with bits of turkey, mashed potatoes, gravy, and the creamed Rocky Mountain oysters. He stood timidly. Ike looked up from his rhubarb pie. Then Mike forced one of his little grins and said, "It must have been something she ate."

CHAPTER 13

THE NEXT DAY Mike's dog got into a porcupine. Stormy was a smart dog, a great cattle dog, but it happened every summer. Papa Vic used to say, "Ain't a question of smartness; it's a question of weakness. That dog's got too strong a weakness." Like the skunks he trapped with apples back in Johnstown.

It had taken them over an hour to remove the quills, and it was late afternoon. Jimbo watched Mike rubbing his fingers through the dog's thick coat. "Jeez, you're a dumb dog," he was saying. Stormy's ears suddenly erected and his eyes became alert. "Want another mouthful?" Mike asked him.

Then a car appeared on the Canyon Creek road, kicking dust behind it for a hundred yards. It came closer and turned into the Bar V. Jimbo recognized it. "That's Zach Thorndike," he said. He waited, but Mike gave no reaction. "I was wondering when he'd turn up around here."

Mike looked at him with an odd expression. "Why was that, buddy boy?"

"Why was that? Just a wild flying hunch is all."

"Ivy League hunch."

"That's it, Mike."

The car came over the cattle guard, and Thorndike parked beside the corral. He got out. "Afternoon," he said. His white shirt was wrinkled and rolled up at the sleeves, and his tie was loosened. He put his hands in his pockets and walked over. Mike was watching him with that expression he sometimes got when it seemed he might do just about anything. There was a tenseness around his mouth and his eyes were alert, neither threatening nor inviting.

"That's a big shepherd," Thorndike said, stopping again.

"Stormy?" Mike worked his hand through the dog's coat. "Stormy got himself into a porky this afternoon."

Thorndike motioned to the small pile of quills and the snout-nosed pliers on the step. "So I see."

"Little procedure we go through 'bout twice a year."

"They never learn, do they?"

"Nope." Mike looked at the dog. "God never give them that capacity 'cause in the wild the first porky they get into kills 'em. Sure as a bullet. Lot slower, too."

"That right?"

Mike was still looking at the dog, scratching it. "Deacon Bueller shot a coyote right there off the bunkhouse steps last fall. Come in when it smelled food, face all swole up and full of quills. They work their way in and break off after a few days, and coyote can't close its mouth or swallow, sometimes can't even see. Starves to death. Nature don't give animals two chances to figure out a porky."

"Hmm." Thorndike abruptly took his hands from his pockets and folded his arms in front of him. His tone changed. "Congratulations on your good fortune," he said, curling his lips in so that his mouth became a thin, dark shadow.

"What good fortune's that?"

Thorndike laughed. "The coal, naturally."

He waited, but Mike said nothing, chewing on a stalk of grass.

"This changes things considerably with regard to our original offer." Again, Mike said nothing.

Thorndike rocked back and forth on his toes. "We had reason to believe that this valley would produce some deposits of coal, but no one could have had any idea how much it has turned out to be. It's fantastic. Do you have any idea how much the value of your property has increased?" Thorndike asked the question rhetorically. "How has your family reacted to the news?"

Thorndike looked at Jimbo. Out of the corner of his eye, Jimbo could see Mike grinning at him. "How much *has* the value of our property increased?" he asked.

"A lot. A great deal."

"How much?" Jimbo repeated.

"All right," said Thorndike. "I'll tell you both. This land is worth about two hundred fifty dollars an acre as cattle land. That's roughly accurate, do you agree?"

Mike shrugged. "Never been up for sale." Then he said, "Seems I recall an offer of nine hundred dollars an acre from some outfit."

Thorndike nodded. "That was only gambling there was coal. Now Titanic is prepared to up that to two thousand dollars an acre. That comes to seven million dollars total."

Jimbo saw Mike smile for an instant, still chewing his stalk of grass. Thorndike clearly didn't feel he had to push the issue. He let the "seven million" hang in the air, and the three of them sat in silence. A magpie flew across the dirt yard and lighted on the fence rail of the corral, and Mike watched it.

"Eight hundred percent," Mike said.

"How's that?" Thorndike asked.

"That's how much the land has appreciated since I took over runnin' this place. Eight hundred percent." He smiled and turned to Jimbo. "You wouldn't fire a man for that?"

"I shouldn't think it would be too presumptuous to say that's more money than you ever envisioned coming into as a cattle rancher," Thorndike said.

Mike looked at him. "Do we get taxed that much more? Our taxes won't go up eight hundred percent, will they, Mr. Thorndike?"

"The company will take care of the taxes."

"Is that right?"

Thorndike was smiling. "Let me just show you the contract. There's lots more. If you want to live on here as foreman, that can be worked out. You raise cattle for the company, we'll pay you a salary. And there's a clause that says Titanic will sell you back the land after the coal has been mined for a dollar an acre."

"After the coal has been mined? When would that be?"

Thorndike shrugged.

"Twenty years?"

"Twenty years might be an outside extreme. It's really impossible to say."

Mike frowned and scratched his dog. Thorndike said, "Would you like to read it? It's an excellent contract for you, the seller. It's a super contract. I've a lot of experience drawing these things up. Let me get it for you." He started away.

"I don't want to read it."

"Let me just get it for you."

"I don't want to read it!"

Thorndike stopped. His whole body sagged.

"I would," Jimbo said.

"The hell you would," Mike snapped.

"I *would*."

Thorndike went quickly to his car. Jimbo could feel Mike glaring at him. "Don't read it," Mike said firmly. "Don't read that stuff, buddy boy."

"Why not? Jesus, Mike."

"You just shouldn't start reading that stuff, is all."

"Well, *somebody* ought to."

"Nobody ought to."

Thorndike came back with the contract. He held it against his chest. "Is there something the matter I can clear up for you?" he asked Mike.

"Everything's perfectly clear."

"We're not looking for an answer today. I wanted to get an initial reaction and leave this thing off so you can go over it with your family and your lawyer. We're open to negotiation, of course. But this is very fair. This is a super contract." He extended it to Jimbo. "Here. We'll talk next week."

"Don't take it, buddy boy."

"I'm taking it. I want to read it." He avoided Mike's eyes and rolled the twelve-page contract into a cone. He felt his face redden. "I'm taking it." He twisted the pages of the contract as tightly around as he could. "Avelyn has a right to see it. So do I." He waited for Mike to rip the contract from his hands, but Mike was still. Jimbo said to Thorndike, "We'll see you later, then. Thanks for your trouble."

"All right. Good evening."

Thorndike left. Avelyn came to the screen, wiping her hands on her apron. "Who was that?"

"Come on out," Mike said.

"Who just left?"

"Zach Thorndike."

Avelyn sensed the tension. "Another offer?"

Neither of them said anything. Then Mike got up and took the contract from Jimbo. He handed it to Avelyn. "Seven million. He'd do better than that, too."

Avelyn glanced at the first page of the document, shaking her head. "*Seven* million." She read the figure in print and kept coming back to it. "Jesus. I've never even thought about that much money." She looked up. Her smile felt foolish. "Well. Well, shouldn't we have a lawyer look at this? I can't understand these things."

"No," Mike said.

"Yes," Jimbo said.

Avelyn glanced from one to the other. Mike's mouth was fixed in a tight frown. She waited.

"We shouldn't," he said. "We shouldn't do a goddamn thing. I'm not going to sell the ranch."

"I'm not saying you should," Jimbo said. "You should at least consider the options, though. You can't make a decision if you don't know what your options are. Just *consider* them."

"I don't need you to tell me how to make a decision, buddy boy. A man starts thinking 'bout what he *might* have, he won't ever be happy with what he's got. I'm happy with what I got. Alls I wanted was to live in this house and raise cattle on this land. If I'd've wanted seven million dollars, I wouldn't have started with cows, that's for sure." He looked at Avelyn. "I told you that."

She nodded.

"So you don't have to tell me how to make a goddamn decision."

Jimbo said, "It's not as simple as yes and no. You're always putting things into black and white. The world doesn't work that way, Mike. They're not going to offer you seven million dollars one day and forget about it the next."

"That's their problem."

Jimbo nearly laughed. "*Their* problem? My God, Mike. They'll bloody well make it *your* problem."

"I ain't gonna worry on crossings twenty miles upstream."

"Twenty miles? You're at one now. You're there now and you don't even know it." Jimbo looked to Avelyn for support, but she said nothing. "Look, there are professional consultants; there are lawyers whose whole occupations are representing landowners in mineral contracts. There are environmental groups who have counselors on their payrolls. There's a lot of knowledge out there at your disposal. Christ, Thorndike's a *professional.* You've got to fight fire with fire, even if you don't want to sell. Titanic Coal is *big* business. You can't fight big business with a popgun that shoots a flag out the end reading, 'I don't want to sell.' "

"Why not?"

"You *can't.*"

"Why not? I own the land. I own the coal."

Jimbo made a frustrated gesture. "Look, if you won't talk with a lawyer, at least let's show the contract to Sam. Sam knows all about this strip-mine stuff. He'd know if you were being raked over the coals."

"Sam'd know," Mike agreed.

Avelyn said, "Talk to Sam, honey. It couldn't possibly do any harm to talk to Sam. We'd all feel better about it."

"I told you what harm it'd be. You start thinkin' about what you *might have,* and there's no end to it." There was an edge to his voice. He was tired.

Mike walked out far enough around the corner of the house where he could see the lone oak tree that grew in the south pasture. He put his hands behind his neck and stretched. The sun was low, and the tree cast a long shadow on the new grass. Jimbo came up beside him. "Remember, buddy boy," Mike said, "when you asked Papa Vic how the hell that oak tree got there, and he gave you this long, serious look and said, 'Gawddamn if I know, Jimmy. How'd it stay there is more like it. I always meant to cut that fat oaker down.' You were just a little bugger. Threatened him with all manner of harm if he ever did."

"I remember. Mike. Sam'll know if Thorndike's being straight with you."

Mike didn't answer. Then he said, "Be about a year now since he went on the television. Oh, he was something that day. Wish you'd've seen that, buddy boy. Tom Aldridge didn't know if he was coming or going."

"I wish I'd seen."

"He give me a call today," Mike said.

"Who? Tom Aldridge?"

Mike nodded. "Wants to come out next week for an interview. Wants to talk about the coal. Billings *Gazette* been spreading news of this damn deposit all week. Had my name in there and Hepp's and Lloyd's."

"When's he coming out?"

Mike shrugged. "Told him I had to think about it. I don't want to talk this thing up a whole lot."

"It'll be talked up with or without you."

" 'Pears so." He turned and came back to the steps by the porch. "I'll talk to Sam," he said.

He walked inside, and the screen door slammed behind. Avelyn, Jimbo, and the dog, Stormy, all turned their heads to watch him go. They stared through the screen for a long time after he was gone, as if waiting for his return.

"He'd be miserable if he sold," Avelyn said. "I don't want him to sell this place."

Jimbo thought for a moment and shrugged. "He won't."

The next day they went to see Sam Benson, and Sam told them three things that Jimbo hadn't fully understood. The first

was that the Bar V was the only outfit in the valley that owned
its coal outright. After 1904, the state sold land to the homesteaders with surface rights only, retaining all mineral rights.

Next, he said to put away any thoughts of using the land for
cattle after the coal had been mined. Reclamation was an un-
proven process in the Great Plains. The topsoil was thin, and
on even minor slopes, erosion was sure to be a problem. And
the grasses the land would be replanted with were not the native
grasses of Wyoming — buffalo grass, Indian brome, side oats
grama, big blue stem, and little blue stem — incredibly hardy
strains, each of which thrived in a different climate condition,
so that the soil was rich with dormant seeds, one of which could
adapt to whatever Nature threw at you. The grasses that would
be used were common alfalfa, timothy, and brome. The land
would be planted, watered, and fertilized until groundcover was
established, and then declared "reclaimed." Whether that
groundcover could then reseed itself after grazing or drought
was anyone's guess, whether it would hold up under the climatic
extremes it was sure to face. It simply wasn't known.

Lastly, Sam told them that if the coal estimates in the survey
were even close, and seventy-five percent of it could be recovered, then Titanic was trying to steal the land. The Bar V
was worth at least twice what had been offered.

CHAPTER 14

IT WAS JUNE. Jimbo was helping Denny clean up a calf in the north pasture. It had gotten its left hind leg hung up in barbed wire, and the wound was jagged and deep. Kneeling across the downed calf, he held its head and front while Denny applied the purple salve into the tear to protect it from the flies. He gave the calf a booster shot, working quickly and surely on the frightened animal. He should be a vet, Jimbo thought. He has that way. They let the calf up, and it ran stiff-legged to its mother, who lumbered forward to greet it, lowing.

Mike and Deacon were coming up the slope. They were talking low, chuckling. Behind them a yellow car with a flasher on its roof was parked inside the gate, and two men were climbing out. They opened the back of the small wagon and busied themselves with some equipment.

"What gives, Mike?" Jimbo called.

"TV crew," he said, grinning. "Tubby Tom Aldridge is comin' up for a chat."

Deacon was winded from the climb. Jimbo asked, "What's he coming all the way up here for?"

"Wants a pretty view," Mike said. "How you doin', old man? You ain't gonna die on us?"

Deacon huffed. "I ain't gonna die."

"Thought you didn't want to talk to the media," Jimbo said.

Mike winked. "Well. I'll talk to this fat fella. Called me about six times last week, so he gets the prize."

Deacon laughed.

Aldridge took a long time coming up the slope. His cameraman, much smaller, in jeans, kept waiting for him. He was out of breath and sweating by the time he reached them. "Tom Aldridge," he said, putting out a pudgy hand for Jimbo to shake.

"Jimbo McKenzie. My cousin, Denny." Denny nodded.

"Gee, I love it in this part of the country!" Aldridge took out a handkerchief and wiped his brow. "Mike was telling me that you were out East when we did your grandfather's interview last year. What a great man. I want to tell you how sorry I was to hear he'd passed on. What an interview that was. They still talk about it at the studio."

"Papa Vic would be glad."

"I'm happy to hear you think so." Aldridge turned to the cameraman, who was rigging up the microphone and battery. "Larry, how we coming?"

Larry waved and went back to his wires. He had tinted glasses and a beard. "All set, T.," he said.

"Larry, don't call me T."

"All set," Larry said.

"All right. Let's do the opener. How about right over here?" Aldridge walked a little bit below the cameraman, so that the valley spread out behind him.

"Looks good. Talk to me."

"Testing one; testing two, three, four, five . . ."

Larry adjusted the sound level. "Got it. We got wind, T. Put on the wind squelcher."

"Larry —"

"Sorry. Wind squelcher." He threw Aldridge the foam cap to slip over the head of the microphone. "All set. Roll when ready."

"Okay. Roll."

The cameraman started the film. Aldridge waited for a few moments, then opened, "Behind me is the Bar V Ranch, as fine a piece of cattleland as can be found in Wyoming. It is thirty-five hundred acres of prime grazing land in the foothills outside of Kearney. The McKenzie family has raised Herefords here for three generations. Now, suddenly, unexpectedly, they have discovered something new about their land that will change their lives and the lives of everyone in Kearney. Coal. The largest individually owned deposit of coal in the state." He held his pose for several more seconds, then broke off. "How was that?"

"A-okay," the cameraman said.

"You want another?"

"Nope."

"All right. Great. Terrif." He came over to them. "Now it's you guys' turn. We'll just talk, okay? This thing's all going to be edited anyway. We'll chat, and Larry will roll the film. Don't worry about Larry. Forget Larry. Talk to me. Got it?"

"I think so," Mike said.

"We'll chat. I'll ask you a little of this, a little of that, and we'll just let it fly. Take it where it goes. Sound good to you guys?"

"Sounds good to me," Mike said.

"Super. Super. Geez, I love it out here. Larry, ready when you are."

"Ready."

"Roll it." Aldridge waited until he could hear the film whirring. "Mike, how long have you lived on the Bar V?"

"Twenty-nine years, not countin' the army."

"And how long has it been in the family?"

" 'Bout seventy-five. My grandfather, Vic McKenzie, was the first white man to settle this valley."

"How many head of cattle do you run?"

Mike stroked his chin. "I don't know. Deac, you know?"

Aldridge extended the microphone to Deacon. Deacon furled his eyebrows and looked down at his fingers. He was counting on them. About every three seconds he paused and said a name. "Elsie . . . Bessie . . . Ferdinand . . ."

"Ferdinand died," Mike said.

"The hell."

"No bull. Hoof and mouth."

"That's a *lotta* bull, ole Ferdinand." Deacon shook his fingers in frustration. "Dang. Lost count."

Aldridge cut in then. "All right. It doesn't matter Larry . . . Larry, stop the camera, huh? We're just warming up, okay? We're going to start for real now. Keep to the point and don't interrupt each other. Okay, Deacon? Okay, Mike? Okay, you other guys? Okay. Go ahead, Larry. Ready when you are."

Larry started the camera. Aldridge walked over to Denny. "Your name is Denny, right?"

Denny started to back away, but Deacon held him. "Relax, Denny. We're just going to chat." He held up the microphone. "Listen. Can you tell me how this discovery of coal has affected your lives?"

Denny shook his head.

"Come on. Try." Aldridge smiled patiently.

"Whyn't you ask someone else?" Mike said. "He's a deaf-mute."

Aldridge shrunk back. "Oh, geez. I didn't know that. God-damn it. Larry, stop the camera." He was staring at Denny. "What's he doing up here if he can't talk?"

"He can see, can't he? I thought ole Den might enjoy seeing himself on the television. 'Sides, he was workin' up here. You come to him."

Aldridge had begun to sweat again. He wiped his brow with a handkerchief. His deep, casual voice assumed an edge. "All right. Here we go again. Ready, Larry? You ready, Deacon?"

Larry started the film. Aldridge waited a few extra seconds to recompose himself. Then he asked, "Deacon, as foreman of this ranch, how has the discovery of coal affected *you*?"

Deacon glowered at him. "I still won't carry the slop bucket for man nor cow, neither one; if that's what you're askin'."

Aldridge thought about that for a moment. No, he stammered. That wasn't what he was asking at all. What he was asking was what the land, the way of life, and the cattle meant to Deacon; rather, that was what he had *meant* to ask. His self-assurance had pretty much faded before their eyes.

Deacon pointed toward a nearby calf. "Yoū see that calf over there? He's my son, Mr. Aldridge. You're asking me how I feel about my son."

"You're that close to the cattle?"

"Not all of them . . ." Then Jimbo noticed Denny was laughing, which for him was a sort of silent, grinning convulsion — though he didn't see why. And Mike, too, his face puffy and scarlet. ". . . Just my son over there. And his mother. But come here, I want to show you somethin' that'll show you how we feel about this land better'n any words." Deacon knelt down, and Aldridge knelt with him. "I'm talkin' about roots . . ."

He was, too. Jimbo saw it then — what had cracked up Mike and Denny so badly that they were stuffing their fists down their throats to choke off the laughter.

". . . I want you should hold somethin' . . ." Deacon and the reporter looked down at the good rich soil, Deacon guiding Aldridge's hand along the ground, between his feet. "I want you should learn somethin' about roots . . ." The camera was whirring, and everyone was staring at the earth between Deacon's feet. "Hold this — " Solemnly, with reverence, Deacon lifted the newsman's hand against his naked penis.

Aldridge pulled back. "Oh, *God!*" With a quick flip of the wrist he hit the penis with his microphone.

"Noooo!" Deacon buckled in pain.

Aldridge was furiously wiping his hand in the dirt. "God, man, you're absolutely *foul.*" He rose and held his hand away from his body like some dead thing. Deacon was groaning at his feet, and Mike was collapsed, helpless, as Larry continued to film. "I can't believe you did that, man. Goddamn, I just can't believe it . . ." He really couldn't. His eyes were as big as saucers. "Goddammit, Larry. Will you stop the camera?"

The news car drove away, two hundred feet of film trailing out the window. Deacon was still curled on his side. "They got me," he moaned. "They got me, boss." He sat up and stared miserably into his lap. "I'm afeared the old boy's dead."

Mike was lying back on his elbows with a grin. "No loss."

"No loss? No *loss?*" Deacon looked down with the bewildered expression of the lost or dispossessed. "Gawd Almighty . . . what a thing to say "

CHAPTER 15

MIKE WAS SIMPLY UNAWED by the whole affair. The size and power of the Titanic Coal Company, the value of the coal, the shifting mood of the community, didn't faze him in the least. They could go their merry ways without him. They could depend on themselves for a change. Jimbo couldn't help admire it. In New York, the world had seemed so immense and unwieldly to him, its workings beyond a single man's control. But seeing Mike's utter independence, his unwavering belief in his ability to cope within his own environment, gave him renewed hope that maybe life wasn't as complicated as it was made out to be.

Four days after the incident with Aldridge, they were all in the arena teaching Mike's new roping horse to back up on command. There was no one better with horses than Mike. Everyone said so. He could train a horse for calf-roping or bulldogging like nobody in the county, and he always had a couple of young ones around to work with. Jimbo liked watching him, helping out when he could. That was how to learn, to watch a man like Mike. That was how he had learned, from Papa Vic. But people said Mike was even better than his grandfather.

Jimbo had roped a calf and was holding it while Mike tapped the young horse on the chest with a switch, calling, "Back! Back!" The rope was tied hard and fast to the saddlehorn, so when the horse backed up, it became taut. Jimbo then threw the calf. If at any time the young horse stepped forward, Mike would call "Back!" to it again and tap it with the switch until it backed up and pulled the rope taut. Then Mike would step away from the horse, and if it held the rope taut and didn't move, Jimbo would release the calf and they'd do it again. The young gray was working very well after a while, and Mike was pleased. They were getting ready to quit when he saw Zach Thorndike watching from the rail.

Mike took the rope off the calf, shooing it away, and led the gray horse over toward Thorndike, walking slowly, Jimbo following.

"Don't stop on my account," Thorndike said. "I'm happy to watch."

"He's had enough," Mike said. "If you try to teach them too much at once, they forget. 'Sides, my brother and me got to go up to Billings pretty quick. Cattleman's meeting. So if you'll — "

"How old is he?"

Mike paused. "Just three."

"He's a beautiful horse."

Mike nodded. He loved to talk horses, and Jimbo could see him debating whether to continue along this line with the likes of Thorndike. "He should work out all right. Good straight legs. Good feet. Good head."

"I don't know much about horses," Thorndike admitted. "I know a little about dogs. You can tell a lot about a dog by looking at its eyes. You can tell about their intelligence. There's a whale of a difference between the smartest puppy in a litter and the dumbest. It has nothing to do with which one looks the best."

Mike looked at the gray gelding. "You can tell about a horse from its eyes. Some don't see nothing, some see things that ain't there, and some see right. Good roping horse has got to be a smart horse. Good racehorse don't. Great racehorse does, though. Difference between a good and a great racehorse is in the head, not the legs. But if a horse ain't smart, he won't be a good roping horse. Sometimes you can tell from the eyes, sometimes you can't."

"This one here's smart?"

"He's got a good head. I bought him with another quarter horse, a black filly. Fella who sold 'em to me said he didn't know which was better. They were just halter-broke is all. Just kept my eye on 'em for a few weeks, and saw this one here had a little better head. That black filly's got better size and runs better, but never would've been the ropin' horse this one'll be. I give her to the wife. This one'll be a helluva ropin' horse. I could get four thousand for this horse tomorrow."

They walked back up to the corral. Mike unsaddled the gray horse and gave it a tin of oats and barley. The black filly, Pasha, came over and tried to put its nose in, but Mike punched it lightly on the snout. "You get out of here." As Pasha leaped away, the gray horse did, too, and Mike drew it back by making a sucking noise with his lips. "That black horse can run," he said. "She can really go." They watched as Mike's gray horse dug at the last few flakes of grain in the tin. Mike turned away and hung the tin back on its peg above the grain bin. "Go on now," he told the horse.

"Have you thought about the offer?" Thorndike said.

"We've thought about it."

"And?"

Mike let him hang for a moment. "Friend of mine tells me you're trying to steal it from me."

"Seven million dollars and we're trying to steal it?" Thorndike laughed.

"That's what he says."

"You've got to be kidding."

"I ain't."

Thorndike said nothing for a long while. They watched the two quarter horses swishing at the flies with their cropped tails. A horsefly landed heavily on Mike's sleeve, and he swatted it.

Then Thorndike said, "The company has authorized me to go as high as three thousand four hundred fifty an acre. That's twelve million dollars."

Mike smiled, then looked over at Jimbo. "Seems ole Sam knew what he was talking about."

"You could buy a place ten times as big as this place," Thorndike said.

"Thirty-five thousand acres? No, I couldn't. Maybe in a desert."

"Five times as big then."

"Sounds like five times as much work."

"You don't strike me as a man afraid to work, McKenzie." Thorndike walked a few steps away from the corral. He put his huge hands in his pockets and stared over to the north pasture, under which lay millions of tons of coal. "Afraid to dream, maybe."

Mike just watched the horses. Jimbo heard the piercing cry of a magpie behind the barn.

"What kind of a man are you, McKenzie?" Thorndike asked.

"A dumb one. A dumb rube."

"I keep asking people in town, 'What do you know about Mike McKenzie?' Everyone gives me a different answer. Some say that you'll leap at selling this place. 'He don't want to work too hard.' Others tell me to forget it. Say, 'He's a McKenzie, ain't he?' What the hell kind of an answer's that, will you tell me?"

"Pretty dumb one. If you're looking for smart answers, you're asking questions in the wrong town."

Thorndike smiled and shook his head. "What you have here may be the single richest private deposit of coal in the United States. That's a fantastic thought. It's a big country."

"Too fantastic for this rube. I'll bet my brother can appreciate it. Can you, buddy boy? You been around."

"Probably better than you can."

"There you go."

Thorndike took a calculator out of his shirt pocket. "Let's figure something out, shall we? It takes thirty acres to run one cow for one year, am I right?"

"Thereabouts. Little less."

"Well, one acre-foot of coal weighs about seventeen hundred fifty tons." He punched that into the calculator. "The coal under your land is supposed to average some fifty feet in thickness." He multiplied. "That comes to eighty-seven thousand five hundred tons of coal under one acre. The thirty acres that support one cow cover . . . two million, six hundred twenty-five thousand tons of coal. Let me see if I'm counting those zeroes right . . . . That's right. Two *million*, six hundred twenty-five thousand tons under land that supports one little cow. Say you didn't want to sell. Say you just wanted to lease us the land. Twenty-five cents a ton in royalties." Thorndike tapped in the figures and multiplied. "Six hundred fifty-six thousand, two hundred fifty dollars. That's what those thirty acres are worth to you for their coal. That, Mr. McKenzie, is the most expensive cow in the world. And we're not talking about thirty acres. We're talking about over two thousand. That's how much of your land has coal beneath it."

"That's some outfit you got there," Mike said, peering at the calculator.

"The point is, McKenzie, with the money this coal can bring you, you and your children and grandchildren will be able to make a finer ranch than you could ever have made of the Bar V. Either here or somewhere else. A better ranch and a better life."

"You got all the arguments, mister. But I got the land." He paused. "I ain't selling it, and I ain't leasing it."

Thorndike lowered his head and scuffed his feet in the dirt. "You'll sell, McKenzie. Sooner or later, you'll sell. Be a lot easier for everyone if it's sooner."

"What's easier ain't always what's best."

"It's not always what's worst, either. Look. There are two things you should think about. First, there is going to be strip-mining in this valley whether *you* sell or not. The state owns the coal on every place but yours, and Titanic has already been granted the lease. That will change the entire character of Canyon Creek. A lot of people will want to live here more than ever because of it, but you and many of your neighbors probably won't. Here's the second thing you should think about. We're not going to buy out some of these smaller outfits who have coal until you sell. They're going to hate you for that."

Thorndike stopped. There was no great tension or ill-feeling between them. He just let that sink in. Then he said, "A lot of people in town have got the smell of big money in their noses. Coal money. They don't want to just smell it. They want to taste it. I'd like to be able to save you and your family the pain and trouble of seeing what that smell does to people. It's not very pretty. That's not a threat on behalf of my company; that's simple human nature, I regret to say.

"Every man has his price. Maybe yours isn't money, McKenzie. Maybe yours is when you learn your friends are no longer your friends. Maybe yours is when your wife stops being talked to down in town, or your brother here is beaten up, or your dog shot. Believe me, people do much worse; and believe me, it is your friends and neighbors who will turn on you the fastest. I don't particularly love this part of my job, but I've been doing it for a long enough time that there are things that I know. And I promise you that before this affair is over, you will be quite happy to sell your ranch to Titanic.

"So . . ." Thorndike nodded to them both, then turned and walked slowly to his car. He started to open the door. Then he stopped and called back to Mike at the corral, "You respect this land, McKenzie. It's your family's land, and I respect that in a man. But the time comes when a man's got to bend." He opened the door and folded his large body into the front seat. He started the engine, calling more loudly through the window: "Just think about it." Then he drove back down the Canyon Creek road.

Mike watched the car out of sight and stared after it for a while without saying anything. Jimbo was watching him. He finally pushed out his lower lip and turned and, with idle curiosity in his voice, asked, "You believe that stuff, buddy boy?"

"I don't know what to believe. Like I said, the man's a professional."

"Well. Got to change for the meeting," Mike said, turning to walk unhurriedly into the house.

CHAPTER 16

THE TIRES HUMMED evenly on the highway. Jimbo watched the great stacks of last year's hay crop, one after another, sitting like loaves in the pastures. They threw long, soft shadows in the grass as the sun began to sneak behind the mountains. It would leave a gentle trail of pink when it had completely disappeared. Western sunsets didn't burn like the sunsets in the farmlands of the Midwest. Like perspiring women, they glowed.

He took a swallow of beer and tried again to get Mike to talk about the coal. "We're expendable, Mike. That's the bloody problem. Cattle ranchers are expendable."

Mike curled his lip, as at a smell. That was all. That was the way Mike felt about discussions like that: he would rather you sat and farted. With him, you could never try to draw a parallel between one period of time and your own, between one class of people and your own. He would curl his lip and give you a look that made you feel petty and cone-headed. So you stopped. Though why? For you were right to try, or what was the point in learning at all? If you didn't try, you were no better off than the ones who knew nothing of what had gone before them, condemned blithely to repeat all the same mistakes. Why, when he was with Mike, did he feel slightly embarrassed about his education? He wondered about Avelyn. He wondered if Mike curled his lip at her, too.

"Go ahead and curl that lip, cowboy," he said. "We're *expendable*." No reaction. "You know that until last spring mining companies up in Montana actually had the power to condemn private lands by right of *eminent domain?* If you're condemnable, you're sure as hell expendable." Still no reaction. "It happened up in Butte in the early sixties. Where Anaconda has that copper mine? Big, open-pit mine, and it started to stretch beneath some of the private homes in the city. The whole damn town was employed by the mine, or someone who worked for the mine, so something had to be done, right? Right, Mike? You listening?"

"I'm a plumb captive audience, buddy boy."

"Good. So the Montana state legislature, which was in Anaconda's pocket, passed a bill giving the company the right of eminent domain. Can you believe that? And not just the one company, or even the one industry, but *all* mining companies. What they were saying was, 'What's good for the mining industry is good for the commonwealth.' There's some pretty good arguments against that, which I won't bore you with, but no one heard any of them, since Anaconda also owned seven newspapers around the state. Can you believe that? *Eminent domain* to a private company! Law was on the books until last spring, when Anaconda lost its influence in the legislature. But just imagine what might happen around these parts if Titanic ever gets the Wyoming legislature in its pocket. Hell, they probably already do."

"Probably," Mike said. His lip had uncurled and he was working it over his Copenhagen.

"Our impassive hero. Unflappable."

Mike pulled out to pass a cattle truck. "Wish your mouth was unflappable," he said.

"Pipe down, Loquacious. You're a captive audience, remember?" He took a long drink of his beer. "The cattlemen aren't the first people around here to be expendable, you know. Indians. Buffalo. Sheepherders. Homesteaders. They were all declared expendable by the goddamned cattlemen, that's the lovely irony of it. By men like yours and my grandfather. They were in places and lands that somebody else more powerful needed. Same as you are now." He waited for a reaction, but Mike continued driving.

"And don't think the bloody national conscience is going to save you," Jimbo said. "Things haven't improved that much since the good old days of buffalo hunts; you know those lovely affairs where they'd skin them and cut out their tongues — the tongues, I take it, were *haute cuisine* — and leave the rest of the carcass to rot while the Injuns were all starving? Oh, these coal folks might not be as tactlessly thorough about expending cattlemen as cattlemen were expending Injuns, but that won't matter to the ones that get in their way. You can bet your Tony Lamas *they'll* be rubbed out. You heard Thorndike back there. What the hell do you think he was talking about?"

"Talked about my brother getting beat up for a while. That was interesting."

Jimbo laughed with mock nervousness and shook a finger at his brother. "Oh, oh, oh . . . what is that? Enmity? Between brothers? No, no. Come on, Mike. We're *communicating*. Exchanging ideas? Remember?"

"You're exchanging ideas, buddy boy. I'm going to the Cattleman's meeting. And I'll tell you right now, it's the first time I ever looked forward to getting there." He nodded and winked.

"Oh, *yes*. The Cattleman's Association. You know what I think of first when I think of the Cattleman's Association?"

"Cowshit."

"Nope. Papa Vic's famous story about rimrocking sheep into the Powder River. Remember that one?"

"Hell, he told it on the television."

"Terrific. Perfect. You see? They were *expendable*." He waited. No reaction. "Three thousand sheep hurtling down two hundred feet — a raft of gray floating off into the sunset — men wiping out animals in order to wipe out other men. Ah! The banner years of the Cattleman's Association, after the land had already been taken from the Injuns and the white men could get down to the business of fighting themselves. Fighting the rustlers; fighting the sheepherders; fighting the homesteaders. Might made right, big brother. You would have done swell."

Jimbo knew he was going a little far now, and he pretended not to notice it when Mike turned his head his way, continuing on: "The law was in the hands of the people, and if a cowboy wanted to change a rustler's ways, all he had to do was hang him up from a railroad trestle. Homesteaders? Hell, cut down his fence around harvest time and let the livestock fatten up for winter. Sheepherders? The hell with freedom of the range! String up your own barbed wire to keep them from grazing to the waterholes. Or hell, if they want water, we'll give them water. Run them off a cliff!"

Jimbo finished his beer. He wanted to back off now and mend fences. He opened another and offered it to Mike, and was relieved when he took it. Then he got himself one. "What the hell are these Cattleman's meetings like, anyway?"

"Guys just go in there and tell jokes and drink, mostly. Bellyache over prices. Once in a blue moon somebody'll show slides of some new breed, or you'll hear about a fool aberration like Lloyd's cattle-yaks." Mike grinned and took a drink of the beer, wiping his mouth afterward on his sleeve. "That old yak bull's still around, you know."

"Is he?" Jimbo asked, thinking, yes, he will talk about this. He will talk about the things he understands and can control.

"I remember the first time I ever saw that critter, I was riding the fenceline with Papa Vic," Mike said. "We come upon a place where that damn yak had plowed through three strands of barbed wire to get on one of our cows. Oh, he was putting the wood to her all right, that cow lowin' real pretty, 'O-o-o-o-w . . .' Papa Vic like to shit. Just as mad as a wet whore, shouting, 'Get off'n her, you! Quit!' Tried to ride right into it with his horse, but the horse is having none of it. So he jumps off and runs at that yak, waving his arms, 'bout red as a radish, and starts kicking dust at the yak. Yak don't care; cow don't care — she's still lowing real pretty — and me, I was all for the yak. Goofy long-haired thing. Then he goddamn takes his *hat* off and starts beating that yak between the horns, yelling to get off the cow! They got those big upturned horns, you know, and he's going after it with a six-ounce straw lid."

Mike took a long drink of beer and smiled. " 'Bout that time I figured I'd best get help, and rode off after Paxton. We come back about ten minutes later, and there's the old man, shinnied up a cottonwood, that yak glowering up from the trunk. Goddamn, if I could bottle the look on Papa Vic's face I'd make a million dollars, buddy boy. Called Lloyd and his yak every name he could think of in fifteen seconds. He knew a few, too. Made Lloyd buy the cow when all was said and done. Good thing, too. Them half-yak, half-Hereford outfits was a disaster. Cost Lloyd a ton, that Asian yak did. The half-yak bulls were sterile. Like a mule. And the females, well, they were fertile, all right, and when you took a cattle-yak cow and bred it with a full-blooded Hereford bull, that quarter-yak calf was a satisfactory piece of livestock. Problem was" — Mike shook his head, chuckling, his eyes growing big — "them half-yak mothers were plumb wild! Cowboy couldn't get near them *or* their calves. Weren't a lick of fear in them. Lloyd went through about three hands that summer who'd flat quit rather than try to work with them cattle-yaks. They'd charge a horse so regular that a fella'd have a rodeo on his hands if his horse just caught wind of 'em." Mike unrolled the window and spat out. "Lloyd, he'd *laugh*. 'They're plumb wild!' he'd say. Took a mother's pride in their spirit. Papa Vic'd look at him like he'd gone ding-y, and'd say, 'One of them critters comes back on my land he'll be just wild enough to die, ole bud.' "

Jimbo smiled. Mike's spirits had soared, and he didn't much want to bring them down. But he had remembered something. "I saw Thorndike's vehicle drive up toward Lloyd's place last week."

Mike glanced at him, then back at the road. "Lloyd won't talk to him."

"He wouldn't have been driving up to see anyone else."

"Well. I'm not worried on Lloyd, buddy boy. He can be right crusty to a fast-talker like Thorndike."

"Maybe. Then again, a dollar sign followed by a lot of zeroes has been known to break through some pretty thick crusts."

Mike looked at him, annoyed. "I know Paxton. He's my roping partner. He's one steady sonofabitch and he don't give a holler about money. He is the softest damn businessman you have ever seen 'cause he'd rather keep a friend than keep a buck. So don't you worry about Lloyd." Mike finished his beer and dropped the can in the back. "And I am sick to death of this goddamn coal business anyhow. Can't a man ever talk about anything else?"

Jimbo smiled. "Sure. Let's talk about beef prices. That's always good for a few laughs."

"You'll hear plenty of talk about beef prices and grain prices and ever' other kind of prices in about ten minutes, buddy boy. The Poor Man's Friend just come back from the big national convention in Denver, and rumor from there is it's time to act. Time to save the little guy. I don't know who they mean by that, but it sure ain't the likes of Iker."

"Too late for the little guy. Small-time rancher is going the way of the small-time anything. Under."

"Bullshit."

"It isn't either. By the time a piece of beef raised by a small-time rancher is on the kitchen table, it has passed through the hands of the feeder, the meat packer, and the grocer. That's too many mouths for one cow to feed. You've got to do it like McDonald's does it, and own every stop along the way. Then you're feeding your own mouth four times with one cow."

"That's pure shit. Cattle business always runs in cycles. Two years ago the price of beef was ninety cents, and a man with one cow in the basement could have made a living. All right. So now we're on a downswing. Grain prices has shot way up, 'bout three times in the past two years, and beef is under forty cents again. So. It'll turn."

"But it'll turn too late for some guys, and nobody'll even notice since they're all expendable anyway."

"That's just who's doing the hollerin', too, buddy boy. Them guys that made a lot of money when the prices shot up, then went out on a limb to buy a baler and a pickup and a new line of bulls all in the same year. Well, their bank payments crop up every year, good or bad, which some of these turkeys don't think about. Interest rates go up a bit, they take out second mortgages so's to dig themselves in deeper, and all of a sudden they're in a bind. Of their own making, seems to me. If beef prices or rainfall was as dependable as mortgage payments. . . . If Gawd had only been a banker, Papa Vic used to say."

"He didn't like bankers. He must have shit when I told him I was going to work at Chemical."

"He didn't shit at all them last few years." Mike smiled. "As I recollect, he said he'd never met a poor banker, and didn't reckon you'd be the first. Said that ole Kenny Roberts up in Billings was poor one time in the Depression and didn't much care for it. Jumped off his barn and only broke his arm. Says to me, 'Michael, them bankers is plumb resilient.' No, he figured you had her licked."

Mike turned into a high school lot. The long, flat-topped building stretched out brick-new with silver letters jutting out from iron pins, spelling Dwight D. Eisenhower High School. Most of the vehicles in the parking lot were pickups, and Jimbo could see a cluster of blue-jeaned cowboys talking by the entrance. They looked out of place against the sterile brick backdrop. Mike turned off the engine. Then he grinned at Jimbo and took off his shirt. Underneath, he was wearing the top of a pair of Valentine's Day pajamas, decorated by red hearts with arrows through them. He then pulled off his boots and slipped his pants off, exposing the pajama bottoms.

"You can't go out of here like that."

"Sure I can." He put his boots back on and opened the door to the Travelall.

"You *can't!* What are you doing!"

"Lost a bet."

"You can't. This is my first goddamn meeting, and I'm not going in if you're dressed like that."

"Wyoming not only beat the University of Montana, they beat the seventeen-point spread. Ike was a big fat center there back when we used to kick their butts. We always make some goofy bet. If he'd lost he would have had to run the meeting in his swimtrunks. That'd been a sight, eh?"

"Mike, you look ridiculous."

"So what? Don't sit with me then. Come on. We're late."

The gymnasium was brightly lit and noisy with the hard echoes of footsteps and talk. Most of the ranchers were already seated in the folding metal chairs, their hats tilted back, boots resting across their knees. Many had come as far as a hundred fifty miles to attend. The NO SMOKING signs taped to the gym's walls were ignored, and a gray haze was beginning to form against the ceiling.

Ike Jessup sat at the front table. His tremendous belly bulged from his shirt like overly yeasted dough. His jowls hung loose and his stubby fingers fiddled with his black-rimmed glasses. Mike came up behind him.

"Hey, Iker." Mike sat down in his lap and planted a kiss on his cheek. "Tell me a story."

"Jesus Christ, McKenzie." Ike turned his face away from Mike's probing lips. "Leave me alone! God Almighty, I've got a meeting to run here!"

Mike laughed and turned a deaf ear to the catcalls as he walked to the back of the gym and took a seat. The attention that had been riveted to the front was now straying, and one grinning face after another turned around to inspect his attire. At five past eight, when Ike took the podium, there was still a buzzing, amused quality to the air, which Ike tried to break with his gavel. "Okay, guys . . ." He kept rapping and his voice whined slightly. "All right now, let's get started. . . . Listen up." Ike's voice was high-pitched for a man of his size, and his words were delivered slowly. "I'd like to start off by reviewin' a few things, and that's what I'm gonna do here real quick . . ." It did not take long for his voice to start to grate and the gym to become uncomfortably warm and smoky. One of the overhead lights began to flicker.

Ike said, "We can't run our ranches on the kind of wild price fluctuations we've seen the last couple of years. You all know that. If a man sold his stock today, he'd realize a fifty-dollar loss on each and every calf, or thereabouts. Same here as it is all over the West. Some industry fella in Denver says cattlemen stand to lose three billion dollars nationwide. That's a fair piece of change. And that's why we're here. Some folks think this association isn't good for much of anything, but at times like these here, if we stick together we can bring change.

"All right. Here's what they're sayin' at the national convention. Prices being so low now, lot of cattle'll be held back this fall. That's if the summer hay crop is big enough to carry the weaner calves through the winter. What that's going to mean is a flood on the market next spring. You can bet on it, and you can bet it'll drive prices still lower. We know all this, but we don't do a thing about it. Well. That's going to change. It's time we acted, and it's time we acted together — *before* all hell breaks loose. You think prices are low right now, just you *wait* till you see them next spring if we don't do something. You'll see low prices all right.

"Sittin' back and waiting for things to change, waitin' for our luck to turn, calls to mind my old Uncle Bob. Uncle Bob had a farm just north of here in sugar-beet country, and ever' year, sure as shootin', folks could count on a good lush crop of sugar beets. So what does Uncle Bob all of a sudden plant one year? Sweet peas. Says he likes the smell.

"Well, sweet peas are a fragile crop, as you all know, but Uncle Bob hits it just right that year and makes a lot of money. So next year when ever'one else is plantin' sugar beets like sane men, he goes ahead with another crop of sweet peas, only this year, just when the vines are spreadin' out nice, the bugs come and spoil the whole crop. So the next year he plants 'em again, only he sprays 'em good, but a hot spell hits up and busts open all the pods, so he loses the whole crop on the ground. But all around ever'one is gettin' steady income from sugar beets, 'cause that was sugar-beet country . . ."

"Ike'll flat eat a sugar beet," Mike said.

"Uncle Bob plants one more crop of sweet peas the next spring and near harvest comes a rainfall that wipes out the whole crop again. And all the while folks are askin' him why he doesn't just go back to sugar beets, and he says, 'Luck's bound to change. . . . Them peas made me rich one year.' Onliest thing was, after three straight busts for crops, he was so broke that he had to sell the farm, and it didn't make no never mind if his luck in sweet peas changed or not.

"The point is — just because prices were high once, don't mean they'll be that way again, and we can't depend on it. What we need is some price stability and security like ever'one else in the damn country has, instead of these wild fluctuations that make a man rich one year and broke the next." There was a general murmur of approval. Mike borrowed Jimbo's handkerchief and blew his nose as loudly as a nose can be blown.

"What cattlemen were sayin' at that national convention is that it's time we stopped just lettin' our lives be manipulated by the goin' price of the market, and time we did a little manipulatin' of our own. It happens on the other end: when prices shot up so high a couple of summers back, the housewives had their husbands eatin' pig and chicken till they went down again. I got a mother-in-law in Dubuque, Iowa, who did just that. Calls up Kathy and says to her either divorce me or send hamburger for Christmas, 'cause she can't afford it. Price was up a nickel so she's up in arms. . . . Well, fair enough! Now prices have swung too far the other way, and I say that if she wants to keep eatin' pig and chicken, that's what she'll get, 'cause the only way she'll be able to put beef on her table is if we *do* send her some — which we won't. It's time we all held back. We hear time and again how people all over the world are starvin', how we should be producin' more to feed 'em; but by God, if they ain't willin' to give us our fair share, then why should we sell them our beef at giveaway prices? We shouldn't, plain and simple. It's time people saw our side. Housewives like my mother-in-law, God bless her, are all over this ignorant country, thinkin' that ever' goddamn cattle rancher is rich on her meat money, instead of realizin' there's a feeder and a packer and a supermarket with a finger in the same pie. That's too many fingers in not enough pie —"

Jimbo caught a look in Mike's eye and an upturning around the corners of his mouth as he suddenly sat up and blurted, "Say, Ike —"

Ike stopped and looked back to them.

"Say, Ike, just how many fingers do fit in a pie?" Mike wore that little, curious smile of his.

"Huh?"

"In a pie, in a pie. About how many fingers would you guess fit comfortably in your normal pie?"

"McKenzie —"

Everyone was looking back. Jimbo edged over to the side of his chair, but Mike went right on. ". . . Or take your mother-in-law's pie, God bless her. 'Bout how many fingers could it take, I wonder?"

Some of the members were laughing now, but Mike just furled his eyebrows and waited. He rolled up the sleeves of his pajamas. Ike said, "This ain't a matter for jokes, McKenzie. I was speaking figuratively —"

"Well, so was I. . . . I was askin' how many fingers did you *figure* could fit in that pie you were talkin' about."

"Take them goofy pajamas off, McKenzie," a voice called from near the front.

"Last time I did that I had to get married."

Ike glowered at him and waited for the snickers to die down. "May I continue?"

"By all means . . . sorry . . . sorry," Mike said, sitting back and spreading his hands in apology. He winked to Jimbo.

"Anyway, the worst part about it is that the packer, the supermarket, and the feed-lot operator can just jack up prices at the other end to meet costs — but we can't ask a steer to eat any less —"

"We can't even ask you that, Iker," Mike said.

He waited for the laughter to stop. "— eat any less and still get fatter. People got to understand that we're not tryin' to get rich, we're just tryin' to make ends meet.

"What they suggested, then, at the convention . . ." He paused there, looking around the room. ". . . was that we slaughter some calves to bring our predicament to the attention of the public." There was a prolonged buzzing, and Ike let it continue. "If the price of beef on the hoof falls one-half a cent below thirty, they're askin' each and every cattleman in the country to slaughter one calf out of fifty. Two percent of the herd."

Chairs began to slide and squeak on the gym floor. Ike waited. "Now, we ain't that low yet, but word is it'll fall that low unless we let the buyers know that's what we're gonna do. One out of fifty ain't much, but it's a start. And associations all over the country are votin' on this proposition right now. We aim to prove that cattlemen can work together on this thing. And I want us to be first. I want them other associations to pick up on our lead. It won't be a happy course of action, but a man's got to make a stand."

He stopped. Many of the ranchers were nodding vigorously. Others were still. Men turned and murmured to others around them. They were men fed up, every one, and some were angry.

Tiny Turner rose. He was six feet eight inches tall, with feet so big that Papa Vic used to point them out to Jimbo and say, "Them shoes of Tiny's is made of ole canoes . . . foller arcars of him for a spell and you can pick up the birchbark, haw-haw-hee . . ." He was another rancher out of Kearney's Canyon Creek area.

"I'm with ya, Ike." He spoke in a slow, deep voice made deeper after listening to Ike. "There ain't a man here likes the notion of killin' good livestock, or couldn't use the money it would bring. But the time's come to act. That's clear. Another year like this and the only spreads in this part of the state will be the ones owned by the railroads, big enough where they can just take a tax loss and laugh it off. Well, I'm tired of hearin' people laugh. I'm ready to take action with you, and if you boys won't follow, in five years there won't be no small ranchers left. That's all." Tiny sat down, his body slowly sinking lower and lower like a curtain falling. He was respected by the others, and suddenly there were a dozen hands in the air, a dozen voices calling. More men rose to support the measure. John Cott from Kearney. Wally Fetters from Buffalo. A lot of men Jimbo didn't know. One at a time; one after another. Ike Jessup hammered away with his gavel — bam-bam-bam, the percussion in a song of excited voices. He called for order. One at a time. You there, go ahead.

Shoot the calves? Jimbo thought; afraid to look over to Mike and see the hate or disgust or whatever would be coloring his face above those ridiculous pajamas. Shoot the calves? The voices began to run into each other, like river rapids. Like a river boiling with sheep, he thought. Yes! Yes! Yes! they cried. Not rimrocking sheep now, but shooting their own calves to drive up prices. Not uniting themselves against other people, but against prices; against a faceless, nameless profit-and-loss margin. Jimbo remembered pictures of dairy farmers pouring milk into the mud during the Depression. But this was different.

Then Ike was saying through the commotion, "Mike McKenzie, you got anything to say before we vote?"

Jimbo looked over to Mike for the first time. His heavy arms were folded. He was biting his lip as if to suppress a grin, and his hard, gray eyes stared in front of him.

"Looks to me like you fellas already made up your minds."

"Speak out if you got somethin' to say, else we're gonna vote on this directly."

"Well, Chrissakes, Ike, I ain't any sort of public speaker, but I'll say what's on my mind if you like. Fact is, I'm kinda lost. Lotta you boys been tellin' me for years how smart you were, and I guess now I see why, 'cause I'm flat lost. I wouldn't be too gawdawful surprised if even my brother here, who's got a degree from one of them fancy eastern universities, isn't a tad lost himself, though he's not apt to admit it. I never felt so dumb in my life. Just sayin' that the price of beef *does* drop as low as you say — and I'll grant you it could — we've all seen it under thirty in the past and lived to tell about it, hard as that is to believe. Just sayin' it *does* get that low, how is shootin' a bunch of calves goin' to turn into a good deal at all? You're going to have to explain that to me one more time, Iker. Maybe use another illustration of your old Uncle Bob. That was a swell story, but I think them sugar beets confused me."

Somebody called to get on with the vote. Somebody else called for him to go back to bed.

Ike said, "Just what aren't you clear about, McKenzie?"

"Well. How exactly shooting some of my stock is going to make me any money. Or make me popular with, say, your mother-in-law, God bless her."

"For one thing it will drive prices up by lowering the supply. Two percent isn't much, but it's something. More important, it'll call attention to our problem."

"Our problem? Christ, Ike, you make it sound like a case of the clap or something."

"It *is* a problem. And this will bring it into the open. What we're aiming for is government guarantees like the Agriculture Department gives the farmers. We've got a lot to gain by this."

Mike held up his hands in apology. "Hold on, now. Be patient. I'm a mite slow, I'll grant you. I can see some of what there is to gain: a few less calves would make branding easier, I can figure that much out. I can think of a couple of tit-sore cows that'd be plumb grateful to have their calves taken away and shot so's they could have some peace and quiet without the little fella nuzzlin' in for breakfast all the time. Shoot, Ike, I'll betcha you were just like that as a tyke, eh? Always givin' your ma a cheap feel and a suck in the supermarket —"

"Just get on with it, McKenzie."

"Let's see. It might be kinda fun to get out some Saturday morning with a boxful of bullets and a pen full of calves — or maybe have 'em in a pit so's afterwards all there'd be left to do would be dump in the dirt — then gather 'round and blast 'em, *kabang-kabang*. That'd be pretty good fun. Give a fella a chance to sight in his rifle 'fore the season. I bet most of you guys'd get a hell of a kick out of that. I know I would. But, hell, guys, there's another side of the coin, too, seems to me.

"First off, I can sell them weaner calves for somethin' when they're still alive. That's one of the things a buyer likes to look for. And even if the prices were so low that I didn't want to sell 'em, I could always *eat* 'em, for Chrissakes. But not even Ike there would eat one after it'd been buried a few days, I don't think. And another thing I'm wondering, is what if them folks you're holdin' back from, the folks you're gonna make eat chicken and pig and fat, tender lamb — what if they all of a sudden find out they can do just fine without beef? Hell, they don't eat it in India. Wouldn't take it from you if you offered it on a tray. What if folks over here decided they didn't care if we went ahead and shot every last one of our cattle?" Mike began to laugh, and a childish glint showed in his eyes. Jimbo felt himself starting to smile with him. "What if someone figured out how to make a Big Mac with a soybean, and we started getting telegrams saying, KILL 'EM ALL, CHICKENSHITS. WE'LL USE THAT LAND FOR SOYBEANS! Any of you guys think of that? Soybeans're a damn fine bean." Mike was nodding and grinning. Some of the ranchers thought he was drunk. "Hell, you boys do what you want. If you can make sense out of balin' hay so's to burn it, well, more power to you. Simple fella like me's got enough headaches with the ordinary methods of his granddad."

An older voice called from the front, "Your granddad would whip your hide . . ." It trailed off.

Mike shrugged and sat down. He was immune to the glares boring in on him. Hepp Fox sat in front of them, and he said bitterly, "Either this here's an association or it ain't an association. We act together on this, McKenzie."

"That like a union, Hepp?"

"We all stick by the vote."

"Like I said, Hepp, I'm not as smart as you fellas. You can stick by anything you want, and you can stick it up anything you want, too. Even in these fine, liberal United States it's still not possible to tell another man what to do with his livestock. Not yet, anyway. As I understand it."

"We stick by the vote, McKenzie," Hepp said, looking around him for support.

"You stick by anything you want, Hepper. My calves are contracted for, and I aim to keep my end of the bargain — that's what I'll stick to."

Another older cowboy whom Jimbo didn't recognize said to Mike angrily, "Vic McKenzie helped form this association. Don't cause his name no disrespect by goin' against it."

Mike stared evenly ahead, an innocent smile on his face. "He joined this association to steal land from the sheepherders. He'd call this group here the Shepherd's Revenge."

Jimbo felt his scalp burning and sweat drip under his arms. A rumbling of disgruntlement spread. Mike seemed impervious to any of it. He met the angry glances that turned back toward him with a relaxed smile. Then the gym began to quiet again as Sam Benson strode slowly to the front.

Sam surveyed the gathering from the podium. He was an old-fashioned, commonsense politician who had ended his statehouse career after failing in his bid for the U.S. Senate last election. His face was creased and the color of old newspaper from a life outdoors. He had a voice that was deep and raspy as an old gate hinge, and when he spoke his right eyelid hung low to avoid the smoke from the cigarette that dangled from his black mouth. He smiled and stretched his arms around the speaker's stand.

"Gawddamn, you can be ornery, Mike McKenzie." He had a broad grin on his face, and he took a drag of his cigarette and waited as the tension eased. "But sometimes you do talk sense." Sam's face turned serious. "More harm than good might come out of this thing. You want publicity, Ike, but the kind of publicity you might get by shootin' good calves may not be the kind you're looking for. Folks around the country like baby animals. Other folks might stroke their chins and say, 'Look at them rich ranchers shootin' hundred-fifty-dollar calves with no more thought than piddlin' off a bridge.' Folks might think we cowboys are so bloodthirsty by nature that now that we've got rid of the Injuns and the outlaws and the buffalo, we're turnin' on our cattle.

"Now I know what I'm talkin' about, and if you go ahead with the plans for this slaughter, no matter what your motives, you're gonna make some powerful enemies. You'll get more publicity'n you ever dreamed of — all of it bad. If ya want to hold back your cattle from the market, well, by Gawd, do it! But don't be playin' Gawd Almighty with your livestock and treatin' 'em in mysterious ways, just 'cause some local Joe from an association down in Colorado is gettin' pressure from his cronies to build a fire at the convention and do somethin' about prices. The damn prices'll take care of themselves if you leave 'em be a spell. Don't be shootin' your calves like crippled-up horses just to hurry 'em along. Some things ain't right no matter what the price.

"I've gotta ask you, like Mike did, what's it gonna prove? So you shoot five, six, eight hundred calves — what then? Even if they shoot eight thousand calves all acrost the country, Gawd help us, it won't make much of a dent on the prices. That's good beef you're talkin' about wastin' — beef your sweat helped raise. If we're gonna sit by a calvin' heifer at four in the mornin', with snow up to our knees and so cold it'd freeze piss to a bucket, just to slaughter and waste the calf she bears, then somethin's amiss somewheres. Then maybe we been out there in the freezin' cold so long our heads've gone numb. If ya don't want your calves, then give 'em away to someone who does, or turn 'em loose. That's my feelin'."

Sam Benson stopped and looked around the room. His strong fingers crushed the cigarette out in the ashtray beside him as his eyes scanned the gym, seeking out each and every man. He said, "But, hell, I don't know all the answers . . ."

Jimbo thought at first he might stop there and let them off the hook — but Sam Benson was a born orator. He dangled his humility before them like Jimbo had always pictured Abe Lincoln doing, then he started up, first slowly, but always rising, picking up his voice in volume and in pace.

"All I'm askin' is that you think about this thing. Think about why Gawd gave every last one of you a strong back and land to work, and healthy cattle that make it through our Gawd-forsaken winters and fatten on grass so sparse that a horse can run through a pasture and never trample a blade. There sure ain't anythin' the matter with makin' money. Even Gawd Almighty in His wisdom knows that. But a man's got to keep his wits about him. Let's set things straight: any of you boys who think there isn't an easier way to make a livin' are dead wrong. None of us would be in this business if we wanted to get rich. We're cattlemen because we love the land, because we love hard work and the life and the outdoors. We're cattlemen especially because it's in our blood, and there ain't nothin' in the world that gives us a better feelin' than seein' a newborn suck milk for the first time. We're cattlemen because we love our heritage, because we love what our fathers did before us and the life they lived, and raisin' stock is as right and natural for you men as an acorn growin' to be an oak. Think about that. You men are livin' tribute to a way of life, to men who helped feed this nation and make it what it is — and if you think that those men ever shot one of their own head just to see it die, for money or any other reason, you're crazy. This land wouldn't have been worth a pound of horsecakes without cattle. Cattle made this part of the country — grazin' on land where you couldn't grow beans. If you got no more respect for the breed than to shoot the younguns and bury 'em 'cause they ain't bringin' in enough money, well . . . then we've lost somethin' dear." He stopped and looked sadly around him, letting the words sink home. "I won't be part of it . . . I can't . . . and you can't either." He walked slowly back and took his seat. The room was silent.

Ike Jessup's fat, hulking frame rose, but he said nothing. He started to speak, his thin mouth opening a couple of times, but could think of nothing and instead stood there dumbfounded.

Then a voice spoke from near the back. It was Tiny Turner's. "No one likes it, Sam; but a man's family comes before his livestock."

Ike was jolted from his speechlessness. "It sure does. You think we like it any better'n you? You think we'll enjoy it, if that's what it comes down to? Chrissakes, man, this is the way it is. We've been pushed into a corner, and if they insist on pushing further, we're gonna fight our way out. There ain't nowhere else to go. If the market falls below thirty, we'll be ready to make a statement, loud and clear, that a lot of folks are gonna listen to. Hopefully, Sam, our voting and other associations voting like we do, will be preventative against the price falling that low. Maybe just knowin' that we mean business will wake people up, then maybe even the damn government will open their eyes. Folks should just get it into their heads that we ain't gonna wait till prices right themselves like Sam there suggests. The cattle industry is through handin' out free lunches!"

Mike cupped his hands around his mouth. "Hell's bells, Iker, anyone can see you don't give away your lunch, for free or for profit, neither one."

"Go ahead and joke, McKenzie. It don't matter to you. You got all that coal beneath your land, and you ain't got to worry. Us little guys, less fortunate —"

"Coal stays right where it is. That ain't got nothing —"

"I'll believe that when I see it. And ain't it nice to know it's there, just in case? Ain't it nice to be able to preach high and mighty from your safe and sound pulpit? Rest of us ranchers, we can't afford a bum year like this. We got payments to meet and mouths to feed . . . and *nothing* to fall back on!"

That silenced Mike. And there was a look that passed across his face for just an instant that was something like realization; that maybe he recalled some of the things Thorndike had said about friends no longer being friends; as if Ike's bringing up the coal was the first he understood of the division between him and the rest of the town. And that relaxed, slightly cynical grin darkened into a scowl while cries of "Vote! Vote! Vote!" resounded through the gym. The ranchers were tired of debate, tired of uncertainty, tired of variables beyond their control. They wanted to reach out and grab something, to strike at something tangible. It was not Mike or the Bar V or the coal that they wanted to strike at, but it seemed that they were all standing in the path of the blow. VOTE! they called from behind tight, nervous lips. VOTE! they urged, almost desperately, louder and louder — not pleased or proud or excited, but with a grim sense of: Let's get it over with. VOTE! They clapped with callused hands.

And Mike, the scowl turned to a contemptuous smile, sat motionless in the midst of the commotion. His eyes were expressionless, gazing stonily ahead, and a ring of whiteness surrounded his lips from the strain of the smile. That whiteness was the only sign of his anger. He just sat there and stared.

They went ahead with it. "All in favor —" with a trembling voice, as if Ike knew he'd won a battle he'd had no business winning. The rows of upstretched arms lined up like a backyard cornpatch, the stalks moving so slightly you could swear they were growing in the sunshine. "Opposed?" — perfunctorily, the matter settled, all arms having been counted but two — but one — Sam Benson's alone now that Mike had left. "Carried!" with purpose, with finality.

CHAPTER 17

AVELYN WAS WAKENED by the stumbling in the hall. A light was on. It flicked off and there was more stumbling, then heavy tiptoeing.

"Michael?"

"Shh, babe."

"It's all right." Her voice had sleep in it. She pulled the covers up. There was uneven hopping, and a boot fell on the floor. He bumped against the dresser.

"Shit."

"Are you drunk?"

"Shh. I'm sorry," he whispered.

"That's all right." The sleep wouldn't leave her voice and she drifted away. Then he was getting into bed and she snuggled toward him. "Cold," she said, feeling his skin. It was still night. She had not been asleep long and she had to think to remember where he'd been. His skin was soft and the pillow and it was all very dreamlike. "Kiss?"

He rolled over and kissed her wetly on the neck, then flopped back down.

"You're drunk."

He rolled again and his lips moved more softly over her cheek and her mouth, kissing. Then he collapsed heavily into his pillow. "I'm drunk."

"How was the meeting?"

"Fucking horseshit."

She did not want to wake up completely, and talking about the meeting would put her to sleep. "Did you get drunk at the meeting?"

"No."

"Where did you?"

"At the Mint. At the Mint Bar. Ole buddy boy and I got drunk at the Mint Bar. I'm sorry, babe."

"Don't be sorry. Is old buddy boy drunk?"

"Yes. Very."

"Sounds like it was a fun meeting."

"It wasn't a fun meeting. It was a horseshit meeting. I don't want to talk about the fucking horseshit meeting."

"Hmm. I love you, fucking horseshit." She was lying against his smooth shoulder and it was safe there and warm. "I was thinking about the rodeo," she said.

He grunted.

"I was thinking it would be fun to enter the pony express race. I could run Pasha as anchor, and maybe that new bay and sorrel pair you got. And maybe your gray horse —"

"Not my gray horse."

"Well, then. Maybe old Rooney."

"You can't take my gray horse. Racing makes a rope horse goofy. Makes any horse goofy."

"Rooney then?"

"That's Denny's bulldogging horse. You ask him."

"And that bay and sorrel?"

"Well."

"You could kind of see what they had."

"I can see what they have without taking 'em out in the fool rodeo. Makes a horse goofy, all those people. What you want to be in the fool rodeo for, babe?"

"I just do. It's all right then?"

"I'm too drunk. Ask me in the mornin'."

"Thank you, Mr. Drunk." She squeezed him around the waist.

"Did I say yes? I didn't say yes."

"Yes, you did," she said, smiling to herself. "You said you'd like to see what they could do."

"I wouldn't mind seeing what they could do."

"You won't forget?"

"Forget what? I didn't make any promises."

"And I promise to win."

Mike thought a moment. "With that stock you damn well better win."

"I will. I promise." She smiled to herself again. There was a wind and the house creaked. "You hear that? You hear the creaking? The dryness does that."

"No."

"You never hear it. You've lived in this house all your life, and you've never heard it creak."

"It don't creak."

"When we were first married, and the wind started making the place groan, this old house could be pretty spooky. I like a house that talks, but this one groans." She squeezed him and lay listening to the wind. Far away she heard barking. She hoped it wouldn't be Stormy going after another porcupine. Mike's breathing became heavy and even. She listened to that and felt herself drifting off. His skin was soft. Then from some ridge the coyotes started.

"Hear that, Michael? Why do they do that? Who are they howling at?" He was asleep, and she pulled the covers over her ears and snuggled in.

"Hey, Ike," Mike said into the phone.

"Don't you 'Hey, Ike' me, you sonofabitch."

"Iker —"

"What's the idea of speaking out at my meeting, making a big fuss about quitting, when you're selling out anyhow? You're a sonofabitch to beat 'em all."

"Who's selling out?"

"You are. You seen today's paper? Says you've come to terms with Titanic for fifteen million. Fifteen goddamn million and you're speaking out about beef prices."

"It ain't true."

"I just wanted to tell you face to face you're a sonofabitch to beat 'em all."

"Ike, that thing in the paper ain't true. I'm not selling."

"Yesterday Jerry Barrow down in Lander was offered hundred thirty dollars for his four-hundred-fifty-pound calves. That's twenty-nine cents a pound, McKenzie. We're gonna slaughter on Friday and you better be there."

"Did you hear me, Ike? I'm not selling. I don't know how that thing got to the paper, but I'm not selling and I'm not negotiating or any other damn thing. You hear me?"

"You sonofabitch. You lying sonofabitch. It's right here in the paper."

"Listen with your ears, man!"

"You gonna be there, McKenzie? Just tell me, yes or no."

"I'm quit of that association. I won't have no part of it. No."

There was a silence at the other end. Mike said, "I ain't gonna argue with you on it. You do what you have to do."

"I'll do that, McKenzie," Ike said. Before hanging up he said, "You can expect to be hearing from some of the boys then."

The phone calls started. One after another, members of the association told him to reconsider before Friday. They wanted a united stand on this thing, and no one liked it any better than the next guy. There weren't going to be any freeloaders in this district. No sonsabitchin' freeloaders with fifteen million bucks in the bank. No sir.

It was getting on everyone's nerves. Avelyn stopped answering. If Mike wasn't in, she would let it ring, or go out to work in the garden, or ride, exercising the quarter horses she would race in the rodeo.

For mealtimes and nights Mike finally hooked up a telephone answering machine. On it he taped his fifteen-second rendition of a Canada goose — first its haunting, crying honk, and then a short furious hiss — followed by a chime tone and ten seconds to leave a message. He would play the messages back in the morning at breakfast. They'd hear the callers breathing and maybe asking in a tentative voice, "That you, McKenzie? You there?" or muttering curses before slamming down the receiver. Mike would laugh and play them back, trying to identify the callers, seeming to enjoy the whole idiotic business, refusing to change his lifestyle any more than that answering machine so everyone could get a little sleep. It was a long week.

The night before the slaughter Lloyd Paxton called.

"You too, eh, partner?" Mike said.

"Me too, what?"

"Want me to be there tomorrow. Want me to throw my stock into the ring."

"I'm not calling on that," Lloyd said.

"Well, that's good news."

"Maybe it is and maybe it ain't," Lloyd said. He paused. "Somebody told me that little bit in the paper about you sellin' weren't true."

"You know me better'n that. Course it ain't true."

"That's a lot of money you're passin' up."

"Sure it is."

"Well. That fella Thorndike come up here a few days back and told me you was gonna sell."

"My brother said he seen him drive up. You ain't got to worry, Lloyd. I'm not selling. 'Bout the only good thing about this calf affair is it's taken my mind off the damn coal for a day or so."

"Yeah. Well, that ain't why I'm calling."

Mike waited.

"We been neighbors a long time, Mike — the McKenzies and the Paxtons. We go back a long ways."

"What happened, Lloyd?"

"Well that Thorndike fella was up here sayin' how you'd agreed to sell your place, and he made me an offer on mine. He offered me six million, Mike. I don't own the coal, you know. Just own the surface. Told me they don't need a surface owner's consent in Wyoming. I looked into it, and that's true. He offered me the six million against, oh, royalties or some damn thing. Twenty-five cents a ton. Hell, I don't know."

"You didn't take it?"

"That's why I'm callin' you."

"Hell, you can't take it."

"Well. I guess if you could come anywhere near it, I'd sell the place to you. That's why I'm callin'."

"Near six *million?*"

"I don't know. I wanted to call."

"You can't sell, Lloyd."

"He don't even need my consent. That's state-owned coal, McKenzie. I'd have to take the whole shootin' match to court."

Mike rubbed his forehead with his fingers. "Hate to see you sell, Lloyd."

"It's a worse deal for you than for me. It's a fair price for me. If you could come anywhere near it, I'd sure like to sell her to you."

"I can't come near that."

"No. Well. It just ain't a very profitable living, as things are now. I don't much care for working myself to death, just to break even. I'm sixty years old now."

"That ain't old. Papa Vic lived to ninety-two."

"Vic was a helluva man." Then: "What you aim to do, Mike?"

"Guess I won't do anything just yet."

"I wanted to tell you myself. Paxtons and McKenzies go way back. Hate to think of you and Avelyn stayin' behind in the mess there's gonna be. You're a young fella. You oughta think about getting a new place somewheres. Seems to me a middle-sized cattle outfit ain't long for this world anyhow. You might just think about taking some of that money Titanic's throwing around and getting yourself a helluva big outfit."

"Just hasn't sunk in you won't be around, Lloyd."

"Yeah. Well." Mike listened into the phone, and the two of them were silent. "Better find yourself a new roping partner," Lloyd said. Then: "He'll have a helluva partner. I guess that's all."

Mike's moods were not susceptible to the moon or the alignment of the stars or the weather. It took a physical, tangible act to change them, a thumb hung up in barbed wire or a knocking engine. Jimbo knew that. He was playing backgammon with

Avelyn, trying to cheer her up from the long week of phone calls, from Mike's stubborn insistence that the phone stay on the hook, that every call be answered. He would not give the other cattlemen even that much satisfaction. Jimbo had made a batch of margaritas, and they were drinking them, rolling the dice, laughing and relaxed for the first time all week, when Mike appeared in the doorway, and in a glance Jimbo saw that something had happened.

"Lloyd's selling out," Mike said. He walked slowly over, poured himself a margarita, and drank most of it right down. "Six million."

They were quiet for a long time. "To Titanic?" Jimbo asked.

"I just never thought he'd sell," Mike said. "I never thought so. They told him I was selling. It was in the paper, and then they told him that. Goddamn, I wish he'd called. He hears that, then he thinks, 'Well, why the hell not? They're throwin' that money around, why the hell not, anyhow?' The livin' ain't profitable, and he's getting old, so why the hell not? Then when ole Lloyd finds out it's just a goddamn lie they've started, well, he's kinda used to that six million. Who cares what his neighbors think? Goddamn him anyway."

"Sit down, hon."

"I'm all right."

"Don't blame Lloyd."

"Well, who the hell should I blame? Who the hell put a gun to his head, anyway? I just didn't think he'd sell. Not him." Mike drank, and they were quiet. Then he said, "And next I s'pose they go to Hepp Fox and Tiny Turner and Jeb Miller and say, 'Now Paxton *and* McKenzie've agreed to sell . . .' and *those* bastards start getting dollar signs swimmin' in their empty heads like the goddamn ninnies they are. Any sonsabitches that'd shoot their own cattle and bury 'em 'cause of bucks'll sure as hell jump at the dollars them coal companies will float their way. Sure as hell."

"Only with those guys they won't buy them out," Jimbo said. He looked at Mike to make sure he was listening. "Mike? You understand that? They won't buy those guys out."

Mike said nothing, so he went on. "Thorndike said he wouldn't buy anyone else out till we sold, remember? You see how they do this? You see how they fuck up a town? They go back to those other Canyon Creek ranchers after telling them how much they're going to be worth, and they say you've backed out. They say you're holding out for more money or something, and till you sell, no one gets any money."

"That's just fine with me, 'cause I ain't selling. I told 'em all that at the meeting. Coal stays where it is."

"Yeah, well, that's how they do it. You see? You tell them you aren't selling, but Titanic tells them you are. So they believe what they want. It doesn't matter that you've never said you'd sell in the first place. All those other guys need to know is if you *did* sell, here's what they'd be worth. Bingo. A fortune. All they end up thinking about is all those bucks Lloyd Paxton got away with, start thinking what a fucking hellish thing it is to put hay up in August anyway, start thinking they could do anything in the damn world they'd want if Mike McKenzie would just sell out. Hell, six million bucks. You put that in municipal bonds and you've got more tax-free income than any of these guys will see in ten years. See how they work it? See how they screw up a town? *You're* the villain. Not Titanic. You. Mike McKenzie. And some guy like Hepp who's never had anything more in his head than marrying a pretty girl like Marge and then holding on to her and his ranch both, all of a sudden gets to thinking about millions of dollars — visions of grandeur, these great lofty delusions — and who knows what goes through his head?"

"Nothing goes through his head but air on a windy day."

"You see, though."

"What the hell do I care what Hepp Fox thinks? I don't give a damn."

"What about Turner or Miller or Will Taylor? Their land has coal, too. Or some guy like Billy Preston who'll be building houses for all those miners?"

"I don't give a damn."

Jimbo shrugged. "They will."

"That's their problem, buddy boy."

"Terrific. Everyone's got a problem but Mike." He poured himself another margarita. "You give a damn, Avelyn?"

She didn't answer.

"Well. Good. Nobody gives a damn. Bottoms up."

"I didn't say that," she said. The phone rang. She started to get up, but Mike was already on his feet.

"You give a damn, buddy boy?" He reached the phone and let it ring again. "You give a damn about what our dear goddamn friends and neighbors think about what we should do with our land and our calves and our goddamn —" He picked up the phone and held it against his stomach. "Maybe we should hold a little poll, find out just exactly what would be the most popular way to handle all this —

"Yeah? . . . Wally, it's good of you to call . . ." Mike had that funny look in his eyes, and Jimbo listened. ". . . a slaughter, you say? Well, I'd be plumb honored . . . Well of course I would . . . No, hell, ain't hardly like me to disappoint my friends and neighbors who've been so goddamn good to me all these years . . . You tell Iker he can depend on me . . . You tell Iker I said so . . ." He hung up.

Jimbo looked at him, amazed. "That was a quick change."

"It's the tequila. It makes you crazy."

"So I see."

Mike finished another drink. "Let's eat, babe. I'm starved."

"So you'll be at the slaughter?" Jimbo said.

"That's what I said. Show everyone I give a damn."

"And tomorrow morning, when you haven't got the tequila to make up your mind for you, will you still want to be at the slaughter?"

Mike gave him a long look. "Why not?"

"I don't know. No reason."

"I'll show, buddy boy. Don't you worry on that."

In the morning it was raining. Jimbo looked out the window to the dirt yard. The ground drank in the drizzle without puddling. The stock truck was gone, and he realized that was the noise that had wakened him.

They had breakfast, then Denny and he put on their rain gear and the two of them drove down to the pit recently dug near the Kearney dump. There was a long line of stock trucks loaded with calves waiting in the muddy drive, and a trickle of foot traffic from town. Beside the pit stood two news crews from national television networks, toting cameras, threading out cable, passing among the spectators who, sensing they were part of an *event,* became giggly and self-conscious. A carnival atmosphere prevailed. The people wore bright yellow slickers and talked loudly in groups of twos and threes. Some calves were bawling in a makeshift pen. The rain fell steadily.

Ike Jessup was orchestrating from the rear of one of the stock trucks, directing traffic, giving instructions. He saw Jimbo and waved him over, motioning for the ranchers around him to clear a path. "Ain't seen your brother," Ike said.

Jimbo looked around. There were dozens of trucks like theirs. "He took off early in the stock truck. I assumed he was headed here."

"Ain't seen him."

"Well, I haven't laid eyes on the old boy this morning, but the last thing he said to me last night was that he'd be here."

Ike frowned. "I'll tell you this, Jimbo. Be a bad deal if he don't show. Real bad deal. I hope he does."

"He said he would, Ike, that's all I can tell you. His Highness must speak for himself."

"Well, he's been speakin' a passel of things I don't believe."

"Like what, Ike?" Jimbo asked, smiling.

Ike's frown deepened. "I just know what I read."

"I hope you know more than that."

"I got to go. You send him over when he shows up. I hope he does. That's what I hope."

Jimbo kept an eye on the road, but there was no sign of Mike. The excitement grew as ten o'clock neared. The crowd grew. Most of the town must have been there, standing in the mud and rain, pushing forward to get a good view of the pit, of the television people. Then Ike Jessup led the first calf to the edge of the pit by a halter. He tied it to a post and got a rifle. The cameras were on him, and he faced them. The calf was standing calmly, showing no particular fear of the rifle. It was just another metal, odorless tool, like a shovel. Ike came closer, raised the gun to his shoulder, and there was a sudden explosion as he shot the calf in the ear. Its legs buckled and it rolled onto its side, jerking spasmodically. Then it stopped and Ike untied the halter and kicked it into the pit.

When the death smell became thick, the calves began to struggle harder, and it took two men to drag them to the edge of the pit. When they were shot, most of the calves dropped as if clubbed, kicking for a few moments and then stopping; but if one jerked about for too long there was another man with a pistol who would shoot it again. Then the halter would be removed and the dead calf would be pushed down the slope, which was worn slick from the sliding carcasses.

They could average three a minute. Each rancher shot as many calves as he had brought. When one area of the pit became too stacked up with carcasses, they moved to another. The television people had filmed the shooting from a number of angles, including from within the pit itself, and they had interviewed Ike and several of the ranchers. They were just preparing to leave when the Bar V truck appeared on the dirt access road.

"There's McKenzie," Ike told a newsman. "There's the fella."

Mike parked the truck a little way off and came right over. "Sorry I'm late, Iker."

"That's all right. Glad you changed your mind."

"How's it going?"

"Goin' all right."

Mike looked around at the people. The steady *bam . . . bam . . . bam* sounded from the pit area. "Helluva crowd."

"There's some media people who'd like to talk to you. How about goin' up next?"

"Sure thing." He nodded to Jimbo. "Mornin,' buddy boy."

"Just back your truck right over," Ike said. "Need to borrow some halters? We got extra halters."

"All set, Iker. Got some kinda runty Black Angus pups all rigged out. Meant to cull them from my herd anyhow."

Jimbo followed Mike to the truck. He could hear bawling from the back. "Where'd you get Angus? We don't even run Angus." He climbed in beside him.

Mike grinned, backing the truck around. His eyes were bloodshot, and Jimbo guessed he had been drinking. "Found some kinda runty ones in a newspaper ad. Just come back from Sheridan." He parked near the pit. "Lead these pups out while I get me a rifle."

He had a funny look. Jimbo went around to the back, attaching the loading ramp, listening to the bizarre, muffled bawling from inside the truck. Something was wrong here. Something. He opened the gate and looked in. There were no calves. In the straw lay Mike's new tape recorder, playing his frightened calf calls, and beside it was a box of six black Labrador puppies with a length of clothesline tied around each one's neck for a leash.

"Bring 'em out, buddy boy. Need some help?" Mike handed the rifle to Ike. "Here you go, Iker. My brother there needs a hand." Mike hopped onto the ramp and climbed into the back. He reappeared, leading one of the puppies, pretending to be struggling. "These goddamn Angus may be runty but they're stout."

"What's goin' on here?" Ike lowered the rifle, and some of the people started laughing. The television people moved closer, and Ike tried to shield their view. Some of the ranchers yelled angrily.

Ike took two steps and grabbed Mike by the arm. His teeth were clenched and he spoke through them. "This better not be one of your jokes, McKenzie."

Mike pulled his arm away. "Ain't no joke."

"What're you doin' with that dog?" he hissed.

"Not dog, Iker. Dogie. Fella sold 'em to me said I was gettin' some nice little *dogies*."

There was more shouting. Ike pushed past Jimbo up the ramp and looked into the back of the truck. He turned red and came back down and shook Mike by the collar. "Goddamn you!"

Mike pushed him away, hard this time. "Goddamn me *what?* Any blind man can see a person can't make any money on that

little runt of a calf, so let's shoot him. Let's *shoot him, Ike!*" Mike
grabbed the rifle off the ground and threw Jimbo the leash, and
Jimbo suddenly saw that he was furious. The puppy was sniffing
around his feet, and Mike kicked it toward the pit. He stepped
back and put the rifle to his shoulder. Ike grabbed his arm again
with a curse, and Mike lowered the gun and swung his arm back
so that Ike stumbled against the truck. "Don't touch me, you!"

He raised the gun again as the puppy clambered against
Jimbo's knees. "Kick him away from you, buddy boy!" Mike's
eye was to the barrel of the rifle. "Goddammit, get him away!"

"Goddammit, don't point that!"

"Yes! That sonofabitch costs too much to feed! Yes!" Mike
turned back to the truck and jerked the box of puppies out of
the back. Jimbo let go of the leash and stepped forward, but
Mike pushed past him and tipped the box so that the puppies
slid down the muddy embankment, tumbling on top of each
other in a pile among the dead calves. Then he kicked the empty
box into the middle of the pit, cursing and raising the rifle to
his eye. A lady screamed at him to stop. The television cameras
whirred. Mike's finger tightened on the trigger, and Jimbo
yelled, "Don't!" He raised the barrel slightly and fired six shots
into the carcass of one of the calves.

There was a stony silence as he lowered the gun. Below, the
Labrador puppies squirmed out of their cluster and ambled over
the carcasses of dead calves, sniffing curiously. One stopped and
licked the blood from an ear. They fell clumsily as they explored.

Mike handed the rifle to Jimbo and lifted the loading ramp
into the back of the truck. He closed the gate. No one moved
or said anything. One of the TV men came forward with his
microphone out, but Mike pushed past him. He walked around
to the door of the cab and started the engine. Then he drove
off.

The ranchers watched the disappearing truck. The talk became loud and bitter. Ike was glaring, working his mouth in and
out like a cow chewing its cud. "That sonofabitch," he said, not
loudly. Someone climbed down into the pit to retrieve the puppies, and Hepp Fox walked past saying just loud enough for
Jimbo to hear, "He's gonna regret that."

The television people left. The crowd left. The ranchers stayed and finished the shooting just after two. Three a minute until the last one was dragged out of the pen and shot; seven hundred eighteen in all. The rain had stopped now, and the bulldozers moved in and covered the pit over. Afterward, the earth was packed down with stones and brush to keep out digging animals.

CHAPTER 18

JIMBO DROVE DENNY out to the Custer Battlefield that afternoon, where the general had made his Last Stand. It was one of Denny's favorite spots. He would walk in the high, brown grass, running his hand over the simple white headstones that marked the dead soldiers. The hills surrounding the memorial were treeless except for the draw where the Sioux had been waiting, and there the tops of an aspen grove showed.

After a while the gunshots stopped ringing in Jimbo's ears, and he listened to the wind as it picked up in the late afternoon. It was a warm, lazy wind, and dry as a scar. He kicked at a sagebrush, smelling its rich, turpentine-like aroma, picking at its twisted leaves, gray-green and powdery. Papa Vic used to talk about sagebrush: . . . *Ain't worth a shit, Jimmy . . . Sagebrush just ain't no good to man nor beast . . . Must be here for a reason, don't know what, but I reckon it's Gawd Almighty actin' in his doggone mysterious ways . . . Rain won't grow it, sun won't burn it, and a cow won't eat it . . . Plumb mysterious . . . Person can watch it, or a person can rub it in his sheets to make 'em smell nice. . . . That's all the sense I ever made of the ole sage. . . .*

There was lots of sage on the mesa. It took over when the grassland was overgrazed. Sagebrush could survive drought as well as a thistle could. Jimbo tugged at one of the little bushes, but its gnarled roots clenched the rocky soil. It wouldn't give an inch. The sagebrush would have broken off in his hands before

162

he could have pulled its roots from the ground. It was a hardy plant.

They were late getting back. Avelyn had held dinner for them, and by the time she served it the roast beef was overcooked. Mike was hungry and pretty testy from waiting. "You boys put in a rough afternoon?" he asked through a potato.

"Stayed to the end of the slaughter."

"I know where you were."

"Then why'd you ask?"

"I didn't ask. I asked if you had a rough afternoon."

"I've had easier."

"I'll bet you have." He heaped a forkful of beef and potatoes into his mouth and wiped the gravy from his lips. "I'll just bet you have. Pick up that baling wire like I asked you?"

"No. Sorry, I forgot."

"You forgot —"

"I'll get it next time I go in."

"If you don't forget."

Jimbo stopped chewing and looked at him. The rest of the table was quiet. "That's right. What's the big deal? We won't need it for three weeks anyway. I'll pick it up."

"Fine. Great."

Avelyn dropped her fork. "Let's enjoy our dinner, shall we?"

"By all means. Enjoy, enjoy. I just happened to forget my chain saw out in the barn, so I figured while I tried to cut my meat I'd pass the time with the kid here about what a hell of a day he put in."

"I'm sorry about the roast beef," she said. "It's my fault."

"If him and Big Den had been back on time for dinner it wouldn't —"

"— The meat's my fault, Michael. I'm very sorry."

Jimbo said, "We drove out to the Custer Battlefield. Denny wanted to go."

"Well, whatever Denny wants —" He held a piece of beef up with his fork. "More meat, Den?"

Jimbo tried to keep his voice even. "Maybe you should take a trip up there sometime. Great little exhibit all about a big powerful general who got himself trapped in an impossible situation through arrogance and pigheadedness."

"That right?"

"What the hell put it into your head to pull that bit with the puppies?" He turned to Avelyn. "He tell you about that?"

"No. What?" She looked at Mike in alarm.

"This crazy sonofabitch comes down there and dumps a box of puppies in there with all the calves. All the *dead* calves. What the hell put that in your head?"

Mike was smiling around his mouthful. "They were dogies. Little dogies."

"Cute, Mike. They hate you for that. They hate your guts."

"Not the first time."

"You embarrassed them. They won't forget that. You couldn't just stay away, could you? You had to have the last word. Then Den and I had to listen to a lot of crap from our great and dear neighbors about what a *sonofabitch* that Mike McKenzie was; how he'd live to regret his precious insolence. . . . So all in all, about the one thing I don't need at dinner is a lot of crap about *baling wire.*"

"What do you mean I'd live to regret it?"

"I don't know. Ike, Hepp Fox, Tiny Turner, Wally Fetters, you name 'em, bub, they were talking. I don't know if they meant anything by it more than trying to sound tough and mad, but I wouldn't count on getting asked to a lot of functions in the near future."

"What'd you tell them?"

"I didn't tell them anything. I told them how blessed upset you'd be to hear they were mad at you."

"You did, eh?"

"Nervous as a pregnant nun."

Mike laughed at that. They calmed down and ate the rest of the meal. Avelyn cleared the table and brought out the ice cream with her homemade fudge sauce, setting it in front of Denny.

"Save a bite, big guy," Deacon told him as he scooped from the fresh half-gallon.

Mike grinned. "Just give him a spoon and bring in somethin' else for the rest of us."

Denny looked up from the mound of ice cream he'd piled into his bowl and saw everyone looking at him in amusement. He glanced around hesitantly, then sheepishly tried to pass his bowl across to Avelyn.

"You keep it. Have some sauce, Denny." He exchanged the ice cream for the sauce and became absorbed with his dessert again. "Leave him alone, why don't you?" Avelyn said.

"You're in a spankin' fine mood," Mike said. "We were joking. He knew that."

"Mike . . ." She paused and rose to return to the kitchen. "You can be so insensitive I wonder how you could possibly know what Denny's thinking."

Denny looked up again, and sensed he was being discussed. Avelyn returned in a moment with the coffee and put it on the hot pad harder than was necessary, then sat down, staring at her placemat. Mike shook his head and muttered, "Jesus."

He turned to Deacon and said, "You don't figure these boys will do anything unreasonable, do you?"

"McKenzie, ain't hardly no chance at all for anyone in that association to act without reason." They smiled, and after a while Deacon went on, "I don't reckon on there being any trouble, though. Lotta talk."

"Let's you and me go in there and hear some of that talk."

"Tonight?"

"Friday night, ain't it? Care to come along, hon?"

"No," she said, still angry.

"How 'bout you, stud?" he asked Jimbo.

"No, thanks. I might catch you down there later."

"I don't know, boss. I don't figure I'd trust the ole stud-buck back home with the wife," Deacon said.

"If I can trust you with the heifers, I might just as well trust ole buddy boy here with Avelyn."

"That's a lovely analogy, Michael. Thank you."

"S'okay."

They left for town around nine o'clock. Jimbo helped Avelyn clear the dishes, then took a Brillo to the roasting pan. "You don't have to do that," she said.

"I don't mind. I want to."

"I'll bet." She managed a smile and went on loading the dishwasher, pushing a dark lock of her hair away from her eyes with the back of her hand. "Thanks, though." She squeezed the back of his neck with her fingers, then went out to the dining room.

He could hear her singing in a small, soft voice. " '. . . if it comes at all this year, my love's up and gone from here, my love's up and gone, and me, I'm bound to stay . . .' " He dried his hands and came out.

"Let's go somewhere and have a drink, want to? Up the road to the Pines."

"Chat with the tourists?"

"They've got a good bar there. Let's do it. Come on. We'll solve the problems of the world."

"Promise?"

"Come on."

"Should I change?"

"You're perfect. Grab a coat."

Avelyn put on a white cotton sweater and they drove up the Canyon Creek road in her station wagon. The Pines was a log inn on Custer Lake that stayed open from the beginning of summer through the end of the hunting season. The walls of the bar were hung with game and various trout — predominantly lake — that had been taken by guests. There were some backpackers and fishermen drinking there, and a couple of forest rangers were at the bar.

"I feel like a Harvey Wallbanger," she said.

Jimbo ordered her one and got a brandy for himself. They were sitting by the deck and could see the dark, still water with its pinpricks of light from the stars. The moon had not risen yet, but the sky across the lake was beginning to glow above the tree line.

"I wish we had a boat," he said. "The whopper lakers bite at night."

She looked at one mounted on the wall. "They're not very attractive."

"No. They fight like old boots, too. But they're wonderful poached with a little sherry."

They sipped their drinks and watched the lake. "I'd like to

put a blind up here this winter," Avelyn said. "This place is so deserted that it must get all sorts of wildlife. Mike says the elk migrate through here."

"They come down out of the mountains." Jimbo sipped his brandy, enjoying the satiny burning. He was watching her eyes. She really had the damnedest eyes. Earlier they had been so vulnerable, and now they were alert and controlled behind those long soft lashes.

"Thanks for bringing me. The house felt a little small tonight."

"To all of us."

She smiled. "Michael can shrink a house as well as anyone."

"When he puts his mind to it."

"He usually won't talk when he's like that. He never would have said anything about those puppies to me. He just said he went there and left without shooting any calves, and thank-you-ma'am-where's-lunch."

"This one won't blow over. He didn't see those guys after he drove off." Jimbo shook his head, a little admiringly. "He courts antagonism so that he can conquer it. I've never met such a man as *mon frère*. It was Lloyd's selling that set him off. He wouldn't have done it if Lloyd hadn't sold."

She smiled. "So what are we going to do with him?"

"I might escape that little dilemma by going to grad school. I got accepted into the University of Montana for this fall."

She sat back and her forehead wrinkled, miming a cry. Then she looked away, but she wasn't kidding now. Her face went blank and lonesome.

"I haven't decided yet," he said.

She looked back, smiling. "Oh, you should go. You've got to go. It's so great you've been accepted."

"I suppose it is."

"Of course it is. That isn't far, anyway. You'll be able to come home and visit all the time." She squeezed his hand. "You're not leaving before the rodeo? I'm going to be in the pony express race, did I tell you? You've got to help. Promise you will. I need three helpers, and Mike's not going to be able to do it because the calf-roping's right after."

"Sounds great. Count me in. Who else? Den?"

"Mike knows a trick we'll practice. He won the race once as a boy. We've got Denny, and Deac . . ."

"Fat ole Deac. That gimp."

Avelyn laughed. "God. I'll miss you, Jimbo McKenzie."

"Well. Missoula isn't far. There's skiing there. We can all take a ski trip over Christmas."

"Mike doesn't ski."

"He can learn."

She laughed. "Oh, wouldn't that be the day?"

"The hell with him then. We'll go without him. I'll teach you to do worm turns."

"They sound filthy. Teach me now."

"You ski them. Like this." Jimbo sat on the floor, then rolled over, flipping his legs around so that he sat back up facing the other way. "That's a worm turn. As long as I'm down here on the floor, will you have another Ballwanger?"

"You've got brandy? I'll join you in a brandy. You seem to be further along." She put some quarters in the jukebox while he got the drinks. She was light-headed and felt like dancing. He came back and peered over her shoulder while she made the selections. "How does a girl who likes Cat Stevens end up with a guy whose favorite song is 'Okie from Muskogee'?"

She stepped on his foot, then took his hand. "Come on. Let's watch the moonrise." She went out to the deck with her drink, and he followed. The moon was still hidden by the hills across the lake. Standing behind her, Jimbo could smell her hair. Then a clear white, perfectly arced ring of the moon rose above the trees.

"There," he said.

"Hmm. Sometimes it seems so peaceful and removed out here." While they were watching the moon, her giddiness had turned to something gentler. "I always thought I'd live in New York City. For a while, anyway. Sow some wild, wonderful oats."

"Worried about growing old, are you?"

She turned to him and smiled. The moon was rising quickly and lit the lake up brightly. "Oh, sometimes."

"You're full of 'sometimes.'"

"Sometimes." She gave him a mischievous look. They were both a little drunk.

"I've never kissed a married woman before."

"It's fantastic."

She was looking at the moon and it made her mouth shine. He kissed her to see what it was like. She didn't stop him. More than that, she kissed him back. Then she caught herself and pulled away.

"What was that for?" she asked, as if she had been taken by surprise. She wasn't angry, though.

"I don't know. For Lent."

She brushed her hair back from her face, her movements light and either flustered or fluttery, Jimbo couldn't tell. "I'd better be more careful around Lent," she said.

"We both should. It is fantastic."

"You've just been too long without."

"That's true too."

They finished their drinks and walked back to the car. She slipped her arm through his, making him feel drunker than he was. He would have liked to kiss her again, but he did not feel quite *that* drunk.

"Do you have a cigarette?" he asked.

"You don't smoke."

"Sometimes I do."

"Well, *I* don't."

"I thought you did everything sometimes."

"Not everything."

They drove back down the road. Avelyn moved her arm to the back of the seat so that her fingers draped against his shoulder. "It's hot in here," he said, unrolling the window a crack.

"Is it?" She was grinning and rubbing the back of his neck with her fingernails.

"God, I bet you were hell. Stop it or I won't be responsible."

"You already aren't."

They were driving by Paxton's when a sharp, cracking shot echoed from somewhere. "Sounds like Lloyd got himself another coyote," he said.

"One less howl then."

She was running her fingertips through his hair, and he sat forward, shaking them away. "Will you behave?"

"Grouch."

Another crack rang out, much closer this time. It was impossible to locate with the echoing.

"What the hell's going on?"

They were both sitting forward, watching, suddenly sober. They turned into the Bar V gate.

"There!" Jimbo pointed.

The headlights of a vehicle flashed on farther down the drive. It began to move. It was coming very fast now, the brights glaring at eye-level through the front window. It seemed to be heading directly toward them, a pickup, and Jimbo leaned on the horn. He shouted when it was a few yards away and veered left. Avelyn tumbled against the door and cried out a warning. The truck roared past. Suddenly the station wagon was dipping toward the ditch. The steering wheel spun from his hands. Something hit him on the head and there was a skidding and scraping on his door. The car crunched to a stop. After a while she was wiping at something wet that had spilled on his face. She was saying something to him over and over, and if she would stop wiping his face he could understand what it was. . . . It was a faraway voice and it made him feel safe and warm, and it was a nice dream to be having since she was there too and it was warm there and he was tired.

He awoke and Mike was pulling him up, through the passenger door. Avelyn was standing in the drive and there was blood on her sweater and her hands. There was blood on the side of his face and it was sticky. The car was lying in the ditch. "You okay, buddy boy? Gawddamn . . . you all right?" Mike asked.

"I'm all right." His head ached. Mike started to say something else but he stopped. He looked puzzled. Jimbo could not remember seeing him so puzzled. They were all standing in the glare of Mike's pickup.

"Was that you?" Jimbo asked him.

Mike shook his head. His eyes were still narrowed with the questions on his mind, but he didn't ask them.

"Who the hell ran us off the road then?"

"I don't know." He was looking at the cut above Jimbo's eye. "You okay?"

"I guess."

"What happened here? What the hell happened?"

"We were coming back from the Pines and someone ran us off the road," Avelyn said. She wiped around Jimbo's cut with her sweater. "He's going to need stitches."

"Who was shooting?" Jimbo asked.

"What shooting?"

"We heard shots."

"What fucking shots?" Mike walked quickly to his glove compartment. He grabbed the flashlight and shone it into the pasture, working the beam back and forth. Then he hurtled the barbed-wire fence. Deacon followed after him.

"You all right?" Jimbo asked her.

"What're they looking for? Jimbo? Why are they stopped like that?"

"They're moving now." They watched them, and pretty soon they stopped again.

"They shot our calves, didn't they?" she said.

"Come here." He held her hands. They were cold and trembling. They watched the light bob in the darkness at Mike's feet as the flashlight dangled from his fingers.

"Are you sure you're all right?" she asked him.

They were coming back and he dropped her hands. "How many?"

Mike shone the light on the two of them, from one to the other. "It's too dark out there. We found four." He walked past them to the truck. "Come on. Get in. I'll drop these guys back at the house and run you down to Saint Vincent's, buddy boy."

Avelyn slid in beside Mike, then Deacon, then Jimbo. Mike rubbed his face with his hands. He unrolled the window and turned away from them all to look out. Then he started the truck, his mouth hard. Jimbo could imagine the thin white line of anger that had showed on his upper lip during that Cattleman's Association meeting, could imagine the whitened knuckles as he gripped the steering wheel and fought to control everything in him that wanted to explode through the windshield with rage — though he couldn't guess whether Avelyn was part of that rage, or if it was all the calves and the coal and the town. And apparently she couldn't either, for she said, "I'm sorry, Michael. Maybe if I'd been here I could have done something."

"May if *I'd* been here," he said.

He drove the quarter mile to the house and rested his forehead and arms on the steering wheel as Deacon and Avelyn got out.

"You boys want company?"

"Get some sleep, hon. We'll be all right."

"You want me to take him?"

Mike looked up from the steering wheel. "I'll take him."

"Be careful, Michael."

Mike nodded and pulled the truck around. She watched it out of sight.

CHAPTER 19

JIMBO WOKE UP with Avelyn throwing open the windows of his stuffy bedroom. He had needed eleven stitches, and they had not gotten home until after four in the morning. His head hurt badly.

"Morning," he said thickly.

"Afternoon, you mean. It's one o'clock." She had put a tray of biscuits and gravy on the chair, and she picked it up and laid it at the foot of the bed without looking at him. She obviously felt awkward. Jimbo sat up, propping the pillows behind him. He felt rumpled to the core, and his eye was swollen so he could not see clearly. He pulled the tray into his lap. She was still standing there, near the bed, looking off somewhere. He pushed at one of the biscuits with his fork.

"They shot six calves in all," she said. "Mike's out there with the backhoe burying them now. The sheriff was here this morning, but there wasn't much he could do."

"No. I guess there wouldn't be."

"Maybe that will be the end of it."

"Maybe." He ate a mouthful.

"Mike got the car out of the ditch. It's dinged up but it's not as bad as all that, really. The windshield's all right."

"Miraculous."

"Deacon's pounding out the dents now."

"I've missed a helluva lot for one morning." He was running

his fork around his plate, scooping up the gravy. She came over and looked at his bandage then. She felt the bump with her fingertips and the pain stopped and something in him said *watch out now.* He pulled back. "That hurts." He forked in the last little bit. "Thanks for bringing up breakfast. Makes a thwack in the noggin almost worth it."

"I'll bet." She carried the tray back down. He watched her leave and remembered kissing her, remembered her slimness and her eyes, alert, bright, with those long soft lashes. Then he pulled himself out of bed and decided that was enough remembering.

After he had dressed, Jimbo drove into town for the baling wire. Mike had decided to cut two hay crops that summer, and the irrigation had already been shut off to give the grass a chance to dry. His eye had gotten used to seeing through the swelling, and the driving took his mind off his headache. There was a construction crew blacktopping the Canyon Creek road coming out of town. The tar smell was thick and acrid and the gravel slapped at the bottom of the truck.

He parked in front of Ziegler's Hardware. "What the hell happened to you, Jimbo?" Ziggy Ziegler asked him. He was in his familiar black apron with the rule in the pocket.

"Little car accident."

"That's a dandy shiner."

"Glad you like it, Zig. You got that baling wire we ordered?"

He went into the back room to get it. Jimbo called after him, "Since when are they paving Canyon Creek?"

Ziggy came back out with the order. "Ain't that somethin'? Started 'er yesterday."

"Didn't hear a thing about it."

"I guess I didn't neither. Be nice to have it paved."

"I kind of liked it the way it was. Bound to get all sorts of high school kids zipping up there in their roadsters with their sweet young things in hand, big night at the lake."

"I guess there'll be that, all right," Ziggy said, filling out the charge. "Need it paved for the coal trucks though."

"What coal trucks are those?"

Ziggy looked up, lowering his glasses. "Coal trucks for the mine they're opening on Paxton's place."

"Not this summer."

"That's what I hear."

"Christ, Zig. He hasn't even moved off yet."

Ziegler turned the slip around for Jimbo to sign. "Well, that's what I hear, anyway. Full steam ahead."

"I'll say. Where the hell are all those guys going to stay?"

"Setting up a trailer camp south of town is what I'm told. Then of course there's Lloyd's place. Hate to see him leave, him and Carol. They been here forever."

"More than sixty years."

"Nice folks, all right. I guess your granddad and Lloyd's dad was the first two into this country. First two to settle." Ziggy leaned back on the shelves behind him. "Ole Vic, I watched him on the television that time. He talked about them old days. God, I laughed. He was some man, your grandpa. I was sweet on Willa when I first moved here. Your Aunt Willa . . ." Ziggy smiled affectionately. "Ole Vic, he brought his business to me right from the start. Well. Imagine this coal mine'll be good for business. That's one thing. Hate to see Lloyd and Carol move on, though. Hate to see that."

"Sad day, all right."

"Miss your grandpa, too. I sure do. Oh, he was a needler. That day on the television, he come through town after, and I told him, 'Vic, don't you forget where you come from, just 'cause you're a celebrity. Don't you forget.' He tells me he'll still get his wire from ole Zig. Had four or five people watch that show right from this store." Ziggy was smiling at the memory.

"Wish I'd seen it."

"Yep. Never saw a man with so many friends as your grandpa." The smile darkened and Ziggy said, "Don't see how your brother Mike could've turned so many friends against him so quick." He looked Jimbo in the eyes. "Heard you had a little trouble at your place."

"Last night."

"Hate to hear folks got to resort to things like that."

"What folks is that?"

"Well, *I* don't know. Small town, you just hear about things."

"Yeah. Well. See you around, Zig."

"You boys take care of yourselves." He said it without a smile, as if he had reason to mean it. Sure, Zig, Jimbo thought. I'll just bet you'll hate to see Lloyd and Carol move out. I'll just bet.

When he got back to the ranch, Sam Benson was there. He and Mike were sitting on the rail of the arena, watching Avelyn exercise Pasha. Sam was smoking a cigarette.

"Pick up the wire?" Mike asked.

Jimbo nodded. "Afternoon, Sam. What brings you out?"

"Just visitin'. Heard about the trouble." He inhaled his cigarette smoke and when he spoke the smoke came out his nose. "That's some shiner."

"Isn't it, though?"

"Got no idea who it might've been, eh?"

"Whoever it was had headlights on his truck that were three feet wide," Jimbo said. "Mike, I thought you were a tracker. I thought you could track anything that moved. Couldn't you find a tread mark of the mad calf-killer's truck and track the mother to his lair?"

"Maybe if they weren't pavin' that road," Mike said.

"I saw that. How'd they start that up so fast?"

Sam said, "County commissioners came up with the funds outta their magic little box. I mean right now. Titanic wants a road, they get a road. All three of them loggerheads is prob'ly on company payroll. One of them seats is up for election in the fall, Jimmy. Sure'd like you to think about running."

"Going to grad school." Jimbo smiled. "Somehow I don't think the McKenzie name would be that great an asset these days."

"Oh, this thing'll blow over," Sam said. "Lots of folks don't want that coal company 'round here. Sure'd like to see you run, Jimmy. Vic always said you'd be the politician in the family."

"That's you, Sam."

"Wish you'd think about it. When this calf business blows over, there's gonna be lots of folks on your side."

"I'm not sure I'm committed to a side, Sam."

Sam cocked an eye toward him. "No? Well, don't wait too long. Them coalhounds ain't stoppin' at the road. There's an energy crisis back East, or ain't you heard?"

Jimbo smiled. "Yes, occasionally we pick up bits and pieces of the twentieth century here in Kearney."

Sam had finished his cigarette and he flicked it into the dirt. "They're buildin' those two coal-fired generating plants down in Gillette already. You better believe them coalhounds work fast. You know how much water them outfits use? Shit. But you mention water tables around 'em and they draw a look blanker than God gave a mule."

Jimbo said, "I was down there a couple of weeks ago. God, what a mess."

"They can do what they will to the damn town," Sam said. "She's a goner. But we ain't got that kinda *water* in this state. That's what they gotta face up to. You ask one of them coal execs what happens when drought comes, and he'll mumble and shuffle his feet and talk about averages. You don't talk about averages; you talk about extremes. Droughts are gonna *come*, all right, and who gets the water? Farmers for irrigatin'? Or them generatin' plants? Not enough for both. Wish you'd think about running for one of them county commissioner seats, Jimmy."

He remembered some of Papa Vic's stories about drought: . . . *Don't even think about callin' this a drought, Jimmy. You flat don't know what a drought is. I lived through a couple or three, worst one back in nineteen hundred eighteen. Lasted two years, and we seen more coloreds in Canyon Creek than we seen rainfalls. Weren't but one colored fella, ole Buck Parsons, and him laid off after that first dry summer. Good hand too, ole Buck. Them colored cowboys was tough as leather. Thing about nineteen eighteen was the grasshoppers. Hoppers in a dust storm make a fella believe in hell right quick. Hide the sun for days and days. I never hated one of Gawd's critters, but why He ever cast His love down on a grasshopper plumb escapes me, Jimmy. Must be a fisherman is my only guess. A trout'll flat eat a hopper, and back in eighteen trout in the Tongue was gettin' so big they'd been eatin' hay if any'd been growin'. Them hoppers come straight from the devil, clackin' through the air, snappin' 'gainst your home, eatin' the grass so's to drive the cattle to chewin' the fence line just to keep the memory of somethin' in their mouths sides their tongues. Lord, we got good springs which made Canyon Creek luckier than most. Damn sight luckier. Even with them grasshoppers in nineteen eighteen, a cow could eat. Might have to eat thistle, but a cow'll eat thistle if it comes down to it, and a thistle'll live through anything, even a cow. Even the blight of the hoppers. Thistles plumb laugh at a grasshopper. Lord, I learned to love a thistle. Can't kill one with a hatchet, never mind drought. And if you think a cow won't eat one, you should've been here when them hungry cows was chewin' on barbed wire just 'cause it felt like thistle . . .*

"The way I figure it," Sam was saying, "the way to stop this goddamn mine from coming in here this summer is to make an issue of the water rights. You talk water rights and folks sit up and take notice. You got springs on this land, am I right?"

Mike nodded. "Six."

"Well that's the ticket, then. Coal's porous, see. Can be an aquifer. And if it ain't actually the coal that's the aquifer, chances are it's sedimentary rock that's down there with the coal — sandstone or limestone or that. When you've got a nonporous rock like slate on either side, it traps the groundwater and by God there's a spring. Here's the thing though, Mike. Once that coal seam is broken into, once it's mined — which is just what they've got in mind for this summer — them springs all the way down the valley dry up. Your six springs, Hepp Fox's springs, Turner's, Miller's, right down the valley. If that coal vein *is* the aquifer, and we can show it is, well, then any mine Titanic plans on digging up at Paxton's is infringing on your water rights. Those springs're your property, Mike. We might be able to get a court injunction to stop this thing 'fore it gets started. That's the only time there is to stop it. Once them springs dry up, once that coal pit starts suckin' in water, there ain't no getting it back. Not now. Not ever."

"I don't know about a court injunction," Mike said.

"We can try, anyway. We can try it."

"I don't know about getting involved with the courts. . . . I don't much care to."

Sam gave him a hard look, and Mike answered it evenly.

"It's how to stop them. It's the only way to stop them. You want to stop them, don't you?"

"I want to run my ranch. That's what I want."

. . . We made it through them dry years 'cause this is good land, and we got good springs. Springs don't feel a drought. Don't know why. Tapwater from Gawd, them springs are. Lotta folks pulled out, but if you had a spring, you had 'er licked. Ate lotsa porkypines in nineteen eighteen. Ate so many them two years, I don't reckon I'd partake if you put one in front of me today. Taste pretty poorly, not like a fat possum. But they'll live through a drought same as a thistle, and if a cow can eat thistle, I guess I can eat a porky, and you could too, though a man with a choice oughta steer clear. It's them springs that can lick a drought, Jimmy, and don't forget it. This is damn good land if you hunker down and hang tough . . .

Sam was saying, "They'll grant us a temporary restraining order. I'm sure of that."

Mike looked down uneasily. "Just don't much like the idea of getting involved with a bunch of lawyers."

"I don't know another way, Mike."

"Don't much like it."

"Unless you *want* to sell —"

"No. I don't want. That's not what I want, Sam. Just don't much want to end up in court half the time." Mike drew the back of his hand across his cheek. "What d'ya think, buddy boy?"

He thought about it, surprised Mike would ask. "You can't risk losing the springs."

"Nope." Then: "Well, let's think on it."

"That's all I'm askin'," Sam said.

"I 'preciate your advice, Sam."

"There's lots at stake for the rest of us, too." He hopped off the fence. "Put some liver on that eye, Jimbo."

"Sambo?" Mike said.

"Yep?"

"Never told you. That was a nice little speech you gave at that meeting. 'Preciate that, too."

"Sorry more didn't come of it." Sam nodded toward the bared mound where Mike had buried the calves. "Let's see this thing stops here. Let's see to that."

Mike said nothing.

"Mike?"

"Come on your land; shoot your stock when nobody's home. . . . Ain't an easy thing to let it stop at."

"Didn't say it'd be easy. Said let's see that it does. We got a bigger fight here."

"That's a big enough fight for me, Sam."

"No, it ain't. No, it ain't, Mike." They looked at each other. Then Sam left.

CHAPTER 20

THE WEATHER TURNED hot and the grass dried. They cut it, turned it, baled it, and stacked it over the next two weeks. Sitting in a mower from first light to dusk — there's your reason to sell, thought Jimbo. That's what will drive a man out as soon as Titanic's millions. Dry and hot, the sun headache-bright even through the Polaroid glasses, up and back, the blades cutting and clacking, turning up the local radio show and the numbing country music full-blast to be heard over the rumbling diesel engine. Up and back, the pasture yawning beyond the one clean swath; the hay slivers working their way into your hair and under your collar, the dust parching your mouth until you chewed at your spit. Then's when you should make your offer, Thorndike, Jimbo thought. At the end of a day like that. He'd sell, all right. But you'd have to get him as he stepped out of the mower, when the whole stifling affair was still fresh upon him. Man forgets pain. Man can't remember real pain, or what mother would ever bear a second child? Up and back, hour after hour, the only breaks coming when you rousted out a badger and could try a shot with the pistol — cocking back the hammer of the .45 and blasting at the scurrying bodies as the tractor bounced along, often missing by thirty feet and more. Or sometimes taking a shot at a sage hen, too dumb even to move, though safe enough in the face of that kind of marksmanship. Then at the end of the day soaking your itching skin in the bath, drinking three cold beers before you even reached for the soap and still not getting clean — that hay dust working its way into everywhere and then staying — so that for two weeks you felt like your underwear was woolen. It was a hell of a time, the haying.

They finished by the Fourth of July, which left them two days before the rodeo weekend to practice for the pony express race. Avelyn had been working with the quarter horses, galloping them a mile every day. They could run, all right, and she could ride them. But the race would be won and lost during the exchanges. So they practiced the little trick Mike had devised as a boy.

The temporary restraining order came through on Friday. Sam Benson called Mike with the news. "Court date's set for the thirty-first," he said.

"What's that mean?"

"Means that's when we'll learn if we get our permanent injunction."

"We got a chance?"

"Sure we do."

"Thorndike called last night," Mike said after a pause. "Upped his offer some."

"Did he now?"

"Eighteen million."

"Holy shit."

"Holy shit is right."

"We got him scared, Mike. We got Titanic running scared."

" 'Pears so."

Sam whistled into the phone. "Eighteen million. I'd say that's what she's worth. I'd say they're offering what she's worth. By God, we've got 'em scared . . ." There was a pause. "Mike?"

"Yeah?"

"You didn't take it?"

Mike breathed a laugh. "Told him to go shit in his hat."

"You're a good boy, Michael. You're a damn fine boy."

Saturday morning of rodeo weekend broke with the same blue, high sky that had been with them the past two weeks. From his bedroom, Jimbo could look out on the south pasture, where the water was teeming through the irrigation ditches again, running down from Custer Lake, watering the shoots that would become the second hay crop. The night air had already been warmed by the first hour of sunlight, and it was going to be scorching at the fairgrounds.

Avelyn was nervous and excited cooking breakfast, burning the bacon and destroying the fried eggs as she turned them. Mike was out hitching the trailer to the pickup. She turned and smiled resignedly at Jimbo, part of her hair having fallen in front of her eyes. "I'm a wreck. Go wake up Deacon for me, will you?"

She was wearing a black tapered shirt with green stitching and pearl-colored snaps, the top two of which were open. Jimbo tossed her an apron. "Before you yolk yourself," he said.

"Oh, damn. The coffee. Get out of here so I can think."

He went over to the bunkhouse and knocked on the door. "Get up, gimp."

There was a muffled response, and he went in. The curtains were drawn but the light from the ceiling was on. Deacon was propped up against the far wall with a bottle of bourbon in his hand, and an empty one lying by his knee. His eyes looked as if they had been glazed with a sugar solution.

"Mornin'."

"Jesus Christ, Deac . . ."

Deacon lifted the bourbon to his lips and took a gulp, then he wiped his mouth and screwed the top back on, setting it beside him with a pat. His movements were jerky and careless. "Is it mornin'?"

"It's eight o'clock." Jimbo was taken aback. "This is a first," he finally noted.

"God, I'm drunk. Let's get drunk."

"I'm not sure I could catch up."

"Sure you could. You always been a real fast runner, buck."

"So what's the occasion?"

Deacon grinned and went through the ritual of opening his bottle, winking, then tossing Jimbo a letter from his shirt pocket when he'd finished his swig. It was an invitation to Deacon's son's wedding. "Sugarbabe brought me this last night. Come in the mail."

"I didn't know you had a son."

"Yup. A big son."

"I didn't even know you'd been *married*."

Deacon was staring vacantly out the open door. "Deacon?" Jimbo asked. "*Were* you married?"

"Course I was married, gooseturd."

Jimbo smiled to look at him. He was sort of rocking sideways along the wall. It was obviously an effort for him to focus.

"Dumb bitch didn't like travelin' around after the rodeos. Couldn't stand the idear of me makin' it with all them broads on the road, and took off 'fore the kid was borned . . . 'fore the kid even showed, for Chrissakes. . . . Fact is, I don't reckon she even knowed she was pregnant. Called me up two months later and says we're divorced fair and proper in Nevada, and that she's gettin' remarried, but she's gonna have a little Deacon. I tol' her that's just nice, just be sure to have little Deacon in Nevada and keep 'im there. She did, too."

Deacon nodded and smiled and took another drink. "Betcha she never even tol' that other guy she's gonna have a kid till it's too late an' he hasn't had time yet to add up the months. Know, buck? I never ever rode in Nevada after that. Thought she might come down and leave the kid in my truck with a note or somethin' . . . or a gawddamn diaper bill. Shit. Cost me a shot at the title one year when I missed Carson City. What the fuck're you smilin' for?"

"You going?"

"Goin'? Who're you kiddin'? Goin'? Paaah!"

"You aren't going?"

"Paaaaah!" He spat. He thumbed his nose.

"You ought to go."

"Paaah . . ." He was tiring; so he just gave a fed-up wave of the hand.

"Don't you want to? He's your son, isn't he?"

Deacon pulled his old baseball cap farther onto his head. "Course I want to. He's my boy, ain't he?"

"Now that you put it that way . . ."

"Awww, shut your trap, buck. You're a wise guy."

"You should go then. He wants you to."

"Gawd, you're ignorant."

Jimbo smiled. Deacon's head lolled from side to side. "He don't want me to. Gawd, if I showed up at his weddin', he'd plumb shit . . ." Deacon started to laugh, but it turned to a cough, then a hacking cough. When it had played itself out he wiped his lips and took a drink of the water jug beside him. "He jest sent this invite so's I'd go get drunk and feel bad and maybe send a nice present. Send some gawddamn money that I ain't got." Deacon held his grizzled face in his hands. "Gawd, I do feel bad."

"You look bad."

"Yeah? Do I look like three miles of bad road?"

"At least."

"You look like a bucket of shit."

Jimbo walked back to the doorway. "Well, who the hell are we going to get to take your place today for the race, have you thought of that?"

"No, I ain't thought of that," he mimicked. "You ain't gettin' no one, 'cause I told the little woman I's gonna help her, an' that's jest what I'm gonna do. Now leave me be."

"You can't even walk."

"Like hell." Deacon put both hands on the bunk bed beside him and began to claw himself to his feet as if his legs were paralyzed. He let go and fell over on his bum hip like a one-legged toy soldier. "You shut up!" he warned. "My leg's asleep." He furiously massaged his thigh, mumbling, "Wake up, wake up." After a minute he tried again. This time he made it to his feet and stood propped against the wall. "There. Fuck you."

"Deac, it'd be easier if I just solicit help from somebody else —"

"Solicit shit!" Deacon stepped toward Jimbo, and suddenly he was stumbling and kind of moaning from low in his gut. He grabbed his shirt on his way by, cursing Jimbo, his breath hot and stinking, stumbling and nearly knocking him over. Deacon dove for the door and disappeared off the doorstep. All that was left in view were his feet. They began to flipper-kick as he heaved.

After several minutes he crawled back, laying his cheek on the doorstep like a poisoned dog come home to die. "That felt good," he said. Then he passed out.

The entrance to the rodeo grounds was glutted with horse trailers waiting to turn into the entrants' parking area. A Coors truck was parked behind the grandstand and a group of cowboys were gathered by its tailgate, where tubs of ice held the beer. Girls in brightly colored shirts and jeans that were cut just to the bottom of their boots were passing out programs as the trucks crept past single file. Mike found a place for the four-horse trailer against the rail at the far side of the arena, and Jimbo, pulling the single-horse trailer with the Travelall, followed him around. They unloaded the horses. All around them cowboys and cowgirls were exercising their horses, trotting them, walking them, their contestant numbers pinned to their backs or their pant legs. They wore new, high-crowned cowboy hats of brushed beaver — the men in browns and beiges, the women in blacks, purples, greens, and yellows — and fancy silver buckles on their belts, hand-tooled with Bobby or Earl or Debbie carved into the back. The saddles were beautiful, heavy and ornate, the leathers polished to a shine, draped with straps and thongs and double-cinched. The rope horses all had their manes cropped, and their tails were either tied up or trimmed. They were handsome animals — dun-coloreds, bays, sorrels, roans, dapple-grays — and their coats glistened in the bright sunlight.

Avelyn and Denny each walked two of the quarter horses to stretch their legs. Mike tied his gray horse to the trailer and leaned against the pickup, tying a new pair of reins to his bridle, the hair on his thick forearms sun-bleached below the short-sleeved white shirt. His hat was back on his head so that the sun glinted off his dark glasses. Deacon had been asleep in the back of the Travelall, drooling against the window. He crawled out, rubbing his eyes. "I'm gettin' a hot dog," he announced, disappearing into the growing crowd.

Mike grinned. "He's goin' off like an elephant to die."

Jimbo was brushing Mike's gray horse. "You going to carry a second loop?"

Mike shook his head. "He'll be twitchy enough in an arena for the first time without an extra thirty feet of grass tied alongside. What the hell. Forty-two guys entered, a man misses his first loop ain't gonna be in the money anyhow."

"That's true."

Mike took out his penknife and cut the new rein down to match his old set. Jimbo said, "Think I'll walk around some. It's been about eight years since I've been to one of these. Can I get you a beer?"

"Sure. Be just nice."

Without Mike there to trigger the connection, Jimbo could pass among the scattered groups without remark. He was grateful for that. He recognized a lot of faces. It was a working man's rodeo, the contestants coming from neighboring towns and ranches, nonprofessionals, there to have a good time and maybe win some money, but mostly to visit with friends. Jimbo had his number pinned to his right leg, and he shuffled his feet and hooked his thumb in his front pockets and smiled inside at his play-acting. The ground was dry and the dust kicked up easily.

There was another beer truck behind the bucking chutes, and Jimbo bought two, then wandered over to a group of cowboys gathered in the shade of the announcer's stand. Deacon was in the midst of them holding court. Someone had bought him a beer, and it had freed his tongue and smoothed out some of his movements, and the young cowboys in the bucking events were well pleased to be listening to a former world champion, drunk or no.

There was a commotion behind the bucking chutes as they drove in the first go-round of bareback broncs, poles clattering, cowboys scrambling, and hooves kicking against the wooden rails. The first bucking horse had balked shy of his chute, and the corral boss cursed loudly, prodding him with a hot-shot. The horse bolted forward with a snort, and they slammed down the gate behind it. Then the next gate and the next gate and the next gate, until the horses were set.

The grandstands were packed now and the colors were ridden in. The grand marshal was introduced over the loudspeaker, and then the rodeo queen rode in with her court, silk sashes tied diagonally across gaudy fringed outfits. Everyone moved toward the arena. Jimbo caught Deacon's eye and waved him over.

"You all right?"

"Settin' just nice," Deacon said. His eyes were terrible.

"Come on. Our event's right after the bareback. You sure you're all right?"

"Sure I am." He belched. "Ate a hot dog."

"I smell it. Come on, let's go."

Avelyn was relieved to see them. The other contestants were milling around — Hepp Fox, who was riding Tiny Turner's horses, Fred Johnson from Big Horn, and Pete Miller, who'd played basketball with Mike in high school. They leaned on the fence and watched the bareback, relaxed and smoking.

"Have you seen Mike anywhere?" Avelyn asked, searching the crowd.

"I've got a beer here for him. He's probably down by the calf pens. He's up right after this." Jimbo saw her concern and smiled. "Don't worry. He's watching."

"You'd think he'd come down and wish us luck." Her eyes were alert and darted nervously, but there was no fear in them. "Think he bet against us?"

"Brother Mike? He knows his horses better than that."

"I'll give you that." Avelyn flashed a grin at him. The bareback was over, and the arena was being cleared. The announcement was made introducing the riders of the pony express race. Avelyn climbed into the saddle of the big sorrel gelding, and Denny and Deacon led the other three horses out into the arena. Jimbo handed her the riding crop, and she slipped it under her arm. "Whack him once at the start, then put it away." She nodded. "Look for Denny, and don't bring them in too fast."

"All right."

"That's all. Go on."

Avelyn spun the sorrel around in a couple of quick turns, then trotted the horse toward the starting line. She was hatless, her hair tied back in a ponytail. The horse snorted and was ducking its head from the noise of the crowd, and she stroked its neck, talking to it softly. She pulled it up beside Hepp Fox, who was also on a beautiful sorrel. Pete Miller was on the outside, and the Big Horn man was on the inside. Avelyn sat easily as the gelding twitched beneath her, turning his head this way and that to relax him. Then the starter raised his gun. Taking the crop in her hand, she steadied the gelding's head. The crowd quieted, then the shot sounded, and the horses bolted forward in unison.

The horses ran to the first turn four abreast, the dust billowing behind and settling slowly like the wake of a boat. It was a half-mile track, and on the backstretch the two sorrels inched ahead of the other two, the black of Avelyn's shirt showing first. Deacon led the black horse they called Rooney, Denny's bulldogging horse, away from the rail, to the edge of the track. Jimbo and Denny stepped into the middle of the track, their arms raised. They had drawn the position farthest down, so looking back up the track, to the far turn, to the top of the homestretch, they could see the other handlers preparing their next horses as the riders bore down on them. Avelyn had a lead on Hepp, the two sorrels kicking up the dust butter-thick, one behind the other, sending the waiting horses into fits as they galloped by. Avelyn slowed the sorrel, homing in on Denny. Jimbo was shouting, "Whoa . . . whoa . . . whoa . . . ," arms upraised, ready to grab the sorrel. She passed Hepp's handlers, closer, closer, still mounted, watching only Denny, when suddenly she was upon them and he grabbed her under the left arm and right leg, lifting her off the moving horse, spinning, and in one fluid motion setting her on Rooney. The reins were tied there on its neck, and before she had even grabbed them Deacon had swatted the black horse and she was on her way. It was one slick exchange, and Jimbo, dragging the sorrel to a stop, saw her gallop away free and clear, with nearly a hundred-yard lead over Hepp. There was no way anyone but a professional could have jumped off of one horse and pulled himself up on the next one in the conventional way as quickly. The trick just required a light rider and a good strong middle man.

Jimbo tied the sorrel to the rail as Deacon got their third

horse, a bay. "Run, you Rooney-coon-tuney!" Deacon yelled. He paled. "No more hollerin', buck," he whispered. "God. I damn near fainted."

"Don't faint."

"Won't holler. Won't faint."

Avelyn held her lead coming into the homestretch. Hepp Fox was second, then Pete Miller, with Johnson far behind, his second horse having bucked free of one of his aides. Old Rooney was tiring, and she gave him a couple of light whacks with the crop. She ran past the other teams, toward Denny's upraised arms, starting to ease up but still coming in too fast. Rooney bumped hard into Jimbo so that he had to throw his arms around its neck to keep from falling. He fumbled for the reins as it veered toward the center of the track, Denny following, reaching for Avelyn, who was poised in the stirrups.

"Haul him down, buck! Haul him down!" Deacon cursed, bringing the bay toward them. Jimbo finally grasped the bridle, and Avelyn leaped to Denny, who swung her behind to the bay, which Deacon had positioned perfectly. She rode off just as Hepp Fox was coming in, comfortably ahead of the others. Hepp leaped off the right side of his horse while it was still on the run, grabbing the saddlehorn of his waiting horse. Once he had a grip, Tiny Turner released it and gave it a whack, the horse galloping off with Hepp still hanging from its left side. Hepp bounced once, twice, then swung himself up by the horn gracefully. It was a quick exchange, and Hepp had picked up ground, though still trailing by some fifty yards.

Deacon untied Pasha, the big black filly. Jimbo was tying Rooney to the rail, wiping its wet neck. "Big furry thing just crawled out from under my hat, creepin' down my face," Deacon said, wide-eyed. "Gawd, it was foul. Know what it was?"

"You okay?"

Deacon shaded his eyes from the sun. "Thought it was a caterpillar. It weren't. Was a drop of my own sweat. Only it weren't a drop. More like a gob."

"Look at that bay run. That's a nice running horse."

Deacon tucked his chin in and tried to belch, but nothing came. "Don't make me run around again."

She was still ahead. Denny and Jimbo moved to the center of the track. Deacon held Pasha. She brought the bay in slower this time — Hepp forty yards back, whipping at the flank of his horse — and Jimbo grabbed it by the bridle. Avelyn jumped to Denny, who grabbed her and swung. But the black filly lurched sideways. Jimbo saw Deacon buckle downward, vomiting in a gushing fountain. Avelyn missed the saddle, grabbing Pasha by the neck as it shied sideways, the filly's hindquarters swinging around and knocking Deacon into the dust and his own mess. Denny grabbed a stirrup. Pasha sidestepped into the fence and rebounded like a billiard ball, knocking Avelyn off balance so that her feet flew underneath the skittish horse. She hung there like a pendant. Then there was a thundering of hooves and a yell from the crowd. Hepp Fox galloped in, leaping off his horse to make the exchange. Pasha shied again at the noise. Avelyn was hanging from her neck, trying to work a leg over the filly's back. Pasha was sidestepping down the track, Denny holding her by the stirrup. Suddenly Hepp raced by with the lead.

As Hepp's horse passed her, Pasha bolted forward, breaking Denny's grip. She was chasing the lead horse. Avelyn still hung underneath, one foot over the top of the saddle.

"Jump!" Jimbo yelled, but he suddenly realized the filly was in a full gallop, going too fast. Avelyn clung to the mane. The crowd went quiet as she tried to pull herself up. She slapped one hand toward the saddle, its smooth leather lacking a grip. Then she grabbed the mane with both hands and eased herself up far enough to work her leg over the saddle. She lay flush against the filly's neck, mounted now, trying to find the stirrups, the crop still in her teeth, slapping the filly with her reins. There was a great cheer as she rounded the turn.

Hepp broke into the backstretch and looked back to see if he were alone. Pasha had sight of the horse ahead and lengthened her strides, the black tail flying behind. The black of Avelyn's shirt was against the filly's back, so that as they came up the backstretch it was impossible to tell where the one stopped and the other began, Avelyn's own hair flying out behind, the two of them working in unison. Ahead, Hepp whipped his horse three times and leaned into the final turn.

The crowd sensed it would be close and the noise began to build. They rounded the far turn, the dust coughing up behind, the filly's nose against the leader's tail. They held that position through the turn, Hepp cleverly keeping his horse in the way of Avelyn's. Avelyn swung Pasha wide, losing half a length. She took the riding crop from her teeth and slapped her once, working her hands up the horse's neck, talking to her now and moving her body to match the horse's stride. The reins were loose and Pasha was running on her own, eyes bulging, flecks of sweat frothing white against her coat. The crowd noise built. Pasha's teeth bared against the bit. There was a tremendous roar as they broke in front of the grandstand, fifty yards to go. She felt the rushing and the heat, heard the screaming. Pasha seemed hardly to touch the ground, soaring, the thundering from the left beside them now and the sounds melding into each other, the cheering and the speed and the hooves, passing under the wire and still not knowing, still not looking up, all those noises disappearing except the one voice — Jimbo's — ringing clearly: "You won! You won! You won!" until that, too, faded behind.

He watched her slow Pasha to a canter around the far turn, and suddenly Denny hoisted him in the air. Jimbo hugged him back. The grandstand buzzed in the aftermath of the finish, and the last two horses came across. He was watching her, unable to take his eyes from her, as she turned the filly and trotted it back. Denny toted him in a silent, circular victory dance, and Deacon still knelt in the dust, soiled and sweat-soaked. The black horse trotted back, its head low, panting, while Avelyn patted its neck. Her face was flushed, glowing. He caught her eye and held it. Then she jumped off Pasha and threw her arms around his neck and kissed him full on the mouth.

CHAPTER 21

THEY DID NOT bother to eat, going straight to the Bison following the rodeo. Mike had won the first go-round of the calf-roping, and Denny took third in the bulldogging, so everyone was in fine spirits. Avelyn was in the front seat, one arm around Mike and the other on Jimbo, leaning across him to whoop out the window as they drove. She looked flushed and perfectly radiant.

The Bison was already jammed when they got there, most of the crowd packed three-deep before the huge wooden bar. The front of it was hand-carved and the top was inlaid with hundreds of silver dollars. On the wall behind the bar were the owner's collection of old spurs, from bizarrely roweled Spanish models to the small, sharply honed ones worn by several past rodeo champions. The walls were shingled inside, and on each shingle was a different Wyoming brand — Flying Hearts, Lazy S's, Double Diamonds. There was a band playing, but no one was dancing yet. The dancing would come later, when the cowboys got their minds off the rodeo and onto other things. But now they were on the rodeo and other rodeos and killing their thirsts. They were seeing men they hadn't seen since last rodeo weekend, and there was much catching up to do.

Mike found a table and ordered a round of tequila. They drank it with salt and lime wedges, toasting Avelyn's race. Jimbo did not much care for the taste of straight tequila, but he ordered the next round so they could toast to Denny and his bulldogging time. Then they had a third round for Mike and his gray horse and the calf-roping. They had forgotten their hunger, and everyone felt wonderful. Tequila can make you forget hunger and most anything else. Jimbo thought of tomorrow's headache as he drank his third, but it was too late then anyway, and the best way was to enjoy it and pay the price later. He could not remember seeing Avelyn in such good spirits, ever. Or maybe it was the way in which he saw her now, or the tequila having silenced the nagging voice that went *watch out* when he looked at her, when he thought about her and the way she had looked on that horse. I had better have another, he thought. It will be a long way down at this rate, and I might just as well enjoy it.

Mike was certainly pleased. "How about that gray horse?" Jimbo asked him. "Is that a horse or is that a horse?"

"That's a horse with four legs, that one."

"Set right up and dropped that calf in its tracks, just like you showed him. By God, you can train a horse." He raised his glass. "To the Great American Cowboy. Alive and well and living in Kearney."

Mike smiled uneasily. "Better slow down there, buddy boy."

"Independent. Self-reliant. Conqueror of the last frontier." He did not know why he had started, but now that he had it seemed to take over by itself, and he was enjoying Mike's uneasiness, and Avelyn, listening, curious. "Who the hell says a man can't take control of his life in his own two hands? Who the hell says the myth is dead?"

"Maybe I should run over for some pizza," Mike said.

"How can the Great American Cowboy eat pizza? Surely you jest. You see? I knew it. He doesn't exist."

"Never mind that. Who wants pizza?"

"Hollywood stuff. The Great American Cowboy was never anything more than a myth, anyway, the last of the white no-mads, looking for something more. Looking for something more to exterminate. What the hell? *Cows* haven't got anything to do with it. What the hell is so romantic about pushing a fucking cow? Exterminating Indians and buffalo — that's what's romantic. So what? So Davy Crockett was the first cowboy. No. Wait. Columbus was the first one. He wiped out a few Injuns. Independent sonofabitch who would have sailed right off the edge of the earth if it weren't for dumb luck."

"Boy, are you full of shit. Who wants some pizza? I'm going."

"Cowboys don't eat pizza. You see? It's a myth."

"How 'bout it, hon? You want to split a large with the works? Denny? Extra cheese?"

"Break my heart, Mike."

"Last chance. I'm takin' orders."

"Hollywood turns the Great American Cowboy into a symbol, and pretty soon everyone starts to believe it. It's fiction. It just so happened the West was the last frontier to go. But it was part of something. It was a natural progression starting back in fourteen ninety-two. It wasn't anything big and special and with a quality, you know . . . something neat . . . something all by itself. It's a great big myth that killed buffalo and wiped out Indians and roamed the range. Freedom. It's all bullshit . . . you listening to this, Mike?"

"No. You want to split a sausage and pepperoni with Denny?"

"Sure. Just listen. The scary thing is that everyone still believes it. All these cowboys around here, all these Saturday night drunks, they all think of themselves as a special strain or something. They all think of themselves as *free*. Independent. Like those first guys. Like maybe Papa Vic was for a while. Or Columbus. Think of that. Think of that sort of freedom. Jesus Christ, you can't even imagine it. But all these bullshitters think of themselves like that, when they're just a part. They're just a part, like everyone else. That other stuff is gone. Part of the myth. You're *labeled* a cowboy, but you're not the symbol. You think you are, but you're not."

"Great. I'm leaving."

"Wait. In a second. You understand? You're just a part, the same way as the corn farmers in Iowa are just a part. That bugs you, doesn't it? A cowboy and a corn farmer part of the same thing. But you are. I'm not talking about you, Mike; I'm talking about the Great American Cowboy. He doesn't roam the range anymore. He isn't free. He's married to his land the same as any old corn farmer. So what's so romantic about it? That's what I want to know. You work from a tractor and bitch about prices the same as any old farmer."

"Nobody said it was romantic. Who the hell's saying it's romantic but you, buddy boy?"

He turned to Avelyn. "Well, isn't it? Would you ever, in your wildest dreams, have married a corn farmer from Iowa?"

She laughed. "Did Gary Cooper ever play a corn farmer?"

"Another Westerner. Is that what Mike is, your Gary Cooper surrogate?"

"The best I could do."

"Can I go now?" Mike asked.

"I thought cowboys were drinkers. I thought at rodeos they sat down and drank. Really, this is going to wind up a damn depressing night. You don't eat pizza." Mike smiled, then got up and left. Jimbo was starting to feel rotten. He looked over to Avelyn. "You know what's funny?"

"You are."

"No. What's funny is that cowboys used to be on the very edge of the frontier. Forward-lookers. Now cowboys are backward-lookers. They're on the rear edge now, tugging like hell to keep from being bypassed, or passed over. They don't care about being left behind, but they don't much want to be exterminated."

"I don't think I like that concept," she said. "Don't be so morbid, Jimbo. Tonight isn't a night to be morbid. It's a wonderful night. We're celebrating."

"I am morbid. I feel rotten," he said, and laid his head on his folded arms till Mike came back with the pizza. Eating made him feel better and beer lifted his spirits again. It was smoky in the bar and some of the couples had started to dance.

Mike said, "Let's go over to the Legion, eh? Maybe watch Iker cut a rug?" Mike forced out his stomach. "He'll dance, won't he? Big ole gut. Partner can't get near him. And them little toothpick legs of his . . . sweatin' like a pig on a spit."

"Ike's a good dancer," Avelyn said.

"Sure he is. Let's go see him. I like to see that Iker sweat. Big ole stain under his arms near down to the waist. Let's go say 'hey' to Iker. Want to, buddy boy?"

"I don't care. Sure."

"Now you're talking. Come on, Denny. Come on, big guy. Where's Deac?"

"He passed out up in Tommy's apartment."

"Let's go then. That gimp can't dance anyhow."

Mike got up, and they edged their way through the bar and outside. The air was clear and cool and the bar sounds filtered into the street in a gay, pleasant way. There were street sounds, too, but they were harsher — whooping from a passing truck, boots clomping on the wooden sidewalk, tires screeching from a stop. The American Legion Club was two buildings down, and there was a group of cowboys standing outside, smoking and drinking their beers out of the heat and stuffiness. It was crowded inside and loud and very smoky. A country-and-western band was playing from a platform, and there was dancing. The large dance floor was bordered on three sides by square wooden tables with maroon Formica tops. They found a booth in the back and ordered drinks.

Mike took off his hat and danced with Avelyn. There were a lot of old couples on the floor, doing the two-step to a slow Hank Williams tune, dancing with mirrorlike precision. Their steps were small and they wasted very little movement. The younger couples were flashier and moved around the floor more quickly, but the old ones moved as one with each other and with the music, as if from memory. The next song was faster, and Mike and Avelyn spun and broke away from each other, jitter-bugging, hands folding and unfolding, Avelyn light and smooth on her feet. Effortless. Jimbo watched her move. Ike Jessup was there, too, the sweat glistening off his cheeks and staining his shirt as Mike had predicted.

Their drinks came, and afterward Jimbo danced with Avelyn. He was shaky on his feet, but she was so easy to lead that he felt fine. They danced several dances and then stumbled through a polka trying not to trip anyone.

When they sat back down, Mike had ordered a fresh round

of drinks. He was drinking bourbon. "You dance like a post, buddy boy," he said.

"I know it. Sorry, Avelyn."

"You were fine. Don't listen to him. Come on, everyone. No more arguments. This is fun. We're celebrating the rodeo."

"You were fine," Mike said. "You were both fine. There's fat Ike. Isn't Ike fine? Hey, Ike! Iker!"

Ike turned and saw him and at first stayed where he was. But Mike called him again and he came over. "Havin' a fun weekend, Iker?"

"Not bad," Ike said.

"Havin' a grand ole weekend to match that belly of yours? Just grand, Iker? Would you say that?"

"No, I wouldn't say that." He turned to Avelyn. "You ran a nice race today. You looked real good."

"Thanks, Ike. How did you do in the team-roping?"

"Not much good. Hey there, Jimbo. Talk to you all later." Ike moved off into the crowd.

Avelyn said, "What do you have to be making fun of his weight all the time for?"

"He's pretty numb about his old gut."

"I don't care. That was rude. After everything that's gone on, I'm surprised he even came over. He was making an effort."

Mike was looking across to the door. "He can't hate me for long, Iker can't. Listen, 'scuse me. I'll be right back." Mike chugged his bourbon. Jimbo got up so he could squeeze out and watched him push through the crowd toward the door.

Avelyn was watching the dancers. She looked quite something with a flush in her cheeks, but there was a sadness there now, as well. The rotten feeling he'd had earlier had disappeared with the dancing, and what was left was more of a dull ache in the pit of his stomach, though it was not so unpleasant because of the liquor. It felt rather nice with the giddiness of the tequila and the dancing. Tomorrow it would not be so pleasant, though. Tomorrow there would be some price-paying, but he did not want to worry about that now. He wanted to watch her and forget about the business of the ache.

Over at the door, Hepp Fox was drinking a beer and talking to Tiny Turner. Mike lowered his eyes and wiped at his nose, wearing that little grin of his. He suddenly knew what he would say and how Hepp would react and saw the whole thing as clearly as if it had already happened; the way you sometimes see an elk come out of the timber before it really does, see the crosshairs click into focus, and the shot, and the frantic jolt and half-dozen steps before it falls. It was like that now with Hepp.

He patted him on the arm. "Nice race today, cowboy." He was wearing that grin, and Hepp met his eyes, not hiding the hate.

Hepp looked away. "Fuck you, buddy," he said.

"Hepper? Hepper?" He waited until Hepp looked at him. "You mess with my calves again . . . I'll tell you this once. You mess with my calves again —" pausing then, still grinning, "I'm gonna have to send the wife over to whip your little tail."

Hepp looked back down, his lips working. Out of the corner of his eye, Mike saw Turner step back. Hepp's jaw jutted, stretching the muscles in his neck, and the hand clenched up and was suddenly moving, up and out, the whole body coming behind it, until it smashed against the side of Mike's face.

There was a thick, smacking sound and Mike's head snapped sideways. Hepp swung again, but it glanced off the top of Mike's head as he ducked. Hepp stumbled, off balance, but Mike was too dazed to see it. There was shouting, and Mike wiped at the blood filling his eye.

Suddenly the two were surrounded by a ring of men. Chairs tipped over as they were shoved aside, as others ran to see the commotion. The side of Mike's face was numb. He wiped at the blood dripping down. It mixed with his sweat and ran into his eye. He squinted as they circled each other, trying to see, still grinning a little and wiping at his eye with his sleeve. Something moved again, and Hepp's fist landed above the same eye and spun Mike's head around violently. He heard Avelyn scream. Men were crying out, cheering. Hepp hit him again, and Mike tried to cover up, tried to blink the blood out of his eye, the blows landing one, two, three on top of his head and against his arms. He was crouched, stalking forward, still not feeling more

than a numbness on the side of his face and a dull thudding on
the back of his head and a ringing in one of his ears. He blinked
at the thickness in his eye, but it wouldn't clear. Suddenly he
lashed upward from his crouch with both fists. He nicked Hepp
with his right. The punches stopped and he saw Hepp with his
good eye and swung quickly with his left, catching him underneath the jaw. Hepp's head flew back. Mike straightened up and
cocked his right arm back, aiming at the head but striking Hepp's
shoulder, driving him backward into the ring of men. They
shouted encouragement to Hepp, and the two of them circled
again, Mike giving up on his eye, closing it and seeing through
the right one. Hepp came again with his right fist, coiling his
body behind it. Mike saw it coming and ducked, so that the blow
missed wildly. It spun him around as Mike's fist drove into the
center of his face, making a splattering sound as the nose flattened. Hepp's legs buckled and his eyes rolled back in his head.

A slurping, gurgling sound came from him as he tried to
breathe. Blood poured down his face and onto his white shirt.
Someone knelt and raised his head so that the blood ran down,
and Hepp's head lolled senselessly from side to side. Mike stood
over him, as if he might rise, twisting his knuckles into the palm
of his left hand, when Tiny Turner stepped out of the crowd
behind him. He was holding a beer bottle, and he lifted it up
and brought it down on the back of Mike's head. The bottle
shattered, and Mike's hands shot up to his head as he fell with
a short cry.

There was a low grunt as he hit the floor. The blood was
seeping through his fingers, Tiny standing over him, letting the
neck of the beer bottle fall from his hand. The crowd was suddenly hushed and everything was still. He stood like that, looking
down, no one moving. Then there was a rush and a terrific
parting in the ring as Denny burst through the crowd and
grabbed the big man from behind. He locked both arms around
his rib cage and bearhugged, leaning back to hoist Turner's six-
foot eight-inch frame completely off the ground. Turner let out
a little cry of surprise, setting his jaw determinedly and beating
at Denny's grip. He kicked backward with his legs at Denny's

shins. Denny staggered in a circle, squeezing. His mouth was open in a grimace, in a silent scream, as one of his hands slid farther up his other forearm, tightening his hold.

Turner's voice suddenly blurted, "Put me down," the words spurting out as if crushed from him. His face and neck were red. His veins popped out. He had no wind left to scream with, and he pried furiously at Denny's hands. His eyes watered and his movements were suddenly jerky and panicked. "Put him down, Denny!" Jimbo shouted. He moved in front of him and grabbed his shoulders. "That's enough! Now!"

Denny stopped his circling. He stood motionless, his arms straining powerfully beneath his shirt, Tiny beating at his hands like a small child. Turner's face was scarlet, his head swiveled back and forth, mouth open, the veins purple, trying to scream. Blood suddenly squirted from his nose.

Mike was on his feet now, prying at one of Denny's arms while Jimbo had the other. They were shouting to him. Two men grabbed at him from behind, tugging at his arms, and Denny stood perfectly still in the center of the ring, his head back, eyes closed, bearhugging the great body in his arms until it suddenly went limp. Then he let it fall.

"Holy God, Denny," Jimbo said, scared. "Jesus."

There was no noise. Turner lay on his back, motionless. Blood flowed from his nose in a stream, and the crimson color of his face turned ash-white. Avelyn was at the front of the ring of men now, and she looked over at Mike, the blood still dripping down his cheek. His mouth hung slack. It was the first time she had ever seen fear on his face. Then, slowly, Turner's body began to convulse, gagging in an effort to regain the air Denny had crushed out; some of the color came back so that he no longer looked like a corpse. Mike just stood there, staring from Turner to Hepp Fox, not proud or pained or anything but tired. Denny was shaking and as pale as Turner had been. Then Mike scanned the faces in the crowd as if he was looking at a bunch of strangers. He put his hand on the back of Denny's neck as he had done that first time, leaving the nursing home, and led him through the crowd, Jimbo and Avelyn following.

Denny had started to sob on the way home. He could not help himself. He stayed out on the porch for a while once they were back, and when Avelyn brought him some milk he was still there sobbing. She led him up to bed then.

When she came back out to tend to Mike's scalp, he was drinking another whiskey. "I thought he'd killed the sonofabitch," Mike said.

"Please don't even say that." She was washing the hair around the cut. It was not a deep cut, but it was jagged and on top of a large bump.

"Well, didn't *you*? Goddamn."

"Just don't. He *could* have. He could just as easily have, coming to your dumb rescue."

"I thought he was dead as a mackerel. I never seen anything like that."

"Oh, you're a stupid man. This is a stupid town." She patted his hair dry and put a gauze pad over the cut. Then she filled an ice bag and put it on top of the gauze. She had already bandaged his eyebrow, but the eye had nearly swollen shut.

"Remember your sister at the wedding?" Mike grinned. "Remember that, hon?"

"I don't know why in hell you should be in any sort of humor to remember anything."

"Remember that? Were you there, buddy boy? She'd fallen — whomp! — facedown on the flagstones running over from the neighbors'. We was all sitting around the living room, that big fancy dinner about two hours away, and Avelyn's sister staggers in with blood all over her face, unable to talk. Looked worse'n Hepp. Looked about like Tiny."

"Can't you stop talking about that?"

Mike laughed and sat forward. "Too damn drunk to talk, that was the thing. Old man Stewart figured she'd been shot in the forehead. Shot full of vodka's more like it. All the women is hollering, and the first thing she says is —" Mike laughed again, really tickled now. "Says, 'I'm all right, Ward. Where's the Beaver?' Says it right to her father, who'd thought she'd been shot in the head. God, I nearly shit. The look he had. All them bridesmaids had been getting soused and watching a 'Leave It to Beaver' rerun. 'Where's the damn Beaver?' Oh, God. Said goofy things like that for about an hour." Mike laughed himself off the armchair. He was sitting on the floor now, leaning against it.

"Oh, just stop it," Avelyn said. "Come on to bed."

"You go ahead. I couldn't sleep anyhow. I'll watch the television with buddy boy here. You want to, buddy boy?"

"Sure. I don't care."

"I thought old Tiny was dead as a mackerel."

Avelyn turned around from the staircase. "Stop saying that! Will you just stop saying that?" She looked very, very tired. "Please come to bed. You're going to feel bad enough in the morning as it is."

"I'll be along. Go on. Quit hounding a man."

"I'm not hounding." She went into the kitchen and put on some hot water. Then she went upstairs.

Jimbo asked, "Head hurting much?"

"Not much," Mike said.

"How's your eye?"

"Don't feel you gotta be a nursemaid, staying up and keeping me company. I'm setting just nice."

"Would you rather stay up alone?"

"I don't give a damn. No, sit down. We'll gab. I can't look at that television with one eye."

Jimbo turned off the set. Mike filled each of their glasses with bourbon. Then he unscrewed the top from the ice bag and took two cubes out for their drinks.

"I ever tell you about the time Ma shot up the game warden's watch?" Mike asked.

"No."

"I didn't?"

"No, you didn't. I don't recall you telling me any stories about Mom."

Mike took a drink and set the ice bag back on his head. "I

guess there's probably a whole passel of stories I never told you. You were such a squirt growing up I guess I never took the time to tell you anything."

"I guess. Well, I'm not a squirt anymore."

Mike coughed. He went into the kitchen to get a glass of water, then came back out and said, "Avelyn's settin' in there drinking coffee."

"Ask her to come in."

"She's mad at me. She wants me to go to bed.".

"Maybe you should."

"No." Then: "You mind me calling you buddy boy?"

"No, hell, I don't care. That's what you call me."

"Yeah. All right. You know, Ma was a helluva shot. She could shoot better than Dad or Papa Vic or any of 'em. Well, one time she was hunting with Dad and Sam Benson, and an elk come out of the timber about two hundred fifty yards away at a dead run. That's a damn tough shot, to kill an elk on the run, but she did it — bang! — one shot. And this warden sees it, but he doesn't see who shot it. Figures it was Dad or Sam, and they'd both bagged their elks that year . . ."

Avelyn came out of the kitchen with her coffee. She had changed into her housecoat, which was white linen with red tulips embroidered down the front. The tulips had long straight stems that reached down to the hem, and the housecoat lay flat over the front of her body. She had combed her hair down for bed, and her feet were bare. "You two. . . . Come to bed."

Jimbo was looking at her and some of the rottenness came back. It had been an all-around rotten evening after starting so well, and her looking so perfectly lovely and sad was not going to help things. The tequila had mostly worn off, and now there was just the exhaustion and a sort of grayness to the light.

"I'm telling the kid a story, babe. Now either shut up and listen or go up to bed."

"That's a nice way to talk," she said.

"Sorry then. I'm telling him about Ma's shooting. She could flat shoot, hon. I wish you'd try to shoot sometime. I wish you'd at least give it a try. You won't even give it a try."

"I don't care about trying."

"How're you going to like it if you don't give it a try?"

"I don't like guns. Please let's not go through this again."

"But how do you *know*? You won't even shoot one to find out."

"I don't like to kill wild animals."

"Shit . . ."

"I don't! It's my business, all right? I've never said a cross word to you about it, or tried to dissuade you from it; so I don't see why you have to look down your nose at —"

"You sure don't mind eating 'em when I bring 'em in, now do you? You set right down like a pig at a slop bucket."

"Jesus, Michael."

"Tell the story, will you?" Jimbo said.

"Right. Sure. So the warden sees that elk fall, and he drives over — or rides, I guess — and asks to see a license. Course, the only license is Ma's, and the warden tells her there's no way in the world she fired that shot. Says, 'Unless your name is Oakley. Your name Oakley?' And she says, 'My name's McKenzie.' And he says, 'Then you didn't fire that shot, and this elk is poached.' And she tells him he's so full of shit his eyes are brown."

Avelyn said, "She didn't tell him that."

Mike stopped and drank his bourbon and wiped his mouth on his still-bloody shirt. He looked at Jimbo and was about to continue when he caught himself and looked back to Avelyn. "Did you know my mother?"

"No."

"Were you maybe sneaking there behind a bush when she was talking to that warden? Just how do you know what she said and what she didn't say?"

"Just tell me this, Mike McKenzie. Did your mother — yes or no — ever in her life tell anyone they were so full of shit their eyes were brown?"

Mike sat forward and started to gesticulate when his ice bag fell off. She broke in and said, "Yes or no — don't lie now."

He waved her away with a deprecating gesture and muttered, "Shit." Jimbo laughed. "Anyway," he went on, "the warden didn't believe her, which makes Ma mad as hell, so she says to take off that watch of his and swing it from that tree about seventy-five yards yonder if he doesn't think she can shoot. It was just bluff, mostly, but the dumb sonofabitch does it. Hangs it by the chain from the bottom branch, then starts it swinging. She was crazy as hell to try it, but she raised her rifle and disintegrated it with one shot. One damn fine shot. The warden just stares at his chain hanging there like a dead snake from the branch and says, 'Nice shot, McKenzie.' Then he climbs back on his horse and rides away. Didn't even take the chain. Dad used to wear that chain sometimes. Didn't have a watch or nothing; just ran it from one vest pocket to the other."

Mike finished his bourbon and rearranged the ice bag. Then he said, "Hon, you could learn to shoot in two days, for Chrissakes. You could be a helluva shot. You're always talking about new challenges; well, you could learn to be a helluva shot."

"I don't want to learn."

"No," he said, finishing his drink. His voice mocked, "Don't want to hurt the wild animals." He started to pour himself another bourbon.

"Honey," she said more gently. "You don't need that. Let's all get some sleep. Your head will feel bad enough as it is."

"Don't tell me what I *don't need*. Whyn't you go to bed?"

"Relax, Mike," Jimbo said.

"You relax." Mike shrugged and took a drink. "Never mind me." Then he said, "One time I was guiding for this rich fart from Florida who was blind as an old dog. Mr. John Tilton. Worst shot in the world. If you'd told him to try to hit the planet Earth, he wouldn't have been able to do it without taking off his foot. Made a deal with me where I was guaranteed five hundred bucks for five days guidin', with another five hundred if we bagged a four-point deer or better. You know how many four-pointers there are around here, buddy boy. Sounded like the easiest thousand I'd ever make till I saw the fella shoot." He stopped and took another drink.

"Don't you know any stories that aren't about hunting?" Avelyn asked. "I've had just about enough violence for one night."

"Violence? What violence? This is a funny story."

"I don't understand how you can be telling stories now at all. Michael? It's late and we're all very tired and I'm asking you, for me, to come to bed. Please?"

"I want to tell this story. I like telling stories, what's wrong with that? This isn't *violent*. This is funny, put everyone in a good mood again. You'll like it, you wait. So I'm guidin' Mr. John Tilton up on these great big bucks where he's shooting from so close I thought the noise would scare them to death. But he misses. Again and again. Wouldn't let me back him up, neither. Had to get it himself. So after four days of this, I've had 'bout enough. He weren't gonna get one. So I go out myself and shoot a four-point deer. Four or five — nothing special but in the money — and then I employ the assistance of old Deac for fifty bucks.

"We strung that buck up from the branch of a tree so's it'd look like it was just standing around browsing; at least we figured it'd look that way to John Tilton, who wore those Coke-bottle glasses that made his eyes look about yea big — " Mike opened his eyes as wide as he could — which was no more than a slit for the eye swollen shut — and made circles around them with his fingers the size of silver dollars.

"The next day I bring him about a hundred yards from the spot we'd hung that deer, and I whisper to him, 'There's one, take a shot at him.' Deacon was off hiding behind the tree.

"So John Tilton asks, 'Can't we get closer?' and I tell him that we can't risk it or he'll spook.

" 'Jesus, Mike, I can't hardly see him,' he says.

" 'Sure you can, he's right there browsing 'neath that old tree. He's got your name written all over his broadside.'

"So John Tilton squints through the scope again and says, 'I'll never hit him, Mike.'

" 'Sure you will, Big John.'

" 'I'm gonna miss,' he says.

"Then I did kind of a sneaky-mean thing — but Christ, I was afraid he might not even *shoot at* that deer. I says, 'Tell you what, John, I'll bet you fifty bucks that you bag that baby. I got that much confidence in you.'

"Well, he looks up at me like I was tooty-fruity nuts, 'cause he's missed fifty shots already that week way easier than that one. But he shrugs his head okay, not seeing how he has much to lose. He puts his rifle to his shoulder and squints through the sight, and he says somethin' like, 'He's movin' around too much.' Can you believe that, hon? That deer was dead, see? So I tell him, 'No, he looks dead still to me.' Then he asks if it looks like he's aimed right. Jesus. Well, he finally shoots, and Deacon was supposed to cut the rope at the crack of the gun, then slip it off as we approached, and skedaddle. There was a gully right there. Thing was, old John Tilton happened to get closer than he usually did and hit the tree Deac was hiding behind, and sent the chicken-livered fart diving for cover. There must've been five full seconds elapse before he cut the deer down. Goddamn, did that look funny. I'm sayin', 'Fall, damn you . . . will you *fall!* — kinda like Hepp must've been saying when he was whalin' on me tonight — '*Fall,* damn you!' — standing to lose not only the five hundred bonus but the fifty-dollar bet besides. Big John just shakes his head and says, 'Shit, I missed him,' but I'm sayin', 'No, you didn't either . . . hold on now, he's gonna fall . . . fall you *gawddamn!!!*' . . . Tilton just staring through the scope, waiting for that buck to run away like all the others did — waiting for something — then all of a sudden — *wonk!* — down it goes, like he'd hit it with a needle full of sodium pentothal. He like to shit. God, I laughed. His face fell a foot.

"He came up with that five-hundred-dollar bonus, all right, and all he ever said about that delayed reaction was, 'Sure is funny how hard some creatures die. That shot was through the heart.'" Mike chuckled. "Right through the fucking heart. I always wondered what would've happened if he *had* hit that buck, and there'd been two bullet holes staring him in the face, when he'd only fired that one shot. Probably would've said the same thing about how some creatures sure died hard."

Avelyn said, "It's true, though. A lot of things die hard. I see what he meant."

"Well, I guess I seen what he *meant,* too, but it was still a pretty dumb thing to say in the light of that buck already bein' stone-cold dead when Big John took his shot at him."

"But *he* didn't know that; so it was *not* a dumb thing to say, Michael. Some things *do* die hard, and he was right whether that one silly buck was dead or not —"

"Well, that one silly buck was the point of the story, babe, and I'll tell you another thing, when I shot him through the heart the day before, he found it plumb *easy* to die, like he couldn't hardly wait for it. That buck dropped quicker'n Molly's drawers when the time came; so it seems to me like maybe dyin's what things do about easiest. People, too. Easiest and best."

"People? What made you say that? Do you think of people in the same way you think of deer?"

Mike pushed his ice bag back, then he removed it and placed it on the floor beside him. "Jesus, you're a pain in the ass to-night."

"Take it easy, Mike," Jimbo said.

"Will you just stop telling me to take it easy? Christ Almighty, you're like a mother hen."

Jimbo and Avelyn glanced at each other, and then Avelyn looked down, embarrassed at Mike's drunkenness. Jimbo got to his feet. "I think it's time we all went to bed."

"Well whyn't you and the little woman go on to bed then? I'm gonna watch some television."

"Come on, Mike. Give her a break."

"What're you takin' her side on this for?"

"I'm not taking sides."

"Well, you sure as hell are. What in the hell are you tryin' to pull here, anyway, stickin' your big Ivy League nose into business that's none of your affairs —"

"— I'm going to bed."

"Mike, that's enough," Avelyn said.

"That's it. Now you take the side of the kid. You two are a pair, you know that?"

"Mike —"

"— a real beaut of a pair. You think I don't got eyes?"

"A cryptic warning from my brother the pugilist. Goodnight, Avelyn."

Jimbo went upstairs. Mike turned the television back on, and

Avelyn sat quietly on the couch. She started to cry. It was silent crying and Mike did not notice for a long while. "What's wrong, hon?"

"What's wrong!" She opened her hands in frustration. She started to go on but her sobbing got in the way, and she waited until she had stopped. She wiped her eyes on the sleeve of her housecoat, then went to get a tissue from the bathroom. She came back and tried to force a smile. Her eyes were red. "This just isn't very much fun anymore."

"What isn't?"

"I know it's not supposed to be fun all the time, but this isn't very much fun ever. Today at the race was the most fun I've had in a long, long time, and look at us now. Michael? Look at us now. You've two gashes in your thick head, Denny's almost killed a man, you've offended your brother deeply, and I'm sitting here in tears. Terrific, eh?"

"You want to go to bed? I'll go to bed now."

"Oh, Mike." She sighed and forced another little smile. "I don't know if I want to go on like this much longer."

"You look tired, hon. We're all flat beat. Let's go to bed and get some sleep."

"Are you listening?"

"Sure I'm listening. Let's go to bed now. Let's go to bed right now and get some sleep."

"Michael, you're not listening. I'm sick of this."

"I'm *listening*. Don't tell me I'm not fucking listening. I'm *listening*. Now let's go to bed and get some sleep. We'll fucking talk about it."

"Why are you swearing at me all of a sudden?" She was crying again.

"I'm not swearing at *you*. I'm just swearing. It's not like I'm swearing at *you*. Christ, let's just go to bed. You've been hounding at me to go to bed, so let's go to fucking bed."

"You're swearing at me."

"I'm not swearing at you! Jesus H. Christ, I'm not swearing at *you*. I'm just swearing. I'm swearing at *God*. I'm swearing at fucking God!"

She had her hands clasped over her ears, and she shook her head violently. "I'm your *wife*, Michael! You don't listen when I ask you to stop swearing . . . you don't listen when I ask you to come to bed . . . you don't listen when I ask you not to be rude —"

"Oh, fuck."

"— and drinking and drinking and drinking yourself into bleary-eyed stupors —"

Mike wheeled and threw his glass against the wall. It shattered and she cried out. "I'm just swearing! It don't mean nothing. I'm just *swearing!*" Her mouth was gaping open and she was crying, clutching her sides, her face collapsed. "I'm just swearing."

Jimbo heard the heavy boots on the kitchen floor and the back door slamming. The truck started up and drove off. The house was silent. After a while she was standing in his doorway, her face still wet. Her voice eased into the silence without breaking it. "Sometimes he drives up to the Parker place and stays there in the cabin. They've got a bunk in there." The light from downstairs silhouetted her form in the doorway.

"You okay?"

Her shoulders heaved in a sigh and her chin dropped slightly. "No." She was crying again. Then: "Please hold me."

She sat down on his bed and he put his arms around her. She wiped the wetness off on his shoulder and laid her cheek there. "Talk to me, Jimbo. Talk to me all night. Do you think you can talk to me all night long?"

"Sure. No problem. We'll talk about Long Island. Want to talk about Long Island?"

"That would be all right." Her voice was tiny.

"We'll talk about that. Long Island is a great place. I've only been there that once, but you can see the lights from New Haven. Long Island really has the prettiest damn lights. Gatsby, the Great Gatsby, he used to have a real thing about the lights on Long Island. Especially one green one. One pretty green one. God, it's a wonderful place."

"It is pretty wonderful sometimes."

"Sure it is."

"My sister's getting married in December. Lisa. The one you got on so well with at the wedding."

"Jeez, that's great."

"Yeah. Her boyfriend talks like Cary Grant. That's what she says. I always hoped you two would get something going."

"Well. A December wedding. That's unusual."

She smiled up at him. "We don't have to talk."

"All right. Avelyn?"

"Don't, Jimbo. Let's not talk. Let me just sit here for a while with you, okay? We don't have to say anything. I'll just sit here for a while, then I'll go off to bed."

"Sure. Do you want to put your feet up and lie down?"

"All right. For a while. Then I'll go to bed."

She fell asleep against his shoulder. Her hair smelled clean and good, and after a while Jimbo fell asleep, too. He woke dazedly when she got up to leave, then he stretched out beneath the covers and fell sound asleep until morning.

CHAPTER 22

TIIERE WAS A song she used to sing to herself the year after she'd met Michael, when everyone was telling her she wasn't in love:

> *There's a young man that I know, his age is twenty-one,*
> *He comes from down in southern Colorado,*
> *Just out of the service, and he's looking for some fun;*
> *Someday soon, going with him, someday soon.*

She had met Michael shortly after his term in the army. He was twenty-four then and from northern Wyoming, but the rest of it had worked. It had made her feel a little wild and carefree, the song did. It had made her feel alive and full and happy. She would go with him. She would.

> *. . . And he loves his damned old rodeo as much as he loves me,*
> *Someday soon, going with him, someday soon . . .*

It was going through her head now, but it was not making her happy and she could not get it to stop. It was making her miserable. There was something terribly haunting about it; something dead; and she had never felt more keenly that she was no longer that girl of nineteen who had wanted to follow him right down the toughest road. It was the girl of nineteen who was dead. It was the open, hopeful, naiveté that made a phrase like "someday soon" so joyful that was dead. She wanted it back. She wanted everything back. She saw the rifle in Mike's saddle scabbard and thought of last year's bear hunt, and she wanted that back, too. She wanted Papa Vic there to give her a little piece of the raw heart and tell her about how Indians got courage. She would have taken a big piece this time, and she would have washed it down with lots of whiskey.

Mike turned around and smiled at her and pointed up toward the huge, molar-shaped peak called Blacktooth. He still had a slightly purplish crescent in the corner of his eye from the fight. There was a faint trace of yellow. The swelling had disappeared and the wound had healed over, and the purple crescent had an oddly flattering effect. He was in high spirits, leading a pack-horse as they rode into the mountains to look for bighorn sheep to photograph. She had never seen one. But she was not very excited about it, and that song that was running through her head was not making things easier.

That night they camped at the foot of Blacktooth, in a meadow where Mike had taken his hunters years ago when going for bighorn. After being ridden all day, the horses were too tired to do anything but eat, and Mike did not bother to hobble them. He built a makeshift corral using poles and standing pine trees, and after they had grazed he put them into it. There was a glacial lake there with a clear, black bottom. The rising trout made its smooth surface dance with rings until dark. Mike cooked dinner and they went to sleep early.

The first day he took her up the western ridge, without success. Bighorn sheep were rare and difficult to find. They were afraid of humans and stayed high in the mountains, where their coloring made them almost impossible to spot unless they were moving or silhouetted against the sky.

At the end of the second day, Mike caught sight of two ewes making their way along the ridge opposite him. They disappeared quickly, but it was so near darkness that he was certain they were bedding down somewhere in the area. There was no time to climb higher to find where they had gone, but two ewes would not travel without a ram. If they were there at dawn tomorrow, they might spot them.

They awoke at five in the morning and climbed partway up the ridge in the darkness. It was cold, and the water they had left in the coffeepot had skimmed over with ice. There was a half-moon, and the trail at first was easy for her, Mike carrying her camera equipment in a pack on his back. The first gray streaks began to show in the east by the time Mike told her they were at the spot where he had seen the sheep. They kept climbing, the chunks of granite cold to the touch. In half an hour they reached a staircaselike ridge, which they traversed, keeping their bodies low to the ground and protected from the view of the ridge opposite. The edge of the sun showed on the horizon, and they moved more quickly. Then Mike stopped and knelt behind a rock, handing Avelyn her pack and motioning her to stay quiet. He leaned over the top of the rock with his binoculars. After a while he edged back down and nodded.

Avelyn attached a 600-millimeter lens to her camera and set its tripod on the flat ledge beside the rock. Then she lay prone, peeking over the rock toward the ridge opposite. There was a grassy spot below them, and at first she did not see the sheep. Their coats were exactly the shade of brown as the dirt and dried grass. Mike handed her the binoculars, and after looking through them for a while, she began to make out their shapes. There were seven in all, and she saw the ram last. He was lying against the boulder at the far side of the grassy area. As the sun cleared the horizon, the shapes became more distinct. Then the ram rose to its feet.

"It' all right," Mike whispered. "He's just going to stretch and feed a little. The others must wait."

Avelyn put her eye to her camera again. The sun had not yet hit the bedding area. She focused on the ram. It had a beautiful head.

Mike studied it through the binoculars. "He's maybe five," he whispered. "He's a big one for one so young. Jesus, he's big. See how his horns curl into just three-quarters of a circle? He's just barely legal. Jesus Christ, what a head. That full round arch to the horns . . . and how thick they are at the base. Two or three years, that's a record head. See how round that arch is? You straighten that out, that's a long set of horns. But he's just barely legal."

"What's legal?" she asked.

"Three-quarters."

She was excited and hoped she wouldn't blur her pictures. She had forgotten the cold. When the sunlight fell on the head of the ram, she began snapping the shots, steadying the huge lens and squeezing the shutter button, holding her breath as best she could. It was a windless morning, and the ram heard the camera clicking. It looked directly at her for a moment, its body broadside. She was thrilled. The ram started away at a run, followed by the ewes and lambs. They raced noiselessly along a narrow ledge, the stones they dislodged seeming to float below them, dropping five hundred feet into a gully. As they disappeared over the top of the ridge, Avelyn photographed the file of sheep silhouetted against the dawn pink. Then she turned and grabbed Mike happily and kissed him. His nose was cold and red.

"Oh, Michael, let's not leave here. Let's stay here and wait for them to come back. They were so beautiful."

"I don't think they'll be back," he said, grinning.

"Let's wait and see. Let's stay here forever. Up on old Blacktooth. What a ghastly name for such a lovely spot. Oh, honey, it makes me happy to be here with you. They were magnificent, weren't they?"

"That ram was. I'd like to shoot that ram in two, three years. Be a record head."

"You and your record head."

"They can run though, can't they? Tippy-toeing along that ridge like nothin'. Five-hundred-foot drop and a three-inch path."

"They were magnificent."

"Well. Glad we run across 'em. You cold? Shit, I am." He rubbed his hands together. "S'pose we'd best think about gettin' back."

"Let's not. Let's stay. A few more days." She squeezed his arm.
"That's what we told 'em."

"Can't we stay? Can't we stay on the old ghastly Blacktooth?"

"Wouldn't be right, babe. They'd come looking. We'll do it again. We'll do it in the fall. Be some snow then."

On the long ride back her mind wandered, her body tired and swaying with the walk of the horse. She thought about Lisa's wedding, and going home for that and staying for Christmas. Lisa had good taste in men. She would have liked to have met her fiancé and give her approval before they were married. After they were married it wouldn't matter, but now Lisa would like to hear that her older sister approved of her intended. Avelyn did not worry about whether she would like him. Everyone else liked him, and if she didn't she would lie about it anyway. A sister is the last person in the world to know who is right for another sister. A sister and a mother. Her mother had always been too busy flirting with Mike to worry about whether he was right for her. That was the smart thing to do. You couldn't know. No one could know, no matter how right or wrong things seemed with people. The best way was to get them to like you, which was at least one headache out of the way.

She wondered where they'd get the money. A trip back East for the two of them would cost a thousand dollars by the time they bought the presents and the plane fare and the rest of it. It was the rest of it that made it fun, that made it worth the trouble. It was the day in the city where you shopped at Bloomingdale's and Saks, then watched the skaters in Rockefeller Center and smelled the sidewalk vendors roasting chestnuts — that bitter, winter smell. Then before the theater, you would stop in at "21" and pretend to have dinner reservations, just to show it to Mike; so he could see the Remingtons and look at the silvertooled saddle they kept in the glass case and watch all the waiters and the people trying to look casual among all the clutter and opulence. Afterward, you'd take a taxi, and if you were lucky it would be a good show, with dancing and songs that would make you think, "I didn't know this was from . . . ," and maybe an actor you recognized. Then you would eat at one of the small ethnic restaurants where you ducked in a plain, oaken door and took two steps down, then were led through the taproom and a small dining room with a fire, through a courtyard to some more dining rooms in the back with wooden booths and dim lighting and narrow aisles for the bow-tied waiters. Or you could go to Rosie O'Grady's and eat among the dancers. Mike would like that more than dim booths and narrow aisles. A good Irish pub that was not too expensive or chic, and was filled with people who danced or sang along to the reels and did not worry about the way they acted. Mike would not sing along, but he would not mind that he had come. He would drink beer and talk, and every so often would look up at what was going on around him with no more than casual interest, as if he did it every day. But he would not seem out of place. And he would not seem out of place in "21" or the theater or wherever they went. That always surprised her. Even in his shirt and tie and wool pants, Mike would look like Mike, just as the city would look like the city. His face would be ruddy and good-looking from working outdoors, and his smile would come just as easily, his gait just as bow-legged and slow. Not even New York City could get him to shake the Wyoming dust from his boots.

Then they could taxi to the Village and listen to some jazz or folk singing and drink Spanish coffee until they got sleepy. All that was what made it worthwhile. That more than the caroling and parties and family dinners and gifts. That more even than the wedding. All that was what you had to do so you could come back to Wyoming and relax and know that you would not want to live that way forever.

Her father would have paid for their trip. Mike wouldn't let him, but if it came to that he would tell her to go ahead without him. She didn't want that. She wanted to go to the wedding, but she wanted to go with Michael. They'd dig up the money somehow. Avelyn smiled then, thinking that Zach Thorndike would give them the money. Zach Thorndike would pay for their plane fare home, and eighteen million dollars to boot. It was ridiculous to be that rich and that poor at the same time. It was silly.

It would have been nice to get a fresh start somewhere, like

Lloyd and Carol did, somewhere like Colorado. Or Jackson Hole. The Grand Tetons. Those were some mountains. Some of her father's friends had bought land around Jackson, or built houses near the ski slopes. She did not care about a house near a ski slope, but to have a ranch nearby and some money left over — that would have been nice. That made sense. Then she would be content to raise a family and make a home. And when the kids were grown, she could run a restaurant or open up a shop . . . or if the photography worked out, start her own studio. When they reached school age, maybe. All that made sense. It would be their own place, and she would get all new furniture and decorate it so that she felt it was her own, and they would not have to worry about plane fares and whether cattle prices slipped for a year or two. And you would not have to worry about raising your children in the shadow of a strip mine. And you would not have to worry about what it would be like to be rich, for you would *be* rich, and all that would be left would be to worry if you were the happier for it. And if you weren't, then you couldn't blame Mike, because *he* wouldn't change. She was sure of that.

Mike wasn't the problem because he had never changed and he never would change. She lost sight of that sometimes, with everything else changing so fast. So that it was like when you were sitting in a waiting train and another train passed slowly by and you didn't know if you were starting up or they were slowing down. You just knew the speeds were different. That was what was happening to her and Mike. They were two trains on parallel tracks, which was what marriage was. You may start out at the same station and travel the same speed and make the same stops a good portion of the way, but you were still not the same train. You were two different trains. You would always be two different trains, no matter what. And because of that, sooner or later one would want to speed ahead or slow down, which is what was happening now. Which was when you had to work at it, she thought. Which was when you had to work like hell to catch up or tug like hell to slow the other down; or just let it go.

They came down through the Custer Forest, passing the reservoir and the Pines, where she and Jimbo had had their drink. She closed her eyes, remembering. That had been fun and impulsive and girlish, something that that girl of nineteen would have done. But it did not really have anything to do with Jimbo. It had to do with the girl of nineteen, which is why she did not feel badly about it anymore. Which is why it was a nice thing to remember. They reached the Canyon Creek road. Ahead they could see a huge road leveler scraping it flat, and behind it a roller, with small groups of construction workers standing off to the side in their hardhats and T-shirts.

"They go fast, those sonsofbitches," Mike said.

They pulled their horses off the road and rode next to the fence. The blacktopping crew was still several miles behind, and they could hear the generator that heated the tar pumping from down the road. The leveling crew was knocking off for the day. None of them spoke as they rode past.

Nearing home, the horses picked up their pace. They reached the Parker place, and Mike suddenly stiffened, stopping his horse and standing up in his stirrups. The packhorse, head down, jolted into him, and the two horses scuffled in a circle. There was a flock of sheep over in the pasture.

"Goddammit, what the hell is that?"

"Look at the sheep," she said.

"Those are goddamn sheep! What the hell are a flock of sheep doing on the Parker place?" Mike was agitated, jerking his neck around, trying to keep his horse still.

"They look nice there. Maybe we should buy some sheep."

"That's our goddamn *land!* What the hell are sheep doing on it? Here. Jesus God, what next?" He handed her the halter to the packhorse and spurred his horse into a run. He galloped down the drive and cut across the pasture. There was a man tending the sheep, but she could see very little of him. Mike pulled his horse up and screamed at him for a while. She couldn't tell what the man was doing. After a while Mike turned the horse and trotted back.

She kicked her horse along. The packhorse was anxious to be moving again, and it walked along beside her. "Can you beat that?" Mike said, coming up and taking the halter rope. "Some ole Injun just comes right onto our land and looses his sheep. Can you beat that?"

"He was an Indian?"

"A one-eyed Injun. Plumb whacko, too. I'd of drove him off right then and there but sonofabitch had a shotgun."

"What?"

"Armed and dangerous and goofy in the head. Told him he'd best be gone by morning or I'd unloose the cavalry."

"Be careful, Michael. Shouldn't the sheriff handle something like that?"

"He's an old man, babe. Probably got drunk and wandered off the reservation. Goddamn, though, why do I always end up with them?"

"Michael?"

"Huh?"

"Thank you for taking me. Thank you for the trip. I needed that."

He grinned that little grin. "Your little bottom sore?"

"I feel good."

"You look good, princess."

She felt herself blushing. He could still make her blush. She smiled and kicked her horse, slapping the packhorse in the rump as she bolted by. It bolted too, and she heard Mike holler from behind. She glanced back over her shoulder, and the packhorse had broken free, Mike in hot pursuit and cursing, the panniers slapping up and down against its sides. Laughing, she turned through the Bar V gate, the thundering, clattering packhorse close behind, and let out a whoop. Inside, she was singing.

*. . . I would follow him right down the toughest road, I know
Someday soon, going with him, someday soon.*

CHAPTER 23

BEFORE LEAVING ON the pack trip, Avelyn had put a note on his bureau:

Jimbo —
   I looked all over town for a card to give you, but none of them seemed quite right, so I came home and found this pretty one that I had from New York — this one's only pretty — nothing special except maybe that it goes from me to you.
   I want to thank you for last week, for listening and talking and being there when I needed someone there. In retrospect it all seems slightly unreal, like a dream. I'm not sure there are words to quite describe how I'm feeling. No — I think a hug might do it. See you when we get back —

                                                              Avelyn

The front of the card was a print of a Japanese screen, softly colored with graceful, swooping birds with feathered tails and distant, brooding mountains and delicate flowers. He had read it several times, vaguely dissatisfied, looking for something more, some deeper meaning that escaped him. He wondered why she had written it, why he kept rereading it. He wished she had used words to describe how she was feeling, for there were many types of hugs. He would have liked to find out which. Then he put away the card and tried not to think about hugs, and that rotten, unsettled feeling returned.

He heard them gallop in, followed by the slamming of screen doors and clumping of boots from downstairs. When he went down, he found Avelyn sitting at the kitchen table, drinking a Tab, her face flushed. She waved hello. Bringing in the last pannier, Mike stumbled over Stormy and cursed, "Goddamn you dog, always gettin' in the road." Avelyn laughed, and Mike set the pannier down, raising his hands up to signal he was rid of it. "You clean it out then, you think it's so damn funny. Broken eggs all over the damn lot. You just have a merry old time cleaning up." He saw Jimbo. "She went and spooked old Jacks just up the road here, and he bucked and kicked and galloped all the way back to the barn, them panniers flying every way but loose. Left a trail of silverware the length of the drive. I'm not kidding, babe, that's the worst thing you can do with a horse, runnin' 'em back to the barn. It really makes me mad."

Avelyn grinned. "Bring 'em in wet!"

"I'll bring you in wet, you little sass." He opened the refrigerator and fished out a beer. "So, buddy boy, what's news? I see you got them ditches just chock-full of water."

Jimbo nodded. "Opened them up a couple days ago. How was your trip? Find some sheep?" he asked her.

"Oh, God, it was so beautiful. Mike took me to seven of them this morning. Way up in the mountains on this sheer black ridge. It was about the most exciting thing I've ever seen. I kept thinking we were lost, we were so high. *I* was lost. Honestly, I don't know how anyone finds anything in those mountains. But he did."

"That's our hero," Jimbo said, winking. "So. Did you get some pictures?"

"Loads," she said, ignoring the remark. "The most beautiful ram!"

"It was a big ram," Mike added. "Be a record head if he lives that long. Nothin' else then, eh?"

"Well, there was one thing. I went down to pick up that barbed wire you ordered. . . . Guess what? Good old Zig, friend and neighbor, doesn't accept charges anymore. Charge account — kaput."

Mike put the beer down. "What'd you say?"

Jimbo smiled. "Clean out your ears, cowboy." He made a face and pretended to tug at something. "Say what? I can't hear you, I've got a banana in my ear."

"And you can knock off the 'cowboy' crap. Just tell me what happened."

"Sure thing, Mike. I went to sign for the barbed wire, and old Zig says he didn't take charges anymore. Overhead seems to have been a problem. I must say he was embarrassed about it."

"Embarrassed?" Mike looked at him disbelievingly.

"I don't think it was old Zig's idea. I imagine the Chamber of Commerce or one of our wonderful Canyon Creek neighbors put him up to it. And I wouldn't be surprised if the same goes for Mailer's and Jerry's Texaco and wherever else we're in the habit of being extended credit. But I can personally vouch that our relationship with the post office is still thriving. Unfortunately. Yesterday a package arrived containing a dismembered prairie dog, as near as I could tell. I don't know. It may have been a rat."

Avelyn put her hand to her mouth. Mike sat down, his eyes slowly hardening. "Anything else?"

"Business as usual."

"Okay. Fine."

Jimbo lowered his eyes and smiled. "I imagined a lot of reactions to this news, but 'okay, fine' wasn't on my list. I shall learn your ways yet, brother Mike."

"There's plenty of hardware stores in Sheridan. Figure I can just as easy open up an account there."

"And the package?"

Mike gave that little grin. "Reckon the prairie dog came out on the short end of that particular stick."

"Indeed he did. You're an incredible man." He glanced at Avelyn, to make sure she had heard Mike's absurd, ostrichlike reactions. This business of the coal was getting out of hand, as the calf slaughter had gotten out of hand, and his only response was to sit there sipping a beer making smart remarks about how they were still, after all, better off than the prairie dog that had arrived in little pieces. He wouldn't accept that the fight had already begun, or that it was a fight he couldn't win by simply standing up and brandishing his fists, face to face, Great American Cowboy–style. His opponent didn't have a face, or it had too many faces. You could not beat it by punching a nose, as Mike had done to Hepp. It was a fight you had to run from, and Mike didn't know how to run away; he didn't have the common sense to. He was fighting progress now; or fate, or something — and Jimbo suddenly thought of the horse in Deacon's photograph, the one that had furiously bucked itself over on him, ruining his leg; how it had pawed up at the sky as it to strike a blow at God. You are fighting like a horse, Mike; like a big dumb brute. Progress is too big for individuals. It steamrolls individuals.

Mike asked, "What're you doing tomorrow, buddy boy? Want to come up and help me throw some loco Injun off the Parker place?"

"He's got a gun, Michael," Avelyn blurted.

"Sounds like great good fun," Jimbo said. "Don't tell me any more about it. I want to be surprised."

"Michael, he's got a gun!"

Mike winked. "Only shoots two arrows at a time, babe. 'Sides, ole buddy boy'll be there to protect me."

"No shit? An Indian?"

"A crazy, one-eyed Injun with a flock of sheep."

Jimbo rubbed his hands together. "Oh, goody-goody-goody. A real live Injun for the Great American Cowboy. This should be fine stuff. The stuff of legend. Now we are talking." He hopped up and hoisted a beer out of the refrigerator. "I'll drink to your health when I'm with you, I'll drink to your health when alone; I'll drink to your health so goddamn much, I'll well nigh ruin my own." He popped open the tab so it sprayed a little into the air, looking down to see Mike smiling there, but Avelyn with a trapped look, a wild-animal look, in her eyes. He couldn't watch it. It was the first time he had seen her scared, as if everything was suddenly clear to her, as if she had seen into the future. He walked quickly through the living room, onto the porch, his ears hot and a swelling of helplessness in his chest.

After a while Avelyn came out, too. The swelling was gone now and just the rottenness remained. "You okay?" she asked.

"Sure I am. Great." He looked at her. She still had that frightened look. She came up beside him and leaned on the rail. Her arm was against his arm, and he felt its warmth.

"What did that look mean, Jimbo? That look you gave me? Why did you look at me like that?"

He did not want to move, but it was impossible for him to think with her touching him like that. He pulled away. "More McKenzie morbidness. It's passed."

"Has it? What was it? It scared me, that look you gave me."

He looked back over the yard, across the pasture, listening to the prairie sounds. "I guess I was thinking how by not actively fighting progress, fighting against it, you were really fighting with it. Which is why it won't ever lose. Why it will always win. It's so much easier to be swept along." He looked at her. "That's how to survive — to be swept along. That's how Papa Vic survived the flood. He was swept along. He rode it out in a washtub."

She smiled, but it faded quickly. "In a wicker basket."

"I thought it was —"

"No. Like Moses." She touched his hand.

"What a strange old man. But he knew how to survive." He was quiet for a while. "I think a lot about how he would handle all this. The coal and all. That old bugger . . . you know, he might just sell. Go find something new. Buy a fleet of shrimp boats." He looked away again, then back. "I got your card."

Avelyn looked down. "I wanted to thank you."

He wondered if that was all, just to thank him. "I think I've got to watch myself around you. I missed you a lot the last three days." She was watching him nervously. He managed a smile. "I can't go around falling in love with my brother's wife, now can I?" Her head was absolutely still, and he pulled his hand away from hers. "I think I'll take a walk. I'll see you at dinner, okay?"

He walked off the porch feeling altogether miserable.

CHAPTER 24

THEY PICKED UP THE barbed wire in Sheridan, and on the way back Mike pulled the pickup into an Indian crafts store on the outskirts of town. "Want your advice on something," he said to Jimbo.

"I'd be honored."

"It's a surprise, though. No flappin' your trap."

Inside, the lady took a necklace out from the glass case, and Mike held it up for him to see. It was made of half-dollar–sized conchas, hand-tooled and oblong in shape. They were strung together on a silver chain intermingled with small turquoise stones. The conchas were not the thick, clunky type that Jimbo had seen in belts, but were thin and delicate. Between each concha was a single bear claw, curving inward, its musky color leading to a simple silver base. At the bottom, a rough turquoise stone hung like a pendant, surrounded by a tight circle of the flecked, tawny feathers from the body of a hawk, laid on a black opal face. It was a stunning piece.

"That's something. Really something, Mike."

"You think? You're better about this kind of stuff than me. Figured I'd surprise her on her birthday."

"Looks to me like you did pretty well on your own. Funny, I never figured you for taste." Jimbo smiled a little, but he did not feel like smiling. He wondered why Mike had brought him in to see it. He wondered if this was Mike's way of saying *watch out* — which he should have been able to do for himself. "No, that'll be a big hit with the little lady."

Mike put a deposit down on the necklace and seemed to be in a good mood as they drove back to Kearney. The grass in the hay fields had turned sandy-colored in the hot July sun, in the dryness. The fresh blacktop on the Canyon Creek road sent off heat waves and smelled of tar. Jimbo remembered the billowing tunnels of dust that used to kick off the old dirt road, choking anything unfortunate enough to be following within a hundred yards. That was a good old road, but the blacktop was easier on a vehicle, that was for sure.

Two miles past the Bar V's gate, Mike turned onto the overgrown road of the Parker place, beeping his horn at a covey of sage hens to make them fly. Instead, they started to run in a great flurry of brownish tweed, circling across the drive, then settling back in the sagebrush and grass. Mike stopped the pickup; no sheep were in sight. "Old One-eyed Jack 'pears to have vacated," he said.

"The brute's got a name, does he?" Jimbo said.

"One-eyed Jack Parker. Claims to be the son of old Not Afraid."

"Is that right? Not Afraid Parker, guide for the Seventh Cavalry?"

"The same." Mike eased the pickup down the grassy drive, toward the bowed, gray barn. The log cabin was still standing, but the shed had been demolished by a cottonwood that had been torn down by one of Wyoming's rare but thundering gales. The grass on the land was long and still green, being naturally irrigated by the spring and a bordering creek. In the fall, it was a good place to hunt field birds.

"Should've heard that goofy Injun," Mike said. "Goddamn. Talking to his sheep like there weren't another soul in the county. 'We're home now, boys, and we ain't leaving.' He was looking off in a faraway sort of manner, holding that old shotgun of his that looked like it'd blow up in your face. . . . Gave me the willies."

"Shotgun, eh? Terrific."

"Balmy as hell. 'We're home now, boys,' he's saying. All these sheep kinda goin' 'baaaa-baaa, shut up, old man, and leave us eat.' "

Mike parked the truck at the bottom of the drive and turned off the engine. "Listen to that there." There was bleating from inside the old barn. "Goddamn him anyway, thinkin' he can hide 'em in the fucking barn." He leaned over Jimbo and opened the glove compartment, pulling out a .44 Magnum that he kept there for hunting.

"Listen, since I'm the only unarmed member of this little parley, maybe I should wait here while you two solve your differences."

Mike grinned, crinkling the sunburned skin around his eyes. "He's an old man, buddy boy. I told Avelyn you'd protect me."

"You're not really going to need that?"

"This guy's loco. I don't know what the hell I might need."

Mike stepped from the truck and looked up to the cabin. The chinking had fallen out from between the logs, and heavy cardboard was tacked up against the paneless windows. Beside the remains of the shed a rusted, horse-drawn mower lay half-hidden in the tall grass, and the homestead's wooden-runnered sleigh for winter feeding was caved in and overturned.

"Says he was born there," Mike said.

"Why don't you leave him be, Mike?"

Mike turned and called up the hill: "Hey, Mr. One-eyed Jack Parker!"

They waited for a moment, then the cabin door slid off its hinge as it was being opened. An old Indian stepped onto the porch, a shotgun slung over his spindly arms. His braided hair hung long beneath a black, weathered cowboy hat. There were beaded tassels at the end of each braid. He had a dark face, wrinkled as a dried-out piece of leather, and his eyepatch was faded from the dust and sun, so that it looked gray. He looked down at them coldly.

Mike started up the hill toward the old man. "Time for talkin's through, Mr. One-eyed Jack Parker! You're gettin' off my land, and I mean now!" Jimbo followed hesitantly.

"Don't you move a goddamn inch — " the Indian yelled, waving his shotgun. Jimbo stopped. Mike moved ahead, whispering back, "He's a bluffer." Then he shouted, "You're gettin' off'n my land!" just before the shotgun blast — high — sent them scurrying back behind the truck. The pellets smacked into the barn and ricocheted into the grass, a few pinging off the bed of the pickup, driving the sheep inside to bleat and carom recklessly off the weathered gray boards.

"You listen, One-eye! I got a gun here; I'm holdin' it right in my hand, and you're gonna get hurt if you don't put down that twelve-gauge. You hear me?" They waited for the old Indian to reply. Jimbo poked his head around the bumper and looked up the hill. "You see him?" Mike asked.

"Yeah."

"What's he doin'?"

"Nothing. Just standing there."

"Got his gun?"

"Yeah."

"Gettin' ready to put it down?"

"Doesn't much look like it. He's reloading. Listen, Mike, this is absurd."

"Goddamn you, One-eye! I mean it now, you put that gun away or you'll get hurt. We can talk this thing over —"

"You said time's for talkin's through!" One-eyed Jack hollered down.

"Old bastard . . ." Mike muttered. "You're fuckin' right it's through! I'm gonna come up there and you're gonna get off'n my land nice and peaceful, and nobody's gonna get hurt. You hear me?" Jimbo still crouched behind the front tire and watched One-eyed Jack. "What's he doing now?" Mike asked.

"He's through reloading . . . he's taking aim, I think."

Mike sat back against the truck and considered. "He hear me?"

"Hard to say."

"Look like he's bluffin'?"

"Not much."

He breathed out a long sigh. "Shit."

"Say, Mike, you thought about letting the sheriff handle this? I'm not certain we're qualified."

"Qualified? Qualified? To throw a crippled-up granddaddy Injun off'n our own property? Shit, buddy boy, sheriff ain't hardly enough help . . . we better round up a posse."

Mike began to stand up, the revolver at his side, as if presenting himself for a duel. ". . . You crazy sonofa—" Jimbo said, but a shot rang out and cut him off. It flew overhead so nearby that they felt the air move. Mike dropped back down behind the truck as the pellets smattered against the barn, sending the sheep baaing and crashing around inside again.

"You loco sonofabitch! You syphilitic bastard!" Mike's face was red and dripping from the heat and his anger. "Jesus Christ, did you see that? I've had it with that fucker! His eyes were so wild with fury that Jimbo didn't know what he had in mind, charging up the hill after the old man with his gun blazing, or what — just knowing that he was going to do something, and he'd do it quickly and without any thought; and that whatever it was, he had no more a chance of stopping him than of growing wings — though he tried.

"Hold on now, Mike —"

"I've had it with you, you old bastard! I'm going into that barn and shooting every one of your goddamn sheep until you throw down that gun! You hear me?"

"He's listening, Mike . . . hold on now —"

"I'm gonna kill 'em all! You hear that? He hear that?"

"I think so."

"Fuck him." With his gun pressed to his thigh, Mike scrambled on hands and knees to the barn and flung the door open, diving inside just ahead of another twelve-gauge shell.

"You all right?" Jimbo asked him.

"Keep your eye on the old fart."

Mike shut the barn door behind him. He fired a gunshot that was followed by a cacophony of bleats and crashes as the frenzied sheep ran before the gunfire, looking for a way out. There was another shot and another animal squeal. Then another. One-eyed Jack stumbled off the porch of the old cabin. His face was frightened, bewildered. It had no white blood in it. It was brown with the features of the Sioux nation, so rounded compared with the sharpness of the Crow tribe Jimbo was used to. The only whiteness in the old man was in his clothes — his jeans, his boots, his cowboy hat — and his voice as he called, "Stop . . . stop it —" his voice a croak from age and dryness and fear. Another shot cracked within the barn.

He dropped his shotgun hesitantly and ran forward on withered, sticklike legs. Jimbo thought he would teeter and fall. "Stop it! Don't ya do it!" he yelled, his voice and steps more frantic as he neared the barn. "Whyn't ya leave 'em be?"

Jimbo ran inside the barn. "Don't, Mike. He's coming . . ."

Mike turned his head toward the old Indian stumbling from the cabin without his gun, and Jimbo saw a look come into his face that was far, far removed from pity; a look he had seen in his boyhood when Mike knocked out the boy who had spat at him in the state basketball tournament, when a glare came into his eyes seeming to dare anyone to touch him. Mike raised his gun and fired one more time into the huddled mass of sheep that pressed against the far corner of the barn. Jimbo saw one jump upward from the impact of the slug, there being no room either forward or sideways. One-eyed Jack saw it, too; Mike had been sure of that, waiting until he was near enough the now-open door to get a clear view. Then the sheep disappeared beneath the hooves of the others.

"I said he's coming!"

"I heard you." He shooed the rest of the flock through the door of the barn. Left behind in the dung-odored gloom were five dead animals clustered together near the far end, their wool fouled by blood and runny droppings.

One-eyed Jack hobbled into the barn, staring at the sheep. He wouldn't look at Mike or Jimbo. He dropped to his knees beside the first carcass and began murmuring in Sioux. The words sounded like names. They sounded like running brooks sound, or wind through the trees. Indian names. They sounded like an old woman's sadness. The old Indian knelt there, speaking over each carcass as in prayer. Then he turned to Mike. "Them sheep done nothin' to you."

"Crapped all over my barn while you were taking potshots at me."

"Piss on ya . . . ain't *your* barn," One-eyed Jack said in an easy western drawl. He looked old and weak beside Mike, now that he didn't have his shotgun.

Mike said, "I own this barn, and I own this land."

"You own nothin'." The Indian turned and walked away from the reeking barn. He stepped stiffly and with a limp. A breeze had picked up, and the grasses around the old homestead shook their seeded heads softly. The sheep that had fled the slaughter were now browsing a short distance away. One-eyed Jack's bony fingers fished into his shirt pocket for his Skoal, and he stuffed a thumbful behind his lower lip. He unzipped his fly and began urinating, his back to them. "You own nothin' . . . this land owns you, McKenzie. You can shake out your pecker and piss on this land,' but you can't own it. . . . You can piss on a soul, but you can't own it. . . . This land's got a soul bigger'n you are ignorant. . . . A person can't own another soul . . . even a white person . . ." He zipped himself back up and glared with his good eye at Mike, then spat a lipful of tobacco juice at his feet. "Piss on you, McKenzie."

Suddenly he turned to Jimbo. "Who the fuck're you?"

"Jimbo McKenzie."

One-eyed Jack Parker smiled a faraway smile that showed off his stained and broken teeth. "You the brother of this ignorant post?" He nodded to Mike, who was suppressing a grin. "Well, piss on you, too. Piss on you all." Instead, he spat at Jimbo's boot, and a dribble of brown saliva dripped down his chin.

"You fellas know Mr. Vic McKenzie?" One-eyed Jack asked. His eyes — his eye — was gone again, staring off from the here and now to where his mind wandered, the sheep and the killing forgotten. "Mr. Vic McKenzie, he came down here years back when my pa and me was tannin' the hide from the fall steer. He seen us and says, 'You Sioux tan better'n the niggers back home.' He says that and asks my pa fer a new pair of chaps fer his boy . . ." One-eyed Jack was looking up at the cabin with a cloudy recollection over his face. His mouth hung open. Jimbo wished he would wipe the brown spittle from his chin.

". . . called me Jackie . . . says, 'Jackie boy, I'm a gonna hold this here land fer you so's you kin buy her back someday . . .' "

He turned back to Jimbo. "Who the fuck're you?" Jimbo didn't say anything. "You weren't that little fella my pa made them chaps fer? You know my pa? Not Afraid Parker? That there's Not Afraid Parker's cabin . . ." He glowered at Mike. "That there's Not Afraid Parker's *barn* . . ." He nodded and crossed his arms. "Only Sioux in the state to own land . . . Not Afraid was a scout . . . scout fer the U.S. Army . . . fer Major Reno of the U.S. Army . . . . That there's Not Afraid Parker's cabin. . . . Weren't legal fer the Sioux to own land off'n the reservation. . . . No Indians could, as I recollect. . . . Piss on you, McKenzie." He spat again toward Mike.

"You were born there?" Jimbo asked him.

"Who the fuck're you?"

"Don't get him goin'," Mike warned. "Got no mind left and he starts talkin' crazy. Can't make any sense to him . . ."

". . . Born right here . . . just piss on you. Mr. Vic McKenzie, he bought the land from Pa so's the gov'ment wouldn't take 'er over. He knew . . . it weren't legal, but it was ours. My pa's buildin' his cabin and tannin' his hides and raisin' his kids made it ours. . . . He's buried here, my pa. Mr. Vic McKenzie says it's all right to bring him over from the reservation and bury him right here. . . . Not Afraid Parker's buried here . . . scout fer Major Reno of the U.S. Army. . . . That's't makes it his . . . just like that ole dead cottonwood. . . . Dyin' on a land's what makes it yours, and you can call it anybody's you like on the legal books, but that don't make it right . . . person can't own somethin' else's soul, no matter how ya dress it up . . . same as you can dress me up like a white man, and learn me to speak like a white man, but it won't make me one by your account or mine. . . . Mr. Vic McKenzie, he says, 'Jackie, you come back someday and I'll sell her to you fair and proper.' You know Mr. Vic McKenzie? Go get him and he'll tell you."

Jimbo said, "He was my grandfather. He's been dead over a year."

"You go get Mr. Vic. He'll tell ya. I got cash money."

"Where you got cash money?" Mike asked.

"I got cash money." He spat another lipful of tobacco juice

at Mike, who skipped back a step. "I used to break them colts fer Mr. Vic . . . two bucks a head and ya can't get 'em broke better. . . . He knows that, too. . . . He's all the time tellin' me, 'Jackie, you're the only Injun I ever seen worth a damn at breakin' a horse, and I'm the only white man I ever seen worth a damn at breakin' a wife . . .' " He grinned and winked obscenely. "Got any whiskey?"

"Nope."

". . . Been dead, eh?" One-eyed Jack fell silent.

Mike said, "You gonna get off this land, or are we gonna take you down to the sheriff?"

"Fuck you and your sheriff, too."

"You gonna get off this land? I'm moving my cows up here first of September, and your sheep ain't gonna be eating any more of my grass."

The old man wagged a finger as gnarled and hard as a cherry twig in Mike's face. "It ain't right what you did to them sheep. It ain't natural. Fuckin' un-natural to treat things like that if you're askin' me, and I say piss on you."

"Them sheep's still here by tomorrow, I'll shoot 'em all."

"Fuckin' un-natural."

"You best be gone by tomorrow."

Mike turned around and went back to the truck. Jimbo waited for a moment, watching the old Indian. Mike backed the truck around and called to him through the window. "You coming?"

Jimbo walked over. "He might leave, but he'll be back."

"Probably. Get in. Crazy pecker."

"What's it matter if he stays?"

"Get in, goddammit. I might need this grass come fall."

"Bullshit. What the hell's it matter?"

"It matters."

"*What's* it matter?"

"Because it *matters!* Now get the hell in. A man's got to look after what's his. Nobody else will."

"That old man —"

"That old man's no different from the next guy. Havin' a goddamn eyepatch and being an Injun don't give a man squatters' rights around here or anywhere else, buddy boy. When you put your foot down, you'd best put it down where you are than where they're going to push you — 'cause they'll try to push you, you can depend on that."

"If you can't see the difference between that old man coming back here to die and the Titanic Coal Company —"

"— you getting in or not?"

"Thanks just the same, I'll walk."

"Suit yourself."

The tires spun in the dirt and the pickup jolted forward. Jimbo kicked at it. It bounced up the drive and then sped along the blacktop, disappearing down the valley.

He walked back. Sam Benson was pulling out just as he reached the Bar V gate, and he told him the news. The judge had removed the temporary restraining order and denied the injunction. Titanic was free to open its strip mine.

CHAPTER 25

THE SLIDES HAD taken two weeks to develop. Avelyn had them in her purse, but she had not yet opened them, wanting to wait until she was home. Now that the Canyon Creek road was paved, it took less than fifteen minutes to drive back to the Bar V from town, even with the slow, flatbed trucks toting their extra-wide loads up the valley. Titanic had started construction on a mammoth dragline up at the mining site which would remove the overburden from the coal, a brute of a machine that was far, far too large to be transported on any public road. It would be a monster when it was finished. There were already several trailers parked in Lloyd's south pasture, strung with telephone wires and electric cables; and a small aluminum hut filled with explosives off by itself, surrounded by a high fence; and a prefabricated, single-story central office building. The place was an anthill of activity, and the traffic on their little road had increased correspondingly.

Avelyn had run into Marjorie Fox at the market. When they saw each other, Marjorie had started to turn back and go to the next aisle. But she came along and they nodded awkwardly and Avelyn asked how she'd been. They hadn't seen each other since the fight. Then she asked about Patty, and that got Marjorie going. Patty'd been running around with the strip-miners, the "scalpers," as Marjorie called them, and Hepp didn't much care for it. It was better than Patty spending time with that married

Billy Preston, but the miners weren't what she'd call "upstandin' gents." She wished that Jimbo would take a liking to her. She didn't see what was the matter with Jimbo. Then Marge had said she had to run, and Avelyn worked up the courage to ask if it was Hepp that didn't want her talking to her, or what. It seemed like no one had much time for her in town anymore, and she wondered if Hepp had said something to Marjorie, or if she really did have to run. And Marjorie's face reddened, and she couldn't meet Avelyn's eyes, finally saying, "It ain't you, hon. Just so you know it ain't you. I got to live with him is the thing." And Avelyn had told her that was all right, that she understood, and started to leave. But Marjorie wanted to talk now. "He's not hisself now," she said of Hepp. "It's always some money thing. Things been pretty tight. Tell me one thing, will you, hon? We keep hearin' different things. Mike ain't gonna sell your place?"

"No. He won't sell."

"Them coal people told us back in June he was all set to sell. Papers signed and everything."

"No. He never was."

"And he ain't gonna? You're sure about that? Why'd they tell us he was then? I wonder why they told us different?" Then she'd said, "They won't buy our place till Mike sells" — straight and simple like that, but with sort of a haunted look, as if she were talking about somebody who was dying. Which is what Marjorie had always felt about living in Kearney anyway. "What you want to stay around here for, hon?" she'd asked.

"Mike's here."

"You tell Mike you've had it up to here with this two-bit town. He'll move along . . ." and she started to get agitated; so that Avelyn knew it had been a hard summer for Marjorie, too. "I told Hepp that. I told him I's gonna spend this winter down south, with or without him. That got his attention, all right. I know it ain't ladylike to talk about your position in the community, but I don't give a damn anymore anyway — he'll either have us out of here by then, or the bank will. I don't give a good goddamn. You tell that Mike McKenzie you're good and fed up. He'll get that pretty little tail in gear. If he don't follow, he ain't worth having around to begin with. I got to run, honey. Hepp'd turn plumb blue if he found I was visiting with you. But I don't give a good goddamn anyway. He can go ahead and hit me, I ain't spending another winter in that house. I told him that." Then she'd said goodbye and left.

Avelyn parked the car and was unloading the groceries. Mike came in and took a Coke from the refrigerator as she was putting things away. He asked her about the trip to town. She told him about running into Marjorie. He was staring out the window above the sink and she wondered if he were listening.

"Hepp doesn't want her talking to me," she said.

"That's a loss."

He was still staring out the window. He wasn't even looking at her. "Oh, just shut up," she said.

Mike looked at her without saying anything. He dried his hands and snapped up his shirt, starting out the door.

"I'm sorry, Michael. But she's my best friend around here. You know that."

"I'm sorry, too."

"They're in rough shape with the bank. It's been no picnic for her, either."

"That's what I hear. Listen, I'm sorry. I'm going to work on that fence in the south pasture. Bring me some lemonade later, okay?"

"Okay."

"Were your pictures of the ram back?"

"Yeah."

"Well?"

"I haven't screwed up my courage enough to look at them."

"We'll have a show tonight."

"All right. Maybe."

She nodded, then watched from the window above the sink as he drove off in the tractor, pulling the spool of wire in the trailer behind. A fly knocked against the pane in buzzing spurts. She turned and stared at the kitchen table, where she had set out the meat and potatoes and carrots and onions for that night's stew. She was tired.

She went to her desk and took out her slide viewer, pressing down the button to test the light. Then she looked at her slides. The long lens had given the film a grainy texture that she liked, and the soft morning light had an orange tint where it fell on the ram. The horizontal ridges around the base of its horns were sharply ringed with fine shadows, and in the background, the foreshortened wall of granite seemed to soar upwards in a sheer face. The ram's breath was steaming. The pictures made her feel full and good inside. She went through them all again, more slowly.

Afterward she went into the mudroom and slipped on her gardening boots. She stopped out front where the roses and marigolds and impatiens were in bloom and pinched off the sun-blackened buds. It would be nice when fall came, she thought. Wyoming's fall did not have the shocking reds and oranges of New England's, but in a subtle way it was the loveliest time of the year. The last week of September the aspen leaves and cottonwoods would begin to change from drab green to drab yellow mottled with green. Then suddenly one morning the mottled yellow would turn to the most extraordinary gold, made the more so by the browns and tans of the dried grassland and cut hay fields that would have curled every pigment of color inside them to lie like a nut for the winter. The dark, rich evergreen color of the pines surrounding the smaller aspen groves made the yellow leaves glow. In the late afternoon, the setting sun shining up the Canyon Creek area toward the Custer National Forest would make the golds that much richer, and the sky a deeper blue. It was then that the Bighorn Mountains to the south took on a purplish tint. That happened only in the fall.

She continued on to the vegetable garden. She knelt in the dirt, setting her weed bucket beside her, and dug her weeding knife between the carrot tops for the tiny weed shoots that were starting to appear. The earth was cool underneath and felt good on her fingers. The soil, compost she had started piling her very first summer, was rich and black. The peat it was mixed with was reddish, and she could see it as she broke the soil apart in her fingers. You needed peat in that dry climate to hold the moisture.

She heard footsteps up from the yard. "How goes the battle?" Jimbo asked.

"Which one?" She shook her ponytail away from her face as she turned her head. When he shrugged, she said, "The battle against weeds is pretty successful for the time being."

"That's good news."

He seemed aloof, wary. He had been that way around her for the past two weeks. Avelyn moved nimbly over the row of carrots and began weeding between the tiny shoots of beets. "And I've seen my photographs of the bighorn sheep," she said, knowing that would be a safe enough subject, reminding them as it did of Mike. Though it also reminded her of that first afternoon after the pack trip, when Jimbo had stood on the porch and said that he'd better be careful, that he couldn't be running around in love with his brother's wife. As if it had happened. As if it were true.

"They're good," she continued. "There's one with the old ram staring right into the camera and his breath looks like it's going to steam up the lens. I think it's the best thing I've ever done . . . the texture of the rock and that dawn light —"

"That's terrific."

"Not that it matters now that I don't have any place to show them. But so what. I've seen it. It's beautiful."

His mind seemed to be drifting. "Show them in town."

She smiled and went back to her weeding. "I didn't tell you? Trudy Miller gave back all my prints. It seems Jeb would like to sell out to Titanic."

"Oh. Well, send them to someplace good. Send them to New York."

Avelyn laughed brightly. "Oh yes. New York should be about right. Look." She moved her fingers quickly, then held up an earthworm, wriggling. "Look at that baby. Six inches easy. Earthworms are terrific for a garden. Earthworms and beetles and we've got them both. In abundance. This is one blessed garden, and I am a terrific little gardener. I am not a bad photographer, but I'm afraid it's only a hobby. I'm a gardener by profession."

"You should show your stuff around. You should put together a portfolio and when you go back for your sister's wedding take a few days to show it around."

She threw her weeding tools into the bucket and stood up, brushing off the knees of her overalls. "You're sweet to say so."

She looked up at him quickly, trying to read what was in his eyes. He averted them. She lowered her head again, walking past him and saying over her shoulder, "I've promised Mike some lemonade. Walk down with me if you like." She jogged to the house and reemerged with a large thermos. Jimbo walked with long, slow strides, his hands in his pockets.

"So tell me of your battles," she said, catching up with him. "Are you all set for your great flight to grad school, escaping the McKenzie name?"

"What gave you that idea?"

"What gave me that idea? Honestly, Jimbo, sometimes you act like you're the only person on the face of the earth who thinks."

"That's preposterous. There are other people who think."

"Just none around here, right? Never mind. We don't have to talk about it. When do you start?"

"All I want to do is get a degree. I'm not escaping."

"All right. Fine. We're not exactly escaping either."

They walked past the family cemetery and the cottonwoods growing beside the spring. Ahead, they could see the tractor, and Mike farther down, working on the fence. Avelyn felt bad about having put Jimbo on the defensive, and she tried to think of something else to say.

"I'm sorry, Jimbo. That was presumptuous. I'm getting so stupid it scares me."

"What was presumptuous?"

He was still on the defensive and she wondered whether to get into it again. "That you were trying to escape the McKenzie name by going to grad school. That was a stupid thing to say."

"No, it wasn't." He walked along slowly. "You're probably right. I've always been an escapist at heart." He smiled.

"Now you're selling yourself short."

"I'm admitting a fault. You're so used to living with Mike, who's never shown weakness in his entire life, that you think admitting to a fault is selling yourself short. It's not."

"You have an odd conception of your brother if you think that."

"Mike's never been weak in his whole life. It isn't in his nature."

"It's in everyone's nature."

"Not brother Mike's."

"Oh, don't be an ass, Jimbo."

"No? I watched him shoot a half-dozen sheep last week to prove he wasn't weak. That was the only purpose he had."

"To prove he *was*," she said.

"It proved he was wrong, not that he was weak. That was the point. He wasn't going to give in — not to Titanic, not to you, not to some crippled-up Indian who was coming home to die. You best make your stand where you are rather than where they're going to push you, 'cause *by Gawd!* they'll sure as hell try to push you, buddy boy! That's what he told me. The Code of the West: Stand pat! Don't you move a gawddamn inch! That's how he thinks he's going to beat this thing."

They had stopped walking. Avelyn looked at him, upset.

"It's true," he said. "And we were talking about this the other night, remember? About Papa Vic? Well, he may have been one of those old buggers who opened up this area, but you can bet *he* wasn't living by any Code that said to *stand pat!* or he never would have gotten this far in the first place. He never would have left Johnstown, Pennsylvania. He'd have stayed right there and rebuilt his old man's general store. That's what Mike would have done. And the next flood to come along would have laced him, the same damn way Titanic Coal's going to lace him. But I don't care about that, 'cause Mike's our goddamn hero. But it's going to lace you, too, pretty lady, if you're around."

Her eyes had welled up with tears. She blinked them down

and saw Mike walking toward them, some way off, his shirt in his hand and his T-shirt wet under the arms and down the front.

"He's coming." She turned her face away.

"I don't care if that's the way *he* wants to fight it. It's *his* goddamn Code. It's not yours. That's what I care about."

Avelyn wiped her face and her eyes on the sleeve of her shirt. "People aren't as strong as they pretend to be. Nobody is. You forget that sometimes."

She turned and took a couple of steps toward Mike. He was wiping beneath his chin with his balled-up shirt. "Anything wrong?" he asked, seeing her expression.

She shook her head, her mouth tight. Jimbo stepped forward. "How's it going with the fence?" he asked.

"All right. Got her licked. That second hay crop's comin' in good." He glanced back to Avelyn. "You all right, hon?"

"I'm fine, Michael." She looked away. "I'm fine. I was just telling Jimbo about the pictures. They came out great. They came out so nicely. Thanks for taking me."

"Well," he nodded, pleased. "Good deal."

Suddenly a loud explosion went off. It was not very nearby, but it was not so far away, either, and a thundering clap echoed between the south ridge and the mesa. They couldn't tell where it had come from, exactly. Jimbo asked whether it was a sonic boom.

Mike frowned. "I've got an idea it could be they're blasting from the mine."

"Not so soon," Avelyn said.

Mike shrugged. "S'pose it could've been something else."

They listened, but it was quiet now. He looked up at the sky, shading his eyes with his hand. "Might have been a plane," he said. They didn't see anything.

"It was so loud," she said, her voice straining. "What if it's that loud all the time?"

"It ain't bad," Mike said. "You get used to it. Could be that was just a plane." He grinned. "Anyway, that's not loud. Loud's a howitzer. You want to hear loud sometime, you go stand around a howitzer. Ever heard one of those, buddy boy? *That's* loud. Goddamn."

Another explosion sounded from up the valley, first a light reverberation, then the sudden clapping of the full blast. Avelyn covered her ears with her hands. "Oh! What are they doing?"

"They're dynamiting the overburden. It is goddamn noisy," Jimbo said.

"It's so *loud.* I'll never get used to something that loud."

"Yeah, you will," Mike said. "It's just you've never heard it before. It'll stop before long."

"How much aggravation do we have to live with? How on earth could I come across more aggravation than we have right here in Kearney! Michael! How much aggravation can there be? Was Vietnam more aggravating?"

Mike looked at her coldly. "I think you'd have found it a lot more aggravating."

Avelyn turned away, thinking: Yes, I'm being spoiled now, but this just isn't a lot of fun anymore. This hasn't been fun for a long time, and I know that isn't everything, but it's something — like the fight with Hepp was something and the calf business was something and the cost of a plane ticket home was something. All of it. You can't live off the past. You know that, don't you, Michael? I know you know that.

She turned back with a game smile. "I'm being a brat, aren't I? It's not your fault about the noise, and I'm blaming you." She glanced at Jimbo. "You see how stupid I'm getting."

"You're not being a brat," Mike said.

"Yes, I am. It's just that it's louder than I thought. And that machine they're building is bigger than I thought. I'll get used to them. I'll try to get used to them. Let's do something fun soon, though." She rubbed her finger along the front of Mike's T-shirt. "The river will be warm enough for tubing. Let's go tubing soon. All of us."

"All right," Mike said. "We'll do that. Be a good way to get out of this heat."

"Good. We'll take a picnic and drink some wine. We'll all go. It'll be fun." She handed Mike the thermos. "Here's your lemonade. I'm going down to look at the creek. I'll see you guys later, okay?"

Walking across the south pasture, she could hear the shrill

buzzing and clacking of the insects in the knee-deep grass and the swishing of the seeded heads against her overalls. Another explosion sounded from the new mine. It rumbled through the heat and down the valley. Then it was still again, and the insect and grass sounds resumed, and the pasture was as it had always been. Since Papa Vic and before. Ahead was Canyon Creek, running beside the winding string of cottonwoods, pressed up against the south ridge. And across the hay fields, soaring up out of the valley floor, the mesa — table-top flat and dotted with distant reddish blotches of grazing cattle. Everything in between was part of the Bar V — McKenzie land — fertile and rich and green with irrigation. You should have been able to grow together on such land. Two people, left to themselves, would surely have been able to grow together. There was so much room in which to grow. Left to themselves.

CHAPTER 26

"**T**IBBS WAS A prankster," Deacon told him, "all the time pullin' stuff on the other guys, all kinda stuff; and he was such a damn good cowboy that the guys never said nothin' about it. Tibbs was just a little guy, but built like the stump of a doggone oak, and with a temper. No, when Tibbs got you, you'd flat been *had*."

Jimbo smiled over his coffee. He could hear the others moving around upstairs, getting dressed. Mike had already left for town to pick up Avelyn's necklace and some supplies, and he had taken the inner tubes along to have them filled.

"But Michael, you know, he's got a temper, too," Deacon went on. "He'd plumb chew your ass off for so much as movin' quick around his ropin' horse. And he'd've been a good calf-roper if he'd stuck with it. He would've, too, if he'd been able to stay out of the army. But that ain't a life for a family man anyhow, buck. Hell, it's good he give it up.

"Well. Tibbs figures he's gonna put some beautiful burr in Michael's pants, kinda give it to the rookie, you know. So at the Frontier Days in Cheyenne he cuts off the tail of his ropin' horse. Trims it right down to the nub, just as short as a little oinker's. Poor thing couldn't chase flies. Oh, buck, you should've seen Mike when he sees it. I thought he'd come to tears. He's about twenty-one or so" — Deacon wagged a finger at him over his coffee — "and he *knows* who's done it. He *knows*. Don't know how. Kinda like he knew it was Hepp that messed with them calves. Was he *mad*. But he doesn't fly off the handle; he just sets tight. Then when Tibbs goes into the chutes for his saddle bronc, Michael borrows some nail polish from one of them sweet young things used to follow him around, and goes back to where Casey's got his pride and joy parked — a new yellow Cadillac. Spankin' new. *Gold,* really. Then he squats down and on the door beneath Tibbs's initials he paints: THE LITTLE QUEER FROM FORT PIERRE. Real neat job. Looked kinda nice, kinda professional. Neat and bright and red. That's where Tibbs was from, Fort Pierre, South Dakota.

"Everyone figures Tibbs'll kill him. That Caddy was his *pride and joy.* He comes up to Michael afterward and looks him straight in the eye. Says: 'Some sonofabitch put nail polish on my new car; you got any idea who that fella might be?'

"And Michael looks him right back, not flinching a muscle, and nods over to his no-tailed horse. 'Nope, Casey, I sure don't. . . . But I've got a hunch we're lookin' for the *same sonofabitch!*' Deacon beamed over his coffee. "Yup, *'the same sonofabitch!'* Ole Michael can be right dry."

Jimbo nodded and smiled. "That he can."

Deacon was adamant about passing up the picnic and tubing expedition. He said he wanted to watch a baseball game. But it was Denny's birthday, and when Mike returned from town he ordered Deacon to come along. Avelyn had already packed the lunches and the wine.

"Gracious goodness me," Deacon said, pursing his lips and fluttering his little finger in front of his nose. "A nice light chablis would be heaven." So they added a case of beer and a bottle of Jack Daniel's to the provisions, and left.

There had been no rain, but the rivers were still high from the snow melting in the mountains. They drove to Cobbs Landing, ten miles west of Kearney, and dropped the truck with the food and drink there. Then they drove the station wagon four miles up the road, where it crossed the Tongue River.

Jimbo hadn't been swimming there since he was a boy. He was wearing a pair of cutoff jeans — they all were, except for

Avelyn, who wore a two-piece swimsuit with a pink button-down shirt open down the front. She had her hair pinned up and she jumped into the river first, crying out from the cold. He watched her. The current was swift and it swirled her along. She called to them to follow.

"I'm not freezing my tail alone," Mike said to Deacon.

Deacon, Jack Daniel's in hand, moved cautiously away from the bank. He was dressed as he would have been for any other day, wearing his baseball cap and heavy boots. "I'm too old. You kids go ahead and have a good time. I'll keep a look-see ahead for trouble spots."

Mike was testing the water. "Ain't no trouble spots."

"Could be a tree down. Could be a fat bull down to drink. Or angry trouts. Fella can't be too careful." He lifted the bottle and took a drink. "Me and Jack Black're happy as a warm muff right here."

"It's only water. You touched some just like it in January with your last bath."

Deacon nodded. "Damn fine memory, too. I'll just lope ahead here and keep my eyes peeled for trouble."

Mike chuckled a little. Then he began to laugh. "You can't swim! You can't fucking swim!"

Deacon stepped another yard back from the bank.

"You can't swim a lick!" Mike waded out to his knees.

"Man were meant to swim, he'd been borned with webbed feet and gills, for Chrissakes."

"You're a sorry lout. You can't swim a lick!"

Jimbo watched the two of them, smiling.

"Well, I can *hear,* anyway. You don't need to tell me again. . . . You're laughin' at me, McKenzie, a growed man paddlin' aroun' in an inner tube like a bloody hubcap . . ."

Mike sprang from the water, tapping Denny to come with him, and the two of them scrambled up the bank after Deacon, who fled pathetically on his gimpy leg.

"Don't do it, McKenzie, damn you! Now fun's fun —" Deacon was banjo-eyed as Mike and Denny dragged him back to the bank of the Tongue.

"High time you learned," Mike told him.

"No, it ain't . . . no, it ain't, I swear." Deacon stomped at Mike's bare feet with his boots, but Mike dodged him. He and Denny each took an arm and a leg and held Deacon suspended like a hammock. Jimbo had, by this time, waded into the shallows, where Avelyn was watching the performance, and Deacon appealed to them. "Sugarbabe . . . buck . . . you help me now! Don't let 'em do this . . . I cain't swim."

"You're gonna learn," Mike said.

"Put me down, boss . . . I'll be your best friend —" Mike laughed at him. "What d'you want me to do, you prick?" Deacon asked, becoming feisty. "You want me to say 'Uncle'?"

"I want you to swim."

"Well, I *cain't* swim! *Uncle! Uncle! UNCLE!!!* Put me *down!*"

"We aim to . . . Ready?"

"I cain't swim!"

"I know that. You're going to learn."

"I got along fine for fifty-six mother-lovin' years without swimmin' a stroke! What do I wanta learn for now?"

Mike grinned. " 'Cause you won't make it the next fifty-six seconds if you don't, ole pal . . ."

"Ole pal, my ass!" But Deacon's feistiness left in the face of the smooth-flowing surface before him. "Don't do it, Mike!"

"Ready, Den?"

"McKenzie! Gawddammit, I *cain't swim!*"

"Just think like a duck . . . think like a duck . . . quack-quaaack-waaaaa-waack-waa-waaaa —"

Deacon started struggling again, trying to hump his suspended body into a defendable position. "I cain't swim!"

"One . . ."

"Gawddammit, don't . . . don't do —"

"Two . . ."

"Quack-quack-quaaackk . . ."

"Three . . ."

They pitched him. There was a great *whoosh* as Deacon sucked in his breath, and he hit the water and sank like a stone, never so much as dog-paddling, never even rebreaking the surface.

They waited for a moment for some sign of a struggle, then Mike dove after him with Denny right behind.

Mike came back up with Deacon in tow. Deacon's face was white and he was too scared and out of breath to curse him or thank him or do anything but stare at him in disbelief. Finally, standing in the shallows, he choked out, "I'm about half full of water, you prick."

"I told you to make like a duck, not a loon."

"I damn near drowned. I'm half full of water." Deacon was panting, and Mike had one arm around him, holding him up. He was grinning. Jimbo was watching, standing beside Avelyn, feeling strangely content. The sun felt good against his skin, warming. A moment later Mike gave out a yelp and dove underwater, resurfacing a few yards downstream to rant and shout at Deacon, calling him a pig, a foul hog, and a grubworm for urinating on his leg. Deacon zipped himself back up and waded to shore, grabbing the bottle of Jack Daniel's and the unclaimed inner tube. "Let's go swimmin'. Let's skedaddle." Still fully dressed, Deacon wiggled himself into the tube like a chicken on a nest, his baseball cap drooped shapelessly on his head, and cast off.

It took nearly two hours to float back to the truck. Deacon, Denny, and Mike formed a flotilla, passing the Jack Daniel's back and forth between them. Avelyn and Jimbo followed, Avelyn's leg draped over the side of his tube to keep him from drifting away. She had knotted the front shirt-tails together around her waist and trailed one hand in the water. Her dark hair was wet. He was telling her college stories about blind dates and southern girls who stayed thin by chewing laxatives. She'd known girls like that. She remembered those days. Every once in a while he would point out a fishing hole.

As they came within sight of Cobbs Landing, Mike broke off a stick from a willow bush and poked a hole in Deacon's tube. The air bubbled out behind him. "Gawddamn you, McKenzie! You're tryin' to drown me!" they heard him yell. Deacon jabbed a finger toward the hole, then ripped off his cap and tried to plug it with that. The tube began to sink lower, losing its shape, and his butt and belly submerged until only Deacon's shoulders and feet were sticking up. He was too drunk to be scared. "Gawddamn. Somebody save me."

"Make like a duck, old man," Mike called.

Deacon began earnestly to quack and splash, but it didn't help. He was sinking lower, and Mike took the last gulp of whiskey and threw him the bottle. "Grab hold of this, lad; she floats!"

Deacon caught the bottle with just his hands and head above water. He disappeared beneath the surface, the bottle hanging up for an instant after he had vanished. Twenty yards downstream he ran aground a sandbar. They heard him before they saw him, sitting there and cursing as if he'd never stopped the whole time he was under. ". . . gawddamn infantile prick . . ." He was still holding the bottle, the flattened tube beneath him. He shook himself and primped like a duck whose feathers had been ruffled, then got up and belched.

They waded ashore, and Avelyn set the platter of sandwiches on the picnic table under the trees. The hot sun was wonderful after being so long in the water. They stretched and dried out. Jimbo was putting together his fly rod as the others got into the cooler of beer. He grabbed his sandwich and started to walk upstream, his flies in the sheepskin band around his hat.

A half mile up there was a rippling stretch that became smooth and deep by the far bank. The river cut underneath the clumps of grass overhanging the bank, and the trout would be lying there in the brightness of midday. He tied on a black, weighted woolly worm and threw it up next to the shore. It drifted down, the leader catching the sunlight and then disappearing, until the floating line was swept up in the faster water and got ready to whiplash. He raised the tip of his rod and drew out the fly, casting again. He worked that stretch with five or six casts, then waded up toward a fencepost that was leaning out into the water, forming a little pool.

Something grabbed his leg, and he turned around just as Avelyn was breaking the surface. He thought at first she was naked, the water splashing up and obscuring the top of her suit, her shirt lying back on the shore and her skin white and slippery.

She laughed at his surprise and dove back in, sliding under the surface with barely a ripple. Then she came up again, her mouth opened in a wide smile.

"You'll ruin the fishing."

"You've had your chance."

"I've had five minutes. Don't move. Big Jumbo lurks beneath that fencepost."

Jimbo withdrew his fly and false-casted several times, finally dropping it well upstream of the pool. The current brought the line down, the leader arcing behind without a ripple. As the line reached the pool he felt a tug, and he struck. The line went taut and didn't budge. He had hooked the fencepost.

Avelyn laughed. "Big Jumbo!"

"Shit." He was flicking the line, trying to dislodge it.

"I'll get it!"

She dove under, then surfaced, otterlike. She was a beautiful swimmer with even, powerful strokes that sliced through the current. She reached the post and unhooked the fly, then released the post and drifted, pointing her arms up and slipping elegantly beneath the surface. She came back up with that wide, breathless smile.

"Watch this!" Avelyn arched her back and neck so that her hair trailed behind in the water, then suddenly tucked her knees up to start an underwater flip. She pointed her toes upward as she was halfway through, then the current caught her and her feet splayed wildly. She twisted to the surface with a pained frown. "I pulled something —"

"Are you all right?"

She drifted with the current until she was in the shallows, then she waded to the far shore, massaging her back. She sat in the grass.

He waded across. "You all right?"

"That was stupid of me," she said. "The current caught me."

"Where is it? Your back?"

She nodded and pointed to the lower left side of her back. "I must've pulled it. I'll be okay."

"Lie down a second. Where is it? There?" Her skin was wet

and firm and cool. He rubbed it gently, watching the brown coarseness of his hand against the white of her back. "That hurt?"

She shook her head. The grass had been grazed short there, and she lay with her cheek flat to the ground.

"Showoff," he said.

"Don't tease. It hurts."

"Is it feeling better? Should I stop?"

"No. It feels good."

"You feel good."

"Careful."

"I don't want to be careful."

She didn't say anything. He kept rubbing her back gently. Her skin was warm now, and soft. The air was not quite still. It moved around them like a touch.

"Avelyn?"

Her eyes were closed. She looked fragile lying there, her arms beneath her. He touched her shoulder. "Avelyn?"

"No. Don't." She looked at him, her eyes frightened by his tone: that vulnerable, trapped look.

There was a thickness in his throat so that the words stuck there, did not want to come, his heart pounding and her lying there so lovely and shy. "I don't care. I love you."

She twisted her head around and lay there, perfectly still, looking at him. Then she pressed her forehead into his chest.

"It's true," he said, his voice breaking.

She squeezed him tightly. "Oh, Jimbo. No."

"I wanted to say it. I wanted to." He held her and smelled her wet hair.

"Oh, Jimbo." She pulled back and looked at him, her eyes miserable. "Oh, you." She stroked his cheek with her hand, then rolled away from him and lay with her head between her elbows. "We can't," she said. "Oh, damn you."

"Avelyn." He touched her shoulder. It was bare and soft and he ran his hand down the smoothness of her back. He was trembling. He pulled his hand away, watching her lying there, her legs long and white and sleek, then he laid his hand on her back again. "I can't help it, Avelyn. I love you." Now that he had said it there was a churning inside and he wanted to say it again.

She rolled over, her eyes glistening. "No, Jimbo. Stop."

He touched her lips with his finger. "I can't stop. I don't want to stop. I can't help it, Avelyn, I love you." His voice was quaking, and something like resignation came into his eyes and he leaned down and kissed her, seeing that trapped animal look, but kissing her anyway, unable to stop himself, unable to think for the pounding in his ears and his chest. Her lips were soft and wet, everything else tense and tight and whirling, then she pushed him gently away, looking up with her eyes wide and blinking.

"Jimbo, we can't. We can't." There was sadness in her voice, and he looked down at her. He was still trembling, not just his hands now, but all over; with a great empty pit inside. "Don't think it's not tempting . . . you're not tempting . . ." she whispered. "But we can't."

"I know we can't," he said quickly, looking away. "I know that. What do you think I've been telling myself for the last month? We can't. But *I* can't, now. *I* can't. You see that?" He looked back at her. "*I* can't. You're too damn lovely to look at. You're too damn lovely to be with." He touched her cheek, then moved his fingers down her neck.

She took his hand in her hand and gently pulled it away. "You've been my strength, Jimbo. Leave me that. You've been such strength for me, you'll never know. I haven't let myself think of it beyond that. What good does it do to think of it beyond that? It ruins everything, you see?"

"It doesn't do any good. I know that. But I'm in love with you." His voice was desperate. "I *am*. I can't help it."

"No, you aren't. Listen to me. Don't shake your head. Listen. It's Mike's wife you've fallen in love with, not me; not Avelyn Stewart. You've put me up on some pedestal with Mike; that's not me you see up there. It's someone else, someone you've created who doesn't really exist. I'm flattered by it, Jimbo. I am. But it's not me. If we had been able to meet five years ago, then I wouldn't question all this. I'm sure we *would* fall in love. But right now it's all mixed up with your past dealings with Mike. It's not Avelyn Stewart you think you're in love with, but Avelyn, Mike's wife. Please, Jimbo, please take this in the right way, because you mean so very much to me."

He turned away from her, stung. His head went light, and he had to close his eyes to steady himself. There was a sour taste in the back of his throat and that great yawning emptiness in his belly. "It isn't true," he stammered.

She took his hand and squeezed it. "Please take it in the way I mean it. Please do. You mean so much to me."

He pulled his hand away. His head felt numb. "That isn't true," he said. Everything that had been tense and whirling was suddenly still. The river still, and the air, and the grass; except the wind was blowing and he listened to that. They sat for a while in silence, Avelyn watching him, her face filled with kindness and regret. The numbness in his head made it impossible for him to think things through very clearly, but there was a nagging feeling in the pit of his stomach that something terribly unfair had happened to him, though he did not quite know whom to blame. He couldn't think. It was unfair and untrue, but he couldn't think what to say to her. It wasn't true.

There was a distant blaring, steady and even. Avelyn's eyes flickered as she heard it. She turned her head and listened. "That's the truck. Mike's honking."

She got up and recrossed the river. He followed her. Avelyn picked up her shirt and moved quickly down the path. The horn continued to blare, louder and louder as they neared. He knows, Jimbo suddenly thought. It sounded like anger, that horn did, Mike's anger, his own, too long pent up and now gushing out in a long angry blast. He knows I have tried to seduce his wife, as he knew about Hepp, as he knew about Tibbs, as he knows about everything. He knows. His heart was beating faster.

Which was why it looked so wrong when they found Mike leaning against the front tire of the truck, his shirt off and his hat tipped low over his eyes, crunching a beer can. He looked up with an expression that was almost peaceful, past Avelyn, straight at Jimbo — something in the eyes not of rage or amusement or sarcasm, but a look Jimbo had never seen on him before. It was of understanding, or sympathy, or sadness; a look that had forgiveness in it and made Jimbo think: he has beaten me again, the sonofabitch. Mike forced a smile and had to yell over the blaring of the horn. "Denny locked himself in there and passed out!"

Jimbo could see Denny's great head slumped forward over the steering wheel. Deacon was lying on his back on the picnic table, his hands over his ears.

"Where are the keys?" Jimbo shouted.

"Truck's got the keys!"

Jimbo walked around the truck, as much to escape from Mike's gaze as to try to wake Denny. "Jesus, he puked all over the side of the door!" He pounded his hand against the glass.

"He can't hear you!" Mike shouted, getting to his feet.

"How much did he drink?"

"Drank it all!"

"He drink the whole case?"

"He had some help!"

Deacon came over, his eyes puffy and his palms pressed against his ears. "That's not doin' pretty things to my head!"

"Ask him to open the door!" Mike shouted.

Deacon went over and, not seeing the vomit, leaned against the door. "Whoops!" Mike said, laughing.

"Goddamn you, boss!"

"Let's rock it," Mike said.

The four of them got on the other side of the truck and rocked it sideways until Denny's head toppled off the horn and crashed against the door with a thump. He jerked upright, utterly confused. Mike was making faces at him. Denny unlocked the door and lay back down on the seat. Then they drove home, stopping on the way to pick up the station wagon.

Late that night Jimbo heard Stormy barking. Mike and Avelyn were still up, and he heard Mike talking to the dog: "Got a coon there, Storm? Got a coyote? That's a coon, eh? Hold on now. Hold on. We'll get him."

He heard Mike bound upstairs, opening the drawer where he kept his pistol, yowling with pleasure as if nothing was wrong or could ever be wrong. "By God, Storm," he was calling to the barking dog, "been a while since you and me treed a coon, eh? I'm gonna loosen up the old larynx . . ." He was downstairs again, his boots heavy on the old floorboards. "Hold on a tick . . ." Then he let out a fearsome call through the screen, an alternating series of dog growls and raccoon squeals and hisses that shook the night. It was what he called his coon squall, which he made by pinching his cheeks and squeezing air around the inside of his mouth, then growling nasally. Jimbo put his book down and came to the head of the stairs. Stormy was pawing the screen, whining to get out, and Mike squalled again, then kicked open the screen. "Go get him, Storm! Get him, boy! Whoooee, that felt nice!" He ran after the dog, the screen slamming behind him.

Jimbo came down. Avelyn was looking out the door, listening as the barking got fainter, and Mike gave another distant squall. She leaned back against him as he came up behind her. "Are we friends again?" she asked softly.

"Of course."

They stood like that for a while, listening to the chase.

"I'm still in love with him, Jimbo; whatever that's worth. It's crazy, but there it is. And he needs me. He needs us both."

"But you're not happpy."

"Part of me isn't."

"A large part."

She shrugged. "For now. So that's something we work on. I'm trying to be practical about this. I know that sounds like hell . . ." She turned and, for the first time, faced him. "But that's how I'm going to be. God knows I wasn't being practical when I married him in the first place . . ." She smiled a little. "But better late than never, right?"

"Sure. Why not?"

They didn't say anything for some time. They were looking out into the night, listening for the barking, which had suddenly stopped. "If you're going to be practical you should ask him to sell," he said.

"He won't sell."

"I thought you understood. I thought that's why you looked so scared the other night. I'd never seen you look scared before, and I thought it was because you understood he can't win this fight."

"He wants to try."

"You don't just try. Once you start something like this, once you hold out on the Titanic Coal Company and the whole bloody town, you can't just call a truce. There's a winner and a loser."

"Well. He thinks he can win."

"No he doesn't. He thinks he can go on like that two hundred million tons of coal doesn't exist."

"I don't care, Jimbo. I'm his wife."

Jimbo stepped back. "Let's get that barrier back where it belongs, eh, McKenzie? End of discussion." A pistol shot shattered the stillness. "One dead coon. One dead thief in the night." She was looking at him, hurt by his remark about barriers. Suddenly he felt bad. "Sorry. The wormwood of self-pity."

She smiled at him. "Poor, sweet Jimbo."

"Yes. Poor devil." He was listening for Mike's victory squall, or Stormy's barking, but there was nothing. "So, have you resigned yourself to living the next twenty years with a dragline peering in like Big Brother? Have you seen it? It's nearly finished. They call their machine Big Wally. That's cute, don't you think?"

"I know. I can see it from the pasture."

"Big Wally. Can you believe how big it is? The damn bucket's as big as a Greyhound bus. The body's as big as our barn. Big Mike and Big Wally. Oh, they'll do fine together."

She was still looking out into the night. "Where do you suppose he is? Could he have missed it? Maybe he only wounded it.'

"Mike? Are you kidding? Mike doesn't *miss*."

Avelyn swung open the door and stepped onto the porch, listening. There was nothing. "Michael?" she called. "Did you get it? Michael?"

She exchanged a glance with Jimbo.

"Come on," he said, crossing the porch. "He's probably passed out in the sagebrush."

They walked into the home pasture, Jimbo leading. There was a partial moon and a breeze just strong enough to stir the grass without breaking the silence. "Michael?" Avelyn called, not too loudly, as if unwilling to shatter the stillness. "You out there, you big mean raccoon?"

Jimbo stopped and Avelyn bumped into him. She gave a little laugh of surprise. They went farther and she called again. "Hey you, Michael? Hey, Stormy? Where are you guys?"

"Raccoon warden coming," Jimbo said.

"You hear anything?" she asked.

"No. Stop here." They listened for a long time. It was cool out and he could feel her shivering. "I don't know where the hell he is. He's probably going to jump out and scare the shit out of us."

"He wouldn't dare. Michael, don't you dare."

"Shh." Jimbo heard a cough. He started toward the fence, then stopped again. Somebody was standing there. He couldn't see his face.

"That you, Mike?"

Jimbo stepped forward. The man turned his head, and as the moonlight caught his profile he saw that it was Mike. There was a large, dark form lying at his feet, and as he came closer he saw it was a horse.

"Michael —?" Avelyn called, frightened.

Mike still didn't say anything. Jimbo could see the pistol hanging loosely from his hand. "What gives, man?" He knelt down and reluctantly touched the horse. It was still warm. As he moved his hand around, it came against a thick, hot wetness. "Goddamn, what is this?"

Avelyn stepped closer, "Michael? What is it?"

Mike said, "Stay away, hon."

"Why? What is it?" She started forward, but Jimbo stood up to block her way. The blood on his fingers got on her arm and she gave a startled cry.

"Better get her back to the house, buddy boy. I got to find my dog."

"Pasha! Is it Pasha?"

"What happened, Mike?" Jimbo asked.

"Oh, Jesus God!"

"Get her out of here, will you? You seen Stormy around?"

"What *happened* here?" Avelyn had pushed past him, and she stood over the horse, her hands covering her mouth.

"They slashed her tendons."

"Who did?"

"I couldn't see. Storm took off after the car." Mike was silent for a while, then he gave a loud whistle with his tongue. He waited, wiping the back of his hand against his chin. "Would've taken more'n one man. This'n didn't like to be handled much. Would've taken one man to hold her. I found a bucket of oats over there."

"Jesus." Avelyn sobbed.

"Slashed her just above the fetlocks . . . clean as a whistle. Down to the bone. Must've used a straight razor or somethin' like that . . ." He looked at Avelyn. "You wouldn't've wanted to see her, hon."

She shook her head, her fist pressed against her mouth.

"Whyn't you take her back, buddy boy? I got to find my dog."

"Are you all right?" Jimbo asked.

"Yeah. Take her back, okay?"

Mike buried Pasha that night. Jimbo heard the backhoe digging in the north pasture, crunching through the sandy soil. And later, after he was finished, the coyotes started up again, howling at the sky.

CHAPTER 27

TITANIC CHRISTENED Big Wally that weekend. The president of the company flew from out East and the governor came up from Cheyenne. It was the largest model ever assembled, over three hundred twenty feet from the tip of the main boom back to the body of the machine. There were two other booms that rose straight above the dragline, one hundred fifty feet in the air. Steel cables six inches thick ran from the tops of those two to the top of the third, which was suspended at an angle and from which the massive excavating bucket hung. After the governor broke a bottle of champagne against the tread of the giant machine, Big Wally gave a demonstration of its skills. From the tip of the largest boom, the excavating bucket was dropped with startling speed into the heap of rock and slate and limestone that had been dynamited off the coal seam. It was then dragged through until the jaws clamped shut, raised, and swung over one of the growing spoil banks. A lever was hit and the bucket flew open, releasing tons of debris with a great *whump!* It was swung back, and the bucket again dropped. *Whump!* A full minute passed between each bucketful. To and fro. To and fro. Big Wally. The pit was already a hundred feet deep from the work of the machine's predecessors, yet now its girdered neck rose that much and more above the plains, peeking out like a hungry steel dinosaur, seeming to reach up toward the sky and scratch it irreverently.

Jimbo watched it at work for a while, then continued up to

the Parker place, hoping to find the Indian. There was no sign of him. In the barn, the five sheep were bloated and rank with decay. As he walked back to the car, another vehicle pulled into the drive. It came all the way down, then whoever it was saw him and started to back up. Jimbo jogged over, and when he saw it was Patty Fox he waved at her to stop.

She was embarrassed. He couldn't imagine what she was doing there, but he didn't particularly care, and made no effort to find out, simply saying hello and explaining that he thought she was someone else. He started to walk away when she called after him, "You won't say nothin' to Hepp, will you?" He gave her a puzzled look. "About seein' me up here and all," she said, looking down nervously.

"Can't think why I'd mention it," he said.

She was definitely uncomfortable, fidgeting with her hands. "There's this fella I meet . . ." She looked up and flashed a smile, brushing a lock of her blonde hair from her face. "Hepp don't like me seein' them boys from the mine."

Jimbo had never known Patty very well, but she had always seemed like a nice enough girl. With a father like she'd had, and a brother like Hepp, he'd always felt a little sorry for her. "Works at the mine, eh?"

"He's a nice boy, though. Name's Roly. Don't say nothin' about it, okay, Jimbo?" She smiled, blushing. "I didn't think no one ever come down here."

"No. Hell, we never do. I was just checking on something."

She started to say something, so he waited. "Hepp don't think them miner boys is good enough for me, is what," she said hesitantly. "I don't know what he's lookin' for. I ain't well-schooled and well-mannered like you. I can't give a boy nothin' special." She shrugged her shoulders, and he didn't know what to say. "Why, for a girl like me, how could I ever expect to get a better fella than that Roly there, huh? He's a good-lookin' boy, makin' good money. How could a girl do better than that? I know he's prob'ly just sportin' around with a girl like me, just someone to pass the time with, but . . . a girl's got a right to make her own mistakes, don't she?"

Jimbo smiled. She looked up to see the smile, then she tilted her head and said, "You're a good guy, Jimbo. You are. You tell that stubborn brother of yours to keep his lookout. Hepp's all the time sayin' crazy things about what he's gonna do. You hear me? You tell him just to keep his head up. He's changed so much, that Hepp. Sometimes I don't know him, you know? All that crazy talk. I know it's just talk, but you tell that Mike to keep a lookout." She shrugged again. "You won't say anything about seein' me?"

"No."

"You're a good guy, Jimbo. You take care of yourself."

"You too."

He drove back up the road to the headgate of the irrigation ditch, which he cranked shut. They would be cutting the second hay crop in a few days, once the grass had dried. He kept thinking about what Patty had told him. That meant it had probably been Hepp who had slashed Avelyn's filly. Hepp and somebody else. He wondered whether he should say anything. Driving back down to the ranch, he thought of Patty waiting for her miner. Roly. There's your modern American cowboy, Mike old man. He's a scalper, not a cattleman. He moves right in and takes your land and sleeps with your women — just like Papa Vic did to that old Welshman farmer — stealing his seed money and taking his daughter Kate away, out West. She died of pneumonia in the same bed he died in sixty-seven years later. Only now, instead of Conestoga wagons, they take your women away in trailers. But you don't think these scalpers know how to survive like those old cowboys? You don't think these guys can adapt, moving from town to town, mine to mine, as strangers? You had bloody well better know how to adapt, without roots. There's your Great American Cowboy. There, working Big Wally.

CHAPTER 28

MIKE HEARD THE grandfather clock chime from the bottom of the stairs. It was late. There was a bluish light in the room from the curtains and the moonlight. The windows were open and it was cool, and outside crickets sounded. Avelyn looked out, her face turned away. She was lying on her back, her dark hair spread over the pillow. He put his hand on her stomach, and the muscles tensed under its weight. Her nightshirt felt silky.

"Not sleepy?" he asked.

"No," she said sadly. He heard the sadness and was quiet for a while, wondering about it. It had been there since the killing of Pasha.

"Wally Fetters got a couple of colts he's been wantin' me to check out," he said. "Thought maybe you'd like to go up there tomorrow with me. Want to do that?"

"You were going to start the haying tomorrow."

"No. Hell, we decided to let 'er dry another day. Forecast says hot and dry all week. Thought maybe you'd like to look at some colts."

"Sure," she said, still sadly. "That'd be all right."

"We'll take the trailer in case there's anything looks good. Maybe he'll swap a couple young ones for my gray horse."

"Not your gray horse, Michael."

"Sure. Ole Wally spoke to me about it at the rodeo. He fancies it, I know that. Might be able to trade him out of a couple of good young ones."

"That's your roping horse."

"Ain't worth what he wants to pay me. Not to me. I'll train me another."

She squeezed his hand, then looked back out the window.

He watched her for a while. "What's wrong then?"

She didn't say anything, but she squeezed his hand and kept looking out the window. "You still thinking about that black filly of yours?"

"No. Not of her."

"What then?"

She didn't say anything, and then she moved her shoulders a little bit in a shrug. "Me, I guess."

Mike propped onto his elbow, watching her nightshirt in the dim light, watching where it folded and the shadows that the folds made and the tightening of the folds over her breasts. Her head was still turned toward the window, and her eyes were shining in earnest.

"I think I want to go home early for Lisa's wedding," she said thickly.

"How early?"

"I don't know. September maybe."

"September?"

"I don't know."

"That's three months early."

Neither spoke for a while. Then she said quietly, "I need to, Michael."

"And afterward?"

"I don't know." She turned to face him now and put her arms around his back and pressed her face into his chest. She was trembling a little.

"What do you mean, you need to?" he asked.

"I don't know. I'm not happy."

"Avelyn?" She didn't answer him, so he went on. "Avelyn, it will be all right. It will."

She didn't answer.

"It will. I know it will."

"I hope it will, too. But saying so doesn't make it so."

"I know that." He put his hand behind her neck and kissed her. He closed his eyes and pulled her light body against his chest and felt the silkiness of the nightshirt against him and the firm softness beneath it with the nipples hard. His hand slid down the back of her nightshirt onto the warm skin of her thigh, then up to the soft curve of her buttocks, everything strong and sleek and toned. He bent his knee and rubbed it against the front of her legs, which were smooth and close together. Then he felt the resistance in her arms, and she turned her head away.

"No, Michael," she said gently. "Please not tonight."

He breathed a long sigh. Then he lay back on his pillow and looked up at the shadows on the ceiling.

"Oh, Michael. Please don't hate me."

"I don't hate you."

"Please don't."

"I don't hate you."

"I have to get away for a while. You understand that? There's no one else. It's me."

"It isn't you."

"It isn't anyone. It's me. It's me and everything else."

"Have you made up your mind then?"

"I think so."

"You're going to go home for a while," he said, as if trying to get used to the idea.

"Yes."

"But not right away."

"Not right away. Not unless you say so."

"No, no. No. Stay." They lay quietly, neither of them looking at the other. "Maybe till buddy boy heads off to school."

She turned her head. "It's not him either, Michael. It's not."

"I know it. It's not either of you."

"It's not."

"I know. I do." Then he asked her, "You going to talk to a lawyer?"

"No, no. Please don't take it that way. I'll just go home early for the wedding. Then we'll see."

"All right. We'll be okay."

"Maybe it will be like a vacation. I'll tell my folks it's a vacation. I just need to now. I need to, Michael. I'm sorry, but I do."

"All right. That's all right. We'll be fine." She had started to cry, and he was suddenly very tired. "It's the right thing. Things'll turn out. They will."

"I'm so sorry, Michael."

"Don't be sorry. Let's get some sleep now. We'll get some sleep now." He was very tired, and the tears were rolling down her face without a sound. "I'm bushed. Don't be sorry. It's not you. It's all these other things. Let's get some sleep now, okay? We'll go look at some colts tomorrow, okay?"

"Um," she said with a nod. She was wiping her face with the sheet.

"Night, hon," he said.

He was awakened by a dream shortly after two o'clock and lay awake the rest of the night thinking. He fell asleep again just before dawn, and when he woke in the morning, Avelyn was out of bed, and he could smell the bacon she was cooking for breakfast. He lay there until the sleepiness had left his head, then he got up and dressed and splashed stinging cold water on his face. That was good cold water. It left his cheeks numb and his fingers tingling and drew his breath up short. He toweled off and when he lifted his head from the towel, he smelled the bacon again and was suddenly famished. They were going up to Fetters's place to look at some colts. Then he remembered about last night and all that went gray again. Gray enough where it wasn't very real, and he wasn't hungry.

CHAPTER 29

IT WAS THE dryness that made that house talk. It made the paint curl off like flaking skin and the shingles crack and the floorboards creak underfoot. If a storm blew in, the house hushed up like a cow lying down before a rain. But no storms did blow in, and the grass cured in the hot August sun.

Jimbo remembered Papa Vic talking about the cattle before a storm: "... *Somethin' in their heads just goes, 'Lord, Lord, I'm a tired old cow ...' and down they go like a man with the gout. Them cows is dumb critters, Jimmy ... dumb as clucks ... but they ain't gonna get hit by lightning very quick. Somethin' just goes: 'Down, Bessie! Down, ole cow!' at the first sign of a storm. A damn sight before the first sign, the Good Lord knowin' it takes a cow a spell longer to negotiate things like layin' down than most critters. Gawd's a funny fella 'bout some things. Teaches a cow to lie down six full hours 'fore the first bolt of lightnin', but He lets 'em walk into a slaughterhouse meek as you please, 'thout hardly a fuss. ... I'm tellin' you, Jimmy, Gawd's a cattleman first, and a Creator second. It's He don't like His beef charred, is what. Me, I think it aids the flavor, but that's an old man's preference. I ain't gonna tell Gawd how to take His beef ...*"

It had been quiet for the past two weeks, peaceful, not quite like normal, but not like things had been, either. Jimbo was starting to think about grad school, about teaching somewhere in a year. Somewhere else. Somewhere different. Then the night before the haying somebody went up and opened the headgate to the irrigation ditch, the one he'd closed last week. By the time they discovered it in the morning, the fields were partially flooded again. It would set the haying back another week, and Mike went into a black mood, cursing and ranting about the delay, finally loading up the pickup with enough 2x4s to frame a small barn with and driving up to that headgate. Jimbo came along, and they cranked the gate back shut, then started nailing the 2x4s across the mouth of the gate with sixteen-penny nails. It would have taken a man a week with a crowbar to open it up again, and afterward Mike nodded with satisfaction, saying, "That'll keep them buggers from foulin' us up again." His entire day had brightened. Another problem solved.

They drove back down toward the ranch, passing Lloyd Paxton's old place where the black, girdered neck of Big Wally peered out of the pit, looking no more or less out of place than if an Apollo rocket had been perched next to the Bar V, ready to fire. But Mike never said anything about it. He drove right past that dragline as if he didn't notice it. If you could do anything about it, you'd notice it, Jimbo thought. You notice one lousy Indian when you can do something about it, but not a dragline. Not Big Wally.

"Who do you figure opened up that gate?" Jimbo asked.

"Well. Like the pregnant whore says, buddy boy, 'Could've been any number of pricks is responsible.' I ain't gonna guess which one."

"Could have been a lot of guys, all right. Could even have been One-eyed Jack Parker. Wonder where he's relocated his flock? He's probably not strong enough to open that gate, though."

Mike shrugged. "Ain't the first time. I remember ten, twelve years back, ole Jake Fox borrowed one of Tiny Turner's horses and lamed it. Don't know how. Probably bit it. Probably sunk his ivories into its hock. That Jake was a bad actor, lot worse'n Hepp, once his missus went rub-a-dub, see-ya-bub with that soap salesman. Well, Jake claimed he returned the horse sound, and Tiny said he lamed it. Man lames your horse oughta replace it, and it's that simple; but Jake, well, he never did have any money, so he lies about it. Says he returned it sound. Couple of weeks later Jake was puttin' in a new culvert over that ditch, 'fore irrigatin' started, and it was layin' in there but not shored up. So Tiny comes up here and opens the gate wide open like a damn fool — damn near washed out every culvert 'tween here and Kearney. *Whooosh!* You could hear that water coming. Washed Jake's culvert clean down to Jeb Miller's place, all twisted into knots. They never did talk after that, Jake and Tiny. Must've been five, six years, 'fore Jake choked on his steak, poor bugger, and they never said boo."

Jimbo looked at him. Mike liked telling that sort of story, a story about a man who could solve a problem with his own two hands, riding up to open up a headgate with his own two hands, or nail one shut, or shoot a bunch of sheep in a barn. Shoot a bunch of calves. Punch a nose. He thought about his conversation with Patty Fox. "I was talking to the unfortunate Miss Patty Fox the other day. Happened to run into her. She says Hepp's been saying all sorts of strange things about you."

"That right?" Mike wore that little grin.

"She just said to keep your head up. Maybe this ditch is what she was talking about, I don't know."

"Could've been Hepp."

"Well. I'll be going up to Missoula before very long. 'I won't be around to protect you no more,' " he said with an exaggerated drawl. "So keep your head up, okay, cowboy?"

Mike smiled again, but it wasn't that little grin this time. He meant it. "Okay, buddy boy. I'll do that."

"Mike?"

"What?"

"That eighteen million dollars still stand?"

Mike turned his head slowly, guessing what he would say next but not quite believing it, his eyes suddenly cold.

"Take it," Jimbo said.

Mike looked back to the road. He said nothing.

"Sell the damn ranch."

"I'm *not* going to sell the damn ranch!"

"Oh, *sell* it. Sell the damn ranch."

"I said I'm not. Shut up about it." He turned into the Bar V drive, his eyes narrowed. "You want me to *now?* You want me to sell out *now?*"

"What's left to prove?"

Mike gave him a look of such confusion, such utter blankness, that Jimbo knew he was wrong, knew that Mike wasn't trying to prove anything, knew there were no roles in his black and white world. He went on: "You'd be set for life with that kind of money."

He was getting angry. "I'd be set, all right, Gawd knows what I'd be set for, but I sure as hell would be *set!*"

"All right, then. Sell it for her sake."

Mike pulled into the yard and parked the truck. He sat there, his hands resting on the steering wheel. "She'd stay then, wouldn't she?" he said.

"Yes." Jimbo waited. "God knows why, but she's still in love with you."

A small smile came across Mike's face. "Well. Good. So am I. But that's something else. That's something different. And that ain't none of your affair."

"No? Well, when is it my affair? When they stop maiming our livestock and start going after us? Then is it my goddamn affair? I'm your *brother.*"

"Then act it." Mike got out of the truck, and Jimbo jumped out and rushed around in front of him.

"Act it? Yes, *all right!*" He raised his fist to the sky, closing his eyes and shouting: "BY GAWD, THIS HERE'S McKENZIE LAND, AND I'M THE TOUGHEST SONOFABITCH ON IT! Right? Isn't that it, Mike? Isn't that how to cope with things? I'm putting up my dukes, by gum, and fighting for this *two-foot scrap* of *dirt,* and you're going to have to bloody well *kill* me to get it!" Mike started to step around him, but Jimbo jumped in his way. "No, Mike, *through* me. Right *over* me. Like a McKenzie." He thought Mike might hit him. Mike stood there, looking down at him. But then he started going around him again, and Jimbo lowered his fists. "They've changed the rules on you, Mike. You can't fight them like that."

Mike stopped. "I'm not fighting anyone."

"Bullshit. You're fighting them just by living here."

Mike nodded. "You're the scholar; so if you say it's so, then it's so. But I'll tell you what, when I stop fighting whoever it is you say I'm fighting just by *living* here, and start fighting by *fighting*, you're gonna notice the difference."

"I doubt it," Jimbo said — thinking: He doesn't even hear me. Mike was heading for the house. "Mike —"

"I'm tired of talking about it."

"So am I. Listen. Just one reason. Give me one reason I can take away with me and brood over, cling to, cherish, why you're not selling. All you've ever told anyone is that you're not. I want one reason."

"I'm dumb. There."

"That's not a reason, that's a state of being."

"It's reason enough."

"Wait." Jimbo dashed in front of him.

"What the hell'd you come back here for? Why the hell'd you ever come back here from the East?" He was angry again.

"I don't know. For this. To have it out with you. Just give me a reason."

"I don't see why you ever came back here to begin with."

"Wait. Tilt your head and grin like you do and say, 'I got my roots here, buddy boy' — so I can answer 'Eighteen million bucks is a pretty deep set of roots' — and you can say, 'Yup.' Do that. Just so I'll know there's a reason."

Mike shook his head. The anger was gone again, and he looked at him for a long time. "You're goofier than the old man was," he said. "You scare the shit out of me. Now move."

Jimbo did. He let Mike go by and into the house, thinking: Jesus, I wish I had another brother. Jesus, I wish I had just one more brother so at least I'd know who was odd — me, with roots that fall out of the ground like nothing, like a tumbleweed — or him, the big oak, who won't budge an inch. Won't even bend. Papa Vic learned to bend. He was a blue spruce, that one. Though by building that home where he did, he wasn't bending much. He built it up high, right into the face of the wind, and challenged: "Blow, mothers." He wasn't going to get caught tucked down in some nook where another flood might get him. Not a second time. He put it up high — a McKenzie home built by McKenzie hands on land that had never been owned by another white man except a McKenzie. That made a difference, too. The frontiers were gone now, and the land had all been taken and white men had owned everything that could be owned; so there was nothing left to leave a trace on that would be yours and no one else's. Maybe that's what it was. Maybe that's why he couldn't sell. A trace of you. A trace of you and your people. It was the same thing that had happened to the Indians.

CHAPTER 30

PATTY FOX LAY back in the grass, the overhead sun full on her face. It was Sunday. The morning shift at the mine would be over soon, and then Roly had the rest of the day off. She was holding a new bottle of wine, and the glass of the bottle was cool in her hand. There was a breeze from the east, and an overcast was building up by the Custer Forest. It looked like rain, maybe. There hadn't been rain all summer. She wondered if that old roof on the cabin would keep the rain out, and thought it would be nice if it did rain that afternoon. We'd just lie there and listen to the rain, she thought.

Someone came over the rise beside the road. Patty watched him. She could tell right off it wasn't Roly, even from way across the field. He sure didn't look anything like Roly. She watched, lying in the grass.

One-eyed Jack Parker's legs stumbled and buckled almost comically as they cut through the tall grasses bleached nearly white from the drought, but he held his head and back erect. He was carrying something in his hand as he headed toward the sagging gray barn. It was a red can with a long, curling spout. The can banged against his leg as he walked. He wore a ceremonial headdress of eagle feathers and beads, and beneath it his braided black hair hung to his shoulders. He had a smoothly tanned buckskin outfit on, and deerskin boots. His face was painted with jagged red stripes, and over his right eye was the incongruous patch.

The Indian cast no shadow as he walked through the field. A strong wind made the grasses blow in waves. Their heavily seeded heads bent down the valley before the approaching storm. Across the field, Patty could hear the old man chanting, his deep, monotonous voice like a murmur on the breeze.

He switched the heavy can to his other hand and nearly tripped as his leg brushed against it. After a few more faltering steps, the old Indian stopped to rest. He turned back up the valley to face the wind, and it blew his feathered headdress out behind him, as if he might soar upward. Patty watched, fascinated. The headdress came just to his shoulders. Even resting, he chanted, and the sounds more resembled moanings than words.

The old man picked up the can again, and his toothpick legs staggered on. It was difficult walking downhill. When he reached the gray barn, again he rested. He stood in its doorway, peering inside at the blackness, chanting in a monotone just louder than the wind. Then he leaned over and picked up the can. He raised it to his knees, pouring its contents around the base of the barn boards, circling to the left. He was silent now. After a long while, he came back around to the door. He crouched and struck a match. The flame trickled left like an opening curtain, until it encircled the barn, licking at the old gray planks.

Patty rose to her feet. She started coming closer, slowly, watching the distant fire. The old Indian walked stiffly up the little rise to the cabin made of logs. Again he hoisted the can, pouring the gasoline onto the dry, dusty wood until it soaked in darkly, circling to the left. One-eyed Jack Parker looked behind him at the crackling flames of the barn being fanned by the breeze. He lit another match and dropped it. It went out and lay smoking on the dilapidated porch of the cabin. Again he lit a match, cupping it in his hands until it caught on the gasoline-soaked logs. Then he watched as the flames encircled the home he was born in. The old man stood back a step and watched the fires burn higher. He reached into his buckskin pocket and fished out a can of tobacco, stuffing a thumbful between his lip and gums, then nodded his head.

Patty was running now. She fell as she ran down the long hill, still holding the wine. One-eyed Jack Parker had begun chanting again, and it was more like a song. He picked up the red can once more, and raised it to his chest with ease, most of the gasoline having been poured out. Still chanting, he tipped it above his head, the liquid running down his braided hair and headdress, across his leathery face, dripping then flowing over his buckskin shirt and pants, staining the light tan to a dark, oily brown. He held the can up like that, his face upturned so it poured on his forehead and tightly shut eye and patch, until the can was empty. He laid it down.

"No! No-o-o-!" Patty called frantically.

The old man was singing louder, and he didn't hear her over the breeze and the flames. The black smoke swirled into the sky. He threw his head back and started to dance, in ungainly steps, hopping from one aging leg to the other as if they pained him. He chanted to the sky with one arm raised — haunting sounds that were barely human, more like the groans of a moored boat at sea.

The old Indian danced up on the flaming porch, still hopping from one foot to the other. The fire had reached the roof and the wind whipped the flames through the air. He hopped down again, chanting.

Patty ran up the last little hill to the yard in front of the cabin. "Get away from there, you!" she yelled, waving her arms so that the Indian finally saw her. "What are you doing? Stop it! Get down here!"

The Indian laughed, circling the little cabin, dancing above and between the burning grasses around its edges. The gray of the barn across the way was hidden by the smoke and orange flames that seared into the blue of the sky. Patty took a few steps closer, but the old man came back around to the front of the cabin and hopped back on the porch. The flames were all around him, and Patty shrank back as the Indian stopped dancing and finished his song.

"Come down here, you!" Patty screamed.

One-eyed Jack stood with his arms outstretched and his head thrown back. "Piss on you, McKenzie!" he shouted at Patty.

"No-o-o!" The flaming porch engulfed the Indian, cutting her scream short. The only sounds were the crackling fury of the blaze and the east wind — then the shattering of glass as Patty threw her bottle of wine at the fire.

The finals of the Johnson County junior rodeo championships were that weekend. Denny had bulldogged a steer in six seconds flat on Saturday to take a 3.6-second lead in the event, and on Sunday Deacon drove him down early so he could tend to his horse. Mike, Avelyn, and Jimbo followed just before noon. The clouds weren't starting to build yet, but the cattle were lying down, and there was a haze to the east, where the wind was coming from.

"Looks like a storm," Jimbo said. He was sitting in the back. Avelyn was in the front seat staring out the window.

Mike nodded. "That'll set the haying back again. I was gonna take the swather up to the north pasture tomorrow. Rain won't do us any good now, late as it is. A few weeks back, might've given us a little better crop." Mike drove farther, then he said, "Won't hurt us, though. Be nice to see a little rain fall. You bring your camera?" he asked Avelyn.

"No. I should have."

"Should we go back? We got time."

"No. I don't feel like concentrating that much."

"Ole Den'll be disappointed. He'd like to see a picture of himself with that trophy."

"I know it, Michael. I just don't feel like concentrating that much this afternoon." She looked back out the window. She had picked up her plane ticket home the day before and was leaving next Friday. They drove the rest of the way in silence.

The stands were filling up early, since there were more people than shaded seats, and they found seats near the top. The men wore new straw hats, and the women shaded their heads with scarves. Children ran up and down the aisles in small packs, armed with cotton candy. The arena was watered before the start to settle the dust, and then the colors were ridden in and the cowboy's prayer was given. The national anthem was played, then the rodeo marshals and queens and their attendants rode back out of the arena, and Wally Fetters, the rodeo announcer, introduced the first bareback rider, Tiny Turner's son, Lyle.

Jimbo could see Deacon behind the young rider's chute, giving him some last-minute instructions, maybe telling him that this particular horse was a rocking-chair bucker, or a spinner, or that he turned left out of the gate. Deacon couldn't keep away from bucking stock at a rodeo. The chute was opened and the horse paused a moment before coming out. Lyle Turner had both spurs in its shoulders when it bucked, and the horse kicked its hind feet high. The young cowboy raked his spurs across the points of the horse's shoulders, keeping his back flat against the hind quarters of the horse, working back and forth with the rhythm of the bucking. After eight seconds the buzzer sounded, and two pickup men galloped up to the bucking horse, the boy leaping off and grabbing the waist of one. It had been a good ride, and the crowd applauded.

Wally Fetters switched off his microphone. He reread the note in his left hand. "This thing for sure?" he asked.

"Patty Fox just called in," his wife said.

Wally Fetters looked back down to the judges, Ike Jessup and Jeb Miller. He wrote down the numbers they had on their slates and totaled them. Sixty-three points. There was your leader. He turned the microphone on again and made the announcement. The young fellow from Buffalo was ready on a horse called Wildfire in chute number two. He looked at the young cowboy on the horse and then back down at the note. Then he said over the loudspeaker: "John Cott. John Cott. Get your tail up here, will you, John? Seems there might be a problem up at Canyon Creek."

CHAPTER 31

THE SKY TO the east was already graying with smoke. It was a bad time for a grass fire — the worst, really — the grass being dry and ready to cut. The wind was gusting. Mike sped flat out up the Canyon Creek road. His face was still, but there was a tightness around his mouth that showed his concern. Neither Jimbo nor Avelyn spoke. They passed the strip mine, the sky looking progressively worse, and Mike said simply, "That's up by the Parker place."

They reached the top of the rise, and as they descended the smoke was suddenly billowing from below. They were a mile from the Parker place when they saw the fire, and that tight, hard line made by Mike's mouth dissolved into a single, quiet "Goddammit."

There was nothing left of the homestead. The fire was blazing on both sides of the road, somehow feeding off itself, leaping twenty feet in the air off grasses three feet high. The roar was terrible, like the roar of an immense wave. The sounds flooded together: the wind and the crackling grass and the whooshing of the flames into the air. And in the midst of all that, Mike's single "Goddammit," not in awe or shock or fear — which is what Jimbo was feeling — but as if that fire was one more pain in the ass after a long series of pains in the ass, none of which merited a greater or lesser reaction than "Goddammit."

Mike stayed there long enough to survey the blaze. It had

spread from the Parker place down to what had been Lloyd Paxton's north pasture, burning as far to the left as they could see. The east wind, which seemed to be building, was driving it down the valley. Birds flew ahead of the approaching blaze, then landed and flew ahead again. The air shimmered in waves a hundred feet in the air.

"Will that make it to the Bar V?" Jimbo asked.

"Wind's sure as hell right."

"How long?"

Mike looked him square in the eye. "Christ, buddy boy, your guess is as good as mine. I've never seen one of these before. Not that big." The truck was speeding back down the road. "Fire's got to go about three miles. That's a good wind. Good gusting wind. Might be there in less'n an hour. Be my guess."

Jimbo looked behind, back to the howling billows of smoke. "They'll never put that out in an hour."

Mike skidded into the drive. "I'm gonna call for help. You saddle up three horses." He parked and threw open the door. "Quick!" he called back.

The horses were in the home pasture, and Jimbo herded them in on foot. He had two saddled when Mike and Avelyn came back out. The horses were jumpy from the smoke.

"Got to push these bulls out onto the road so's they don't stampede through every fence between here and town. Those other horses, too."

Mike had his saddle on his hip and threw it on old Jacks without bothering with a blanket.

"Who'd you call?" Jimbo asked.

"Got back to Wally Fetters at the fairgrounds and told him to put out a cry for men and shovels. They're going to get word to the park service and county commissioners and God knows who else about the size of this fire. That wind don't shift, it's likely to roll all the way to town, high as this grass is."

"What about the house, Michael?" Avelyn asked.

"The house? Jesus, if it gets that far, we might just as well let it burn. I'm worried on our grassland."

There were eighteen Hereford bulls and four horses still in

the home pasture. Mike, Avelyn, and Jimbo galloped out there and worked them through the corral gate, onto the drive. They got behind them and, shouting and waving, pushed them toward the road, Stormy running up and down their flank, nipping at the heels of any bull that tried to veer away. The bulls swiped at the dog with their heavy, down-curled horns.

The livestock spilled onto the road and turned their heads to the east, up the valley. They sniffed at the smoke, eyes wide. The horses snorted at each other, and the bulls pawed the ground.

Deacon's truck was coming. "What's it look like, boss?" he yelled, alarmed.

"Not too good." Mike looked back up the valley. The flames were still hidden by the rise of the road, but the smoke no longer just blackened the sky. It was hovering over the ground like a mist.

"What about the rest of the herd?" Deacon asked.

"Fire won't get up to the mesa. When the smoke gets up there, we might lose a bunch of 'em in the fence. Ain't got time to get them all down here, Deac. Best leave 'em be." Mike peered down the road. "Where're them men I called for? How're we gonna stop this thing without men?"

Deacon shook his head. "There's a few of 'em took off to the station. Johnny Cott got on the loudspeaker and called for volunteers. There should be some comin' on along." Deacon took off his baseball cap and said, "McKenzie, you want I should drive on up to the Custer ditch and open up the headgate? Give us some water down here?"

Mike shook his head. "Take you two days, Deac. We nailed 'er shut, ole buddy boy and I."

"How we gonna stop this thing?" Deacon asked, squinting.

Mike stared down the road. A few cars were coming up from town, driving past and turning into Titanic's mining complex. "Looks like Titanic's callin' in the troops."

"Their buildings aren't in danger," Jimbo said. "Those spoil banks will stop any fire."

Mike nodded. "Mine'll stop the fire from spreadin' clear to

the south ridge. I figure that makes the house and barn and that safe." Deacon agreed, and Mike pointed to the north pasture, where three huge loaflike stacks of hay were penned in. "It's that feed right there and our hay crop we've got to worry on. Fire gets that far, and we lose two years' hay crops. Dry as that grass is, she'll go in ten minutes." He looked across the north pasture, as if envisioning the prospect. It was over a mile wide, and it would take more than the four of them to protect it.

"We're going to need help," Jimbo said.

Nobody said anything. Several more miners came by and turned into the strip mine farther up. Then they saw the small town firetruck coming up the road. John Cott was driving, Ike Jessup beside him. Sam Benson stood in the back with his oldest boy and John Cott's oldest boy and Eddie Foyt, who owned the icehouse. They were holding shovels and peering over the roof of the cab toward the fire. Mike kicked his horse into the road as the truck came to a stop. That was it then, Jimbo thought. Six of them. Those goddamn bastards. Just the six of them. Not even Tommy Phelps. Not that goddamn Jerry Tate with his gas station they had gone to for twenty years of gas and oil changes and tune-ups. Not the Prestons or Turners or Millers or Zieglers or any of them.

Mike swung off his horse and wiped his forehead with his palm. His voice was soft, but it cut through the distant sound of the flames and wind. "Where're the damn men? Where're the damn men, John?"

John Cott lowered his eyes, making it easy to guess; though Jimbo saw Mike was too mad to guess.

"You're in charge of this fool outfit, John. Now where're the damn men? Where're the goddamn men and shovels we're gonna need to put this fire out with, huh? Where're all the men?"

"Mike —" Jimbo started.

". . . The great Canyon Creek firemen's association. Biggest damn fire in fifty years, and you show up with half a dozen men and boys while the others watch a rodeo —"

"Mike —"

"Ain't that somethin', buddy boy? Ain't this Canyon Creek

area somethin' else? Neighbors all beating off on a rock when the time comes to save their grassland, waiting for the county trucks or state trucks or anyone but them so's they can watch the rodeo cowboys; knowing fuckin' well John Cott can strap her down with his six volunteers with their bladders full of piss —"

"Jesus, Mike, shut up," Jimbo told him.

"It's you, McKenzie," John Cott said firmly. "You're the reason nobody's fightin' this thing." Mike looked at him for a long time, letting the words sink in. John Cott lowered his eyes, but he was mad, too. His voice was tight. "Lotta folks want this fire to tear right through your ranch and you, too, to put it bluntlike. These fellas here come up 'cause they figure they're your friends. They figure you'd do the same for them. There's a whole lotta folks wanta see you plumb wiped out, so don't go layin' into us." His right hand gripped the steering wheel and made his knuckles white.

"It's okay, John. Ain't your fault." Mike turned to Avelyn and gave her a short shake of his head.

"We're going up to take a look at it," John Cott said.

"It's a bad fire."

"We'll fall back here after we take a look."

"Person might be able to backfire it up at Lloyd's old north pasture. Need men to control the backfire, though." Mike motioned up to the valley. "There's men up at that mine."

"You want me to ask 'em?" Cott asked.

Mike smiled and shrugged. "No, I'll ask 'em. They're the pricks that probably started it." He turned to Jimbo. "Let's take a ride, eh?"

He climbed back on his horse and kicked it up the road. Jimbo followed at a gallop. When they cleared the rise in the road, the upper end of Canyon Creek suddenly broadened before them. The entire eastern horizon was in flames. The fire had spread with awesome speed. The firetruck charged by, its single nozzle comical in the face of a fire that size. The whole scene looked so extraordinary, Jimbo thought. So *unnatural*. He felt he was watching another fire in another valley. The flames and smoke and the speed of the horses hid all landmarks from him, except now as he looked ahead, he saw the giant, steel-girdered booms of Big Wally towering above the smoke and flames — stark black gashes in the gray-brown sky. He couldn't take his eyes from it. No inferno's going to bother you, eh, big guy? He imagined Big Wally with two great eyes peering down with curiosity and a little disdain at the blaze that was no threat to its steel body. You're not going to lose any sleep over this business, you big, invincible bastard.

They rode under the arch reading TITANIC COAL COM-PANY in black block letters. Mike galloped ahead, down the road toward the prefabricated office buildings and the strip mine beyond. The mine was quiet, but there were men milling at its edge. Jimbo had never been this close to it before. The field that had once stretched smoothly up the valley was now heaped into barren banks, and it seemed a beaten thing. The men there trod over it like conquerors. They were more imposing than if they had been milling in an untouched field, as if by using that machine to tear apart the land they had proved themselves more powerful than it. They seemed not only unafraid but nearly unconscious of the fire that burned toward them.

Mike rode up to the miners and yelled, "Who's in charge here?" His horse was frothy with sweat, and his own face was dripping. He looked much smaller than the pit and the crowd of men and Big Wally. Much different. "Who's in charge here?" he asked again, in a voice that made the crowd of miners all turn their yellow hardhats toward him and look. There was an urgency in it that was so far removed from politeness or friendship or fear or anger or whatever else one usually hears in a man's voice that they all looked up, and one of them pointed.

"At the office. Name's Barsotti."

Mike reined his horse around, spurring it into a gallop once again, riding past the huge black pit to the white prefabricated rectangular office beyond, where Lloyd's corrals had been. There was a short, dark-haired, thick-armed man talking with a group of men in the parking lot, pointing, giving some orders.

His shirt-sleeves were rolled up over the elbows, and his hair was thick and mussed back. Mike pulled up suddenly, jumping from his horse, and the man stopped, removing his sunglasses.

"Barsotti in there?"

"I'm Barsotti."

"You in charge of these men?"

"Who's asking?"

"Name's McKenzie. Fella said you were in charge."

"You the McKenzie that lives right over there? You that McKenzie?"

"That's right."

"Well now. I see. What can I do for you?"

"I know how to stop this fire," Mike said.

"I'd say you've got one hell of a chance to prove it," Barsotti said.

"I need your help."

Barsotti folded his arms then, and a slow smile spread across his thick lips. Jimbo saw that the smile was not friendly and that the man would not help and would not be nice about not helping.

"I'll talk to him, Mike," Jimbo said. "Let me talk to him."

"Who the fuck are you, his muscleman?" Barsotti turned to the men he was talking to before. "Hey, none of you guys go too far, eh?"

Mike held up his hand "I know how to stop this fire. I don't care how the hell it got started, but I know how to stop it. I need your help."

"You implying some of my men had something to do with starting this fire?" the man asked.

"I said I don't care about that."

"You got your nerve, McKenzie, coming here saying my men started this fire, then asking me for help."

"I said I don't care who started it, I don't know and I don't care. I know how to stop it. We can backfire it. We need your men."

"You need my men, eh?"

"We can burn a fifty-yard strip across the valley, one that we can control. When that other —" He nodded toward the blaze less than a mile away. It was fully visible now, burning across the horizon. The wind was driving it forward in leaps. "— When that other reaches it, she'll burn out. Won't be nothing left to burn."

"Where would you backfire?" Barsotti asked.

"We'll start right here, burn due north across the road, and stop it at my north pasture. Your mine here will stop it at the south end. That's a bad fire. We've gotta get goin'. We need men."

"What about your men from town?" the man asked with deliberate slowness.

"They ain't up here."

He waited. "Where are they?"

"They ain't here's all I know. We got ten men. We need fifty."

"You're about forty short, sounds like, McKenzie. I'm not authorized to give you forty men."

"I'm not asking that you *give* them to me. I'm asking that you put them to backfiring right here on your company land."

"Burning the company grass."

"The company grass is gonna get burned anyway, buddy."

"No can do, McKenzie. These men have got to stay here and protect the office buildings. We've got our own pumps, and we need the men to work them when the fire gets here."

"There's a hundred men down there. You don't need them all."

"I don't know that."

"There's a lot of grassland's gonna burn. Maybe homes, too."

"That's just not my concern."

"You're living here now, pal. It's your concern. I'm telling you, it's your concern."

"You'll pay 'em, McKenzie? These men are here on overtime."

"I'll pay 'em."

Barsotti grinned. He held up his hand, counting. "Well, seeing how it's *you*, Mr. McKenzie, from right next door — I imagine you could get these boys to save your ass for about two hundred dollars an hour. Hundred men, two hundred an hour, twenty thousand bucks. Cash. In advance." He laughed. "Just give it to me, McKenzie. I'll see they get it."

Jimbo stepped in between them. "Let's go, Mike. Never mind."

He felt Mike tense as he started to push him away. Mike glared at Barsotti. He took a step backward, then resisted again, about to say something. "Come on, Mike, come on. What else did you expect?" Jimbo said. "There isn't one of these guys who would have helped us. Come on now." Mike slowly turned and remounted his horse. He gave it a kick with his heels and it bolted beneath him, already nervous from the thickening smoke.

CHAPTER 32

THEY HAD LOST twenty minutes. The grassfire had forced the half-dozen volunteers back to reorganize in front of the Bar V. Their faces were lined with grime, their eyes red from the smoke, and their backs wet with sweat. The temperature had risen twenty degrees from the heat of the fire, and Ike Jessup and Eddie Foyt cooled their faces in Canyon Creek. John Cott yelled to Mike as Mike jumped off his horse and whacked it down the road, still saddled.

"We can't stop this'n, McKenzie. Wind's too big. Too fucking *big!*"

The storm coming in from the east was chasing the fire on. "Can't stop her . . ." John Cott called, wiping the sweat from his thin brow with the three fingers of his right hand. His forehead and arms were black with smoke and soot. "If the creek were higher or them ditches were runnin', might be able to dam them and flood the field. That might work. Can't do 'er alone, though. I called on the radio for them fireplanes, but till then best we can hope for is to save your place. She's movin' fast, Mike, real fast —"

"We can backfire her," Mike yelled. The wind had picked up and the sound of the fire was rising in the air, really rising, as if it were directly above them instead of a half mile away. It was coming quickly. "Let's backfire her, John. We can stop it there at the ditch . . ."

They were yelling at each other to make themselves heard. "Wind's too big! You'd never control the backfire. Never."

"We can stop it at the ditch!" Mike pointed to the three-foot-deep irrigation ditch running along the edge of the north pasture. It was about four feet across. "I'll start the backfire fifty yards up on Thorndike's land. We'll stop it there! At the ditch!"

John Cott shook his head. "Need water to control a backfire that size! Got but one portable pump. The rest of these lines need an outlet. Truck's water tank is too damn small to use 'gainst a fire this size!"

"We got shovels!"

"Mike, we don't have the men to use them!"

"We got men! Ten good men! We'll backfire her and stop it right there!"

"God damn you! We can't do it without more help! To hell with your grass! I'm telling you, man, you'd better worry on saving your place!" Mike shook his head. John Cott made a sweeping gesture behind him. "We ain't got the men! Will you listen? Will you look at that?"

The fire had spread all the way across the valley. The roar was terrible, and the smoke billowed up thickly to hide the upper end of the valley. The sky wasn't just gray now; it was a muddy brown, as if the land itself were being consumed.

"We can do it, John! We'll set up the hose by the house. We'll leave the truck there. Hell, Avelyn can work the hose, can't you, babe? Sure you can. That'll save the house and barn if the fire ever gets there — but it won't! It won't! The strip mine will block it on the south end! It can't burn that! We just got to worry on the north end, here, from the road to the base of the mesa!"

Cott was shaking his head. "You'd best worry on your place, man! We can't save the grass!"

"The truck and Avelyn stays by the house! We can stop this thing! We can stop it here at the ditch! These men can stop it!"

Mike wasn't talking just to John Cott anymore, he was shouting to the men around the firetruck. To Ike and Sam and Eddie and the two boys, and Jimbo, too. They'd seen the fire up close, and they didn't believe they could stop it. It was terrifying to fight something that big with a shovel.

"Yes! We can stop this thing with a backfire! Line up behind that irrigation ditch and dig like hell! Stop it there! We'll backfire her! The backfire we can control! Won't be like that other. We'll hold it right there and let it burn itself out . . . right there!" Mike ran over and jumped into the ditch with both feet and began shoveling at the grass on the other side. He dug furiously, widening it. The others watched him. Then Sam went and jumped in beside Mike and started digging, too. One by one, the others followed, spreading themselves out, digging at the bank.

"What about the bulldozer?" Jimbo asked.

Mike stopped shoveling and wiped at his sweat. "Jesus Christ, the *bulldozer*," he said excitedly. "Go get Denny and the bulldozer. Jesus Christ, yes. And tell Deacon to drive my pickup over with some cans of gasoline to start this thing. *We can stop it!*"

Jimbo ran across the field to the house. When he and Deacon returned in the pickup, the men were spaced every couple of hundred yards, digging at the banks of the ditch, piling up dirt and knocking down the grass. There was still water in the ditch in places, and the rest of it was muddy. The fire was sweeping toward them, moving quickly, less than a mile away. The entire horizon was in flames.

Denny came with the bulldozer. He crossed the Canyon Creek road and lowered its plow, gouging a path in front of the irrigation ditch, toward the mesa. The soil was rocky and difficult to break through. He could plow ahead about thirty feet before the dirt had built up too high, and he had to back up and start again. The men dug harder when they saw the bulldozer. This, at least, was a weapon. If they all had bulldozers instead of shovels, there'd be no question of stopping this thing.

The fire was past the strip mine now, burning only to the north of the road, as Mike had thought. Mike climbed into the back of the pickup, where there were three cans of gasoline. Deacon drove a short way up the road, then turned into Lloyd Paxton's north pasture. He drove slowly across, Mike pouring the first can in a continuous stream until it was empty. Then Deacon stopped the truck and Mike lit the trail of gasoline. A trickle of flame skirted toward the road. He did the same with the second can of gasoline, continuing across the pasture. He lit it, and from the ditch Jimbo could see the second orange flicker dancing across toward the first, which was beginning to grow. The wind was blowing in swirling gusts. The truck looked small as the billowing flames of the main fire rose behind it, sending the heat shimmering now hundreds of feet in the air. Flocks of birds led the blaze on, shooting into the sky and flying ahead of the grass fire, then landing and waiting and winging off again. The air was alive with insects — grasshoppers and dragonflies — whose noisy flights were drowned out by the crackling grass and the wind.

Mike emptied the last gasoline can. It ran dry three-quarters of the way across the pasture. That was all right, Jimbo thought. It was too wide an area as it was, with this few men. Already the first section of the backfire was in full blaze and closing toward the ditch. There would be nothing left for the main fire to consume when it got to that section, but he wondered if they could control the backfire. John Cott was nearest the road, and then came his son, then Ike Jessup, Sam Benson's son, Sam Benson, and Eddie Foyt. Avelyn was across the road with the firetruck. It didn't look like the fire would get over there, but with a wind change, you never knew. He tried to see her but he couldn't. He could barely see the truck through the drifting smoke. Don't start thinking about her, he thought. You have enough on your hands without thinking about her.

Mike ran back to the ditch. Deacon drove the pickup a short way down the road and parked it, then he limped up the hill and started digging in the slot between Jimbo and Mike. The main fire was a half mile away now, and Jimbo looked at his watch. It had been forty-five minutes since they'd spotted the fire.

"You okay, old man?" Mike yelled to Deacon.

"Okay here, boss . . ." Deacon was panting from the heat and the walk up the hill. He turned and shouted toward Jimbo. "Gird your festering loins, buck. Gonna be hotter'n French love 'round here 'fore long."

Jimbo had found a section of the ditch that was still filled with two inches of water. He stopped shoveling for a moment and rested. The main fire was only a couple of hundred yards behind the backfire Mike had set, moving much more quickly than the smaller blaze, seeming to pick up momentum as it came downhill. He heard Mike yell something to Deacon, but they were too far away for him to tell what it was. They were too damn far apart was the problem. Denny was bulldozing up from the road, which meant that the Cotts and Ike Jessup could push closer to the Bensons and the Bensons closer to Eddie Foyt, and Foyt closer to him. I'm not pushing anywhere, Jimbo thought. I'm staying right here with this water. He began shoveling at the grass on the other side of the ditch again. He didn't know if the ditch would slow the fire down or not. Maybe it would. Maybe if they dug out all these tall grasses on the edge of the ditch, the fire would get there and turn back. Maybe it didn't matter that they were all so far apart, because the fire wasn't going to get across that ditch anyway. It was getting hot, though. The flames of the backfire were still thirty yards away, and they were already bloody hot. He stopped digging long enough to wipe the sweat from his chin. Maybe the ditch wouldn't even slow it down one iota. Jesus, it was getting hot. All this would have worked if we'd started an hour ago, he thought. Then that bulldozer would have had time to clear a swath across the whole pasture. Or we could have put out one backfire at a time. That would have been the way to do it. Start one backfire, maybe a quarter mile long, and use all ten men to put it out. Then start the second, put it out; then the third, and put it out. That'd be the right way. That or get more men. He was sweating heavily as he shoveled. Jesus Christ, this ditch isn't going to stop this thing, he thought, feeling the heat.

Jimbo was shoveling at the flames themselves now, throwing mud from the ditch toward the burning grass. The main fire raged behind the smaller backfire, as if the flames were coming in ascending waves, unbelievably immense, the entire horizon blazing orange and black. He wondered how anything could ever grow on that soil again — how there could even be soil — knee-deep in the ditch and flinging mud at the backfire, which hadn't yet built the momentum and fury of the first blaze and shied back from the ditch. He heard Mike yell over to Deacon again.

"You okay, old man?"

"Okay here, boss."

Jimbo could not tell if things elsewhere at the ditch were okay or not. He could not even tell if they were okay where he was, being responsible not only for the few square feet he could shovel at once, but for fifty yards on either side, too. Too damn much space between them, he thought. Come on, ditch. Come on, you ditch. He started running, up and down, trying to keep up with the backfire, shoveling mud and water and dirt at the flames that seemed to pause for another attack, then creep forward the instant his attention turned elsewhere.

The flames soared ten feet in the air. It was too hot to shovel from the ditch now, and Jimbo jumped back and waited and felt the aching in his shoulders for the first time, the coughing in his lungs, then heard Mike yell something to Deacon. Deacon called back, "Okay here, boss . . . by Gawd, it's a hot'n . . ."

The wind gusted, and a flame leaped like a small boy across the ditch. Jimbo whacked it out with the bottom of his shovel. Another patch of grass burst into flames over the ditch, then another, and a third. He ran up and down the bank, beating at the flames and cursing the wind, the sweat and smoke burning his eyes. He stamped with his feet and the shovel, wondering if the backfire were winning now, the wind not only fanning the flames across the ditch, but the smoke and the heat. Jesus, that was hot! Jesus God, he thought, I wish I had a hat, the air so searing it seemed his hair might burst on fire. He coughed and stumbled and ran along the ditch, unthinking, trying both to fight and to escape the burning in his eyes. He rubbed at his eyes to ease the stinging, then opened them, not knowing where he was or where he had started from. He did not know where the road was or where Mike was or Deacon, but he saw the flames and he whacked at them.

Suddenly Mike's voice yelled from much closer than before: "You okay, old man?" And from not more than a few yards away: "Okay here, boss."

Jimbo turned and headed the other way, the stinging in his eyes and the smoke making it impossible to see. He wanted to run. Jesus, this moved fast. Jesus, this fire. If he could keep it down or pat or something, so long as it wasn't ragingly out of control and racing across the hay field. Some of the flames were five and ten feet over the ditch, and he beat at them, cursing the impotence of the shovel. What if it circled behind Mike or Deacon or Sam? The way that wind was gusting every which way . . . Jesus, it's hot. Jesus, this fire. He beat at the flames and could no longer see the ditch. He wondered what he would do if it got out of control. Then you will give up, he thought. Then you will get your ass out of here quickly without waiting for the order, because Mike will die fighting this fire. Jesus, he wished he had a hat.

A dullness settled over his arms and back and head. He began coughing harder, stumbling from the smoke. He fell. It was cooler on the ground, clearer. He picked himself up, flinging mud and dirt with the shovel, flinging it behind him, toward the heat. Flinging it machinelike. Just flinging it. A voice inside him seemed to laugh at the futility. It was too deep inside to hear the laughter, though he could feel that it was there in his gut, the way you can feel the very lowest notes of a church organ.

This fire is out of control. It is winning. It is winning by a lot. Then that laughter. He shoveled and stamped and fought for his breath, unsure of what was happening anywhere else along the ditch, seeing the flames raging to the left and the right and in front of him, and wanting to hear a sound besides the sound of fire — hearing only that laughing voice inside him, laughing at the hopelessness; so that he no longer just *felt* it was lost but knew it. That mocking laugh. And then it was no longer a laugh he heard but a voice telling him: STOP. YOU'VE DONE YOUR BEST. NOW STOP.

He stopped shoveling and backed away from the flames, holding his arms up to shield his eyes from the heat. His hands were blistered and raw. He did not know if he had been shoveling for ten minutes or an hour, but his hands were raw and his shoulders sore, and he wanted to breathe. He wanted to breathe clean air that would not scorch his lungs. He must breathe.

Jimbo turned and ran. His legs pumped, and he gulped the smoky air, gasping and coughing. His face was tight and dry, as if whatever was inside had been baked too long and might explode and gush out if it didn't cool. He ran, and after a hundred yards he stopped. He stood there panting, gasping, spitting out bile.

Jimbo turned back to the fire. He wiped the sweat and soot and stinging tears from his face. The smoke was blowing down the valley high above him. It was the first time he could see more than ten yards to either side of him since the backfire had reached the ditch.

The main fire still raged behind the backfire, its terrific heat igniting willow bushes along the creekbed from thirty feet away. It had not yet reached the area where Mike had started the backfire, where the grass was all burned out and smoldering. Watching, Jimbo wondered if the gusts of wind could somehow carry the huge crests of flame across the charred stretch, or if the fire could possibly feed off the land itself, steamrolling over the backfire to swallow them all up in an incendiary avalanche. He rubbed his eyes and breathed with his mouth pressed against his cotton sleeve. The bile taste in his mouth was wretched.

On the left side, toward the mesa, the valley was burning up. But on the right side the backfire seemed to be under control. It had not crossed the road, and Denny's bulldozer had prevented it from advancing beyond the ditch. Jimbo could see him sitting on the yellow-now-black machine, driving not ahead of, but right into, the flames of the backfire, plowing them under. We can do it, he suddenly thought. We can stop it. The middle section was still bad, but it was not out of control. The Bensons and Eddie Foyt had fallen back some twenty yards from the ditch, but they were still fighting it. Denny's bulldozer would be able to help them before long. Mike and Deacon were almost where they had started, though the fire had broken through them in spears. If they fell back they could help the others. They could control that middle section without losing too much grassland. And then there would be only that left flank to battle. We can stop it, he thought. If we stop it in the middle, we can stop it.

Jimbo ran back to the center section of the ditch. The backfire was not coming in a wall of flame now, but in scattered shafts. Deacon and Mike were nearly surrounded by the columns of fire that had gone beyond the ditch.

"Mike!" Jimbo yelled. "Mike!" The rushing of the fire drowned out his voice, and he ran to him. Mike was still in the ditch, beating at the flames with his shovel. His face was red with heat and black where the smoke had mixed with his sweat. The heat was searing. He grabbed Mike's arm, and Mike looked up at him.

"Let's move back!" Jimbo shouted. "Let's set up a new line!"

Mike shook his head and pulled his arm away. "Swing that shovel, buddy boy!"

"Goddammit! You'll get trapped here!" Mike was beating at the fire, and Jimbo retreated twenty yards back, to the farthermost flames. He shouted, "Mike! Come here! We'll hold it right here! Give that up and we can hold her here!"

Mike kept throwing dirt and whacking at the fire by the ditch. He kept his arms high, shielding his face. He looked back at Jimbo and nodded encouragingly, then he yelled over to Deacon, who was battling on the other side of a fifty-foot stretch of flames, "You okay, old man?"

Deacon answered back, "Okay here, boss . . ." his voice flat and tired.

Deacon had been driven back a short way from the irrigation ditch, and he hobbled back and forth, beating at the fire. His face and hands were black. There was an advancing spear of flame between him and Mike, and Jimbo started throwing dirt there. He kept his face tucked behind his shoulder, and felt the extreme heat on the side of his body. He shoveled and beat at the flames, stamping and kicking, listening for Denny's bulldozer. If they could keep that section of the backfire from going farther, then they could stop it. Then there would be only that left section, and they could surround that, all of them. The main fire would have reached that charred section by now and burned out. They could stop this backfire. He shoveled and his mouth was dry and he listened for the bulldozer. He was too tired to think anymore, but he knew that they could do it if he would shovel. You will win this if you shovel. You will stop this fire if you shovel.

The fire seemed to stall, seemed to pull back suddenly; so that he thought, *you are winning.* But the wind had changed. It had shifted to the south, so it was gusting across the valley, not down it. The fire was consolidating. Jimbo was too dazed and tired to realize what was happening, that the fire was closing behind Deacon and Mike, that they were fighting from inside shrinking boxes of fire. *Keep at it man, you're beating it!* He shoveled blindly, numbly, his eyes pressed tightly shut against the heat and smoke. He was elated. *You're beating it! It's stopping!*

He heard a cry — from where? — and looked up to see Deacon crumple to his knees, then topple over. Deacon clutched at his chest and made a choking sound, his mouth hanging open in shock or anger or confusion. Jimbo could just see him through the flames. He was lying on his side, his face contorted in pain, his hands gripping at his chest. Lying still.

"Deacon! Deacon, get up! Deacon!"

Mike hadn't seen him yet. He hadn't even seen that he was entrapped by the fire. "You okay, old man?" he called. Then he looked around him, seeing the box of flames. "Deacon — watch out, man! You okay? She's shifting on us!"

Jimbo tried to get to where Deacon was lying. A gust of wind put ten more feet of the fire between them and singed his face. He ran around to the other side, shouting. There was no way through. He came back toward Mike. "Mike! Mike, he's hurt! Can you get to him? I can't get through! He's hurt!"

Mike shouted over to Deacon again. The flames were too thick between them for Mike to see. "Where is he?" he screamed back to Jimbo.

Jimbo could barely see him anymore. He pointed. "Over there! He's hurt! Mike! Right there! I can't get to him!"

Mike leaped into the air, trying to see above the flames. Deacon was lying on his side, still. Mike looked around quickly, then turned and dove into the irrigation ditch. He rolled onto his back, covering it with mud, then began to crawl on his belly as the fire raged above him on the banks. He stopped and crouched in the ditch, shielding his face. Through the fire, thirty feet away, he saw Deacon. He knelt down and covered the rest of his body with mud.

"Wait!" Jimbo yelled, knowing what he wanted to try but that he couldn't make it. "Wait, Mike! I'll get the firetruck! You dumb Mike bastard! Wait!"

Mike was sprinting through the fire, his dripping arms wrapped around his face, the orange and smoke engulfing him until he was little more than a flash of movement at the heart of the blaze, like a shadow or gust of smoke. He suddenly burst into the little clearing, his shirt smoldering, rolling into the dirt and scrubbing his hands furiously over his face and neck. He leaped back to his feet, swinging around to get his bearings. Jimbo called, "Michael! Goddamn you, Michael! Michael! Goddamn, answer me!"

"Okay here, buddy boy!"

Jimbo ran up and down the firewall, waiting for a shadow, a sign of movement, something, screaming: "Run, you Mike bastard! You hear me? Get out of there!" He wondered if he had fallen. Not Mike. He couldn't have fallen. Anyone but Mike would have fallen, but not Mike. "Run, you! Answer me! *Where are you!*" A hundred yards toward the road he found a path to the irrigation ditch. He dove through the smoldering flames to the mud and shallow water. It was too hot to raise up his head, so he kept it low, his chin in the mud, crawling. He thought his shirt had caught fire and flipped onto his back, rubbing it in the mud, then over to his belly again. He scooped mud onto his neck and the top of his hair, onto his face, and coated it on his shoulders and arms. Then he rose to his knees.

Mike and Deacon lay in a motionless heap at the bottom of the ditch, some twenty yards off. Mike was cradling the old cowboy's face against his chest, protecting it from the flames. "Mike? You all right, fella? You and Deac all right?"

Jimbo slid back to his belly and crawled closer. The fire crackled above them, but the smoke was less thick down in the ditch. "Mike? Mike? You okay?"

Mike heard him and looked up. His face and hands were

blistered and caked brown and black from the mud. One of his lips was split, and the red gash showed through the grime and soot and mud. "Go on and get help for him, buddy boy," he said.

Jimbo nodded. He turned to crawl away.

"You be careful now, little brother," Mike said.

Jimbo stopped. He looked back at the two of them. They were there, all right. They were real.

When he was beyond the flames, he sprinted the quarter mile to the house, where the firetruck waited.

Mike didn't move from the ditch. He lay there with his eyes glazed, holding Deacon in his arms until the firetruck broke through. Deacon was conscious, his breathing weak but steady. He lay curled quietly, every once in a while muttering a curse: ". . . Gawddamn ticker . . . Gawddamn quittin' ticker . . ."

Ike Jessup and John Cott lifted Deacon into the truck, then came back for Mike. The fire had moved well beyond the ditch now, and there were only a few scattered tufts burning nearby. Mike waved them back. "Get goin' with him — I'm okay. Get goin' with Deac."

Mike sat in the ditch and watched as they drove across the smoking pasture, onto the road, and down the valley. Then he turned his head and watched the advancing grass fire. There was nothing left to do but watch. Even Denny came back when his bulldozer quit on him — his face and hands blistered like everyone else's, his eyebrows burned bare. The fire blossomed full again and steamrolled down the valley. When it reached the haystacks, the flames reached seventy and eighty feet, and burning hay gusted into the air. Some of it blew across the road, where it smoldered and smoked, then ignited another grass fire in the south pasture. The fire spread in the south pasture, burning toward Hepp Fox's. Avelyn, Denny, and Jimbo watched it, utterly helpless and too tired and morbidly fascinated to turn away. They watched it burn their grassland for half an hour, then abruptly the wind died down and the fire slowed. A single-engined fireplane appeared and flew low over the front of the fire, spewing down a heavy white chemical. The plane made pass after pass over the grass fire, perhaps a dozen in all, then they could see the two county firetrucks coming up the road. The plane flew off and men with canisters strapped on their backs poured out of the trucks, sending long streams of flame repellents into the burning grass. The fire was out within an hour.

The other men left. Jimbo walked across the south pasture. Half had been destroyed by the fire, and it still smoked and smoldered. It felt hot through his boots. He turned and walked along the road, toward town. He walked slowly, trying to clear his head. The miners were driving back to their homes now, and he stayed on the side of the road. He looked around for his horse. It was somewhere down there, still saddled. So was Mike's. So were the other horses, and the bulls.

The north pasture looked like a charred wasteland, and they would need to buy feed to get the cattle through the winter. Through the fall, even. You could buy hay. It was expensive this year, but Mike would probably spend the money. Or you could sell the stock, but as low as prices were, you didn't want to sell now. Or you could truck the cattle to someone else's grassland. That would work. Trade spring calves for fall and winter grass. That's what Mike could do — strike a deal with someone in Colorado or somewhere for the use of his grassland. That'd be the best way probably. Mike could do that.

Except that he wouldn't. There was too little left to hold onto any longer. He would sell, and that would be the end of it. Mike would finally sell. Then the strip mine and the valley and the town could go permanently to hell.

CHAPTER 33

MIKE CAME BACK to the house and stood there with what Avelyn called his faraway expression.

"Sit down," she told him. "I'm going to get you some ice." She came back in a minute with a wet towel wrapped around some ice cubes, and she patted it on his forehead and temples, then held it against the split in his lip. Mike wasn't numb or exhausted or angry like the rest of them. He was distracted. He was in another time or place, not thinking about the fire any longer. Wherever he was, Avelyn let him stay there.

He sat like that for a while, letting her clean his face, feeling the ice soothe his blistered, stinging skin. Then he rose and went into the sitting room and opened up the gun case. He took out the .44 Magnum revolver and put it in his pants, then tucked his shirt over it. He opened the bottom of the case and snapped the lid off the plastic box of shells and pulled six out, one at a time, slipping them into his shirt pocket. He put the box back onto the bottom shelf and saw the package with Avelyn's necklace wrapped inside. He pulled that package out too and shut the case.

He went back into the living room, where Avelyn was still sitting on the arm of his chair, staring out the window, her hand cupped beneath the wet towel to catch the dripping. He put the package on the table behind her.

"I'm gonna go check out the damage, hon. There's something there on the table for you when you feel like it."

She turned around to look. "What is it?"

"Just something. Something to cheer you up when you feel like it. I'm going to go check out the damage now."

"You don't have to do that now. You're exhausted, Michael. Come sit down for a while."

"I won't be long."

"Don't go yet."

"It'll be dark soon." Then he asked, "You okay?"

"I'm okay."

"All right." He stepped out onto the porch, and tapped the screen from the outside. "See you, hon."

"I'm okay," she said.

Avelyn watched him walk over the ridge. She figured there was more to it than checking the damage — not only from that faraway expression, but because he had turned and told her, "See you, hon." Just short and simple like that, but more than he would have said had he really been going to check on the damage. He wouldn't have said anything then. So she had answered, "I'm okay" — wanting in her way to let him know that she was — okay — and so to go ahead with the other. Maybe he would sell the ranch. Maybe that's what it was.

Mike walked up the valley. The ground was black and gray from charred grass and ashes. It was still smoking. He stepped over the fallen barbed wire that had separated the Bar V from Lloyd Paxton's, so that now he was on Titanic's land and heading toward the strip mine. He walked with his eyes straight ahead, every once in a while glancing up to the black, girdered neck of Big Wally.

It was drizzling. He came to the pit of the strip mine and stood at its edge, looking down at the naked black coal seam a hundred feet below him. The drizzle felt good on his face and hair. It was deserted now, the trucks lined up in neat rows in the pit with the loading shovels towering above them, and Big Wally above them. Above everything. He looked over the area for several minutes, thinking things through. Then he heard something behind him. Mike spun around, his hand moving toward the Magnum under his shirt. It was Denny.

"Get out of here," Mike said.

Denny shook his head.

"Get *out* of here."

Denny didn't move. He stared him straight in the eyes.

"I'm not asking you, Denny. I'm telling you. Get out of here. Now."

Denny shook his head again.

Mike crossed his arms and glared into his cousin's face and saw that he was not leaving. He shook his head and cursed. Denny stared him back.

"I don't give a damn. Come on."

They walked around to the other side of the pit. The strip mine was silent and sprawling in the dusk, except for the constant humming of the generators working the pumps. They headed toward a small aluminum hut that was off by itself, surrounded by a ten-foot fence. The rain continued to fall, a soft rain that cooled rather than drenched.

When they reached the hut, Mike pulled on his work gloves, motioning Denny to stay where he was. He clambered up the crosshatched fence and over the top three barbed-wire strands, dropping behind the sign that read DANGER — HIGH EXPLOSIVES in red block letters. The storage shack was in the center of the restricted area, its door locked. Mike put his gloved fist through the window. The tinkling of glass on the cement floor sounded above the rainfall and the gusting of the wind. He reached through and unlocked the door and went inside.

The explosives were pretty much the same as those he had used in the army. He looked them over, and came out with a box filled with ammonium nitrate fuel-oil mixtures, which he tossed over the fence to Denny. Then he brought out a small box of detonators. He went back in one more time and came out with the blasting machine and wire fuses. Then he climbed back over the fence. It was almost dark.

Hepp Fox got into his pickup and started the engine. The grass fire was out now. He had come back from the rodeo and watched it tear through McKenzie's pasture, waiting with Tiny Turner and the Prestons and the Millers and Tate and he couldn't remember who else — all of them having come up to help. They'd watched and waited, prepared to save his grassland where McKenzie couldn't save his own, when suddenly the wind had died down and the firefighters came and that little plane flew over, and they stopped it. They put it out. Just like that. And then they'd stood there, looking over the ruin that had been McKenzie's north pasture, shaking their fists in triumph and cheering their lungs out, telling each other, "The sonofabitch, by God, it's just right for him!" There's one fight you lost, Mike McKenzie, he thought. A damn big fight you lost.

Now that goddamn Patty. Marjorie had seen her driving up the valley two days already that week, late in the afternoon, late enough so that the mine had closed down and the miners were getting off work. They must have been meeting at the mine, her and her miner fella. He'd told her to stay away from that type. There must have been a shack up there with a cot in it. Some little place. He headed up the road, his foot leaning more heavily on the accelerator at the thought. Jesus, riffraff like that just gets a girl in trouble, then heads on down the road. Billy had had enough sense to keep her out of trouble anyway.

Hepp slowed down at the gate leading down to the mine site. It was nearing dark. He wondered what he'd do if he found her in one of those little buildings down there, some buck-naked miner lying on top of her. . . . He went on down the drive, past Lloyd's old place, and parked the truck in front of the mine's small office building. He checked the door there and it was locked. The lights inside the building were off, and he tried to peek in a window. It was too dark to see anything. The area was deserted, and the rain was beginning to pick up.

He walked behind the building, toward the mine itself. There was another shack across the way. He stopped and watched it. The door was open. He wondered what he would do if he found her with her fella in that shack, and thought about going back to the truck for his rifle. It would not be such a good thing to be caught trespassing with a rifle, he thought. But he could sure give that miner fella some scare.

He walked closer to the pit. He was watching the shack, and someone came out of the door. Hepp knelt and ducked his head. It was a man, carrying a box. He couldn't see Patty. Then he saw another man take the box from over the fence. They were stealing something. The first man climbed back over the fence, leaving the door of the shack open behind him, and they started toward the pit. When they were a hundred yards away, Hepp saw it was McKenzie and his deaf-mute cousin. They set down their loads beside that one immense dragline in the center of the pit, then went back to the shack. They each picked up another box and came back to the pit, this time setting them down and staying. It was getting dark, and suddenly the light standards surrounding the pit automatically clicked on. McKenzie and his cousin flattened and were still. They were listening. Hepp looked around nervously. In a moment, McKenzie stood up again, jimmying open the boxes quickly. The rain continued to fall, and the wind was beginning to pick up again, as it had blown all afternoon.

Denny reached into the crate and handed the grayish, polyethylene bags to Mike, who carefully placed them under the hull of the machine. He put four bags at each of the four corners of the dragline. Then he took the detonators and fitted them onto the packs of the ammonium nitrate fuel-oil mixtures, running a wire back from each to a central fuse. He began to splice the wires together. His hands had been steady and sure throughout, but now that he was splicing the wires, they were trembling. His shirt was wet from the drizzle and he felt chilled. He laid the four fuses on his knee and shook his hands violently at his sides to relax them. When he picked the fuses up again, his hands were steadier, and he spliced the wires. Mike checked the splice, then took a roll of tape from one of the boxes and, tearing off a small strip, taped around the splice to protect it from the wetness. Then he laid it on the ground and began stripping the fuse back. It was coiled in his left hand like a lasso, and he stripped it off with his right hand while backing away. The fuse uncoiled for about one hundred fifty feet. Mike took the blasting machine from the box Denny had carried and put it on top of the seam of coal. The floor of the pit was smooth and flat from the trucks driving across it. He spliced the fuse to the blasting machine. The sky was dark now, the moon and stars hidden by the summer storm, but the pit was lit up by the lights.

Mike caught Denny's eye. He gave him a quick nod to tell him they were ready, motioning with his finger to the switch that would set the explosion off. Denny nodded back and knelt beside him.

"You get goin' now, big guy," Mike said. "Get the hell out of here in case this thing don't go just exactly like I planned it —" He pointed away from the dragline. "Go on . . . I'll catch up to you."

Denny shook his head.

Mike said, "Get goin' now, I told you. Get started back home." Denny looked at him, unsure. Mike said, "We're too close to this thing. Little fella like me can duck. You'll get your damn head blown off. Go on. I'll catch up."

Denny shook his head.

"I'm not asking. I'm not going to set it off till you leave. Get goin'. Go home. Now get goin'." Denny started off reluctantly. "I'll catch up to you . . . there you go."

He watched him go.

Hepp Fox opened the door of the truck and pulled his rifle from its rack. By the inside light he found the open box of shells behind the seat and grabbed three. He shut the door too quickly and knocked two of the shells from his hand. He looked down for them. There was a light standard on the other side of the pickup, and the ground around him was in a dark shadow. He cursed and turned and walked back toward the pit, breaking into a jog. He clutched the one shell, slipping it into the chamber as he went. Ain't no one can blame a man for shooting a thief, you dumb sonofabitch McKenzie, he was thinking.

Denny climbed up the coal ramp and out of the pit. When he was gone, Mike turned back to face that giant machine. He looked up its great steel body to the towering shadow of the boom, which disappeared above the light standards into the blackness of the night. He wished he was another hundred feet away, but there was nothing to do about that now. His thumb rested against the detonating switch, and he wondered for a moment if Titanic would build another such monster after this one was gone.

Eighty yards away, Hepp Fox raised the 30.06 to his shoulder. Denny saw something glint beneath the light standard. He stepped toward it, peering. There was another glint, and he saw it was a piece of metal. It was still now. It was a rifle. There was a man there. Denny started running, his mouth opened and silent.

Hepp Fox looked through the scope. In the dim light, his eye took several seconds to focus on McKenzie. He wondered what was going on down there — where that Denny'd gone off to. That didn't matter. He wouldn't see nothing. The crosshairs came together at the center of the back. He raised the barrel a fraction. You should have sold, he was thinking. That little prig brother of yours will sell quick enough. He breathed out and held his breath. It was steady now. He blinked and then he squeezed the trigger. There was a flash of light and the rifle recoiled. The shot rang out so loudly that it startled him.

Something struck Mike from behind and he pitched forward, losing control of the blasting machine. Then he heard the shot. The air in his lungs was crushed out as his torso twisted, and he fell. He tried to breathe.

Running, Denny saw the explosion of light and saw Mike falling and a noise sounded from his throat like an animal noise, a curdling shriek as in fear. Hepp was kneeling forty yards away, frozen — frozen from the shock that the gun had fired and McKenzie had actually fallen, or maybe from that horrible yell in the dark, the sight of Denny all fury and quickness coming toward him. He raised his rifle to fire again. It clicked empty. Denny was upon him, picking him up in his huge hands and shaking him until the gun fell, still shrieking like an animal, gripping Hepp against his chest with one arm while Hepp beat at his face and neck. He held him there, squeezing, using his other arm to stop the blows falling around his head, pressing with his forearm against Hepp's face, pushing the head back. He slipped his forearm under Hepp's chin now. Hepp gurgled for air, eyes wide with helplessness, suspended off the ground. He hit at Denny's face, then stopped hitting, and Denny felt the neck strain and snap, not hearing the little squeal that came last. The noise coming from Denny's throat now was a whining, whimpering cry. The body became limp, and he released it.

Mike moved his hand. He was lying on his side in the mud, reaching for the detonating box that had fallen. Someone was running. They were close now. Then he heard a funny sound like the sound a rabbit makes in the jaws of a coyote, almost like a baby's cry. It was Denny. He knelt down, stroking Mike's forehead, wiping at the wetness and splattered dirt, looking down at the hole in his chest and the redness there. He had never heard Denny make sounds before.

"Kick it here, Denny," Mike said. His lips barely moved and Denny couldn't understand him. "Kick the box here." Denny held him and looked down at him, and Mike pointed. "Kick the box here, big guy."

Denny understood that time, and started to reach for it with his bare hand. Mike touched his arm to stop him and pointed to his boot. "Kick it, Den. Use your foot."

Denny laid Mike's head onto his reaching arm and walked over to the box. He looked back to see Mike nod as he moved his foot behind it. Then he slid it along the ground until Mike could reach it and hold it in his hand.

"Now go get help, big guy," he said slowly, careful to turn his head so Denny could see his lips. "Go . . . get . . . help. Go."

Denny shook his head, no. He reached down to lift Mike into his arms.

"No, Denny," Mike said quietly. "You'll kill me if you move me. Go get Avelyn. Go."

Denny started away twice and turned around. Mike nodded his head. Then he sprinted off into the darkness.

Mike lay with his head on his arm. He coughed, spitting blood.

It was uncomfortable to breathe, but there wasn't any pain. The worst things never had any pain. He coughed and tasted his own blood and felt it warm in his lungs. He's far enough away by now, he thought. I'd better blast this now, before it's too late. He was not sure how much longer he wou d be conscious. He was tired. It's easy as hell to die, he thought. It's about what creatures do best. He remembered saying that to Avelyn and how mad she got. I'd better blast this now. Then he flicked the switch with his thumb.

The force of the explosion sent the blasting machine shooting backward, and hot air scorched over him. Flames shot into the air, the eastern sky lighting up like an early dawn, the red and white reflecting off the clouds. One after another, the charges went off. Chunks of the dragline screamed out of the pit like shrapnel. Then the explosions stopped and there was a great hissing of escaping heat. Titanic's massive earth-moving machine was now a blazing carcass of twisted steel, a fifty-foot flame shooting up where the booms had been.

Mike reopened his eyes. It was dark now and he had been lying there a long time. He was tired, and in a little while he would not be tired anymore. It didn't frighten him, knowing he was dying. The things that frightened you were the things you didn't know. Night noises in the jungle in Vietnam had scared the hell out of him. They could be anything. You never knew, was the thing. Avelyn would be frightened now because Denny would not be able to tell her what she wanted to know. She would have heard the blast and then she would see Denny, and that's when she would get really frightened, because he could not tell her. Don't start thinking about her now, he thought. Don't start now. You were doing fine. He thought about her opening the box and seeing the necklace. Don't start now, he thought. Think about Big Wally. Think about that. Jesus Christ, did that thing go up.

They drove into the strip-mine area just behind the car from the Custer ranger station. Jimbo recognized Hepp's pickup. He parked and they ran down to the edge of the pit, passing Hepp's body on the way, the head bent grotesquely back beneath the shoulders and the rifle off to the side. Avelyn raised her hand to her mouth with a silent cry, understanding for the first time just what Denny's hysterics had meant — though from the first sound of the explosion she had known that was Mike. Sirens were whining up the Canyon Creek road, cutting through the drizzle and the hissing of the burning dragline. Then they saw a small group of men in the pit gathered beneath a light standard, the miners who were lodged in Lloyd Paxton's old house.

Jimbo pushed through them. Barsotti, the foreman, was holding Mike, pressing a bloody handkerchief against the hole in his chest. Mike's eyes were half-open. Barsotti was muttering, "My God . . ." and blotting at the wound.

Mike saw Jimbo and grinned that little grin of his. There was no pain. He coughed and a trickle of blood spilled from the corner of his mouth. Avelyn broke between the men and cried out, falling around Mike hysterically, trying to hold him, his blood smearing her shirt. Jimbo knelt, wiping the mud from Mike's face and cradling his head in his lap. Mike looked at him, still grinning a little, talking to him with his eyes. Jimbo wiped the blood from the corner of his mouth, and Mike coughed again. The ambulance sirens were closer now.

"Mike . . . for Chrissakes, Mike —" Mike's face dissolved into a blur, and he blinked the tears down so he could see him clearly.

"I'm fightin' now, buddy boy . . ." he whispered.

"You sure are, cowboy . . ."

"I got blind-sided . . ."

Jimbo nodded. He pressed his cheek next to Mike's, and he kissed him. Jimbo was crying.

Mike turned his head and let the blood drool out of his mouth. Then he grinned and said, "She's all yours now, buddy boy . . ."

"No, Mike . . ." Jimbo held him, but then Mike's eyes wandered above him.

"Where's . . . Avelyn?"

"Right here, Michael."

"There you are . . ."

"I'm right here." She was weeping, but she could control her face enough to smile and to talk.

"You open your present?" he said hoarsely.

She nodded, biting her lip. "It's so lovely, Michael. It's so very, very lovely. Michael, sweet."

"You don't look so happy about it. I wanted to see your face when you opened it." It was tiring him to talk.

"I am happy. I'm very happy. Now you'll have to take me to shows and such. You'll regret giving it to me. You'll want it back, but I won't give it back to you."

"No. Don't. It's yours."

"Ssh, now." She held him and saw the ambulance drivers pushing through the men, and the sheriff behind them. "I love you, sweet. My sweet. I love you."

Mike managed a smile. His face had lost its color. It looked gray. "I'm tired," he said.

She hugged his head and rocked. "Yes. Yes. I know it. You hush now." She pressed her cheek on his head and smelled the wetness of his hair. The ambulance man was pulling on her shoulder. She didn't want to let go. She rubbed her cheek against the top of his head, and then the sheriff pulled her gently by both arms so the ambulance men could lay him on the stretcher. Mike was still conscious.

"What happened here, Mike?" the sheriff asked, leaning his head close.

Mike looked at him, trying to think clearly.

"What happened, Mike? Who killed Hepp?"

He was on the stretcher now, and they started to lift it.

"I did," Mike said

"No, you didn't," the sheriff said. "Tell me what happened. Who else was here, Mike?"

"Me. Me and him. Then I blew it up." He turned his head back to Avelyn. "Avelyn." He just wanted to say it.

"Yes, Michael. Michael. Oh, love. I'm right here." She took his hand.

"Go on now," the sheriff said to the driver.

They put Mike into the back of the ambulance. Avelyn climbed in beside him, and they drove away. Jimbo listened to its siren down the valley through the raw and chilly night. The burning dragline hissed in the rain. Jimbo was twisting his fingers. He looked around, and near him was a miner with both arms around a blonde-haired girl. It was Patty Fox. Her face was buried in the man's chest. Jimbo stepped toward them. "Mike's dead," he said. "He's dead now."

CHAPTER 34

AVELYN WAS SO completely shattered that there was no time to think of his own loss. He could hear her at night through the walls, crying, and in the mornings she would rise very late and look as if she'd had no sleep at all. He was small comfort to her, though he tried. Her parents flew out. It was better then, but it was still very bad for her at night, sleeping in that bed, and she seemed grateful for the mornings. Jimbo handled the funeral arrangements, as he had for Papa Vic. There were lots of things to attend to, and those first days passed quickly. For him, the nights were deep and dreamless.

The ceremony was held in the little plot beneath the cotton-woods. Sam Benson was there with his family; and Deacon, who had been released from the hospital that morning. John Cott was there. Denny's mother, Aunt Willa, had someone drive her up from the nursing home in Gillette. She was still tiny, withered. Her face drooped terribly from the paralysis on her left side. It was a strange sight: the right side of her face with tears streaming down, filled with sympathy, sharing Avelyn's pain; while that left side stared blankly, without emotion, impassive, like a beaten thing. Jimbo was watching her. He couldn't watch the other, the coffin poised there on its straps. He couldn't listen to the words being spoken. So he watched Aunt Willa and those two faces — the one beaten, and the other so far from being beaten that it was sharing the pain. Accepting the pain. Like that old house of Papa Vic's up there on the ridge facing anything God and Nature wanted to throw at it. And then the numbness that had carried him through those first few days began to disappear. A welling started to build in his chest and suddenly he was sobbing. The sobs came in short little heaves which eased the pressure in his chest. But it built up again very quickly, and there was little use trying to control it. When the service ended he walked away from the people, and the sobbing came harder. Michael, he was thinking. Mike, this lousy goddamn world. You poor Michael. He had no control over these thoughts or the heaving in his chest or the twisting in his face. The pressure was easing, but it would build up again when he thought, You poor Michael sonofabitch. Then Avelyn came over — it was she who was strong now — and let him hold her and press his face into her shoulder until it was all out. Then she put her arm around his waist and walked him up to the house.

He was all right then. He washed his face and came out to talk with the people who had come. Aunt Willa was in her wheelchair with Denny hovering protectively at her side, and Jimbo thanked her for being there.

She said to him, "Papa Vic always thought you'd make the best rancher in the family."

He smiled politely and said, "No, I think it was my brother."

"It was you," she said out of the side of her mouth. "Your grandfather used to talk about it."

"Well. I'll be going back to school soon."

She made no response. "Mike was set in his ways, bless him."

"They were good ways."

"Good ways become old ways before long," Aunt Willa said. "Papa Vic would say it."

It was late. The grandfather clock chimed four from the bottom of the stairs, and Jimbo rolled onto his back. He opened his eyes. To the east, he thought he could see some gray. He would have liked to have slept longer, but now that he was awake he wished the dawn would hurry. He thought about the old Indian, One-eyed Jack Parker. He had arranged for him to be buried beside his father on the Parker Place. Dying on a place's what makes it yours, he thought. That land's yours now, Mr. One-eyed Jack Parker. That's Parker land.

His mind was racing now, and there was no sense fighting it. He thought of the old black porter who had seated him when he was coming home by train, seated him backward with a toothy grin and his smooth walnut skin and a rhythmic "You won' know where's you goin', but you sure knows where you been." He was right about that. After all that had happened, he was still right as rain about that. He had never known where he was going. He had always questioned where he had been, where he was, where Mike was — spending so much time challenging Mike's direction and veering away from it, that he had never been able to figure out a direction of his own. Of *his*. So that now that Mike was gone, he had lost his bearings. He had always been so determined to steer clear of that shadow that now it had disappeared he was dangling in limbo. He felt empty and lost and what good did it do to change things now? If he had accepted Mike's road instead of challenging him every step of the way, if he had tried to understand it instead of being one more thorn, one more needling pain in his side, none of this would have happened. One more thief sucking away at that strength. He thought, What lousy life is this, that won't give us a second chance to show love?

It had been nearly four weeks since the fire. When the wind picked up, the air was still hazy with ashes, but two heavy rains had washed most of them into the soil. Deacon was still not allowed to do any heavy work, so there was plenty to keep Denny and Jimbo busy. He had told the university that he wouldn't enroll until spring. There were too many things to get in order. They had to find feed for the cattle and rebuild the fences and feeding stations. They had to till and fertilize the pastures.

Avelyn kept the house and harvested the vegetables from the garden. Her parents had wanted her to come back East with them, but she'd wanted to wait. She'd wanted to stay a little longer. She was better now, although there was little of her light, vibrant laughter that had once carried through the house. But she started talking again, especially in the early morning when she made their breakfast as the sun streaked the land with a cool orange, her biscuits and steaming gravy warming the kitchen with their smell. She would set the biscuits on the table in that dawn quiet, when even the softest clatter of a plate seemed harsh after the night's stillness, like the first cold running faucet in the morning. Then they would eat, and Jimbo would watch her and listen to her talk about home or Mike or things past, but never about the future beyond her chores that day, or theirs.

Except one day in early fall she said, "I wonder when Thorndike will come?"

"I don't know," he said.

"It won't be too long, I imagine."

"No. I shouldn't think so."

They had never talked about what to do with the ranch. Jimbo was content without fully knowing why. Content to have her company; content working the ranch, rebuilding; content to be committing himself to something besides himself. To something tangible. Though there was a nagging doubt in his mind when he thought about the coal. It hadn't gone anywhere. The town was still the town. The mine was in operation again, if lacking that monstrous dragline. So he wondered if all this rebuilding wasn't just delaying the inevitable; or worse, a trip back along the same futile road.

They took a trip to the Custer Battlefield. Avelyn and Jimbo stood on a small knoll above the rows of white headstones, watching Denny walk ahead of them. They stopped. The battlefield had always given Jimbo an eerie feeling of history, as if spirits brushed the grasses with marching legs. The grasses grew high around the headstones, swaying. This was not a cemetery. This was a battlefield where headstones had been left behind.

It was a cool day. Avelyn sat in the grass and the wind blew her hair across her face. She shook it back and turned her face into the wind.

"I'll be going home, Jimbo."

She turned her face to him for as long as it took for the wind to blow her hair across her eyes again, then she looked back into the breeze. She was still so lovely. He was standing with his hands in his pockets. "When?" he asked.

She lifted her shoulders. "Soon."

He watched her, thinking all sorts of thoughts. Finally, he said, "He's well rid of me and the ranch and the goddamn town." Then he softened his voice. "But he got a hell of a deal losing you."

She made a sad smile. "So did I."

Jimbo paused. "You were right, you know."

"About what?"

"At the river."

She remembered. It seemed like a very long time ago.

"I wouldn't let myself love Mike, so I fell in love with you. That sounds funny. I don't understand it. Now I want to tell him that I love him. So I'll tell you."

He took his hand from his pocket and she reached up and squeezed it. "I want to tell him, too."

He couldn't picture her in New York City, or wherever. He didn't try to. "What should we do about the ranch?"

"Whatever you like."

"Should we sell it?"

"Only if you want to. I don't care about the money. I wouldn't keep it. I truly wouldn't."

"That might change. Time changes things."

"Yes. There's that to hope for. But I wouldn't keep it. Truly. Do what's right for you, Jimbo. You decide. I'm going home. That's all the decision-making I'm good for. And I shall miss you, Jimbo McKenzie." She stood and kissed him on the cheek and then walked down the slope through the waist-high grasses.

It took her three days to pack. She said goodbye to Denny and Deacon, trailing a waving hand behind to the horses and cows as Jimbo drove down the drive and turned onto the Canyon Creek road. They drove for a while in silence.

"Thorndike called this morning," Jimbo said.

"I'm glad I shall miss him. Is he coming?"

"He wanted me to check the springs in the south pasture. It seems that their mine is all of a sudden sucking great fountains of water."

"Really?"

"He's prepared to drill us a well." He paused. "And he wants to talk about an offer."

She squeezed his arm. "That's your decision."

He nodded. They drove awhile. At Billings he turned onto the airport road, driving on top of the bluffs that looked down on the winding muddy Yellowstone as it emerged from the wheat fields and flowed into town. Then she said, "But I'll worry about you if you decide not to sell. I'll worry that those same terrible things will start up again. I can't help it, Jimbo. I will. I don't see what would be different."

"I don't know," he said, wondering.

Then he turned into the airport.

CHAPTER 35

JIMBO STOPPED THE car on the access road, walking through the newly built gate and across the tilled pasture. It looked different after the fire. The willow bushes along the creek had all been burned, and that one sole oak tree was now a charred stump. The grass in the pasture would grow back by next summer, but those willow bushes would take longer. They were pretty in the spring, flaring up orange before they came into their foliage. The moose who had used them for cover would probably feed elsewhere now.

He reached the spring. That pipe that had dripped water into the U-shaped copper trough winter and spring for the past fifty years was still now. The last of the springwater sat in buggy pools, drying in the hot Indian-summer sun. Sam was right then, he thought. The coal vein had been the aquifer.

He drove back, trying very hard not to think about Avelyn, not to think about what the ranch would be like without her or Mike or Papa Vic. He had not said a very good goodbye. He remembered seeing her suddenly walking up the steps of the plane, stopping at the top to look back and catch his eye, blowing a quick kiss, then ducking inside. He tried to remember how she had looked, exactly how, but he couldn't. That was probably for the best.

He remembered that Jacks had thrown a shoe, and he walked out and brought him in from the home pasture. Mike's old roping horse. He tied Jacks in the barn's shoeing stall and got out Mike's box of tools. He tied on the leather shoeing apron, then moved the anvil closer and cleaned the horse's foot of the manure and mud caked in the hoof. Then he rasped and clipped it flat. He was talking to the horse in a quiet voice. "You be good now, Jacks. You be nice." He had just begun to fit the shoe when he felt the horse's weight lean heavily down, felt the straining in his thighs and back. He began to sweat. "You quit that, Jacks boy," he muttered through the nails in his mouth. He removed one and tapped it in with the hammer. "You be nice now. I'm no fencepost."

The horse continued to lean against him, and he dropped its leg, straightening up. "It's me. Little Jimbo."

Jacks turned his head as if to listen. Jimbo rested for a spell. Then he picked up the hind leg again and laid it across his thigh. He tapped in two more nails. Jacks began to lean again, and Jimbo strained. Suddenly he lost his balance, and the horse's leg slipped free. It landed on his boot.

"Owww! Jesus Christ!"

Jimbo dropped the hammer and hobbled out of the barn. It was excruciating. He tried to walk off the pain, cursing under his breath. He had walked around the yard twice when a car drove up. Thorndike got out. Jimbo untied his shoeing apron and tossed it on a peg in the barn.

"Hello, McKenzie."

"Hello."

Thorndike's manner was pleasant, but he wasn't smiling. Jimbo's foot throbbed. "Doing a little shoeing, are you?"

"Very little."

"Nice-looking animal."

"Old Jacks. A real bugger."

There was a pause, an end to the amenities. "Have a chance to check on those springs?"

"They're dry, all right," Jimbo said.

"I was afraid of that. You can't believe the inflow we're getting. We've had to bring up extra pumps from Cheyenne."

Jimbo was looking down at the dirt, shifting his weight on and off his sore foot. "That's what happens when you tear a half-mile hole in the ground. You can't just take it out and put it back in like a goddamn piece of pie."

"That's true enough." Thorndike shifted to a friendlier tone. "Anyway, we're sending a crew up here tomorrow or the next day to drill you a well —"

"A well?" Jimbo interrupted.

"Yes. There'll be a crew up here soon as possible."

"Christ, a well isn't a spring. It takes electricity to run a well. You'll have to run power up there."

"We'll pay for all that. Don't worry about the expenses."

"I'm not worried about the goddamned expenses. I'm worried about our *water*. A well isn't a spring."

"A well isn't dry either. McKenzie, I can't get the company to bring the spring back. Surely you understand that. It's something of a bad break for us, too. But we're going to get you back your water."

Jimbo was quiet for a while. He wondered what he ought to do. "You going to dig all those fellas wells whose springs went dry?"

"Every one."

He thought some more. "What if the wells go dry? A big strip mine like that can just act like a vacuum on all the subsurface water. What happens then? You sink them deeper?"

"I suppose. Listen, this isn't what I came out here to discuss with you —"

"Well, let's discuss it. You're fooling with our water rights. That's no doubt occurred to you, but it's just occurring to me. That spring didn't just *run* dry. It wasn't like an Act of God or something. It was sucked dry by that mine of yours. I can sue you for that —"

"Jimbo —"

"My grandfather used to tell me stories about the droughts this area's had. He said the only reason we lived through them was because of our springs. This land always has had good springs. Now that mine's sucked them dry."

"Listen to me —"

"Folks around here are scared to death of drought, Mr. Thorndike. Scared to death."

"I want to talk about something else."

"You tell those well-diggers of yours to stay home. I don't want their damn well. You tell them that."

Thorndike looked at him impatiently. "Jimbo . . . " Then he softened his voice. "You can't fight something like this. You can't fight something like this and win. You learned that, tragically."

"Maybe that old court system of ours will tie things up for a while though, eh? Maybe we'll be so long in court protesting a little matter of water rights your company will get tired of it and go dig somebody else's coal."

"I didn't come to argue over water rights. I came to make you an offer. Are you ready to listen?"

He waited. Jimbo made no movement, but he was listening. He listened as Thorndike told him how this could have been avoided, how he was sorry and the town was sorry and he was no doubt sorry too; how the whole fucking business had been a bad deal from the start. Which was true, Jimbo thought, and a pretty good choice of words at that. Because the deal *had* been bad, the cards had been stacked by Whoever it was that was in charge of those things; so there wasn't anything anybody could have done about it. There wasn't anything that could have been avoided no matter how the hand had been played, because maybe you've only got so many cards to fiddle with, and when you lay them down they only read one way. So no matter how badly everybody felt, how sorry everyone was, it all came down to one thing: it was a bad deal.

Thorndike was shaking his head. "Anyway, we're all very sorry . . ." Then he paused and after a good sincere frown he extended the same offer that he had to Mike, the same offer that had precipitated all those things that everyone was so sorry about — Mike having turned it down. He stood there with his arms folded, and Jimbo listened carefully as he said, ". . . eighteen million dollars —" and let it hang.

He had never really pictured this moment. Never really imagined what it would be like to have the power to sell or not with a simple yes or no. So now he stood there, trying to think of what and how to answer, trying to think of reasons to or not to, wondering why he had not decided earlier. He hadn't. He really hadn't. Two drops of sweat beaded up and rolled down his flanks from under his arms, and his foot throbbed angrily. Then he came to a decision. It was his decision and he was absolutely sure about it. It was his. "As my brother would have said, and I apologize for his phrasing — go shit in your hat, Thorndike."

Jimbo grinned at the bigger man's expression. Thorndike's mouth was moving like a fish's. He looked a little like Denny. "Now shoo-shoo-shoo," Jimbo said. "I've business to attend to."

There was a broom by the door of the barn, and he took it and swept it at Thorndike's feet, as if they were scraps of paper. The dust blew up around the cuffs of his trousers, and Thorndike hopped back. "Be gone with you," Jimbo said, sweeping. "I'll see you in court." He followed as Thorndike retreated to his car, brushing away his footsteps with the broom. Then he watched the car out the drive.

Jimbo turned around. He felt light-headed and giddy. He saw the horse. "Goddamn you, Jacks. Goddamn your sleepy ass." He walked back to the barn, untied the halter, and led Jacks into the yard. The gate to the home pasture was open. "You shit in your hat, too, horse." Then he booted the horse, and Jacks skirted off sideways, pulling the halter rope from his hands and fleeing through the gate.

Jimbo sat down. He sat in the dust of the yard, feeling his sore foot. After a while he stood and walked a few steps toward the north pasture, looking to the mesa beyond, up where the grass still grew long 'cause Gawd's got real tender feet. Okay, old man, he thought. We try her again.

Which is when he saw Denny. He was standing next to the barn, his thick mouth breaking into a broad, slow grin. He came toward him, and a glint came into his eyes, a glint like — Jimbo couldn't remember when he had seen such a glint. He backed away as his cousin neared.

"You stay away from me now, mammoth one . . . You behave . . . Stay back now, Den!" Then Denny reached forward and, wrapping his great arms around him, hugged him off his feet.

The plane wasn't crowded. No one flew out of Billings on a weekday. Not in October. Avelyn sat next to the window. The seat next to her was empty, but an elderly woman in the aisle seat glanced at her with concern while she had her cry. It must have looked like a healthy cry because the lady said nothing. Avelyn hadn't had a good cry since the night of the funeral. But when Jimbo waved from the gate and walked back into the terminal, something inside her let go.

After a while she stopped and stared at the vast plains passing below. She started to think a little. She had not let herself think too much in the past few weeks, but it was rather nice now. She thought about Jimbo and Deacon and the ranch. When she thought about the ranch, it wasn't the way it was now, but the way it was in the spring when the grass was new and still greenish, and the calves were little milk addicts. Before the branding. That was the best time of year. Then she thought about Michael, and she pictured him in that same time of year, with his shirt off and his muscles gleaming with sweat, sweating from his forehead and temples, his gray eyes smiling beneath his stained straw hat. If she had started to cry then, it would not have been a good cry but a wretched one. So Avelyn thought about the coal company and the coal. Then she thought about Papa Vic. You had to go back to Papa Vic to make any sense at all out of the McKenzies — at least to find out what made you proud to be · one, and what gave Mike and even Jimbo that strength. It was Papa Vic, not the land. Mike hadn't known that. It was the grandfather. The land was nothing but a semifertile tract that had been cursed with a thick black seam of coal. Millions of years ago, that coal had been swamplife, ferns and mosses and horsetails. Growing and dying and growing and dying and sinking to the bottom of the marsh, where it was turned into peat. Ferns and mosses and horsetails, the kind that still grew in the marsh, pretty plants that the moose fed on. Then the peatbogs themselves submerged, and the sea deposited sandstone and limestone which compacted the peat into coal. All that for a seam of coal. Which made her wonder about God or Fate or Whatever it was that was supposed to have a hand in all this and make some sense where she could not. She hadn't honestly tried very hard, though. As Papa Vic used to say, "If Gawd had wanted me to worry about what went on in His head, He would have put more into mine."

That was probably true.